THE PERFECT CHRISTMAS VILLAGE

ALSO BY BELLA OSBORNE

The Girls
The Library

THE PERFECT CHRISTMAS VILLAGE

Bella Osborne

An Aria Book

First published in the UK in 2023 by Head of Zeus,
part of Bloomsbury Publishing Plc

Copyright © Bella Osborne, 2023

9 7 5 3 1 2 4 6 8

A catalogue record for this book is available from the British Library.

ISBN (PB): 9781837930012
ISBN (E): 9781804542675

Cover design: HoZ; illustration: Harry Woodgate

Typeset by Siliconchips Services Ltd UK

Printed and bound in Great Britain by
CPI Group (UK) Ltd, Croydon CR0 4YY

Head of Zeus
First Floor East
5–8 Hardwick Street
London EC1R 4RG
WWW.HEADOFZEUS.COM

For Lesley Elder – life coach extraordinaire and
without whom I wouldn't be an author

THE VILLAGE OF HOLLY CROSS

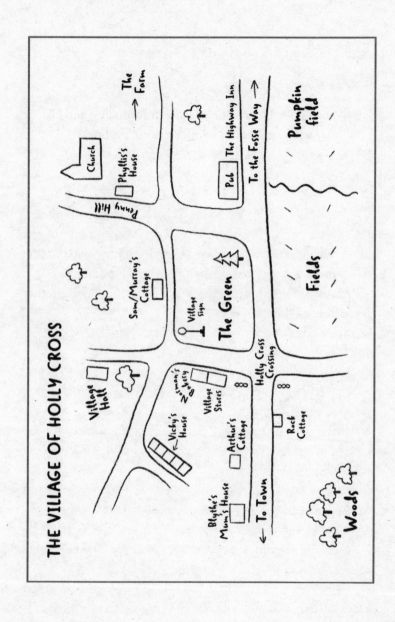

Prologue

The Holly Cross Christmas Fayre was in full swing and Blythe was enjoying a chat with Murray, one of the older village residents, when the two elderly sisters from Rock Cottage approached the stall he was manning.

'Murray, we're after a hook-up,' said one, as the other nodded her agreement.

Blythe almost spat out her hot chocolate. 'A hook-up?' she asked.

'For our front door,' the lady explained.

'Is this what you're after?' asked Murray, holding up a plastic hook.

Blythe was still giggling to herself as the sisters moved on and Murray adjusted the many ivy- and moss-covered wreaths in front of him.

'At least that's one sale,' said Murray. 'Leonora has spent hours making these wreaths and nobody is interested.'

'Maybe people will buy one as they leave, save carrying it around all evening,' said Blythe, hopefully. Murray didn't look convinced.

Holly Cross was a picture of twinkling lights and happy faces. Blythe watched the other local residents all happily chatting, some jangling charity collection buckets, others buying presents and some petting the live reindeer that were part of this year's Christmas display. Every year Holly Cross was turned into a winter wonderland and folk travelled from all over to see it and, in the process, the village raised money for charity and had a lot of fun at the same time.

Murray gave her a nudge. 'Next ones to get married – you mark my words,' he said, nodding in the direction of Norman, the local baker, and his friend Phyllis who were sharing a joke.

'No way. Norman and Phyllis?'

'You heard it here first,' he said.

The jolly scene was interrupted by a massive bang as an old white van backfired. Everyone turned. Phyllis squealed and two reindeer leapt so high Blythe thought they were taking flight. The Brownies gasped as the reindeer cleared the temporary fencing and ran amok around the fayre. Their shocked handler was fully occupied with hanging on to the other two reindeer who seemed keen to join their mates who were charging in between stalls creating havoc.

'Baubles!' shouted Murray.

'On it!' replied Blythe dashing off to try to save some as they tumbled to the ground.

Twenty minutes of madness followed as everyone tried to corral the creatures until Murray had the idea to get everyone onto the other side of the green and let the animals calm down. It worked because the reindeer then became distracted by what was on the stalls. One was happily munching on a stick of sprouts while the other was busy eating its way through something else.

'My wreaths!' hollered Leonora, pointing at the reindeer who was happily chewing on his second one.

There really was nothing quite like a Holly Cross Christmas, thought Blythe.

I

29th May

Blythe watched Amir stick his aubergine to the wall. In actual fact she'd fantasised about doing something similar, although that had involved a staple gun and quite a bit of screaming on Amir's part. This was an even bigger nightmare, even though the aubergine in question was only on a sticker. It meant Amir had broken Blythe's almost record-breaking sales run at Happy Homes Estate Agency. In the Warwickshire company's thirty-four-year history no single sales representative had achieved the most sales every month for a whole year. But this month Blythe had been on track to achieve just that until Amir had set out to ruin things.

He adjusted his sticker on the wall chart. It was so appropriate he'd chosen aubergines to record his sales. She looked at her row of unicorn stickers, one short of Amir's eggplants. She now needed just one more to tie for first for this month, keep her crown and go down in history. It wasn't up there with walking on the moon or even the first mooning (incidentally recorded by a Roman soldier in 66AD who mooned and caused a riot where thousands died). But it was notable in the history of Happy Homes estate agents or at least it would be if bloody Amir hadn't made it his mission to derail her plans.

'No hard feelings, eh?' said Amir, giving her shoulder an unwelcome squeeze.

Blythe tried to slap on a smile but instead she bared her teeth and Amir retracted his arm to a safe distance. 'It's not the end of May,' she said, her voice coming out as a low grumble.

Amir huffed a derisory laugh. 'It is the last *working* day of May. Face it, Blythe. I won.'

'But it's not just this month. It's the year. I was about to—'

'Yeah. Sorry about that,' he said, sounding about as sincere as an MP apologising for having an affair.

Blythe opened her mouth but before she could say anything their boss, Ludo, barrelled out of his office and enveloped Amir in a bear hug. 'Is this what I think it is?' Ludo's bright eyes were at odds with the rest of his grey appearance. 'Have you done it, lad?'

Amir wobbled his head. 'If you mean, have I produced a record month of sales and beaten Blythe. Then yes I have.' He looked smugger than the Cheshire cat in a grinning contest.

'By one sodding sale,' she muttered under her breath.

'That's fantastic,' said Ludo. 'And, Blythe, you had such a fabulous run. Well done to you too. I'll get the champagne.'

'Hey. Hang on!' said Blythe, quite loudly, making Ludo do a pirouette any ballet dancer would have been proud of. She had everyone's attention. 'The month's not over.' She checked her watch. Ludo nodded encouragingly at her. 'There's still a whole working hour today and then there's… more hours tomorrow.'

'It's Sunday tomorrow and Monday's a Bank Holiday.' Amir lifted his chin. 'Do you have any planned viewings?' he asked. 'Any offers out waiting to be accepted? Anything that's likely to come in before the clock ticks over into June?' His stare was icy. They'd been fierce rivals since he'd joined six months ago and now he was challenging her position as top sales representative and Ludo's favourite – she wasn't sure which hurt her the most.

She racked her brains for any properties on her books that were anywhere close to a sale. There really wasn't anything. Then she mentally went through her list of potential buyers. She'd been chasing a young couple who were trying to sort out their deposit but because each time she rang it kept going to voicemail she feared they were screening her calls. Blythe scanned her client list for someone else. Anyone. 'There's that guy from London, Sam Ashton.' She felt her cheek twitch at the mention of him.

Amir's Cheshire cat grin broadened. 'The bloke who you call every week with properties matching his criteria and he pooh-poohs every single one?'

'I thought you said he was a time-waster,' chipped in Heather, the office junior.

Blythe widened her eyes at Heather. She needed her onside because if Amir did any more swaggering he was going to slip a disc. 'No, that was someone else.'

'You said there was a WOTs file. And that WOTs stood for Waste of Timers.' Heather looked confused. Blythe giggled nervously. Heather flicked through her notebook where she'd jotted down meticulous training notes and read out loud. 'For some people, looking for their ideal home is a hobby. Ask the right questions to ascertain if they are delusional, dilly-dallying, time-wasters or simply fu—'

'Fantastic notes there, Heather,' cut in Blythe, before Ludo's eyebrows jumped so high they merged with his receding hairline. 'But that's not Mr Ashton.'

'But…' Heather held up her notebook in front of Blythe who snatched it from her, closed it, put it on the desk and sat on it.

'Excellent. So in summary. There's still everything to play for and we'll find out on Monday who has won for this month.' Blythe ignored Amir's smug expression and focused on Ludo who she could see was torn between mollifying her and celebrating Amir's achievement.

'Fair enough,' said Ludo, giving Blythe an indulgent smile. 'Amir, well done. Whatever happens on Tuesday, that's a fantastic sales sheet.'

Amir smacked Ludo on the back. 'All in a day's work.' He put on his knock-off Ray-Bans. 'If it's okay with you I'm going to call it a day. Anyone want to join me in the pub?' He twisted to eyeball Blythe. 'I'm celebrating.'

There were murmurs of agreement but not from Blythe. 'I'm too busy, *working*. But you enjoy it.'

'Don't worry I will,' he said, and he sauntered out of the office.

Blythe realised she was clenching her teeth. She knew she was clutching at straws and not the robust, plastic unenvironmentally friendly, last-for-a-million-years type – her straws were flimsy, paper and decidedly soggy. But they were all she had.

*

After an hour of scouring her property and potential client lists and reviewing the company inbox, just in case a buyer had happened to drop in, she knew she was facing defeat. She'd worked so hard and couldn't face that it might now be for nothing because petty Amir had decided to get off his butt for one month and put a spanner in the works. She'd pulled out all the stops last month, even selling her own house in record time, forcing her to move back in with her mum and stepdad while she found somewhere else. And this month she'd worked all hours. She really couldn't have done more.

The office was empty and the street outside was quiet as most people had rushed home to enjoy another glorious summer's evening. But Blythe wasn't joining them. She was stubborn and wasn't going to give up just yet. She checked her phone for the umpteenth time: still no reply from the young couple. The only other vague possibility was Mr Ashton. The client she had had on her books for almost five months and who had never actually visited any of the properties she had suggested. She was going to give him one last try.

Blythe went through their property portfolio and packaged up the best homes that ticked Mr Ashton's numerous 'must have' boxes and she pressed send on the email. She made herself a coffee, figuring that would provide enough elapsed time before she called him.

She dialled Sam Ashton's number and with each ring her optimism lost another life like a hero dying in a computer game. 'Don't go to voicemail,' she whispered, in the hope the God of property sales was looking kindly on her.

'Sam Ashton.'

Blythe threw up her free hand in delight before focusing hard. 'Hi, Mr Ashton. It's Blythe Littlewood from Happy Homes estate agents. I'm sorry it's late but I—'

He spoke over her. 'Sorry, I'm in the middle of some—'

'That's fine, I don't need your time now but I do need it tomorrow,' she butted in. Keen not to lose her opportunity she spoke as fast as she could. 'I've just sent you a fabulous selection of our top properties, which all meet your exacting criteria. You're going to be spoiled for choice. So have a look tonight and let's talk offers tomorrow. I'll come in to the office specially.' Blythe grimaced and crossed her fingers. She was a very rare species, an almost mythical creature like the unicorn; she was an honest estate agent with scruples and a conscience. It was something Ludo had instilled in her and which made the agency the most trusted in the area. She'd never been this pushy before and it didn't sit well with her, but needs must. Amir had driven her to this. She glanced at the wall chart and the mass of aubergines. She knew where she'd like to shove a particularly large—

Sam Ashton interrupted her thoughts by sighing heavily into the phone. 'Fine. Ten tomorrow?' Blythe blinked. Had she heard that right? Was he taking the bait? 'Miss Littlewood, are you still there?'

'Er, sorry. Of course. Yes. Absolutely. Ten o'clock sharp tomorrow. Thank you, Mr…' The line went dead. Rude. Blythe put the phone down, slumped back in her office chair and punched the air. It was a very soggy straw but it was all she had and she was going to cling on to it for all she was worth.

2

30th May

Blythe wasn't sure how she ended up being out of bed so early on a Sunday morning. When she'd lived in town she only saw her friend Vicky once or twice a week but now she'd had to move back in with her mum and her stepdad, Greg, Vicky lived just around the corner. It was one of a number of benefits that had softened the impact of her break-up. A sigh escaped as she thought about her ex now playing happy families with someone ten years older than her. That had been a blow to her ego. She was missing him less, which was a good thing. She'd sold the house they'd shared in double quick time – partly because it matched the buyer but mainly because she needed to get away from all the 'what might have been' memories. But that was in the past and Blythe had to concentrate on getting back on her feet. Usually Sundays were for long lazy lie-ins, snuggling on the sofa with a good book and the occasional hangover, although today she was careering around their sleepy village being dragged along by a huge bear of a dog.

'Vicky, explain to me again why we're doing this,' said Blythe, holding on tight to the ridiculously large fluffy grey and white dog who was named Princess but appeared to have no comprehension of that fact.

'So I can get a good reference from the owner,' said Vicky, grimacing like she was losing in a tug o' war competition as Princess's brother battled to wrench her arm from its socket.

'Yeah, that's the bit I don't get.' Vicky was a single mum to her daughter, Eden. She worked part-time in the local candle factory. How walking the owner's dogs would get her a good reference for a job, Blythe had no idea.

'It's my new business venture – dog walking,' said Vicky proudly, although she looked like she was skiing behind the old English sheepdog rather than walking it.

'Then we're getting paid for this?' Blythe felt a fraction better about her early start.

'Not exactly,' said Vicky. 'But if we do a good job they might be my first client.' She briefly grinned at Blythe before the dog jerked forward and she went flying, landing in a heap on the path. Thankfully she was still hanging on to the lead. 'Barnaby!' she yelled, making the dog bound back and jump all over her. 'Oof!' Vicky rolled onto her front but the dog found it was even more fun to tug on her ponytail. 'Barnaby, sit. Siiiit!' Barnaby ignored her.

Despite the large dogs it was always nice to have a walk through the scenic landscape that surrounded the village of Holly Cross. Nestled in the Warwickshire countryside it was where Blythe and Vicky had grown up. The village and its inhabitants held a special place in Blythe's heart. And whilst it hadn't been on her life plan to move back in with her mum and stepdad she was enjoying the feeling of being cosseted that they and the village gave her. Although she could do without them kissing at breakfast – it was enough to put anyone off their muesli. And worse than that it made her feel like a child again. All those mortifying moments when she'd walked in on her mum and Greg kissing and all the times Greg had insisted on picking her up from parties.

Blythe held on tight to her charge who was keen to join in. 'Would you be walking these two on a regular basis then?'

'Daily.' Vicky tried crawling away. 'Sit, Barnaby. Bloody well sit!'

'On your own?' asked Blythe, trying hard not to let it show on her face how much of a bad idea she thought this was.

Vicky wriggled away from the giant dog's slobbering jaws and got to her feet. 'Once they get used to me they'll be a lot calmer, I'm sure.'

'I'm not,' said Blythe under her breath as they carried on their walk. 'They'll eat you alive given half a chance.'

'I was sorry to hear about Murray dying,' said Vicky, pulling a sad face.

Blythe was interested how Vicky had made the connection because Murray was an elderly gent from their village who had recently passed away from old age and had not been eaten by out-of-control furry demons. 'Me too,' agreed Blythe. 'I know he was in his eighties but it was still a shock. Does that sound daft?'

'No.' Vicky shook her head and Barnaby tried to jump up and bite her ponytail. 'You two were mates.'

The phrase made Blythe raise an eyebrow. But on some level Vicky was right. Blythe had been popping round to Murray's on a regular basis. Partly because when Murray was away she fed the semi-feral cat who frequented his garden and partly because she enjoyed having a cuppa and a natter with the old man. Because he wasn't just an old man; he was someone with a wealth of life experience, a listening ear and somebody who offered sound advice. Blythe was really going to miss him. 'I guess we *were* mates. He always seemed happy. Never let anything get him down.'

'His funeral was held last week up in Manchester somewhere; that's what people were saying in the pub. I don't think anyone from Holly Cross went.'

'That is sad. I wonder why—' But Blythe didn't get to finish her sentence before the two dogs started to play-fight, tangling their leads and wrapping up the two young women like they were about to be kidnapped.

Once they had managed to untangle themselves, which actually took quite a while because both dogs thought it was a fun game and kept circling them and making things worse, they were able to continue on their country hike. 'How do you feel this is going then?' asked Blythe, now holding on to Princess's lead with both hands.

Vicky wrinkled her nose. 'Not quite as easy as I'd hoped.'

'Maybe you could walk them separately,' suggested Blythe.

'Not cost-effective. I need to do six walks a day to earn enough money from this, but if I walk multiple dogs at a time it could be a gold mine.' Vicky looked genuinely excited at the prospect.

'Would it not be easier to get some extra hours at the factory?' asked Blythe.

'They have been really good but next step is back to full-time working, which I can't do. I could fit the dog walking around my shifts and do it before and after school with Eden.'

'With Eden?' Images of the five-year-old flying behind Princess loomed large in Blythe's mind.

'Yeah. Fab mum and daughter time plus I would be my own boss and as most people are out at work all day they don't really care what time their dog is walked as long as they are taken out and get some exercise. And, who knows, if this really takes off I could then be employing other dog walkers and making shedloads without even having to leave the house.'

'Is there that much money in it?' Blythe was intrigued.

'Ten pounds a time soon adds up!'

Vicky looked thrilled and Blythe didn't have the heart to give her a reality check. Blythe swapped hands with the lead three times before she could get a look at her watch. 'I'll need to head back soon because I've got to have a shower and go into the office.'

'On a Sunday?'

Blythe brought Vicky up to speed on the whole sorry situation of Amir trying to snatch away her record-breaking sales achievement.

'He sounds like a shit,' said Vicky.

'I think that's a fair summary.' Blythe puffed out a breath. 'In any other situation I wouldn't begrudge him. I really wouldn't, but I've worked my bum off this last year. If I'm honest I'm surprised Ludo brought him in. With the sales I've been doing it's not like it warranted someone else. But Ludo said that was exactly why we needed another senior negotiator: because I was in danger of being overworked.'

'Don't you believe him?'

'Ludo is the most honest person I know. So I know he

genuinely thought bringing Amir in was the right thing to do. I don't trust Amir though.'

'Is Amir dishonest?'

'I don't have any evidence but a few things don't add up. And to get that many sales in one month when he'd been jogging along at almost half that many until now seems fishy to me.'

'But you got almost that many,' pointed out Vicky.

'Almost.' Blythe noisily sucked in air. 'I can't believe I got so close.'

'Oh well, never mind,' said Vicky breezily, making Blythe do a double take.

'Never mind?'

'Yeah.' Vicky shrugged. 'I know you wanted to set a new sales record but it doesn't really make any difference. Does it?'

'I would be the irrefutable top agent.'

'Ooh, like Danger Mouse,' said Vicky with a giggle, but the look Blythe was giving her made her put on a pretend serious face. 'I know you want to prove to your real dad that—'

Blythe was stunned. The mention of Hugh brought her up short, or it would have done if Princess would have let up her pulling for a second. Her dad had taught her many things: the importance of being professional, not to mix business with pleasure, and that no matter how much you loved someone they could still just walk out of your life. Twelve months of record sales was something her father, a London property guru, had said was impossible.

'What? It's got nothing to do with him. Nothing at all,' said Blythe, although it had set her wondering what it might be like to get a little praise from her father.

'Oh, okay. Sure.'

'I just want to be the best I can be. That's all. And I just need two more sales.' It was so frustrating.

'This cockney customer bloke...' began Vicky.

Blythe laughed. 'Just because he's from London doesn't make him a cockney.'

'Don't most of them speak like they're on *EastEnders*? You ain't my muvver; apples and pears; Gawd blimey, Mary Poppins.' Vicky's cockney accent was on a par with her business ideas.

'Obviously not. His accent is sort of neutral.' She'd spoken to him so many times. Mainly he sounded terse or bored and for some reason she guessed he was a similar age to her parents.

'Is he likely to put in an offer on a house over the phone?' asked Vicky.

'Probably not. I mean it does happen once in a blue moon with overseas clients and investors but I think that's about as likely as Barnaby listening to a command.' Although at the sound of his name Barnaby whipped around in Blythe's direction, spinning Vicky around like a top. His sister barked excitedly, making Blythe jump, and in a moment of confusion the lead was snatched from her hand. 'Nooooo!' she shouted, as Princess raced off with Barnaby close behind despite the fact he was dragging Vicky along with him.

Blythe gave chase but Princess was fast. She charged into long grass and apart from popping up a couple of times she then disappeared.

'Find her, Barnaby,' instructed Vicky. For the first time that day Barnaby sat down.

*

They searched and searched and eventually Blythe spotted a flash of white fur deep in the thicket. 'She's here!' she called although Vicky and Barnaby were nowhere in sight. Blythe pushed her way through the overgrown bushes and brambles, scratching her arms and at one point getting a bramble caught in her long hair, which she had to tug free. Eventually she found herself a few feet away from the dog.

'Come here, Princess,' she said, in the cheeriest voice she could muster.

Princess barked at her and danced up and down the small patch of earth on the other side of a tangle of brambles.

'Come on,' encouraged Blythe clapping her hands together. Princess stared at Blythe and then at the brambles. 'Really? You're scared of spiking your paws. Is that it?' Princess's tongue lolled out of her mouth as she panted. 'Seriously. For a very big dog you are a complete wimp.' Blythe checked her watch. She was running out of time fast. But then she could get away with not having a shower as nobody else would be in the office and it was only a phone call with Mr Ashton. Still she needed to get a move on – Sam Ashton was her last hope of at least landing a draw with Amir.

Princess barked and broke Blythe's train of thought. 'I'll come to you then,' she said, wondering why she was talking to a dog who clearly wasn't very bright if she'd managed to get herself surrounded by thorny bushes. Blythe stamped onto the brambles nearest to her, and they sprang back in protest and adhered themselves to her jeans. 'Bloody hell,' she grumbled trying to yank her clothes free. The more she stamped them down the more they attached themselves to her – they were nature's Velcro. Princess got bored and lay down with a hearty huff. 'If you think I'm carrying you out of here you can think again,' she told the mutt. Blythe stamped down on uneven ground, toppled, and reached out to stop herself falling. Unfortunately what she grabbed was another thorny section. 'Arghhhhhh!' She let go sharpish and as she fell she tried to avoid the brambles but instead landed in a pile of nettles.

A huffing and puffing behind her announced Vicky's arrival. 'There you are! What are you lying down for?'

'Princess won't walk on the brambles.' Blythe shook her head but before she could explain further Princess stood up and, using Blythe as a bridge, she trotted out of the bramble thicket to join Vicky and Barnaby. 'Good idea,' said Vicky, grabbing Princess's lead and looking impressed.

'I didn't intend her to... oh, never mind,' said Blythe.

They eventually returned the giant hounds to their owner who seemed pleased with the long walk they'd had but didn't even so much as tip Vicky, although she was buoyed up that she had at least one potential client for her new business. Blythe had left Vicky to it and dashed home, got straight in her car and set off. Thankfully town was quiet. Blythe hurriedly parked her car, grabbed her bag and headed for the office, marvelling at the stinging sensation in her arms and neck thanks to the nettles and thorns. She could have done the phone call from home but then she'd likely have her mum and stepdad hovering in the background, which wouldn't sound very professional, and anyway all the information was on her desk computer because Ludo worried about data protection and wouldn't let them have laptops that could be stolen. And there was still the remote chance Mr Ashton may ask some detailed questions or want more information emailing. If she was going to give this last straw her full attention then it was best that she was at her desk with everything she needed to hand. Blythe vowed that if Mr Ashton didn't buy anything today then she was going to move him to the WOTs file.

Blythe pulled out her office keys and was about to open up as her phone rang. It was Vicky. 'Hi, Vicky, is it urgent because I have to call Ashton dead on ten?'

'Sure. I wanted you to know I have my first clients! I'm going to be walking Barnaby and Princess daily!'

'Congratulations, I think,' said Blythe, screwing up her features at the thought of the giant beasts and feeling something sting in her cheek. 'We'll celebrate later. I've got to go because I want to get ready for this client.'

'I thought you said he was a waste of time?'

'I did and I know it's pointless because he's a time-wasting numpty who is likely never going to buy anything but I have to try.'

'Well, I hope he buys the biggest house you have,' said Vicky. Blythe was aware of someone standing on the pavement very close to her. She glanced over her shoulder and a casually dressed man in his late twenties smiled back at her. In actual fact he looked quite amused at something. Blythe ignored him. She turned the key and shot inside the office.

'Thanks, Vicky. I've gotta go. I'll catch you later.'

'Pub?'

'If you like. Bye.'

Blythe ended the call, hit the on button on her computer

and went through to the back to grab a quick coffee. While she was waiting for the kettle to boil she heard someone try the door. 'Sorry we're closed!' she called, adding under her breath, 'which is why the closed sign is up.' Some people were dumb. She hastily made a coffee and dashed back to her desk to pull up the property details so she could see which of Mr Ashton's criteria she was going to focus on with each of them. She checked the time. Dead on ten o'clock she picked up her phone to dial his number and it sprang into life. It was Mr Ashton, which was quite annoying because even after everything she wasn't late calling him.

She composed herself for her last-ditch attempt at getting a May sale and put on her most professional voice. 'Good morning, Mr Ashton, bang on time. I had my phone in my hand. Which of the properties I sent would you like to know more about first?'

'I was hoping I could have a sit-down.'

What did that mean? Blythe closed her eyes so she could concentrate. 'The Regency semi in Leamington has a beautiful window seat…' She paused while she brought the details up on her screen.

'O-kay. But I'd be happy with that chair there.'

Blythe peered at the photos on her screen. 'I'm sorry, which chair?'

There was a tap on the glass door. 'That one.'

Blythe was preparing a scowl for whoever was at the door until she saw it was the man from earlier. He now had a mobile held to his ear and he was pointing at her. 'Crap,' she said, and then realised her mistake. 'I'm so sorry. Are you?' She pointed to the man outside and he nodded. Blythe stood up so fast she knocked her chair over and bumped her desk, spilling her coffee and hurting her thigh. 'Well, this is a lovely surprise...' She wondered why she now sounded like her grandmother. She shoved the phone into her neck while she wrestled with the door. She snatched it open and the man outside beamed an amused smile at her.

'Mr Ashton?' she said.

'Hi Blythe, call me Sam,' he said, ending the call and offering her a hand to shake.

Blythe shook hands and then realised she must have looked like an idiot as she still had her phone tucked into her neck. She quickly shoved it in her pocket. 'Come in. Sit down. Can I get you a coffee?' she said, the whole time wondering why the hell he was there in person.

'No coffee for me. I just had one while I was waiting for you to open.'

Blythe raced around to her side of the desk and sat down, which was when she noticed the spilled coffee. She grabbed a handful of tissues from the box on her desk and began mopping. 'I'm sorry, I wasn't expecting you,' she said.

'Oh, I thought we said ten o'clock?'

'For a phone call.' She knew she was pulling that tense-emoji face she did in awkward situations but it was hard not to.

'I thought we were viewing all those houses you sent me.' Sam frowned hard. 'I've come up from London especially to see them.'

This was the best and worst news in one sentence. The chances of him actually making an offer on a property over the phone had been minuscule so now she had a real chance of selling one and setting a new sales record. She had desperately wanted to show him properties but he'd always said he was too busy to travel up and now he was here and she had no appointments booked in with vendors. *Don't panic*, she told herself, while a mini version of her inside her brain had a total meltdown. 'And see properties is exactly what we will do,' she told him firmly. Although she did not want him sitting there while she grovelled to vendors to let her view their property on a Sunday morning with a moment's notice. 'How about you have a little mooch around the town. Get a feel for the place while I make some calls?'

'I don't think—'

'You could grab another coffee, see the sights. There's a clock tower, the church is stunning and—'

He seemed to sense her desperation for him to clear off. 'I'll be back in twenty minutes.' He checked his watch, stood up and left.

At the sound of the door closing Blythe puffed out a breath she'd been holding in and slumped back in her chair. This was a nightmare. Sam opened the door again and she sat bolt upright, almost giving herself whiplash. Blythe pasted on a smile.

'If we're visiting people, you might want to…' He waved a finger in a circle motion around her head. He grinned at her and closed the door.

What was that about? She picked up her phone and flipped the camera so she could see herself. Her usually straight golden hair was like a mad professor's but with added leaves and twigs. There was a smudge of dirt on her forehead and a scratch covered in dried blood on her cheek. 'Arghhhhhhh!'

3

30th May

Blythe may not have given off the professional image she'd been hoping for but at least after a few frantic phone calls she now had four viewings lined up. Thankfully despite the short notice, in a slow-moving market, vendors were still keen to sell even if it meant tidying up and changing out of their pyjamas on a Sunday.

Blythe pulled the last of the foliage from her long hair, quickly put it up into a rough bun and dashed out of the toilets to see Sam hovering outside the shop. She watched him for a moment. He wasn't at all how she'd pictured him from their many phone conversations. But now she thought about it those interactions had been pretty one-sided – she'd been the one doing all the talking with the occasional clipped comment from him, reminding her of her stepdad when she was trying to talk to him whilst the football was on.

Whilst he might have sounded a little bit like her stepdad he definitely didn't look like him. Sam was very tall with the sort of dark stubble on his jaw that had her wondering if he was growing a beard or just liked his stubble extra-long. He pushed his sun-streaked hair off his face, making her think he usually wore it shorter. When he turned to look through the glass she rapidly gathered up her things. Blythe joined him outside feeling a little more like she was back in control and that the game was certainly still afoot. If she could actually get Sam inside some of these homes she stood an excellent chance of landing a sale. It was all to play for.

She went through the hastily arranged viewings as they walked to her car and she explained that she also had calls out for two more properties that, worst case, she would just call on and see if they could accommodate a viewing. It wasn't ideal but they could always say no. 'These are some of the best properties in the area. You're going to be spoiled for choice.' She glanced at Sam for a reaction but he was still looking at the details of the first property they were going to.

'This one's a bit modern,' he said.

Blythe always avoided confirming any doubts; she preferred to focus on the positives. 'It's in your ideal location. Close to the countryside, but convenient for the town and the motorway networks. It has four bedrooms so you could easily use one of those as a home office and it has a lovely garden.' She was mentally ticking off Sam's requirements list in her head as she reeled off the house's best features.

'Hmm.' Not the most encouraging response but it wasn't a straight no, so there was still hope.

Blythe bleeped her car open and they got in.

Sam folded himself into the car. A little too late Blythe realised she'd pushed the passenger seat forward to get something in the back a few days previously and not bothered to return it to a neutral position. Sam's knees were wedged against the glove box.

'Whoops, sorry,' said Blythe. She automatically went to pull the lever under the seat. Sam looked alarmed at where she was putting her hand. 'Sorry,' she repeated as she pulled the lever and Sam was catapulted backwards at speed. He now looked like he was sat in the back but she wasn't groping around his thighs again. Sam seemed to make her small car feel minuscule; his head was almost touching the roof. At least it was a short drive to property one.

She pulled up as close to the place as she could and they got out. Blythe could tell Sam wasn't impressed by the way he was scowling up and down the street. 'It's quite a busy road. You can't see that from the photographs.'

'It's always good to assess that sort of thing from inside the property because often once you're in the house any road noise diminishes,' said Blythe, ushering him along.

As it turned out there was actually more noise inside the property. The owner opened the door with a screaming toddler and a selection of toys in his arms. 'Hi, sorry come in. My wife is away on business so I've not really had a chance to tidy up but you're welcome to look around.' He handed Blythe a doll so he could shake Sam's proffered hand.

Blythe slapped on a smile. This was not a good start. Negotiating the toy-strewn hallway was harder than an army assault course. 'Actually, could you take your shoes off please? Cream carpets,' the owner added by way of explanation. Blythe and Sam did as requested. She noted his Star Wars socks. Blythe knew the house layout and had already mapped out in her head which order to view the rooms. In his requirements Sam had majored on needing a designated room as an office and for it to be an easy drive to the nearest motorway junction – she wondered what he did for a living and she filed that for discussion later as it might be something she could use.

They went upstairs and she pointed out that it had been recently decorated. The first floor looked like the place had been burgled. Toys were scattered everywhere. There was a pile of wet towels on the bathroom floor and the once shiny white tiles were covered in what looked like blue paint. She saw Sam's eyes widen at the sight.

'It's just those bath crayons; it'll rinse off,' she said, giving it a rub with her finger and smearing more blue across the tile. 'Anyway, master bedroom is a great size and has an en suite.' She pushed open the door to see a toilet with the lid up and a large floating turd bobbing on the surface. She swiftly shut the lid and pointed at the shower to pull Sam's attention, which worked. 'Rainfall shower. Right, let's take a look at the other bedrooms and see which would make the best home office.'

She waxed lyrical about the light, built-in storage and the fact that one bedroom was at the back of the house so was quietest. Sam didn't say anything. Complete silence. She'd have preferred it if he'd been negative because at least then she could counter his objections, but nothing was hard to manage. They went back downstairs and she did get a nod in both the kitchen and lounge so all was not lost. Out in the garden she painted a little aspirational living picture. 'This corner here is the perfect suntrap. Ideal for a summer's evening, perhaps a barbecue and a few drinks with friends. Time to relax and unwind after a busy week. Can you imagine sitting out here and kicking back?'

'It's quite small,' said Sam.

'It will certainly be easy to manage.'

'And you can hear the road.'

'But you wouldn't over the laughter of friends.' She gave a little chuckle as a demonstration. 'Would you like to see any of the rooms again or ask the vendor any questions?'

'Yeah…' Hope soared in Blythe's heart. Questions showed interest; they were a good thing. She steered him into the living room where the owner was trying to put the scattered parts of a Mr Potato Head in a toy box while the toddler screamed and threw them out again. Sam stepped forward just as the toddler chucked something down and Sam trod on it. 'Ow!' Sam staggered about on one leg, his features screwed up in pain.

'Lego,' said the owner, with a sympathetic look on his face. 'Almost the worst pain known to man. Second only to knob in zipper.'

Blythe blinked at him. This was why she preferred to conduct viewings without the owners present. 'You had a question, Sam?'

Sam gingerly returned his foot to the floor. 'What's the broadband like here?' he asked.

'Shocking,' said the owner.

Blythe wanted to shake him. 'But that can be upgraded,' she said quickly.

'Nah, we're on the best there is and it's still crap.' Blythe glared at him and he seemed to get the message. 'But the pub's great. Well, the beer is, the food not so much.' Men were unbelievable.

'Right, we'd best be off but I'll be in touch,' said Blythe, keen to move on. 'Thanks again for letting us view at short notice.'

Sam wasn't going to make an offer on this house and the sooner they found one he was going to buy the better.

4

30th May

Vicky loved living in Holly Cross – so much so that when her parents had decided to move away to the seaside she had insisted on staying. She missed them, and the lack of childcare was tricky, but it was nice to have a little place for her and Eden. And whilst on paper she'd known the rent and other bills would be a stretch financially the reality was even more of a challenge. She had no wiggle room for Eden needing two pairs of shoes in one term or being invited to parties where it was expected she'd take a present. There was no spare cash for luxuries. She didn't want to live like that and certainly wanted a little more for her daughter.

Vicky was very pleased with how her first dog walk had gone. After mulling over a number of business ideas she'd hit on the dog walking. She loved dogs, needed an additional income and wanted some regular exercise as she had a big liking for cheese, chocolate and cake, so this was the perfect solution.

It had been particularly good to get out of the house that morning because it was the first time Eden had been to stay at her parents' new house, and she missed her. It was just the two of them and Eden was Vicky's world. While she'd been hanging on to Barnaby's lead with two hands, she'd not been able to check her phone every two seconds to see if her parents had messaged. Of course they hadn't. After she'd panicked last night that she'd not heard anything and had catastrophised it in her mind until she was certain the reason she'd not had an update from them was because Eden had been rushed to hospital, she'd rung her mum in a stressed-out state. Her mum had calmed her down and explained they'd been at the park most of the day.

Instead of offering to message Vicky regularly her mum said it was best if she assumed everything was wonderful unless she heard otherwise. Her daughter was away for the whole weekend, and Vicky knew it was going to seem like a lot longer. Eden was just five years old – she was bound to worry about her. Just thinking about something happening to her daughter brought on a sense of dread.

When she'd cleaned and tidied the little house and all the washing up was done, Vicky decided she'd have a go at conjuring up some business names and maybe even design a logo. It killed an hour and she was quite pleased with her efforts. So much so that she printed some off and decided to pop round to the local pub to seek a consensus on the best name and see if she could drum up some business. The sooner she got more clients on her list the sooner she would start earning some extra money.

The Highway Inn was always busy at weekends. As a desi pub it was a destination in its own right because the food was so good. Desi pubs were a Midlands phenomenon where Asian cuisine met classic English pub, and a gastro revolution had been born. Vicky had to agree that beer and curry was a winning combination.

'What can I get you, Vicky?' asked Sarvan, who ran the pub with his wife Jassi.

'Just a tap water and some advice.' Vicky spread out her printed sheets while Sarvan got her drink.

When he placed it on the bar the colourful printouts caught his eye. 'What do we have here?'

'My new business venture. I think having the right business name is really important. It needs to say what it is but also be memorable. Which of these do you think stands out?'

Sarvan read the examples and his eyes widened as they moved across the page. 'Rollover and Beg, Bone Sweet Bone, Shaggy Bitch, Doggy Style…' Sarvan did a slow blink as if composing his question in his mind. 'What sort of business is it?'

Vicky tilted her head in question. 'Dog walking obviously. Why?'

Blythe's day went from bad to worse. The second property was an immediate no from Sam because it was next to a school. The third property ticked a lot of boxes but was definitely something even Blythe would struggle to class as a project. It was a full renovation, which was already above Sam's price limit. House number four had the perfect location: a village twenty minutes from the motorway junction Sam wanted to be close to, and it was also a cute cottage with a courtyard.

They stood in the farmhouse-style kitchen. 'Well?' asked Blythe.

'I love it,' said Sam.

'Fantastic!' she said, already mentally slapping another unicorn on the sales chart.

'But it's not for me.'

Blythe felt like she'd been kicked by a unicorn. 'Why? Why? Why?' She was losing her patience. Which was unusual for her. Usually she was focused on finding people their perfect home and that was what mattered and gave her a real sense of job satisfaction, but today that was a bit lacking and she felt bad because of it. Thanks to Amir's sneaky tactics she was focusing on the sale and not on the client. She was a bit shocked with herself. Ludo had taught her better and one day she very much hoped to be able to take over the running of the agency from him. Despite the competition, Sam Ashton still deserved to get the five-star service she gave everyone else.

Sam twisted his lips. 'It doesn't feel right. I love the period features, the layout and location, but it's not going to work.' He looked skywards.

'Okay. Why do you think that is? Because it has everything on your must-have list.'

Sam wobbled his head and she knew he was going to challenge her statement. 'It's only two bedrooms so if I use one as an office I have no spare bedroom.'

'They are two good double bedrooms so you could have a sofa bed in the second one as well as a desk.' In her mind she mentally ticked off that objection.

'I was hoping for a proper garden not just some hardstanding.'

'It's a courtyard garden. Some planters would make a world of difference.' She was straw clutching again.

'And then there's this,' said Sam, at last lifting his hand to knock on the ceiling. The very low ceiling that was causing him to stoop like a giant in a doll's house.

Blythe huffed out a breath. She knew when she was beaten. She smiled. 'I feared that might be a problem.'

Sam smiled back. 'If you could find me this cottage but just a bit bigger, I'd be putting in an offer.'

The words were like an aphrodisiac. Surely there was somewhere else. 'Right, let's go to the next house. It's not exactly like this and they might not let us view it. But have a look from the outside.' It would also give her some thinking time. She was mentally scrolling through previous valuations and properties Happy Homes had had on their books in the past. Perhaps one of those would fit the bill and maybe they were ready to move again. All very flimsy, but flimsy was all she had.

They thanked the owners, got back in the car and headed off. The route to the next property took them through Holly Cross. As Blythe came into the village, she passed her parents' house. Her stepdad was mowing the lawn and seeing her car he waved and came striding over. Blythe pulled up.

'Someone you know?' asked Sam.

'My stepdad,' replied Blythe, putting on her hazard lights and buzzing down her window. 'I'm with a client, Greg. I'll be back later.' She thought it best to pre-empt his conversation.

'Hello,' said Greg, reaching inside to shake Sam's hand. 'Has she found your ideal home yet?'

'We're still looking.'

'She's their star negotiator you know.'

'I didn't know that,' said Sam, raising an eyebrow at

Blythe. 'I'm after somewhere like this.' Sam pointed past Greg at their chocolate-box property. I don't suppose your house is for sale, is it?'

Blythe looked hopefully at Greg. She had not long ago sold her own home to clients, which was why she was back at home. That and a need to recharge thanks to a nasty relationship break-up. She was keeping an eye out for her ideal property and like Sam she'd know it when she saw it.

Greg shook his head and laughed. 'Only way I'm leaving here is in a box. Sorry, young man. Thanks for the compliment though.'

'Right, bye then,' said Blythe.

'Just a sec,' said Greg. 'Your mum is making her spag bol for dinner.' He grimaced.

Blythe pulled a face to match Greg's. 'Okay. Thanks for the warning. And now I have to go,' she said, and with a smile she shooed Greg away from her car.

'She'll find you the right place. Mark my words. Top negotiator,' he said with a cheery wave. Greg always went a bit over the top with the compliments. If only her real father was half as encouraging.

Blythe checked the road was clear – although there was very little traffic in Holly Cross – indicated and waved as they drove away. Sam's head was on a swivel. 'This is a gorgeous village. You're very lucky to live here.'

'It's only temporary. But yeah, it is really lovely. Close community, good primary school, great pub and easy access to the motorway.' Why was she selling him a place with no available properties?

'If somewhere comes up here I'd definitely be interested.'

A thought struck her. Blythe slammed on her brakes.

Sam almost banged his head on the dashboard. 'Hold on, I've had an idea,' said Blythe, as hope and excitement blossomed in her gut. She slammed the car in reverse and in a slightly wobbly line she sped backwards to Greg.

After swinging the car onto the driveway, she abandoned it and raced into the house. A couple of minutes later she came back to find Greg and Sam discussing football teams. 'Wait until you see this one,' said Blythe to Sam.

Sam said his goodbyes to Greg and wound up the passenger window.

'We don't need the car; we can walk from here,' she said, opening the door and striding off with a spring in her step.

'What are you up to?' called Greg.

'I'll tell you later. Bye,' she said with a wave, and Sam jogged to catch her up.

'Which property is this one?' asked Sam. 'Because I left all the details in your passenger footwell.'

'Ahh, this is very new to the market and we don't have details for it yet.'

'You've got me intrigued,' said Sam.

'Good,' said Blythe.

They walked down the gentle hill, over the crossroads that gave the village its name and around the green. As they passed the village stores and bakery, Norman was locking up and he flagged her down. 'Can you make use of a tiger and a crusty?' he asked. She saw Sam smirk.

'Always, Norman – any discount?'

He laughed good-naturedly. 'Half price. I'll add them to your bill,' he said, handing her two wrapped parcels.

'Thanks,' she said, taking them and handing them straight to Sam. 'Sniff those,' she instructed. Sam did as she suggested as they continued to walk through the village. 'Fresh bread. You can't beat it. He still makes it daily. And his cream horns are to die for. This is a very special village.'

'I'm beginning to sense that.'

'You like Christmas right?' she asked casually as they crossed the road.

Sam pulled his chin into his chest. 'Can't stand it. It's over-commercialised hype. Months of cynical advertising aimed at winding kids up into a frenzy about some cheaply made tat their parents will spend the rest of the year paying for. It guilts people into over-spending only to be disappointed because their expectations were so high. Then they're depressed and in debt. And don't get me started on the whole massive Santa lie thing. Christmas really is the worst.'

Blythe laughed then noted his stony expression. 'You're joking, right?'

'I'm deadly serious.'

She realised some faiths didn't celebrate it. 'Is it... um... a religious thing?'

'Not at all. It's a common-sense thing. Why would you build up one single day to such heights? You're always going to be disappointed. It's like a collective madness falls over this country in the last quarter of the year. I steer completely clear of it.' He motioned his hands as if he were drawing a line.

Blythe hadn't been expecting such a vehement and negative torrent. 'Right. That's a definite no to Christmas then.'

'Sorry. It's just one of my pet hates. Why do you ask?'

This was the moment for her to tell him. She swallowed

hard. Or she could tell him later, see if he liked the house then explain it to him, she reasoned. Yes, that was a good idea. 'I was just going to say that they decorate the green with lights at Christmas and it looks really pretty.' Sam didn't say anything but he was watching her closely like he suspected something was up. 'But you like curry, right?'

'I love a good curry.'

She breathed a sigh of relief. 'Then you'll love our local pub.' She pointed to the Highway Inn on the other side of the village green.

They passed the ornate village sign and the higgledy-piggledy cottages that encircled the heart of the village. Across the way a horse whinnied in its field as if on cue – it was picture-perfect.

'Here we are,' announced Blythe, and she stood back so Sam could take in the property. Blythe could have written the details then and there – *accessed through a canopied porch and dark oak entrance door, this is a once-in-a-lifetime opportunity to purchase this magnificent three-bedroom thatched house with single garage set within the heart of Warwickshire Conservation Area. Built in the 1920s, the property occupies a double-width plot with gardens extending to approximately half an acre, with the house nestling beautifully within them. Throughout the property are leaded Crittall windows, exposed beams and all principal rooms enjoy views into the beautiful, established gardens with other rooms overlooking the famous Holly Cross village green.*

Sam looked at the house and Blythe held her breath while she watched him. 'It's in excellent order throughout.'

'The thatch will need replacing within the next two years.'

'Looks okay to me but a survey will confirm that.'

'Trust me, three years tops,' said Sam. 'Is it in my price range?'

'Like I said it's new to the market. We haven't confirmed a price yet but I would value it at the top end of your budget.' Sam's cheek twitched. 'But it's worth every penny. Take a look inside.'

Blythe unlocked the front door and let Sam go in first. She directed him into the living room with its stone fireplace, window seat and bay window that looked out over the green. Then back into the hallway to view the dining room, generous kitchen, utility room and cloakroom. 'It's a bit quirky because there's a further living room or snug through here, which would make the perfect home office. She led the way through a latched door, down two small steps and into a square room with an inglenook fireplace and French windows out onto the large garden. It was a bit dated with a hotchpotch of old furniture but it was clean and tidy.

Sam went to the windows and looked out on the garden and the willow tree waving gently at them in the breeze. It looked like someone had recently mowed the lawn; that was handy. 'On the first floor is a principal bedroom with en suite, two further double bedrooms, airing cupboard, a family bathroom and access to loft space.' At last a smile spread across Sam's face. And Blythe knew she'd nailed it.

5

1st June

'What do you mean you've sold Murray's house?'
Ludo's already ruddy complexion had found a new
level on the colour chart.

Blythe had called him on Monday to tell him she'd beaten
Amir because Sam had fallen for a Holly Cross property
and thanks to an evening phone call from the first-time
buyers who had just landed at Heathrow she had secured
the two sales she needed by the end of May. The only slight
problem was that it was Tuesday morning and she was now
back in the office having to explain which house Sam was
buying and her boss was not as overjoyed as she'd imagined
he would be.

'I had a copy of Murray's keys because he was away a lot
and I was driving through Holly Cross and I realised it was
the perfect house for Sam... Mr Ashton.'

Ludo ran his hands over where his hair used to be. 'But
it's not on our books. We have no instruction to sell it. No
remit. It's not ours to sell.' He looked increasingly alarmed
by his own words.

'*Technically*, we don't.' She held up her palms to stop
Ludo's protests, which were coming thick and fast.

'But Murray died, and he lived alone so the house will need to be sold. We're just being proactive.' It had sounded better in her head when she'd justified her actions to herself. Saying it out loud, even she could see that she'd crossed a line. A line Ludo had always been very clear about. 'It'll be fine. I just need to find out who is acting for Murray's estate, offer our services, which they're bound to accept because we already have a buyer. It should be a no-brainer.' Ludo's brow was puckered with worry but worse than that he looked disappointed. 'Ludo, it'll be fine. Trust me.'

'I did,' said Ludo. He opened his mouth to say something else but a tap on his office door stopped him. They both turned to look.

Amir was frowning at them. Blythe had been so looking forward to this moment. 'Could I have a word?' asked Amir, popping his head around the door. 'It's about the chart.'

'Do you mean the two additional sales I secured this weekend?' asked Blythe, trying hard not to sound as smug as she felt, but failing. 'I'm sorry, Amir, but there will be other opportunities for you. Breaking the record was really important to me. I hope you understand.'

'You can't have won.' Amir's frown deepened. 'Where did you—'

'Hold fire, both of you,' said Ludo waving his arms. 'The competition is off.'

'What?' said Blythe and Amir in unison.

'I blame myself.' Ludo shook his head. 'When I set up Happy Homes I never intended to create this dangerous level of competitiveness. It's always been about doing the right thing for the client. Striving to avoid being the cliché everyone expects estate agents to be.' He looked from Blythe to Amir who was still standing in the doorway looking confused. 'It has to stop.'

It was like she'd been winded by his words. 'But I beat the sales record.' Her voice sounded pathetic even to her own ears. All this time she had been striving to prove herself to her father and Ludo. To do the impossible and have the highest sales every month for a whole year and now he was calling a halt to it all. She'd already emailed her father to tell him. Blythe could feel tears building behind her eyes and she took a deep breath to steady herself.

'So nobody won then. I can live with that,' said Amir. 'What about the monthly bonus for the top number of sales. What's happening with that?' asked Amir.

Ludo rolled his lips together and shook his head. 'It all has to be revised.'

'Of course,' said Amir. 'But what about this month?'

'I need to think everything through, so for now there's no bonus until I work out where I went wrong,' said Ludo.

Amir didn't look pleased. 'But I was in the lead when the last working day ended so technically I should receive it. And I need to pay the balance on my holiday so—'

'Amir!' Ludo raised his voice. Ludo never raised his voice.

Amir pulled his head back in surprise. 'Sure, let me know,' he said backing out of the room.

There was a long awkward pause. Ludo stared at the carpet.

'I'm sorry,' said Blythe, her voice feeble. 'I'll sort everything out about Murray's house sale. I can put it all straight. I promise.' She wasn't sure how, but she would find a way.

★

As Eden had gone to a friend's for tea and to watch a new release on Disney Plus, Blythe had dragged Vicky to the pub. Sitting in the bar with Vicky, Blythe tried to mentally tick off who in the village would know a bit more about Murray. Blythe had spent half her day ringing round local solicitors, trying to find out who was dealing with Murray's estate, and she'd drawn a blank. She'd been reckless and stupid and now she had an excited buyer but potentially no way to sell him the house of his dreams.

Blythe held her head in her hands. 'It's a mess.'

'Yep, it is,' replied Vicky.

Blythe peeped through her fingers. 'Thanks.'

'I'm not being mean. I'm just agreeing with you. But it doesn't mean you can't sort it out.'

'But if I can't find who is managing Murray's estate I'm screwed.'

'I suppose they'll have to sell the cottage at some point, so hopefully they'll pick Happy Homes as their estate agent.'

'I'm not that lucky,' said Blythe. 'But I will leave my details on the kitchen table in case someone comes to empty the place. Assuming there is someone.'

'Somebody organised his funeral,' said Vicky, making Blythe's head snap up.

'You're right. If I can find out who that was then I would have the next of kin. You're a genius.' Blythe got on her phone but a few minutes later she realised there were no details about Murray's funeral on the internet. It was another dead end. 'Do you remember who told you that Murray was buried in Manchester?'

Vicky scrunched up her features in thought. 'Could have been Sarvan. Not sure.'

Blythe looked at her empty glass and Vicky's. 'Do you want another drink?'

Vicky checked her watch. 'Eden's out until seven thirty. So, yes please. I'll have a snowball.' Vicky grinned at her.

'You're joking? When have you ever drunk snowballs?'

'Never, but that's why I want to try one. I'm branching out. Widening my horizons. I've lived in this village my whole life and it's time to spread my wings.'

'And a snowball will do that, will it?'

Vicky narrowed her eyes at her friend. 'It's a start.'

'One snowball coming right up.' Blythe took the empties back to the bar. It was busy and she had to wait.

One of the older regulars, Arthur, was sitting on a stool staring into his half-empty pint. 'Hi, Arthur, how are you?'

'I'm fine thank you,' he said, although the deep sigh that followed told her otherwise.

'You sure?'

'Just feeling my age today. That's all.' Arthur was in his eighties but generally seemed in rude health. He strode around the village with the gusto of a much younger man. But tonight he did look deflated and frailer than usual. He pulled a smile from somewhere. 'How about you?'

'Not great.'

'Oh dear, why ever is that?' He turned his body towards her and looked genuinely interested.

'I've sold a house.'

'Isn't that a good thing?' asked Arthur.

'Usually it is but I've done a really daft thing.' She bit her lip.

'Go on,' he encouraged.

'I found the perfect house for a buyer and the buyer is perfect for the house. He absolutely loves it. But I didn't get the um… owner's permission to sell it.'

'And they don't want to sell?'

Blythe sucked her lip. 'It's not that. I actually think they will be very happy to sell. I just don't know who the owner is.' Arthur was looking decidedly puzzled. It was time to own up. 'The house is Murray's.'

Arthur looked suitably shocked. 'Oh, I see.' Then his expression changed to something worse than shocked, he looked disappointed – it was the same expression she'd seen on Ludo. She felt awful.

'I know it was a stupid thing to do. But I just thought Murray's house would have to be sold anyway and this buyer had a really unique set of requirements, which Murray's place could satisfy. It seemed like the perfect match. So I showed him the house and he fell completely in love with it.' She was about to try to explain further in an attempt to change Arthur's expression but Sarvan appeared to take her drinks order, distracting her. She had a brief chat with Sarvan about Murray, but he couldn't remember who had told him about Murray's funeral, and he had no further details so they moved on to the delightfully warm weather. Blythe paid and turned to take her drinks back to Vicky. 'Take care, Arthur. Thanks for listening,' she said, moving away from the bar.

'I can make a few enquiries,' he said.

'Sorry?' Blythe spun around, sloshing her Diet Coke but managing to contain the snowball in its fancy glass.

'I used to be a solicitor's clerk and I still know a few people locally.'

'Thanks. I'm not being funny but anyone I've spoken to today has given me a straight brush-off because they won't divulge who their clients are. Even if they're dead.' Which did seem a little extreme to Blythe especially as what she had done would be a benefit to them.

'That is true, but if you have someone who would love the house like Murray did then I feel we should do what we can.' He gave a wan smile.

'Thank you, Arthur. That would be great.' At this stage she was grateful for any and all assistance, however unlikely it was. 'And in the meantime, if you could keep an eye out for anyone putting up a for sale sign in Murray's garden...'

'Will do,' he said, and he turned back to his receding pint.

6

Vicky waited outside the village hall with all the dads who had been sent to collect their offspring from Rainbows and Brownies. It seemed to be an unwritten rule that mums dropped off and dads picked up. But that was not the case for her. She was both mum and dad – always had been. It was just one more thing she had to do. The situation may have been different if she and Owen had stayed together. The thought of him made her shudder and the dad next to her gave her a cautious glance before quietly taking a sly step away from her. That was fine. It was best if men kept away from her. She'd decided that long ago thanks to Owen. Eden came skipping out with her friend who ran off the moment she spotted her dad. She wondered if Eden noticed things like that?

'Hi, sweetie, how was Rainbows?' she asked.

Eden beamed a smile. Her two front baby teeth were missing. She was growing up. 'It was fun. Look, I made this myself!' Eden excitedly thrust a clear bag at Vicky containing a lumpy brown substance, which worryingly did look like she'd made it herself.

Vicky recoiled. 'Wow. What have you got there?' It looked exactly like what she'd been picking up on her dog walks.

Eden's grin broadened. 'It's chocolate fudge! Do you want to try some?'

As unappetising as it looked the first rule of parenting was that you could never refuse to try your child's cooking, however bad it appeared. 'Of course I do.'

'Mia is going on holiday on an aeroplane,' said Eden, wide-eyed. It was moments like this that Vicky felt like a bad mum. She couldn't give Eden what other parents could. She knew lavish holidays weren't everything but she hated the thought of Eden missing out, of her feeling somehow lesser than her friends.

'That's nice for her,' said Vicky.

'She's going to America to a place called...' Eden paused with a lump of brown on her finger as she puckered her forehead in thought '...Vagina!' she announced with gusto.

'Virginia,' corrected Vicky.

'She's going to ride a horse like a cowboy, sleep in a wigwam and go to theme parks with really scary rides!'

Yep, Vicky couldn't compete with that. 'Once I've built up the dog-walking business we might be able to go on a little holiday,' said Vicky, thinking out loud.

'To America?' Eden's voice was almost a gasp.

'No, sorry, that's really expensive. I was thinking a caravan in Devon would be fun.'

Eden's slopey shoulders said she didn't agree.

They walked along with Eden dipping her finger in the fudge bag. 'Snowy Owl says people should walk their

47

own dogs and that Hot Dogs sounds like you're opening a McDonald's.' Eden laughed. 'Silly Snowy Owl. McDonald's sell burgers not hot dogs.'

Vicky wished Snowy Owl would keep her beak to herself especially as Vicky was proud she'd finally settled on a name for her new business and had spent quite a few hours printing out flyers she was going to distribute around Holly Cross and the neighbouring villages. Over the next few days the plan was to walk Princess and Barnaby and deliver the flyers at the same time – two birds, one stone.

Amir was regaling Blythe with his top tips for wooing clients, making her want to ram Blu-Tack in her ears, when she was interrupted by her mobile vibrating. She glanced at the screen and a mix of delight and trepidation permeated her system – it was her father. His calls were rare and almost always scheduled. This was an impromptu phone call.

'Sorry, I need to take this,' she said, waving for Amir to get his backside off her desk. Amir looked put out but left anyway, most likely to bestow his knowledge on some other poor soul.

'Hi, Dad, this is a nice surprise. How are you?'

'Busy. I assume you're still working for Ludo Chadwick.'

She shouldn't have been thrown by the lack of usual pleasantries, but she was. Her father was a very focused individual and sometimes he overlooked things like chit-chat. But then perhaps she was being overly sensitive; he had explained he was busy.

'I am, can I help you with something?' She'd been working her way up the ladder at Happy Homes estate agents since university in the hope of impressing her father – the London property specialist – maybe, at last, this was her opportunity. She'd had no reply to the email she'd sent about her record-breaking year of sales.

'Of course. I'm sure you can. Hence my phone call.' Blythe's spirit soared. This was the moment she had waited years for. An acknowledgement from her father that she was competent in his eyes. It was an unexpectedly emotional moment, making her swallow hard before regaining focus. She had to get this right.

'What do you need help with?'

'Have you got a mobile number for Ludo?'

'Yes, of course. I'll email it to you right away.' She put the phone under her chin and fired off an email. That was easy. She steeled herself for the big request. 'What else can I help with?'

'That was all. Thanks.'

Blythe blinked. Surely that wasn't the only reason he'd called her. 'Oh, right. So how've you been?' She could feel her shoulders drooping with disappointment.

'Busy, like I said. I'm afraid I can't chat. Do we have a call in the diary?'

'Not for another couple of weeks.' Her voice was gloomier than Eeyore's.

'That's great.' He sounded chipper at the prospect. 'I'll speak to you then, Blythe. And thank you, you've been most helpful.' The line went dead. She liked to think she could brush off her father's limited interactions and how they made her feel, and sometimes she could, but not today. That feeling that she was never good enough. That however hard she tried he never noticed, praised or rewarded her.

And after calls like this one it was like a part of her returned to that dejected little girl whose daddy had walked out and never come back. The six-year-old he'd had a conversation with earlier that morning when she'd caught him putting a case in the car when her mum was at work. And who told her it was a secret. A little holiday. But she mustn't mention it to mummy. She'd been so excited she'd turned the garage upside down hunting for her bucket and spade.

But it had all been in vain when her mum had returned from a long shift at the supermarket only for her husband to tell her he was leaving while Blythe watched from the top of the stairs.

Blythe decided to go home via Murray's house. She was still feeding the cat anyway, so she could write a nice note and leave it on the kitchen table with her business card – just in case whoever had inherited the property popped by. She let herself in and walked through the hallway, but a couple of paces in she sensed something was different. She reversed back. She glanced around: coat stand, mirror, Murray's slippers and the small telephone table – everything was in place. She shrugged her shoulders and carried on through to the kitchen. She got out the big piece of paper where she'd jotted down key information, namely that she had a very keen buyer for the property and could they call her as a matter of urgency. She positioned it so it was unmissable and placed her business card next to it for good measure. In the utility room she got what she needed out of the cupboard and slipped out the back door. Blythe sat down on the ancient garden furniture and waited.

She liked this time of the evening. The sun was slipping away but it was still warm. The village was quiet, except for the birds having an argument in the trees about who was roosting where. It was a lovely garden. Big patches of it were left for wildflowers. They looked so pretty, but Murray had explained that wasn't why he liked them. Murray was a birdwatcher and the wildflowers encouraged insects and that was like a bird buffet. She'd once seen a woodpecker in his garden and also late one spring evening she'd seen a hedgehog. But it wasn't birds or hedgehogs she was waiting to see tonight.

There was a rustle in the bushes and out strolled a lythe ginger-striped cat. 'Good evening, Turpin,' she said.

Turpin ignored her and instead headed straight for the food bowl. Each night Blythe was moving the bowl nearer and nearer to her and he hadn't seemed to notice. The cat was semi-feral and Murray's garden was his home. Murray had taken care of him but when he had been away on birdwatching trips he'd enlisted Blythe to call in and feed Turpin. Since Murray had died she'd just carried on.

She missed Murray. She wondered what he would say if she were able to talk him through her current predicament. He was all for practical solutions, which was fine, but given she was working her way through funeral directors in the Manchester area and having no luck, she wasn't sure even Murray would have the ideal solution to this one. She'd discovered Manchester was a very big city and she had no idea whereabouts Murray had been buried or even if Manchester was correct, as that had just been what someone in the pub had said. And now nobody was even sure who in the pub had said it, but it had somehow become fact.

This was what happened in a little village. Someone said something and it got embellished and before you knew it the molehill was Ben Nevis.

The sound of Turpin munching his dinner brought her back to the garden. Murray had got as far as stroking Turpin but because, until recently, Blythe's visits had been sporadic, Turpin was still getting to know her. A couple of times he'd had his dinner and then settled down on the chair next to her for a snooze and that had felt like progress.

While Turpin was fully occupied with wolfing down his food Blythe leaned nearer and nearer, her fingertips almost touching his back. Her phone sprang into life, making them both jump. Turpin ran halfway up the garden, turned to scowl at her and then gave her a flick of his tail, which Blythe took to be the feline equivalent of giving her the finger.

She checked her phone. It was Sam Ashton calling. She answered it. 'Hi, Sam, what can I do for you?'

'I wasn't expecting you to answer. I thought it would go to voicemail,' he said. Blythe wished she'd let that happen because each time she spoke to him she felt bad about the situation. If she didn't track down who had inherited Murray's cottage soon, she was going to have to tell Sam that the deal was off.

'I'm at the house now, actually.' She wasn't sure why she told him that.

'Is there a problem?'

'No, just checking a couple of things.'

'I thought for a moment the thatch was on fire or something dreadful like that,' he said. Blythe felt bad for thinking that if it did burn down that would save her having to admit to Sam what she'd done.

'No, it's fine. Completely beautiful,' she said, almost sighing at the sight of a bat swooping around the trees.

'Good. I've been thinking. You said it was a death sale, right?'

Blythe didn't like his turn of phrase. 'Yes, the gentleman who lived here died.'

'Do you know if they want to keep the furniture?'

Blythe shut her eyes. When she'd set this up she hadn't realised that she'd have to lie to people. She was rubbish at lying. 'I don't know, Sam.' That was at least an honest answer.

'Could you ask them? Because I'm thinking usually in a case like this they get in a house-clearance firm and it all gets skipped, which is such a shame. I'd be happy to make an offer for it all. I'm hoping we can come to an arrangement because if I take it lock, stock and barrel that saves them a job.'

Blythe thought about the old chairs and bits and bobs. She hadn't thought of Sam as the sort of person who would favour carved wood and wing-backed chairs. 'Can you leave it with me?' she asked, rubbing a hand over her face.

'Great. Thanks, Blythe. I don't suppose anyone is talking dates yet at your end, are they? My solicitor said he hasn't had any engagement yet.'

'Er, no dates as yet, Sam, but I promise I'll keep you posted.'

They said goodbye and she could tell how different he sounded. Gone was the curt, bored man she'd first dealt with, replaced by an enthusiastic one who had found his dream home and was hoping to set a moving-in date. *Eurgh*, she hated herself.

Blythe waited to see if Turpin would return but he didn't so she took the food inside. Murray had always been very clear about not leaving any food out for fear of attracting rats. She washed up the bowl and walked through to the front door. She halted in the hallway and scanned everything. Her eye was drawn to a small wooden seagull ornament. She picked it up and remembered chatting to Murray about it. How he'd knocked it off the little table so many times reaching for the phone but he couldn't bear to move it as it greeted him when he walked into the cottage.

Blythe studied the glue mark around the bird's beak. 'Poor little seagull.' She swallowed down a lump. Then she heard Murray's soft voice correcting her. 'It's a kittiwake.' And despite feeling a little tinge of sadness, it made her smile.

7

17th June

Things were decidedly frosty in the office. Blythe had come in to find that the monthly sales charts had been taken down and so had the Agent of the Year certificates, which had covered the last ten years. Clearly Ludo was serious about making changes. She hated that she was responsible for him rethinking the way he'd been running his business after all these years. The other staff were blaming her and apart from the odd stilted good morning she was being blanked. Blythe did find this a bit odd because seeing as she had been the top agent anyway it was really only her who was missing out now that the scheme had been dismantled, but as nobody was talking to her she didn't have an opportunity to put this case across.

She spent the day focusing on doing the job to the best of her ability. She couldn't bear the thought of disappointing Ludo further. Ludo had even reassigned Heather, the office junior, to Amir for the next part of her training, which had been another body blow. She was determined to put things right. Blythe had rung all the local solicitors and funeral companies again and they either didn't know anything about Murray or completely refused to tell her either way. She was fast realising she was going to have to come clean to Sam. The thought of it made something hit the bottom of her stomach like an out-of-date Christmas pudding.

A small part of her had been hoping that something else would come on to their books that would be even better for him than Murray's place, but she knew that was impossible. The cottage was completely perfect for Sam; nothing else was going to top it. Which meant she had to call him and explain the situation she'd got them both into. She was putting off making that phone call. She'd not covered all the Manchester area solicitors or funeral directors yet, so maybe she'd exhaust those first before she spoke to Sam. Although exactly how long that was going to take was uncertain.

Amir was buzzing around the office looking ridiculously pleased with himself, presumably because he'd come back from a successful viewing. Part of her wanted to know what he had sold but most of her didn't want to show any interest. It was him who had triggered this mess. If he'd not set out to stop her hitting the record she wouldn't even have been working on a Sunday let alone selling properties that weren't for sale.

Amir tapped on Ludo's door, said something inaudible and returned to the middle of the office. 'Can I have everyone's attention?' he asked, puffing himself up like a pigeon on heat. Blythe reluctantly stopped typing and looked up. 'I have some exciting news,' he said. Blythe noticed Heather hanging off his every word. He gave a dramatic pause and she wanted to shout at him to hurry it along. Her mobile rang just as he spoke and everyone grumbled.

'Good afternoon, Bly...' Everyone was glaring at her. 'Sorry,' she said with a wince and she took the call outside.

'Hello? Is that Blythe Littlewood?' asked the caller.

'Yes, sorry about that. How can I help?' Blythe peered through the glass window in an attempt to work out what the big news was that Amir was announcing.

'I'm from Ashley, Bennett and Wake solicitors and we've been instructed to deal with the sale of the property 32 The Green, Holly Cross.'

At the name of the village Blythe tuned back in. 'I'm sorry, which property was this?'

'Thirty-two The Green, Holly Cross,' they repeated.

'You're dealing with Murray Henderson's estate? Oh my goodness, thank you so, so much for getting in touch.' Relief washed over her like gravy over a roast dinner.

'I understand you already have a buyer for the property. Is that correct?'

'Yes, it's a Mr Sam Ashton. I can email over all his details. He's very keen to proceed quickly if we can.' She was desperate to make up some of the time she'd made him lose.

'That shouldn't be an issue.'

'Oh, and Mr Ashton would like to make an offer for the entire contents too. Could you speak to your client about that as well, please, and let me know?'

'Absolutely.'

'Thank you. Can I ask who put you in touch with me?' Blythe was keen to find out if it was Arthur's old network, her many desperate phone calls to solicitors and funeral parlours, or the note she'd left on the kitchen table.

'I'm afraid our client would prefer it if we didn't share any unnecessary information. I'm sure you understand.'

She didn't understand at all, but she really didn't care because now she would be able to sell Sam Ashton his dream home and hopefully start to repair the situation at work and in particular with Ludo. She thanked the solicitor again and ended the call – things were definitely looking up.

Blythe walked back inside the office feeling like she'd grown at least a foot in height. She could hold her head up now. She'd resolved the problem. Lots of smiling faces turned her way and their smiles faltered.

'What was this big news then, Amir?' she asked, returning to her desk and swinging gently from side to side in her swivel chair.

'I'm taking on the additional role of office manager.'

Blythe spun herself so violently in his direction that she threw herself off her chair and came back down to earth with a bump.

Vicky was beyond pleased with the response she'd had to her flyers. Her problem now was scheduling everyone in, labelling house keys and keeping track of payments. Although the five dachshunds currently using her as a maypole was a more pressing problem. They all had names beginning with C, which she couldn't remember, and although she had been assured that they were all very well trained they were refusing to respond to her commands. Perhaps it was the doggy equivalent of a school trip when normally-well-behaved children got overexcited to the point of vomiting just due to being outside their usual environment. She had to admit when she'd met the dogs in their home they had all been obedient and calm. That wasn't the case now.

After the incident where Princess had briefly run off when she'd been out with Blythe, Vicky was terrified of losing a dog. This situation with five leads wrapped around her legs and five small dogs all pinned to her ankles was quite the opposite. She decided that logically if she turned the other way to the dogs she would become untangled. Unfortunately the dogs seemed to want to follow so they all turned in circles together. After a few moments she started to feel dizzy.

Vicky loved the dogs and she was sure she'd lost a couple of centimetres off her waist with all the walking, but she had to admit it wasn't the easy money she'd thought it would be. That caravan holiday in Devon wasn't looking like it would be any time soon.

'Are you all right there?' asked Norman, carrying a loaf from the bakery. 'Can I give you a hand?' he asked, as his image spun past her at speed whilst she did another pirouette.

'No thanks, I'm fine,' said Vicky. She'd always been fiercely independent. Two of the dogs raced around to see who was approaching, tightening the lead around her legs and making her topple. 'Argh!'

Norman stepped forward just in time to steady her.

'Thank you,' said Vicky, glad of the hand that gripped her arm. The dogs focused their attention on Norman, giving her a chance to stand still for a moment and rearrange the mass of leads.

'What's this I hear about new blood coming to the village?' Norman cocked an ear expectantly.

'Oh, Murray's old place you mean?'

'Someone said it had been bought by that chap off the telly with all the animals. Now that would be good for your business. Wouldn't it?'

Right at that moment, Vicky couldn't think of anything worse.

8

24th September

The last Friday in September

After all the shenanigans it was finally completion day on Murray's old cottage. Blythe was looking forward to handing over the keys to Sam Ashton and finally drawing a line under the fiasco. Everything had thankfully settled down at work. She was no longer a pariah. Things with Ludo had improved. She was still unhappy that Amir had been made office manager although Ludo insisted it only meant he'd taken on some additional admin. Amir was borderline unbearable because he seemed to think he was now Blythe's boss and they were banging heads on a daily basis. But not today. Today she was hoping everything was going to go smoothly for Sam. As soon as she got the call that the money had changed hands she hotfooted it over to Holly Cross with the keys.

Holly Cross looked particularly pretty in its autumn colours as Blythe drove into the village. The fields that encircled it had all been harvested and were now being ploughed ready to repeat the whole cycle again. The trees were just on the turn, making Blythe happy with the thought that winter was on its way. Sam Ashton was standing by a large van when she pulled up.

'Congratulations, you are now the owner of 32 The Green,' she said handing him two sets of keys, a small welcome pack and a bottle of champagne; the latter was something she had bought with her own money and went a little way to make her feel better for the lie she'd told, although thankfully now Sam would never have to know about that whole debacle.

'Thanks,' he said. He looked really happy and that made all the hassle almost worth it. Despite the fact her actions had all been about winning the sales competition her instinct to match the right property to the right buyer had kicked in, and seeing someone in a home they would love was always the best part of the job for Blythe.

She delayed her departure because she was keen to see what Sam's stuff looked like, especially as he was keeping all of Murray's furniture too. 'You'd best get moved in,' she said, as two men got out of the cab of the van and came to the back of the vehicle. One of the men opened up the back of the van and Blythe had to do a double take. The van was completely empty. She looked at Sam for an explanation.

'We need to get everything out of the cottage first and over to my warehouse,' he explained, handing a set of keys to one of the men.

'Right. Are you in the antiques business?'

'I supply pretty much anything and everything for film and television sets.' Sam pulled a business card from his pocket and handed it to her.

'Cool.' Now she sounded like an idiot. 'I'll look out for Murray's foot stool in the next Hollywood blockbuster.'

'It's actually going to be used in a wartime saga the BBC are filming in the new year,' said Sam.

'That is actually very cool,' said Blythe, wishing she could come up with something more intelligent to say. The other men came down the path carrying Murray's sofa and Blythe felt a little pang of sadness. She'd had a connection with Murray – he'd been like an adopted grandfather – and she was also very fond of Turpin, but this was where she needed to walk away. And if she didn't go soon she was in danger of getting a bit emotional. 'I'll leave you to it. I hope you'll be very happy here.'

'I'm sure I will,' said Sam, looking over his new home with pride. They smiled at each other before Blythe got in her car and Sam went inside.

A thought struck her; she'd meant to explain about Turpin so she waited for Sam to come out again. He appeared carrying Murray's coat stand. Blythe buzzed down her window and called over. 'Sam! I forgot to mention. Look out for Turpin.'

Sam paused and frowned hard. 'Who's Turpin?'

Blythe didn't like the look on his face. If he didn't like Christmas who knew what else he wasn't in favour of. Perhaps it was best if she let him discover his squatter for himself. 'I left you a note but you'll find out later tonight.'

Sam put down the stand and held up his hands in confusion. 'Is Turpin a neighbour?' She shook her head. 'A highwayman's ghost?' he asked, looking a little wary.

'You'll see,' she said, and she drove off.

Blythe wasn't sure why she was walking an overweight Shih Tzu at seven o'clock that night but Vicky had rung her in a bit of a flap as a client had been delayed getting home from work and they didn't want their dog having to cross its legs. As Eden was in her pyjamas and about to go to bed Vicky could hardly take her out on a walk, so she'd called on Blythe. She'd been slightly put out Vicky had assumed she had nothing better to do on a Friday night but the reality was that she really didn't.

It was a nice evening. There was a gentle breeze but it wasn't too chilly and Vicky had said once around the village would be enough. Blythe decided to stroll past Murray's and see what Sam was up to. It would always be Murray's in her mind. Sam was standing next to another removal van. Darn it, if she'd been a few minutes earlier she might have got to gawp at his furniture. She walked across the green and watched the van drive off. Sam was just going inside the front door.

'How's your day gone?' she asked, walking up the path, her chubby charge waddling along beside her.

'Tiring but I'm in,' he said. 'I'm already getting junk mail – I had a letter about joining some committee.' Blythe's stomach clenched; she knew exactly what that was and Sam wasn't going to like it one little bit. He crouched down to the small dog and gave it a fuss. 'Is this yours?'

'No, long story.' They smiled at each other and Blythe felt suddenly self-conscious under his gaze – or was that some remaining guilt seeping out? 'Anyway, I'm glad the move has gone well and that you'll be very happy here. Bye.' She made her way past the cottage and the little dog started to pant as he shot her accusatory looks. 'It's for your own good,' she told it.

She was level with Murray's garden gate when she heard Sam yell. 'Help!' He sounded distressed.

She instantly opened the gate and went down the side of the garage with the poor little dog's legs going super-fast to keep up with her. 'Whatever's the matter?' she called.

'I'm being attacked. Come quick.'

She dashed into the back garden. The sight that met her was a surprise and she had to work hard not to burst out laughing. Sam was bent over with Turpin standing on his back.

'He just leapt on me and he won't—argh!' At the sight of the small dog Turpin clearly felt the need to cling on a bit tighter.

On seeing the cat the little dog started to bark excitedly. This was not a good situation. 'Hang on,' said Blythe. 'I'll work something out.'

'Hang on?' repeated Sam, incredulous.

'I was talking to Turpin.'

'That's what he's doing very effectively. I can't shift him.'

Blythe took a garden chair and walked around to the side of the house so that Sam and Turpin were no longer in view. She tied the lead to the chair, patted the little dog and then rushed back to Sam.

As she approached Turpin hissed at her. 'Come on, it's me. I'm not scary,' she told him.

'Maybe just a little,' muttered Sam.

She ignored him. She tried to stroke Turpin but he cowered and dug his claws in a little more, making Sam flinch. 'I've got an idea. Back in a mo,' she said.

'No, don't go,' said Sam, but she was already inside the cottage.

Blythe quickly returned with a bowl of cat food and Turpin lifted his nose and had a good sniff. 'Dinner time,' she said, placing the bowl on the ground by the patio furniture. 'If you come over to the table, Sam, it'll be easier for him to jump on that to get down.'

'And we obviously want to make things easier for the cat,' he grumbled, but he did do as she suggested.

Turpin hopped onto the table and then to the grass and started to tuck into his meal. Sam straightened out his spine. 'Ow. That hurt.'

'Sam, meet Turpin.'

'We've met,' said Sam. 'We don't like each other. But I can see why he's called Turpin – he assaults unsuspecting people.' Sam tried to rub at his back where the cat had clawed him.

'Actually, that's not why he's called Turpin. Legend has it that the famous highwayman Dick Turpin used to work the Fosse Way.' She indicated the nearby ancient Roman road to the east of the village with a wave of her hand. 'And after a hard day of robbing people he would take shelter at the Highway Inn. When the authorities came looking for him, the innkeeper would hide Turpin's horse in the cellar and Dick would hide in a nook inside the huge fireplace. And that's where this cat used to curl up. Phyllis thinks he's Dick Turpin reincarnated. The pub landlord thinks he's a pain in the bum because he kept leaving sooty paw prints over everything and everyone. Plus in the winter there's regularly a lit fire in the fireplace so it wasn't the safest place for him to hide. For his own good he's barred from the pub.' Turpin gave a sad mew as if he understood what she was saying.

'So he belong to the cottage's previous owner?'

'Not exactly. He's semi-feral and kind of lives in your garden. Murray always fed him and I've been carrying on with that since he died. I did leave you a note in the utility,' she said. 'Sorry if he was a bit of a shock. I'm sure you'll get used to each other. Here's my set of keys.'

Sam pulled a face as he took them. 'I'm not after a pet. But I can take him to the rescue.'

Blythe couldn't help the sharp intake of breath. In Blythe's last conversation with Murray she'd promised to take good care of Turpin. Granted the context had been because Murray was going away for a week, as he often did, but as Murray had not come home she'd felt it was down to her to carry on looking after Turpin. 'I don't think he'd do well at the rescue. He's not the sort of cuddly kitty most people are after. I'm not sure he's even house-trained.' What would happen to a feline like Turpin at the cat rescue anyway? He wasn't exactly friendly and barely tolerated being stroked – who wanted a cat like that? Blythe feared they would have no alternative but to put him down, which seemed like a drastic solution. 'Surely you could cut him some slack.'

'I'm not really a cat person,' said Sam. 'I'm sure he'll find a good home.'

'He's never been someone's pet. He's an outdoor cat. I doubt he would cope at a rescue centre; they probably wouldn't even be able to catch him.'

Sam shrugged. 'I'm sorry but he's not living here.'

'Okay. How about if I feed him?' offered Blythe, but Sam was frowning. 'You'll not have to do anything. I'll come round and I'll try to lure him to my parents' house. I'll move the food a bit closer each night.' She mimed moving the bowl and Turpin hissed at her.

'That'll take a while.'

'At least let me try. I think the rescue would be a death sentence for him.' She went to stroke Turpin and he took a swipe at her.

Sam took a long while before answering. 'Fine.' He handed her back her keys. 'As long as he's not going to be a nuisance. We'll need to—'

His sentence was cut short by an awful clattering sound as the Shih Tzu came belting around the side of the house dragging the garden chair behind it and Turpin fled into the bushes.

9

2nd October

The first Holly Cross Christmas Committee meeting of the year was always a bit of an occasion. Attended by the great and the good of Holly Cross, all were enticed to show up by Norman's iced buns. Blythe took a seat and put her bag on one for Vicky, who was setting Eden up on a separate table with some colouring. She joined the others already assembled around the meeting table with Leonora, the formidable chair of the committee, at the head. Phyllis sat to her left as she was the HCCC secretary – a slight woman with a shock of grey hair who had a soft spot for Norman.

Norman opened up the cake boxes he'd placed in the middle. 'Usual buns and I'm trying out a passionfruit curd in the éclairs so all feedback welcomed,' he said, as hands came from every angle to grab one. He seemed pleased by the eager response.

'I suppose now is a good time to go through notices while you're all busy eating,' said Leonora. She didn't wait for replies. 'Last year we had more visitors than ever and raised the most money we ever have for charity, which is something we want to continue this year. At the post-event meeting in January we talked about improvements we wanted to see this year, which were an online presence, Christmas Olympics, sexy Santas—' there was a moment where Leonora eyed Phyllis over her glasses before continuing '—definitely no live reindeers and the end of Murray's dodgy flickering lights. Ah, well, that leads me on to my next point. We have lost a key member of this committee in Murray—'

'We'll all miss Murray,' said Norman, and there was a forlorn ripple of agreement.

'Lovely man. Very sad,' said Vicky, whilst licking cream off her fingers. 'Those éclairs are bloody gorgeous, Norman,' she added.

'Thank you.' He smiled broadly.

'He'll be sorely missed,' said Greg, giving a nod in Blythe's direction.

'Funny he was buried in Manchester though,' said Vicky.

'I don't think funny is the right word,' said Arthur.

'My apologies,' said Vicky. 'It's odd though, right?' She looked around the table.

Norman gave a Gallic shrug. 'I assume he had family there.'

'I've got family in Stockport,' said Phyllis. 'That's near Manchester.'

'But you'll not be buried there will you?' asked Vicky.

'No, I've got my plot booked in the churchyard,' said Phyllis proudly.

'Do we need to do that?' asked Arthur, looking concerned.

'Always wise to book ahead,' said Leonora, who was a staunch forward planner of the obsessive kind. 'But I think we're going off at a tangent. Can we focus—'

'Are we expecting anyone else?' asked Phyllis, checking her notes.

'Sarvan said he'd try to get away but the pub car park was full so he might not make it,' said Leonora, as Vicky's hand crept towards the cakes. 'But I'm hoping Mr Ashton will be joining us.'

Blythe's head shot up. When she'd asked Sam whether he liked Christmas he'd replied with a passionate rant about why he hated it. She'd meant to break it to him about Holly Cross's special association with the festive season but with the hassle of having to track down who had inherited Murray's property, the fact that Sam was buying a house in the most Christmassy village in the country had slipped her mind. The last thing he would want to be a member of was the Holly Cross Christmas Committee. Most of the members who were on the committee were only there because they were mildly terrified of Leonora, so nobody who hated Christmas was going to voluntarily sign up.

'Who's Mr Ashton?' asked Phyllis.

'New owner of Murray's old place,' said Leonora. 'He's in the film industry apparently,' she added.

'Ooh, is he someone famous?' asked Phyllis, who had been hoping for some time that Holly Cross would get its very own celebrity.

'I heard he was that chap off the telly with all the animals,' said Norman.

'I heard Mr Ashton was in films,' said Leonora with authority.

'Ashton? Wasn't he married to Demi Moore?' asked Norman, offering the last éclair to Phyllis much to everyone else's chagrin.

'That's Ashton Kutcher. The new resident is Sam Ashton,' explained Blythe.

'You never said he was famous,' said Vicky, looking accusatorially at Blythe whilst helping herself to an iced bun.

'He's not. He supplies props for film sets.' There was a collective sigh of disappointment.

'Does he know anyone famous?' asked Leonora. 'That might be useful for the lights switch-on.' She jotted down some notes.

'Ooh, Ryan Reynolds. I love him,' said Vicky.

'Or Sean Connery,' said Phyllis, clapping her hands.

'Did he say he was coming to the meeting?' Blythe asked Leonora.

'Sean Connery?' asked Phyllis excitedly.

'I think he's dead,' said Vicky. Heads around the table nodded. Phyllis looked shocked.

'No, Sam. Is Sam Ashton coming to the meeting?' Blythe felt that sometimes committee meetings were harder than they needed to be.

'I've not managed to catch him but I put a note through his door. It'll be nice to get some fresh blood on the committee and some new ideas.' There were murmurs of agreement around the table. Most likely because the more people Leonora had to boss around the easier it was for everyone else.

'I quite like to keep with tradition,' said Arthur, nibbling on an iced bun.

'But if we don't move forward we move backwards,' said Leonora forcefully. Leonora had two focuses in life: her prize-winning roses and the committee.

Vicky was frowning. 'Wouldn't we just stay where we were?'

'But if everything else moves forward and we don't...' explained Norman.

'I don't get it,' said Vicky. Eden came to show them the picture she'd drawn and Blythe took a photo. Pictures of Eden and the occasional coffee were all Blythe ever posted on her Facebook page these days.

Leonora shuffled her papers to gain everyone's attention. 'Anyway, let's crack on. I can catch up with Sarvan and Mr Ashton afterwards.'

'I'll update him. Sam. Mr Ashton,' said Blythe. 'If you like.'

'Someone's keen,' said Vicky, with a wink.

'Not really. Just trying to be helpful.' Blythe couldn't make eye contact with her friend.

'I think it's best if I do it,' said Leonora. 'First impressions and all that. I'm sure you understand.' It was hard not to take offence at Leonora sometimes.

'Actually, I'll be there anyway because of Turpin so...'

'Fine,' said Leonora dismissively. Blythe puffed out a breath – the time to come clean about Christmas in Holly Cross had arrived.

That evening Blythe was due round at Sam's to feed Turpin. After a slightly stilted text exchange Sam had conceded that for the time being it made sense to leave the cat food and dishes in his utility, which was great because she would have felt like a prize idiot carrying them across the village. When she got there she wasn't sure what to do. With Murray she'd let herself in but now she was there it didn't seem right. She went to the door and knocked.

A puzzled-looking Sam opened the door. 'The side gate is open.'

'Fine, I'll use the tradesman's entrance,' she said, still a bit miffed at Sam's lack of compassion for Turpin.

'Don't be daft. Come through. It's fine.' He stood back and she jutted out her chin as she walked into the hallway. She was actually very keen to see how things looked inside now he'd moved his stuff in, but she also didn't want him to see that she was being downright nosy so she did super-quick fleeting glances into the rooms off the hall as she passed. She didn't see much but what she did catch sight of was all very tasteful.

She went through to the utility. Nothing much had changed there, only the addition of a laundry basket on the counter. Blythe had a sneaky peak inside.

'Someone called Leonora…' began Sam, making Blythe jump and knock the basket to the floor where an array of clothes tumbled out.

'I'm so sorry,' said Blythe, hastily grabbing up the garments until she realised she now had Sam's underpants in her hand. She dropped them quickly. Then felt that maybe that was rude but was too rigid with embarrassment to pick them up again.

Sam grinned at her. 'You won't catch anything. They're clean. I've just not got around to sorting them out yet. He leaned past her to collect up the items and return the basket to the worktop.

'I'll be out of your hair in a moment. Well, I usually sit in the garden for a bit and talk to Turpin.' Now she'd said it out loud she realised it made her sound a bit of a crackpot or – possibly even worse – a bit of a sad case. 'Is that weird?'

'I'll be working, so it doesn't bother me.'

'Great.' She gave a tight smile before sorting out Turpin's food and taking it outside.

Blythe sat and waited. There was no sign of the cat. He had run off at high speed the previous evening thanks to the rude interruption of the Shih Tzu and the garden chair. She hoped it hadn't scared him off. Despite his hissing she had felt he was beginning to trust her. The garden was looking lovely. All the roses had been dead-headed and it looked like the apple tree had been pruned.

Sam joined her outside. 'Did you want a coffee or something while you wait?'

'Tea, please. If it's not too much trouble.'

'I know my way around a kettle,' he said, before disappearing inside. He returned a short while afterwards with two mugs. She hadn't realised he was going to join her. He pulled up a chair and sat down facing into the garden the same as Blythe.

'You've got to work quickly. The garden looks good.'

'This is the first time I've been out here,' he said.

'Oh, right.' That was odd. She realised now that the garden had looked perfect all through the summer. 'One of the neighbours must have been taking care of it and mowing the lawn. It's the sort of thing people here do for each other.'

'Holly Cross seems like a close community. I've had another invitation to a village committee meeting,' he said. A prickly sensation spread across Blythe's skin.

'Village committee?'

'Yeah. Handwritten note no less. I'll probably go along to the next one. Show willing,' he said with a smile.

Blythe frowned. 'It was the HCCC meeting.'

'CCC?' he said with a grimace. 'Sounds like the KKK but without the pointy hats?'

'Actually, no, nothing like that. Look Sam, the thing is—' But she was interrupted by something moving in her eyeline. The hanging basket was swaying and yet there was no breeze. A furry ginger leg appeared over the edge of the basket as Turpin stretched. He must have got onto the garage roof and climbed into it from there.

'There he is,' said Sam, spotting him too. 'I think those flowers are past their best now.' He pointed to the squashed remains in the swinging basket as Turpin leapt onto the wheelie bin and then to the ground. Turpin paused to eye Sam suspiciously before continuing over to his bowl and starting to eat.

'If we're going to be virtual neighbours, perhaps we should get to know each other a little better,' said Blythe.

Sam pulled his chin in. 'Ah, awkward, you seem like a lovely woman but I'm just out of a relationship and—'

'Goodness. No!' Blythe held up her hand for emphasis. 'I meant we should talk to each other, get to know each other. Nothing else.'

Sam was looking confused. 'Why would we do that if not to date?'

'Because you're going to be living in the village. You're part of the community now. It's okay, I was just being friendly. If you'd rather not...'

He seemed to relax a little. 'Okay. I'm originally from Kent. I dropped out of university and I hate Marmite.'

'And Christmas,' she said tentatively.

'That's right.' His jaw tensed.

'Because it seems a shame that you're missing out on all the festivities and what really is a lovely time of the year.' His expression hadn't softened so she tried to sell it a bit better. 'I mean, who doesn't love getting together with family and friends over roast turkey and a cracker.'

'It's just not my kind of thing,' he said at last.

She nodded. 'But maybe it could be.'

He was looking perplexed. 'What is it with you and Christmas? Do you have a side hustle going in Christmas trees or elf outfits?'

'Hmm.' This was it. It was time to come clean. 'The thing is that in Holly Cross we celebrate Christmas.'

Sam sighed out a breath. 'That's fine. I'm sure it won't interfere with me.' He picked up his mug and Blythe waited until it was safely back on the table before she continued.

'You see Holly Cross is the Christmas village.' He shook his head as if not following what she was saying. 'It's famous for its Christmas lights and Christmas trees and Christmas fayre and…' With each word Sam's complexion seemed to go darker but that could have been a timely cloud.

'When you say famous?'

'People travel to see the lights. If you google Holly Cross Christmas…'

Sam already had his phone out and Blythe knew the second the pictures had loaded because his eyes popped wide like he'd sat on something sharp. 'Bloody hell!'

Sam paced up and down the patio. Each time he neared Turpin, the cat gave a low warning hiss. 'I can't bloody believe this.' Sam raked a hand through his hair, making a bit stick up at an odd angle but Blythe didn't feel it was a good moment to point it out. 'This is a nightmare.'

'I'm really sorry,' she said. 'But do you think there's the tiniest possibility that you're over-reacting? Because it's just a few weeks of the year and—'

'Weeks?' Sam was virtually shouting and his eyebrows were pulled so tight he almost had a monobrow. 'This just gets worse. And I'm not over-reacting. You sold this house under false pretences.' He jolted as if a memory had actually struck him. 'You even asked me if I liked Christmas and, if I remember rightly, I explained fairly categorically that I didn't. And yet, you said nothing and went ahead and sold me this cottage.'

'Because this is the perfect property for you,' said Blythe.

'Not if it's in the middle of the most Christmassy village in the world.'

Blythe wobbled her head. 'Most Christmassy in this country. There's a place in America that...' Sam was glaring so hard it was quite unnerving. 'That's probably not relevant.'

'There should have been some sort of disclaimer or it should have come up on the searches,' said Sam as he continued his pacing.

Blythe failed to hide a snort. 'It's not dry rot. It's a few festivities to raise money for charity. All you need to do is put a few lights up.' She remembered Murray's elaborate display from the previous year. 'And a sign or two, and maybe a couple of moving figures on the lawn.'

'Moving figures?' Abject horror was written all over his face.

'You don't have to buy anything. It's all in the shed. You bought it as part of the contents.' Blythe gave a smile but it quickly faded thanks to Sam's rising colour. Blythe quickly went to her photos on her phone and pulled up some from the previous Christmas to show Sam. She held out her phone so he was at arm's length. 'Murray's... your cottage is kind of central to the display because it faces the green, which is sort of the epicentre of the celebrations.'

It wasn't hard to read Sam's feelings as he stared at the pictures. She scrolled through a few but his anger levels appeared to be notching up with each swipe so she stopped.

'I have bought a house in the middle of the village from hell. I'm going to be living in actual hell.' He shook his head like a dog in the rain.

'I'd encourage you to be open-minded about this, Sam. Holly Cross is a delightful place to live, it ticks *all* your boxes and the fact that the locals celebrate Christmas really is a minor thing.' She emphasised *minor* by pinching her thumb and finger together.

Sam's nostrils flared as he exhaled. 'Not to me, it's not.'

There was an uncomfortable silence broken only by Turpin licking his bowl so hard that it moved and scraped along the patio. Blythe hadn't expected Sam to shrug and say 'Great, fetch me a Santa hat. Where do I sign up?' But she also hadn't imagined he'd react quite this badly. He was incredibly cross and obviously upset. Which made her really want to know why he was so anti Christmas, but given his current state she wasn't brave enough to ask.

Blythe stood up. 'I am truly sorry. If I'd thought for a moment it would bother you this much then I would have told you.'

'Would you?' Sam narrowed his eyes.

Blythe thought for a second. She didn't like to see anyone in this much turmoil, and it was even worse to know that she'd created it. She opened her mouth to reply but Sam got there first. 'Your silence speaks volumes. Of course you wouldn't have told me. You would have wanted your commission and that's all that matters to people like you.'

Okay, it was fine that he was cross but now he was borderline rude. 'People like me?'

'Bloody estate agents. You're all the same. Can't be trusted.'

'Now hang on—'

'I'd like you to leave,' cut in Sam, staring her down.

There was a moment where Blythe considered arguing with him but in truth she knew it was hard to defend her actions. What Sam didn't know was that this was genuinely the first time in her whole career that she had done anything like this. She had always stuck to Ludo's rules, been honest and open with clients, until Amir had taken up the challenge of stopping her setting the sales record. It had been the one and only time she'd bent the rules to get what she wanted and ultimately it had all been for nothing. She wished she could turn back the clock because all she had done was to let Ludo down and upset a client. Although it was likely Sam would still have bought the cottage even if he'd known about the Christmas connection – she was convinced of that, but now they'd never know.

'Fine,' said Blythe, snatching up Turpin's licked-clean bowl and making the cat hop out of the way. She went to storm off but spun around. 'If it's any consolation, you don't hate me as much as I hate myself right now.'

Sam held her gaze. 'It's not.'

10

2nd October

'Shhh,' said Vicky as she opened the door to Blythe. 'I've just put Eden to bed after three stories and a record-breaking number of cuddles.'

'Okay,' whispered Blythe, holding aloft a bottle of wine as she went in.

'I'll have water if that's okay? Wine equals calories and I might have overdosed on Norman's cakes.' Vicky rubbed her middle as they went through to the kitchen and she shut the door so they could speak at normal volume.

'I think we all did.'

'What's the emergency wine for?' asked Vicky, getting herself a glass of water and joining Blythe at her tiny kitchen table.

'Sam sodding Ashton,' said Blythe, pouring herself a glass of wine.

'Has he turned you down?' Vicky leaned forward, intrigued.

'What? No.' Blythe did a double take. 'Blimey, Vick, did you think I'd hit on the guy when he's just moved into the village?'

'I may have binge-watched too much *Bridgerton*. Come

on, tell me all about this Sam bloke. It's been a while since we've had an eligible bachelor in the village,' said Vicky.

Blythe puffed out a breath. 'Not much to tell really. About our age. Very tall. Nice eyes. But he takes the hump easily and he's not a cat person.' Vicky wrinkled her nose at that. She was a big animal lover so anybody who wasn't was never going to meet the mark in her eyes. 'Oh, and he absolutely hates Christmas,' added Blythe.

Vicky spluttered a laugh. 'What on earth was he thinking by buying a house in Holly Cross?' She watched her friend's expression change. 'He doesn't know what happens here at Christmas, does he?'

'Long story but no he's not exactly got the full picture.' Blythe winced at her own words.

'He will notice soon enough when the whole village is lit up like Piccadilly Circus.'

'I'm kind of hoping I can win him round before then because he's massively over-reacting isn't he?'

'Hmm.' Vicky pondered what she'd heard. 'Good luck turning him from Scrooge to Santa in twelve weeks.'

Blythe fixed her with a glint in her eye. 'Are you saying you don't think I can change his mind?'

'I think it's a long shot but I'd like to see you do it.'

'Is that a challenge?'

Vicky pressed her lips together. 'If you like. If you fail, you buy me those fancy Christmas crackers I've always liked.'

'And what if I win?'

'Then it's homemade crackers with the insides of loo rolls for everyone and I'll make you a personalised set,' said Vicky.

'Deal.' And they clinked their glasses.

Vicky sipped her water and looked longingly at the wine.

'Anyway, how are things with you?' asked Blythe.

'I'll start with the good things, because I always like to be positive,' said Vicky. 'I now have twelve dogs signed up to Hot Dogs.' Vicky puffed out a breath. 'Otherwise it's same old same old. It's like I have two lives. One where everything is perfect when I'm with Eden and we do mummy and daughter stuff and then the other one where I hate every dull minute of packing boxes at the candle factory.' The one good thing about her job at the factory was that she didn't have to think about it. Candles trundled along one side of her and she picked them up with her left hand, gave them a quick quality check and put them in a box before that went off on another conveyer belt the other side of her. She could do it with her eyes closed. She had actually done that experiment to prove that she could but it hadn't worked so well for the quality control aspect of her role. The factory wasn't the most modern but the job wasn't taxing and it paid her enough.

'But it pays the bills,' said Blythe.

'Only just. How's your job?'

'Ludo still thinks I'm a liability and I'm not sure how I'm going to win him round. Amir is an even bigger arse now he's got a sign on his desk that says office manager. Oh, and guess who has friended me on Facebook?'

'Father Christmas.' Vicky opened the sharing bag of crisps and took a handful, only half listening to Blythe.

'Nope, one more guess. It's a blast from the past,' offered Blythe as a hint.

That piqued Vicky's interest. 'Not that bloke from the

German sausage stand who you snogged at the Christmas fayre?'

'Klaus? Not him. He stank of onions. No, the person who has friended me on Facebook is...' She gave a long enough pause to make Vicky turn to look at her. 'Owen.'

'Owen who?' asked Vicky, but as soon as the words had left her lips she knew.

'Owen Hockley who you went out with for, like, a million years. I was really pleased to hear from him and thought you would be too. I had a bit of a stalk on his page and it looks like he's doing all right for himself. He's got a little business as a handyman. He's living near Oxford, looks typically blokey with a huge TV and black sofas. His status says he's single—'

'Please tell me you've not accepted his friend request?' Vicky didn't often feel anxious but she was at that moment. She didn't want Owen anywhere near her little bubble and the thought that he was trying to connect with people she knew unnerved her.

'It was all a long time ago,' said Blythe, taking a crisp.

'Bloody hell, Blythe. You've friended him. Haven't you?'

'I wanted to know what he was up to. He looks pretty hot too. Not that I'm interested. But you and he were super cute together back in the day. Catching up with old friends doesn't do any harm.'

Harm was exactly what it could do. Vicky felt a mild panic set in. 'Can you just unfriend him, please?'

'If it bothers you that much, of course I will.' Blythe gave Vicky a friendly nudge.

'Go on then.'

'What now?'

'Yes now.' Vicky waited. The sooner the connection to Owen Hockley was broken the better.

Vicky didn't usually dwell on things but the mention of Owen was playing on her mind the next day at work. As she checked and boxed candles she replayed the conversation with Blythe, which had unlocked many memories of the boy she used to date. Some of them happy, some of them a shitstorm. Their relationship had been a tumultuous one and had ended badly. Now he was poking around in her corner of the world and that bothered her. Was it just an old friend trying to reconnect or was he onto her? She could have shaken Blythe for friending him but to be fair to her she only knew half the story. A story Vicky wouldn't be telling anyone ever.

She tried to refocus on her job and block out all things Owen. As factories went it wasn't the worst. The chicken factory she'd very briefly worked in held that title. The smell there had been stomach-churning. The candle factory smelled of cardboard and patchouli. Patchouli featured in a lot of their candles and especially their most popular creation called 'a happy home', which it seemed everyone wanted. Perhaps buying the candle was a step on the road to happiness for some buyers or sadly as close as others would ever get. Vicky had bought a couple with her discount but only lit them when people came round because they were still pricey.

The thrum of the belts was oddly soothing. Some of the other workers wore headphones and listened to music but Vicky liked the rhythm of the factory. Usually she used her time for thinking about what to cook for tea or something Eden had said at breakfast. She was going through a phase of asking a lot of questions. This morning's classic had been: 'Mummy, why do fingers have little knees?' How long would it be before Eden started asking other questions? Ones that Vicky didn't have the answers to.

She had decided a long time ago that some things were best left in the past and she stood by the decisions she had made at the time. They might not have been good decisions but once made Vicky wasn't one to change her mind. Case in point, it had been Vicky's decision that the father's name on Eden's birth certificate should say *unknown*. She'd told Blythe that the father was a temporary worker at the factory who had been hired to help with the Christmas rush. A nice enough guy, not the brightest, hence his nickname of Dim Wick, and not someone she wanted butting into her life for evermore. Blythe had accepted her story and her decision, and like the true friend she was had pledged to support Vicky however she could. For the past five years she had been true to her word. But the truth was that whilst her baby's father could well have been Dim Wick it could also have been Owen Hockley – Vicky just didn't know.

Later that day Blythe waved a stalk whilst standing outside Sam's kitchen window. He scowled at her whilst drying his hands. He threw down the towel and came to join her in the back garden.

'I come in peace,' she said, waving it again. 'It's a figurative olive branch.'

'There's a sprout on it.' He pointed at the small green vegetable clinging to the stalk.

'Which is why it's figurative.' She stopped waving it. 'I'm not sure where to get hold of an actual olive branch so I improvised. And it worked.'

'I'd not go that far,' said Sam, his voice gruff.

'But you *are* talking to me. That's a start.' She tried giving him her best smile but his expression didn't change. 'I wondered if I could buy you a pint… as an apology.' He opened his mouth but she continued in case he was going to refuse her. 'I'm sure we can resolve this like adults. What do you say?'

'Full forgiveness in exchange for one pint? I don't want people thinking I'm cheap.'

She shrugged one shoulder. 'Understandable. How about a curry to go with the pint? But that's my final offer.'

'Okay. But this doesn't mean you're off the hook.'

'Absolutely not,' she said, although she was pretty sure it did and it meant step one of her plan to win the bet and get Sam to love Christmas was in motion.

The pub was busy but they found a small table in the back room near the real fire that fed two rooms. The doorways and ceilings were low but Blythe reminded Sam at the last moment so he just missed banging his head. They took their seats and she watched him look around and take in his surroundings. The pub took cosy to the extreme with its mismatched furniture, some ornate, some utilitarian, bare herringbone brick walls and gnarled dark oak beams. Where there were patches of rugged plastered walls they were painted white and dotted with a mix of black and white prints of the pub, both old and new, including a few taken at Christmas. It was quaint and quirky without being kitsch. Sarvan and Jassi had worked hard to update the pub but retain its olde-worlde charm, and they'd nailed it.

'It's a nice pub, isn't it?' said Blythe, handing Sam a menu.

'Yeah, it's bigger than it looks from outside.'

'This bit was the stables. They converted and attached it just before the war. When the new owners took over they made a memory book. It was a way of them getting to know people in the village but it also preserved all the memories and the stories about the pub's history.'

'Nice idea.' Sam was nodding, and Blythe took that as a good sign.

'It's a close community. On the run-up to Christmas we all—' Sam was holding up his palm and frowning, making him look like a grumpy traffic cop. 'What?'

'I hope you've not brought me here to wear me down, because I might not be moving house but I'm not taking part in any of this Christmas fiasco.'

'Fiasco is a bit harsh. It raises a lot of money for charity.'

'Great, let me know where to donate but I still don't want to be involved. I'm thinking about getting away from here for Christmas. Maybe hire somewhere on a remote Scottish island or take a foreign holiday.'

Blythe bit her lip and nodded. She knew now wasn't the time to point out that because his cottage was centre stage opposite the village green it was pretty much the focus point of the lights and decorations, with most events either kicking off from or taking place just outside his front door.

They ordered their meals and things relaxed a little. Blythe got Sam talking about his business in between tucking into his desi mixed grill of seekh kebab, chicken tikka and lamb chops.

'How did you get started?' she asked.

'I worked for a thatcher. The roofing kind, not the politician.'

'Ah, so that's how you knew about Murray's cottage roof.'

'It's not often that kind of knowledge comes in handy but I know I can replace it myself when I need to. Anyway, I was working on a cottage in Devon when this guy started taking photos. That's not unusual but he watched us for ages and then he came back the next day. I asked him why he was so interested and he said he was working with a film company who needed to build a thatched village for a Netflix series and they wanted to know how to do it. I told him he needed a skilled craftsman so he hired me. Building that set I realised there were a lot of props they bought in and then dispensed with afterwards. I made them an offer for some of it and within weeks it was being used on another production.'

'That's why you have the warehouse.' Everything was starting to make sense.

'Warehouse space in London is premium-priced. The one I have here is a much better central location, way bigger and far cheaper,' he said, finishing his meal and leaning back in his seat.

'Do you get to meet any of the actors? Phyllis, who lives around the corner from you, would love some celebrity gossip.'

'Rarely. We do most of our job before the actors are brought in and then if we need to do anything more we work at night so we don't interrupt filming. Although I have shared some crisps with Ralph Fiennes.'

'Cool.' She was impressed. 'I once saw Ian Beale in Marks & Spencer's – or the actor who plays him anyway,' she said, feeling she had to share her only celebrity encounter, which if she was honest was unsubstantiated because she hadn't seen the actor's face; only that the woman on the checkout pointed at a man in a flat cap leaving the store, excitedly telling her she was sure it was the *EastEnders* actor.

'That's cool too,' Sam said, although she felt he was humouring her. 'Thanks for the meal. That was exceptional.'

'Am I forgiven?' she asked.

But before he could answer Leonora appeared at their table, pulled over a spare chair and sat down. 'You must be Mr Ashton. Welcome.' She thrust out a hand for Sam to shake. 'Leonora Clarke, chair of the HCCC.'

Blythe watched the dread appear on Sam's face. 'Call me Sam but I'm really not—'

'Has Blythe been telling you about your starring role in the Christmas celebrations?' asked Leonora forcefully.

'No, you see—' began Blythe.

'Why ever not? I thought you said you'd speak to him. Goodness, I knew I should have handled this myself. Mr Ashton, Sam, we need to meet as a matter of urgency. You will need to attend committee meetings. They aren't onerous – two hours once a week.' Sam looked horrified at the prospect. 'There's a lot to do,' added Leonora.

Sam stared at Blythe, pulled in his bottom lip and gave an almost imperceptible shake of his head. 'I've already explained to Blythe that neither I nor my property will be taking part.'

Leonora's head recoiled so fast she looked like a startled tortoise retreating into its shell. 'What?! But, but, but…' She sounded like a broken moped.

'Sorry,' said Sam, getting to his feet. He stared Blythe down. 'I can't believe I fell for your friendly chat, when all you were doing was planning an ambush. There was me thinking you were half decent after all. How wrong was I?' He turned and left.

11

16th October

10 weeks until Christmas

Blythe had lots of things on her mind as both home and work were giving her grief, mainly the ongoing stand-off between Sam and the Holly Cross Christmas Committee, trying to organise the sexy Santa dinner, plus Amir who was trying to undermine her at work at every opportunity. Since he'd walked out of the pub, Sam Ashton had virtually ignored Blythe. He'd made sure he was out or on the phone when she called round to feed Turpin and only gave her the most cursory of acknowledgements if they passed each other in the village. She didn't really care what Sam Ashton thought of her; however, she *did* care about the Holly Cross Christmas display and more importantly the indomitable force that was Leonora. She also hated the idea of losing a bet.

The moment Blythe walked into the village hall Leonora was locked on to her like a scarf-wearing missile. 'Blythe! What are you doing about Sam Ashton?'

Blythe wasn't going head-to-head with Leonora so she sidestepped her and the issue. 'I'm not doing anything. It's up to him whether he takes part or not.' She pulled out a chair and tried to start a conversation with Arthur about how best to replace the scary inflatable snowman from last year's display. The thing had massive eyebrows worthy of any *Love Island* contestant.

Leonora pulled out the chair at the head of the table, making a skin-crawling screech across the floor and instantly diminishing the chatter. 'I must insist,' said Leonora. 'It's you who sold him the cottage without full disclosure of the commitment that came with the property. Buying here is tantamount to a binding contract to participate.' There were a few nodding heads around the table although most were trying to avoid eye contact.

'Leonora, whilst the committee members are all committed to a Holly Cross Christmas, in all its charitable intent and madness, I'm afraid not everyone feels the same.' Leonora opened her mouth but Blythe continued, 'And however much we would want any new Holly Cross residents to enter into the spirit of the village displays, we cannot force them to participate and buying a property here certainly doesn't constitute a contract, binding or otherwise.'

Thankfully Norman, Vicky and Princess the dog chose that moment to enter the hall, although it appeared Princess's attendance wasn't wanted. 'Heel! Stay! Stop!' yelled Vicky, as the large dog excitedly careered around the hall bumping into chairs, tables and Leonora's flip chart. Leonora gasped as the flip chart toppled but thankfully Blythe stuck out her hand and grabbed it when it was a centimetre off landing on Leonora's head. Leonora glared at Blythe as if it was her who had tried to bludgeon her with it.

'You're welcome,' said Blythe under her breath, righting the board.

'I am so sorry,' said Vicky, now hanging on to Princess's collar as the dog tried to snatch the cake boxes Norman was clutching protectively. 'I'll just tie her up outside,' she added, but Princess didn't look like she had plans to be parted from the cake boxes.

'Here,' said Blythe, passing her friend a bone-shaped dog biscuit. She had it in her coat pocket from the last dog walk she'd done for Vicky.

'Lifesaver,' mouthed Vicky, waving the biscuit under Princess's nose and finally grabbing her attention.

After the dog had been encouraged outside and everyone had chosen a cake – custard tart or blueberry cheesecake slice – Leonora tapped her flip chart to bring everyone to order.

'We are T minus thirty days,' began Leonora, revealing her first flip sheet with a flourish.

'Does T stand for turkey?' asked Phyllis hopefully.

'No, it's the day when we kick off all the Christmas preparations,' explained Leonora with a furrowed brow.

'Should that be KO minus thirty days then?' asked Vicky, to mutters of agreement.

'T minus is a recognised project term; it stands for time remaining,' explained Leonora, which was met with a cumulative round of ahhs from the committee members. 'And it means we need to focus. This year it feels like we are all adrift.' She scowled at Blythe. 'Which is unfortunate given we have never had more riding on our display.'

'Ooh, are we adding more reindeers?' asked Phyllis, clapping her hands together. 'I love the ones riding across the church roof. Not the real ones.' Phyllis shuddered.

'I loved rampaging Rudolph,' said Vicky, but she seemed to be alone on that one.

'No, it's definitely not reindeer.' Irritation evident in

Leonora's words and eye-rolls. 'I have an announcement to make.'

'You're resigning,' said Vicky with glee, before drastically changing her expression to overdramatic sad face. 'Which would be soooo sad,' she added, with a fake wobbly lip.

Faces around the table looked hopeful. 'Of course I'm not resigning. I'd never abandon you all.' Leonora seemed puzzled at the very thought. 'Anyway, my big announcement is that I have entered us into a national competition to find the United Kingdom's most perfect Christmas village.' Leonora turned over the next sheet on her flip chart and revealed a multicoloured sheet that elaborately declared: *Holly Cross IS the UK's most perfect Christmas village.* 'It would mean publicity, newspaper coverage, perhaps even television...' she looked off into the middle distance as she found her stride '...world recognition, accolades, royal honours, perhaps even a blue plaque.'

'How exciting,' said Phyllis.

'There are quite a few places in the country who already unofficially claim that title,' said Norman. 'I expect there will be stiff competition.'

A few shoulders slumped. Not Leonora's – hers now displayed a certain defiant rigidity. 'But we literally *are* the most perfect Christmas village. We just need to prove it. Here's how we're going to win,' she said, flipping over to the next sheet with a dramatic swish.

Everyone stared at the very long list that covered two columns. 'It's about doing what we do every year but doing more of it and better. If we're going to win, we need everyone on board. And that includes Sam Ashton.' Leonora stared at Blythe.

'Fine.' Blythe held up her hands in surrender. 'I'll speak to him again.'

'Excuse me!' called someone from the doorway. 'There's a dog here eating its way through a plant pot.'

'I swear that dog is part goat!' said Vicky, rushing from the hall.

Vicky and Princess caught up with Blythe following the meeting (after Vicky had apologised profusely for Princess eating the plant and chewing half the plastic pot it was in). 'Have you heard any more from Owen?' asked Vicky. She'd considered talking about the weather first to make it less obvious but she needed to know because it had been playing on her mind. Or more accurately she'd been unable to think of much else than Owen Hockley and the mess he could make of her and Eden's happy little life. Every scenario she had imagined had ended in disaster. What if he was Eden's father? Would he want shared custody? What would that mean to a five-year-old who'd never set eyes on the man? It was all too much to deal with.

'Heard from him?' queried Blythe.

'Yes. Another Facebook friend request, phone call, carrier pigeon? Heard from him in any way, shape or form?' asked Vicky with growing anxiety.

'No. You watched me unfriend him. And anyway it's just Owen. Easy-going slightly dozy Owen. He's not turned into a mad axe murderer since he moved away. Well, at least he's not added it to his profile.' Blythe laughed but Vicky was stony-faced. 'Are you okay? Because you're acting weird.'

'Me? I'm fine. What about you? Are *you* okay?' asked Vicky, overtaking Blythe as Princess pulled hard on her lead.

'I'm just not looking forward to speaking to Sam *again*. He hates Christmas so it's completely pointless. I'm wasting my time and it's borderline begging when you ask someone the same thing more than three times.'

'What about giving Sam an incentive?' called back Vicky, who now found herself quite a way ahead of Blythe. 'Come on, catch up!' she yelled.

Blythe increased her pace. 'What sort of incentive?' Blythe was looking puzzled.

'You can't expect me to think of everything. Oh, I know. You'll buy him something nice. A big turkey if he joins in.'

'This is not *A Christmas Carol* and he is definitely not Tiny Tim. More like Scrooge but less happy-go-lucky.' Blythe looked despondent.

'What would Scrooge want?' asked Vicky, as the dog did an emergency stop to sniff a lamp post, almost making Vicky trip over the top of her. At least the unscheduled sniff stop gave Blythe a chance to catch them up.

'Scrooge wants everyone to go away and leave him alone so he can happily ignore the Christmas celebrations,' said Blythe.

'Ahh... That's what he *thinks* he wants, but really deep down he wants to be part of a family,' said Vicky, very pleased with how unexpectedly her suggestion was starting to make sense. 'Like old Ebenezer, Sam has forgotten how to have fun and enjoy Christmas. He just needs reminding.'

'Basically, you're saying to solve Sam's deep-rooted hatred of all things festive all I need is a Ouija board to conjure up the ghosts of Christmases past, present and future and he'll be dancing in the streets in his nightgown come lights switch-on day. Is that right?'

'Exactly.' Vicky held up a fist triumphantly until Princess pulled on her lead and she lurched up the street. 'There has to be a reason for it. It's not natural to hate Christmas that much. Discover the root, uncover the solution.' Vicky was amazed at her own insightfulness. Sometimes she really had it.

'You want me to delve into his past and find out why he hates Christmas?'

'Might be a good place to start,' yelled back Vicky, as Princess bounded off and she had to run to keep up. 'Then you could sell him the many benefits of joining in with the village celebrations, possibly through the medium of song, and build up to the full production with Muppets. I bloody love that version.' She realised she'd lost it again.

'Are you okay?' Blythe's voice was faint as she was now some distance behind.

Vicky was panting with the effort of keeping up with the dog. 'Not really, no! Have you got any more dog biscuits?'

12

17th October

Ludo was deep in conversation with Amir when Blythe entered the office. Immediately she was suspicious. 'Morning. Is this a briefing or just a blokey chat?' she asked.

'We're discussing long-term business strategy,' said Amir.

'That sounds like it should be something that involves everyone or at least the senior team.' Blythe looked to Ludo to confirm her thoughts.

Ludo stood up. 'It was more of a general discussion about whether or not it's worth checking the building applications to the council on a regular basis to pick up any developers early on.'

'We have great relationships with local developers and some of the bigger nationals too, so I think anything more would be duplication and therefore a waste of time,' said Blythe, pointedly. She'd nurtured those relationships and they worked well for them. She made a mental note to give all her local building contacts a courtesy call before Amir did.

'I'm leading on it so it's my time I'd be wasting. Although I obviously won't be,' said Amir, returning to his desk. 'Thanks for your support, Ludo. I really appreciate it.'

'Ludo, can I have a word?' asked Blythe, leading the way into his office.

Ludo followed and shut the door. 'Amir's not the devil, you know. You could cut him a bit of slack.' Ludo looked weather-beaten as he slumped into his sumptuous leather chair and Blythe sat down opposite – her back straight. She should have had this conversation with Ludo weeks ago. Things hadn't improved since the whole monthly sales record debacle.

'He might not be the devil but he is trying to undermine me at every turn.'

Ludo leaned forward onto his large desk and steepled his fingers. 'How so?'

His question had put her on the spot. 'Well...' She paused for a moment to think. 'He mapped out the campaign to leaflet the new estate without consulting me and only when I found out about it did he then agree to have half the leaflets printed with my details, otherwise all the leads would have gone his way.'

'A simple oversight. In future the main office number will go on all leaflets then it's the luck of the draw as to who answers the call. So that's resolved. What else?'

Blythe chewed the inside of her mouth and thought. 'He's got two monitors on his desk and they're both bigger than mine.' She was convinced he'd only ordered two that size so she couldn't see what he was up to behind them.

'The old one was pixelating and he says it's easier with two. You're very welcome to order another monitor if you want one.' Ludo was so reasonable it was actually infuriating.

'No, thanks, I don't need two monitors. *Nobody* needs

two monitors. That's my point.' She wasn't entirely sure if it *was* her point but it was something that annoyed her. 'He bought Heather an emotional thesaurus to use when she was creating listings. That's for writing fiction, not fact-based property details.' She folded her arms.

'It was just a joke and to be honest her copy has improved since she's been using it,' said Ludo, and annoyingly Blythe had to admit that was true.

'But it implies that we make stuff up and that goes against everything you've taught me.'

The phone rang and Ludo looked relieved to be interrupted. 'Maybe don't worry about everyone else. Just focus on what you're doing,' he said. What did that mean? Was he telling her to butt out? Or worse still that he had her lumped in the same dishonest pot as Amir?

'I am fo—'

'Sorry, I need to take this,' said Ludo, picking up the phone.

It was clear Blythe still had a lot to sort out.

Ludo had valued a particular property as senior valuer but it was on Blythe's books, so she needed to go out and meet the vendors and get them to sign the paperwork so that Happy Homes could deal with the sale. She liked this part because she was basically nosy and loved to look around other people's homes. From a professional perspective she was also looking for unique selling points and aspects of the property she would want to highlight to any prospective buyers. From the outside it was a fairly standard Nineteen-Seventies build – solid and conventional but in need of a little TLC – a trimmed hedge and newly painted front door were easy fixes to increase the kerb appeal of a property. She'd had a few clients who wouldn't even step inside a house because they hated how it looked from the outside.

Blythe rang the doorbell, which triggered loud barking from inside. Eventually the door opened to reveal a man in his sixties who appeared to have just got out of bed. He scowled at Blythe whilst the giant black dog barked ferociously, revealing a vast number of large teeth.

'Good morning, Mr Smith, I'm Blythe from Happy Homes estate agents.' Usually at this stage any scowl disappeared but not today. He just stared at her. 'He's a good guard dog,' she said, trying to engage with the man.

'Bitch.' Blythe was astonished. 'Honey is a bitch,' clarified Mr Smith.

'Oh, my apologies, Honey. Isn't she a sweetie?' she said, raising her voice above the dog's snarls. 'I've got the paperwork for you to sign.' Still no response. 'If I could come in?'

'Post it,' he snapped, and went to shut the door.

'I'd rather not.' She was almost shouting. 'I've come all the way from town and I think my boss explained that we need to take a few photographs. Listings with internal pictures do sell much quicker. It'll only take a few minutes.' She hoped her pleading smile would do the trick.

Mr Smith shook his head and let go of the door. Thankfully he didn't let go of the dog but towed Honey away by her collar, leaving Blythe to shut the door. Once she was inside the smell was very obvious. Difficult to identify at first – she put it down to a combination of unwashed dog with a hint of mould. The hallway was fairly standard but the midpoint floral border indicated it hadn't been redecorated since the Nineties. She followed him into the kitchen but only got a brief glimpse as he let go of the dog, making her step quickly out of the way. He shook his head at her. 'This way.'

The living room was like walking into a cave. She had to blink to get her eyes to adjust to the lack of light. 'Shall I draw the curtains?' she offered.

'If you like.'

Blythe made her way in the general direction of the window, banged her shin on an unseen coffee table but contained her yelp. She flung the curtains open, creating a cloud of dust – goodness only knew how long they had been untouched. Light flooded in, highlighting the swirling dust particles. She stifled a cough as she breathed some in. The windowsill revealed a collection of small dusty horse ornaments, a vase of dead flowers encased in dried-out green slime and a selection of lifeless flies.

She turned around; the rest of the room wasn't quite as untouched as the windowsill but it wasn't a pretty sight. Although it was a good size, it was cluttered and her eyes were drawn to a particularly large ominous stain in the middle of the beige carpet. Was that gravy or blood? Oh well, it could be covered up with a nice rug.

'Right,' she said, as brightly as she could manage. 'I can offer you a few tips that will help your house to be seen in its very best light and secure an early sale.' She glanced around trying to find somewhere to sit. Apart from the small spot on the sofa Mr Smith was occupying every other seat was taken by boxes, papers and in the case of one of the chairs a glass case containing a taxidermy fox. She decided to perch on the arm of the chair next to the fox.

Mr Smith was watching her. 'I don't want to sell,' he said, bluntly.

'We do get rather attached to places, don't we? I don't think I've got the details of the sort of property you're looking to move to. I can do that now as well so we can find you the perfect new home.'

'I don't want to move.'

'Err.' Even Blythe wasn't sure how to counter that. 'Have you changed your mind about selling?'

'I never wanted to sell. It's the wife.'

'Ahh, I see. And is Mrs Smith here?'

'Huh!' he said vehemently, almost making Blythe topple off her chair arm. 'She left me four years ago.'

A lot of things were starting to make sense. Acrimonious divorces were always tricky ones to deal with. The resident spouse could make it very difficult to sell the property and she had a feeling Mr Smith was going to be one of those clients. But then divorce and moving house were two of the most stressful things you could do in life and Blythe saw it as her job to make the process as stress-free for him as possible.

'I know this all feels a bit daunting right now but Happy Homes will be there every step, and whilst I'm sure you have many special memories of this house, we want to get the best possible price for you so that you can start afresh and find the perfect home to make new memories in.'

'There are no special memories here,' he said, and his eyes drifted to the worrying stain on the carpet. She would be earning every penny of the commission on this one.

*

Blythe had put Mr Smith to the back of her mind and had been mulling over Vicky's suggestion of how to tackle Sam. Not the one about recreating the *Muppet Christmas Carol* but the idea that she should try to get to the bottom of Sam's hatred for all things festive. She knew that confronting it head on would likely not have him opening up to her. She was, after all, not his most favourite person. She needed to be subtle, to coax it out of him almost without him knowing, and she had a plan to do it.

Sam was already scowling when he opened his front door. Not a good start. 'Hiya, Sam. It's Halloween crafts day in the village hall on Saturday and I wondered if you'd like to come.' He opened his mouth but she carried on. 'It usually turns into a bit of a party because there's hot dogs and punch. Might be a good opportunity for you to meet a few other residents.'

'Halloween is weeks away.'

Not the response she'd hoped for but still a response. 'Two weeks. It's to get the children in the spirit of things with making broomsticks, autumn wreaths, scary masks – that sort of thing.'

'Don't tell me the village is big on Halloween as well as Christmas.' He sighed heavily.

She didn't like his tone. 'Big? It's huge. We turn Holly Cross into a ghost town and recreate Michael Jackson's "Thriller" video on the green.' His eyes widened. 'Has Leonora not dropped off your zombie costume yet?'

He wagged a finger at her. 'You're joking. You almost had me there. I don't suppose the Christmas thing is an elaborate hoax too by any luck?'

'No, that's very real. We use events to bring the community

together throughout the year. There's the Valentine's dinner, Easter Egg Hunt, Summer Fete, Harvest Festival Ball and at Halloween all the children dress up and go trick-or-treating. It's a lovely evening.'

'Not in my experience. Kids high on sugar, banging on your front door, kicking pumpkins up the street and egging your house – not my idea of fun. Anyway trick-or-treating is basically begging with menaces.' He gave her a broad smile.

'What is wrong with you?' It came out more forcefully than she would have liked and it certainly wasn't the subtle coaxing of finding out his underlying Christmas issues that she'd planned.

Sam pulled his head in. 'What's wrong with me? What's wrong with this village? Do you think it's normal to decorate your house every five minutes? To do everything together? Because it's not.'

'It's called community and more importantly it's fun. You should try it sometime.' They were snapping at each other now.

He looked genuinely hurt by her words. 'I'm fun!'

'Prove it.' She put her hands on her hips. 'Pumpkin picking and Halloween crafts are from ten until two thirty Saturday.' She slapped a leaflet against his chest and stormed off.

13

23rd October

Vicky loved Halloween probably even more than she loved Christmas but she daren't mention that to Leonora. Leonora was fully focused on Christmas and generally gave the Halloween events a wide berth. No one person was really in charge of Halloween; it just sort of happened with the help of everyone getting involved. Sarvan and Jassi from the pub were a big part of Halloween as the Highway Inn was usually decked out in spooky trimmings and the focus for adults on Halloween because they always did a themed buffet and special cocktails – quite the money spinner. It had got Vicky thinking that perhaps she was missing an opportunity. She lived in a village that people travelled to for events throughout the year. There had to be some way of her using that to make a bit more extra cash – she just had to figure out how.

Eden was also a fan of Halloween, mainly because of the unlimited sweets, and had been pondering over her costume for some weeks. She had whittled it down to witch, vampire or a character from *Paw Patrol*. Vicky was hoping she'd go for witch because that was the easiest costume to source and also the cheapest as she had accessories from previous years.

'Blythe!' yelled Eden, the moment they set foot on the village hall steps.

'Hey, lovely. Are you excited?'

'I am. This year I'm going to be a vampire Marshall on a broom!' she declared, before running off to join the other children.

'What's a vampire marshal?' asked Blythe, hugging her friend in greeting.

'Marshall is a character from *Paw Patrol*. It looks like I'll be making a vampire dog costume this year.' Vicky was already wondering exactly what that would look like.

'I met a vampire dog the other day. She went by the name of Honey. Looked like she'd rip your throat out on command.'

'Nice. Does she need a dog walker?' asked Vicky. Business was business and if she could walk Princess she could probably walk any dog.

'Don't think so.'

Sarvan came over and greeted them both warmly. 'You guys know there's soup back at the hall after the pumpkin picking? And the usual buffet on Halloween at the pub?' He held up a leaflet for the latter.

'We'll be there,' said Blythe.

'What's the soup?' asked Vicky.

'Spicy pumpkin of course,' he said, with a grin. 'Or witch's brew with eye of toad for the kids.' Vicky gave him a look. 'Creamy tomato with spinach croutons,' he added.

They chatted as more and more people arrived. Everyone in the village with children had turned out and most of the other residents too. It didn't matter that their kids had grown up and left home; it was still fun to get together with others and watch the children choose their pumpkins.

The church clock chimed ten and without any instruction the group began moving away from the hall. Blythe scanned the crowd.

'Who are you looking for?' asked Vicky, checking she still had Eden in her sights. The village was supremely safe and everyone looked out for each other, but still a mother's instinct was to keep them under subtle surveillance.

'I invited Sam,' she said with a twist of her lips. 'What a waste of time that was.'

'Did you grill him about why he hates Christmas? Unleash the spirits? Whoooo,' said Vicky, doing a Scooby-Doo-worthy impression of a ghost.

'Sort of.'

Vicky was chuffed that Blythe had run with her suggestion. Most people didn't take her seriously. That didn't bother her – she'd always been her own person – but it was nice to think that perhaps sometimes she did have good ideas. 'What did you find out?'

Blythe was looking over her shoulder as they walked away from the village hall. 'That we wind each other up very fast.'

'No big revelation then?'

'Only that it's not just Christmas; he also hates Halloween and anything community-related.' Blythe puffed out a breath. 'We ended up virtually shouting at each other.'

'Oh well. His loss,' said Vicky, linking her arm with Blythe's.

'I thought that too but Christmas means so much to this

community and to me, and whilst I'm not one to side with Leonora I have to admit that if his cottage isn't decorated it is going to completely ruin this year's display, along with our chances of winning the competition.'

'You'll win him round,' said Vicky.

'But what if I don't?' Blythe sounded genuinely worried at the prospect.

'Then I get posh crackers,' said Vicky.

'But everyone will blame me. And do you know what? They'll be right. It'll be all my fault. I brought the miserable git into the village, all because I was so caught up in achieving that stupid sales record.'

'Don't beat yourself up. And try not to let this Sam get to you. For a start he's not even met me yet and I can be very persuasive. I'm sure we'll think of a way to win him round,' said Vicky, although off the top her head she was out of ideas.

Free events like this one were a godsend to Vicky. Eden bounced around excitedly and Vicky couldn't help feeling like the luckiest person alive. Yes, she'd like a bit more cash in her life but she had the most wonderful little girl and that was really all that mattered.

Arthur was waiting to greet everyone when they arrived at the allotments. Many years ago the local farmer had donated part of a field to the village for allotments and, whilst they had been hugely popular for a while, their interest had waned over the last ten years. Arthur had come up with the idea of turning over half the allotments to pumpkins and the local school as an outdoor classroom, and the decision had been a huge success.

Arthur was in his wellies standing in front of the hedge that hid the field from the road. It was sad to see Arthur standing alone as this was something he had always done with Murray. 'Hi, Arthur, how are you?' asked Vicky giving him a hug.

'Oh, I'm fine,' he said, forcing a smile.

Blythe squeezed his arm. 'I'm missing Murray today too,' she said. A tear formed in Arthur's eye and he nodded his understanding.

'Right. Just in case anyone is new to this.' Arthur raised his voice above the chatter of the crowd. 'Hopefully you're all wearing wellies because it's a bit muddy in places. Remember the biggest isn't always the best.'

'Hear, hear!' called someone from the back.

Arthur continued. 'Don't lift a pumpkin by the stalk because it may break and you'll damage your pumpkin. Once you've chosen one get an adult to cut the stalk, leaving at least two inches. Secateurs are on the bench and are for use by sensible adults only.'

'We don't have any of those,' someone shouted.

'Then you motley crew will have to do,' said Arthur. 'One pumpkin per child. If you'd like any extras, then please make a donation. Bring your pumpkin to me for checking and weighing and let me know if you find any rotten ones.'

'I like finding the rotten ones,' shouted Eden. 'We get to give those to the pigs at the farm.'

'That's my girl,' said Vicky proudly.

The children all gathered around. 'No running, no squabbling and no tantrums,' said Arthur firmly. 'And that applies to you children too.' Everyone laughed. 'Off you go!' he shouted, and the eager bunch made their way behind the bush and into the field. The gasps from the children as they saw the pumpkins always made Vicky's heart soar. Oh, to still have that level of excitement for something so simple.

Blythe usually loved pumpkin day in the village but she was struggling today. She watched the kids diligently check out all the orange squashes. They had a bumper crop this year and she knew Murray would have been proud of them. As Eden identified the pumpkins that had squishy spots and were therefore destined to be a pig's dinner, Blythe carried them back to where Arthur was making a pile for the farmer to collect later.

'Penny for them,' said Arthur, appearing at her side.

'Oh, you know.' She forced a brief smile. 'Murray would have been puffed up with pride at the sight of this lot today.'

'That he would,' Arthur agreed. They both watched one of the smaller children insist on carrying his pumpkin as his attentive father hovered nearby. These children were making memories they would cherish for a lifetime. Blythe wished sulky Sam was there to see it. Arthur cleared his throat and interrupted Blythe's thoughts.

'How's the new guy settling into Murray's old place?'

Blythe instantly felt her mood change at the thought of Sam. 'He moved in a few weeks back. He doesn't speak much even though I go around every night to feed Turpin. We can barely say a civil word to each other before it turns into a snarking spat. And he flatly refuses to join in with anything in the village.'

'Is he not happy there?' asked Arthur.

She turned to see his look of concern. This wasn't something she'd really considered. 'I don't know.' Mulling this over made her feel less irritated with Sam and back to feeling guilty about selling him the cottage without full disclosure of the nature of Holly Cross. 'He could probably be happier I guess.'

'And what could we do to help, do you think?' Arthur was the loveliest.

'I invited him to come today but he's not turned up.' She thought back to their mini slanging match on Sam's doorstep. Perhaps it wasn't the most thoughtfully delivered invitation she'd ever given out.

'I hope he's all right,' said Arthur. 'Perhaps he was a little daunted by it. Not everyone has your confidence.'

Blythe didn't think that was an issue with Sam. 'He's probably just being the misery he is.'

'That's a little uncharitable,' said Arthur, and she was surprised by his reprimand. 'That's not like you, Blythe. You don't usually shy away from a challenge.' Arthur's words prodded at her but before she could come up with a response he was in demand to supervise a particularly large pumpkin.

Arthur was right; she was tenacious and normally she never gave up on a challenge. She decided right there that Sam Ashton wasn't going to change that. And even if it was only for crackers a bet was a bet. When the others headed back to the village hall with their pumpkins, some being carried reverently, others in bags, and a selection in Arthur's wheelbarrow, Blythe peeled off towards the green.

She'd given herself a talking-to and she was going to stay calm, not let Sam wind her up, and she would show him what an awesome place to live Holly Cross was – even if it pushed her to the limits of civility. She'd chosen a nice pumpkin, made a donation to Arthur and carried it up to Sam's front door. She took a deep breath and knocked. Sam was smiling when he answered the door but she saw it slide from his face. She didn't like that she had that effect on him and vowed to change that.

'Hi, Sam, how are you?'

He eyed her and the pumpkin she was hugging warily. 'Fine thanks. What can I do for you?'

'How's Turpin?'

He narrowed his eyes at her. 'Stalking a fat pigeon last time I saw him. Why?'

'I just wanted to check that you're both doing okay.'

'Ri-ight. Anything else?' He nodded at the pumpkin.

'Yes. I got you this. And I wondered if you'd like to come to the village hall and carve it. There's also Sarvan's speciality on offer – spicy pumpkin soup.'

Sam looked mightily suspicious. 'I stopped carving pumpkins when I was about eleven so I'll give it a miss if that's okay. Thanks anyway.' He went to shut the door.

'What are you doing for lunch?' she asked, hastily.

There was a long pause, but Blythe was happy to wait it out. At last Sam spoke. 'I'll probably make a sandwich. Why?'

'Wouldn't homemade soup be nicer?'

'What's going on?' he asked.

'Here's the thing. Holly Cross is a friendly village.' She ignored his puckered brow that said otherwise. 'Perhaps you've not seen it at its best in that respect and I would like you to meet a few people. Get to know your neighbours. Become part of the community.'

'I don't know. I'm kinda busy.'

'Twenty-four hours a day?' The irritation was creeping back in and she pulled herself up. She softened her voice. 'Surely not all day every day? Even you need a break sometimes. Come on. What do you say?' She held up the pumpkin like a peace offering.

'If it means that much to you—'

'It does,' she said, emphatically.

He rubbed his chin as if thinking it over. 'I'll come on one condition.'

'Name it.'

'You stop going on about Christmas.'

Now that was going to be tricky.

14

23rd October

Vicky and Eden were pondering options for their pumpkin whilst finishing off their soup. 'I like the traditional look: big scary eyes and jagged teeth,' said Vicky, because she knew how to carve those. That was how she'd been carving pumpkins for as long as she could remember and had managed to persuade Eden for the last few years that they were the best sort of pumpkins too. However, now Eden was a little older and influenced by the world around her, she had much bigger ideas.

'Oscar says he's going to carve his into a 3D octopus and Millie is doing a unicorn.'

They sounded complicated to Vicky. 'You don't want to copy them. You want yours to be different. How about one with big scary eyes and—'

'But I like *Paw Patrol*, so Marshall or Everest or—'

'*Paw Patrol* isn't very Halloweeny though,' butted in Vicky, to stop her daughter from listing off every character. 'A pumpkin is meant to scare people,' she added, pulling a monster face for effect.

Eden fixed her with a serious look. 'No, it's not. It's to tell trick-or-treaters which houses have the best sweets.'

Vicky was about to put her right when Blythe walked in followed by a drop-dead gorgeous man who could only be the new guy. Vicky was aware she was staring so she put down her soup bowl and went to say hi.

'You must be Sam,' she said. 'Come here.' And she pulled him into a hug. Blythe looked alarmed but it had been her who wanted to show Sam how friendly the village was. Although he did look a little startled when she let him go. 'Welcome to Holly Cross,' she said. 'I'm Vicky.'

'Hello, Vicky.' Sam gave an unsure smile.

'You've got a little...' Blythe was pointing at Vicky's face.

'What?'

'There's soup on your chin, Mum,' said Eden.

Vicky hastily snatched up a serviette. Great first impression. 'Whoops.' She rubbed around her mouth. 'Did Blythe drag you down here to carve pumpkins with the kids?'

'It looks that way,' said Sam scanning the room as a lump of pumpkin pulp sailed through the air and plopped at his feet.

'It's for adults too,' said Blythe. Her eyes were getting wider and wider. 'And we'd best get on with that.' Blythe held up a pumpkin and nodded towards the carving table where children were already diligently chiselling away with plastic tools.

Vicky got the feeling Blythe was on edge. Oh well, at least she'd given Sam a warm welcome.

Blythe loved Vicky but being wrapped in a bear hug by a complete stranger with soup around her face, however well-intentioned, maybe wasn't the best impression of the folk of Holly Cross. She scanned the tables as they approached. Lots of children were squeezed around the biggest table and pumpkin innards were flying in all directions whilst parents tried to scoop them into the buckets provided. They'd give that a miss. One table had Norman and Phyllis and her grandson who appeared to be carving a doughnut into his. Whilst she adored Norman and Phyllis they were both committee members and very keen on Christmas so she feared it wouldn't be long before the subject cropped up. She gave them a wave and carried on by to join Jassi who was assisting their seven-year-old twins whilst also helping Sarvan serve the soup.

'Can we join you?' asked Blythe.

'Have a seat,' said Jassi, pulling out a chair. Blythe introduced everyone and they settled down with their pumpkins. Blythe handed Sam some tools.

'You moved up from London didn't you?' asked Jassi.

'Yeah, Shoreditch.'

'How are you settling in?' asked Jassi.

Blythe was quite keen to hear his response. Despite everything, she very much wanted Sam to feel at home in the village.

'Fine, thanks.' Sam concentrated on his pumpkin while Jassi and Blythe exchanged looks.

'We moved here from Sparkhill, Birmingham. It's a big change coming from a city to a little place like this. We weren't sure if we'd like it or if the locals would like us, but it's been brilliant. Everyone's been so supportive. Kal has congenital nephrotic syndrome, which is long hand for dodgy kidneys.' Jassi ruffled the hair of the nearest twin.

'Sorry to hear that,' said Sam.

'This year HCCC are raising money for the renal department at our local hospital to help Kal and people like him.'

Jassi squeezed Blythe's hand 'The villagers are lovely, the kids are happy and business is booming.' Blythe was very grateful to Jassi for trying to engage with the newcomer.

Sam nodded but said nothing. 'Sam runs his own business too,' said Blythe, desperately trying to keep the conversation going.

'What do you do?' asked Jassi.

'Film props,' said Sam.

'Must be interesting,' she said, intercepting a scoop of pumpkin seeds one of the twins was wielding in Sam's direction.

'I like it,' said Sam.

Blythe was inwardly rejoicing at him uttering a whole sentence. Was this progress? 'He's got a warehouse near here,' added Blythe.

'I rent one,' corrected Sam. Maybe she didn't need him to speak whole sentences. As long as he was there that was the important thing.

They settled down to carving their pumpkins and Blythe felt that although it had all been a little stilted Sam would hopefully be picking up on the community vibes. Sarvan was collecting in bowls and receiving lots of compliments about the soup and was imparting that he never measured his spices so it was different every time he made it. Arthur was diligently collecting waste pumpkin in buckets and ferrying it out to his waiting wheelbarrows to add to the pigs' tea and was talking to people in between trips.

And the children were chatting and giggling excitedly as their creations came to life. Blythe started to relax.

They carved in silence for a while. Blythe helped the twins with some tricky bits and Sam quietly chiselled away. She wanted to see what he was carving on his pumpkin but didn't want to put him off so she kept to her side of the table.

The chair next to Blythe was hastily pulled out and someone sat down. It was Christmas Carol. Blythe was instantly on edge as Sam glanced up and locked eyes with the smiling reindeer on Carol's jumper.

'Hello, you must be the elusive Mr Ashton. I'm Carol,' she said, offering a hand for him to shake. 'Everyone calls me Christmas Carol.' She chortled at her own joke and gave a shimmy so that the tiny bells on her jumper jingled. Blythe's shoulders tensed.

Sam wiped his hands on a cloth and shook with Carol. 'Sam. Pleased to meet you.'

'We are all very pleased to meet you.' Sam went back to his pumpkin. Blythe was about to breathe a sigh of relief but Carol spoke again and Blythe froze. 'You're a difficult man to track down. I'm sure Blythe here has explained all about Holly Cross Christmas...' She paused to look at Blythe.

'Well, I've mentioned it but Sam's a very busy person. And today we're just doing pumpkins so—'

'We're all busy people,' said Carol. 'Next HCCC meeting is Thursday at seven o'clock. Leonora has a long list with your name on, so you'd better show up this time. No more excuses or we'll think you don't want to take part.'

The tension in Blythe's shoulders was spreading up her

neck. She watched Sam slowly look up from his pumpkin. 'Sorry,' she mouthed.

Sam put down his carving tool and put the lid back on his pumpkin. 'I won't be at the meeting next Thursday, Carol. Or any other Christmas-related gathering. I don't celebrate Christmas. I'm sure you'll all respect my decision.' He shot a warning look at Blythe before picking up his pumpkin and leaving.

By Thursday night what Sam had said on pumpkin day was all around the village and from the look on Leonora's face it had also reached her. She stormed into the village hall as if her brogues were on fire. She wrestled her flip chart over to the table and sat down with a thud. 'I'm sorry I'm late but I've been trying to get a response from Sam Ashton. I needed a definitive answer to all the rumours currently circulating the village.' Blythe was wishing she hadn't gone to the meeting but everyone knew where she lived so she'd figured she would only have been delaying the inevitable confrontation.

'I finally got to speak to the man and do you know what he said?' She scanned the table and her eyes fixed on Blythe, making her feel even more uncomfortable.

'Ooh,' said Phyllis. 'Did he give you Sean Connery's phone number?' There were awkward looks around the table. 'Wouldn't that be something if we could get him to switch on the Christmas lights this year,' she added.

'It'd be a miracle,' muttered Vicky through her jam tart.

'No,' said Leonora looking even more irritated. 'Sam Ashton told me that he can't abide Christmas.' There was a well-timed gasp from someone at the other end of the table.

'In fact he hates everything about it. And he's sorry he ever purchased a property here.'

'Umm, so why did he then?' asked Norman.

'Because Blythe failed to tell him about Holly Cross's long-standing Christmas traditions. She tricked him into buying Murray's cottage.' Another unhelpful gasp.

'Tricked is a little unfair,' said Blythe, finally finding her voice. Leonora opened her mouth wide. Blythe held up her palms. 'But I take full responsibility for the fact he wasn't made aware of what happens here at Christmas. In my defence I wasn't expecting him to be quite as anti the festive season as he evidently is.'

Greg cleared his throat. 'The fact that he isn't into Christmas isn't Blythe's fault. At the end of the day anyone can buy a place here. There's no prerequisite that says they have to love Christmas.'

'Thanks, Greg, I've got this,' said Blythe before turning back to Leonora. 'I know it means things will have to be a little bit different this year but it doesn't mean we can't produce an award-winning display. I think we just need to think through what we *can* do rather than what we can't and calmly work towards that.'

'Calm!' shouted Leonora. 'I've devoted months of my life to the celebrations and this year was to be my ultimate accolade. But thanks to you the centre of the display, the key cottage, our focal point, will not be joining in. There will be a huge, ugly, obvious gap in the festivities. And that is entirely down to you.' Leonora slammed her hands down on the table, making everyone jump. 'You've ruined everything!'

It definitely wasn't the response Blythe had hoped for.

15

30th October

On her way into work the day before Halloween, Blythe stopped at Sam's cottage. He was quick to answer the door. She was now very familiar with the way he greeted her – a broad smile was instantly flipped upside down at the sight of her.

'I don't want a fight.' She held up her hands in mock surrender. 'And I really don't care if you join in with Halloween or not. You won't be alone if you don't, because the Bennetts have seven-month-old twins and they won't be and nor will Mrs Devonshire because anything spooky gives her nightmares. They won't be putting up any decorations or pumpkins so the kids won't knock. But if you did want to join in and light up the pumpkin you carved you'll need a safety candle. You forgot to take yours on pumpkin day.' She handed him the battery tea light and he stared at it like she'd just handed him a lit firework. 'It's safer than a candle. Especially with all the thatched cottages.' She pointed upwards – like he needed reminding that he lived in one.

'Right,' said Sam, as usual not giving anything away.

'It's actually a really fun evening. All the kids love it and there's no egging of houses or any antisocial behaviour.

It's just about people checking out everyone's pumpkins, giving out a few sweets and wishing each other a happy Halloween.' Sam didn't respond. 'Oh, and the headless highwayman's ghost usually appears about midnight.'

Sam's eyes widened. 'What? Oh, you're joking.' He didn't look as if he found her very funny.

'Anyway, I'll be by to feed Turpin a bit earlier than usual tomorrow so I've got time to go home and get changed.'

Sam smirked. 'Are you dressing up for Halloween?'

'Yes, every year I'm a sexy devil in horns, a bright red basque and matching hot pants.'

He blinked as if trying to rid the image from his mind. 'Really?'

'No, but it'll be chilly so I'll put on a few more layers. You're very welcome to join us.' She looked hopefully at him.

'No, you're all right.'

'Maybe in the pub afterwards for the buffet and themed cocktails? Anyway as always it's up to you. Bye.' She darted back to her car not giving him a chance to say no for a second time.

It was halloween and Blythe had had quite a slow day at work. She wasn't fond of those because they dragged. She had one trip out of the office to do a viewing for a vendor who preferred the estate agent to do the guided tours. Blythe liked it that way too. Some people were very good at showing round prospective buyers. Sometimes they were the perfect ones to sell their house because they had an attachment to it and could paint a picture of what it was like to live there. Little anecdotes like 'we love to sit in this corner of the garden and watch the sunset with a glass of wine' were worth their weight in gold in her business. But for many vendor clients professional viewings were part of the service they expected from a quality estate agent and that was where Blythe came into her own.

Today's property was a lovely one. Well maintained, clean and comfortable, it was owned by a high-flying couple who were looking to move up the property ladder, most likely more for financial gain than for space, because with only two of them they definitely didn't need four bedrooms. They kept their home spotless so there was nothing Blythe needed to do, but she still arrived at the property fifteen minutes early so she had a chance to give it the once-over. Today, however, her master plan was thwarted as the prospective buyers were already parked outside.

'Sorry, we're a bit early. We weren't sure how long it would take us to get here,' said the smiley woman getting out of her car. 'It's a lovely house,' she added, looking like she'd already bought it. Hopefully this would be an easy sale.

'That's fine. Let's go in, shall we?' asked Blythe, leading the way with the key in her hand. 'New double glazing and front door two years ago,' she pointed out as she opened the door and was still talking over her shoulder as she stepped inside. 'Conservatory added at the back at the same time which really does— Whoa!' Blythe walked straight into something or – as she thought as she turned around – someone. She jumped in fright as a face loomed in front of hers. 'What the?' She panicked and forcefully pushed the face away. As the life-size cardboard cut-out of Justin

Bieber fell she realised her mistake. 'Oh my word, that gave me a start,' she said, putting her hand to her thumping heart as she tried to quickly regain her composure and any shred of professionalism that remained. 'Sorry about that,' she said to her client as she tried to right Justin, who she now noticed had a broken neck thanks to her hard shove. His head kept flopping down, which wasn't good.

'It's okay. It was quite funny,' said the woman. 'Looks like someone has had a bit of a party.' She pointed through the hallway into the open-plan living space where balloons and garlands adorned abandoned bottles and glasses. Bugger, thought Blythe.

Vicky was sitting on her bed laughing so hard she thought she might rupture something. 'You decapitated Justin Bieber,' she spluttered.

'Not exactly.' Blythe shook her head. 'It was still attached but not by much. Thank goodness the owners were more bothered that they'd forgotten about the viewing and for leaving the place in a state. That definitely got me out of sourcing another Justin. That would have been an interesting one to explain on my expenses claim.'

Vicky took a breath to calm the giggles. 'You should have brought him tonight.'

'Who?' asked Blythe.

'Nearly-headless Justin. We could have taken him trick-or-treating. Although a complete Justin is probably scarier.' She shivered at the thought. Vicky wasn't a fan.

'Come on, Mum!' yelled Eden from downstairs.

'Eden's been ready since four o'clock,' said Vicky, putting

on her giant alien head. She didn't see why you had to stop dressing up once you were an adult. If she was going out on Halloween then she was entering into the full spirit of things. She wasn't alone; quite a few of the village residents dressed up. Blythe wasn't one of them. 'Are you sure you don't want Eden's witch's hat from last year?'

'Certain. Come on,' she said, leading the way back downstairs.

Thanks to the foam head Vicky couldn't see where she was going and missed her footing. 'Cra—'

Blythe spun around and grabbed hold of her.

'I'm fine. I'm fine,' she announced, hanging on to the rail and righting herself. 'For a moment there I thought I was going to get Biebered,' she said, setting off her giggles again.

Eden was waiting for them at the bottom. 'What are you doing?' she asked with her hands on her hips. Vicky had struggled with Eden's outfit because they couldn't agree on exactly how to put together the vampire-Marshall concept and Vicky was also restricted by cost. Some of the children in Eden's class had their pick of outfits because Mum and Dad could afford to buy them whatever they wanted. Vicky couldn't do that but she also didn't believe that was what Halloween was about anyway. Homemade outfits were more in the spirit of the evening and a darn sight cheaper.

Eden was wearing a furry trapper hat Vicky had found in a charity shop and had added felt ears to. Thanks to face paint Eden had bushy eyebrows, a shiny black nose and a beard. A red jumper and the *Paw Patrol* backpack she got for her birthday completed the look that Vicky was calling Were-Patrol.

'You look amazing,' said Blythe, planting a kiss on Eden's hat.

'No, I don't,' said Eden, with a fierce pout.

'Oh... um...' Blythe looked unsure what to say.

'I look super scary so I'll scare people into giving me lots and lots of sweets.'

Vicky was relieved. 'You are super scary. Come here, strange earth creature.' She grabbed her squealing daughter and after a tickle fight and a cuddle they headed for the door.

Thankfully it was a dry evening and not too cold. Not that the children ever noticed. They were far too busy running around. Many of the houses they visited had made a real effort with their decorations. One had fake cobwebs all over their front garden and a giant spider guarding their front door. Another had a skeleton with flashing red eyes that reared up as they approached and scared Blythe, which Eden couldn't stop laughing at. All the houses they visited proudly had their pumpkins on display.

This year Arthur's pumpkin had *Happy Halloween* carved into it. Eden knocked on the door and it opened a crack. 'Who dares to wake the Mummy?' asked Arthur, in a croaky voice.

Eden giggled. 'It's me, Eden. I'm a Were-Marshall from *Paw Patrol*,' she shouted, through the gap.

'Oh, that's okay then,' said Arthur, in his normal voice, opening the door fully to reveal himself wrapped from head to toe in white toilet roll. He offered Eden a bowl of chocolate bars and while she was mulling over her options he spoke to Vicky and Blythe. 'Evening, ladies.'

'Hi, Arthur,' said Vicky. 'Great costume. I might nick that idea for next year.' She loved something she could do on a budget.

'Top tip,' said Arthur, handing them each a mini Mars bar. 'Buy the quilted because the cheap stuff breaks and you end up looking like the Andrex puppy with sheets left all over the house.' He shook his head wisely.

'Happy Halloween, Arthur,' said Blythe.

'Thank you,' said Eden, taking something from the bowl. 'Happy Halloween!' she called, as she skipped off to the next house.

On their rounds they encountered all manner of outfits and folk chorusing 'Happy Halloween!' It really was a cheerful party atmosphere that met them wherever they went and none more so than at Phyllis's; she had made a bucketful of green jelly and hidden the sweets in there for the children to dig out, which they all thought was the best thing ever. Some of the younger ones were slightly confused and also took a handful of jelly thinking that was the treat.

'Aww, I got slimed,' said Eden, as she happily shook jelly from her hands.

They turned onto the green and Sam's cottage came into view. 'Well, well, well,' said Vicky, pointing ahead.

16

31st October

Outside Sam's cottage was not one but three carved pumpkins all flickering away merrily. He'd carved two of them as simple ghosts and the one in front of those was Pac-Man. Blythe couldn't help but smile at the sight. Was Mr Ashton finally warming up to Holly Cross? Eden ran ahead and knocked. A smiling Sam opened the door and held out a large bowl as if fending off an anticipated attack.

'Trick or treat?!' shouted Eden, who already had her face in the bowl hunting for her next sugar hit.

'Hi, Eden,' said Sam. Blythe was impressed that he'd remembered the little girl's name. He leaned closer to Eden. 'The good stuff is at the bottom.'

She rooted further down and pulled out a big bag of chocolate buttons. 'Thank you. Happy Halloween!' She quickly departed with her loot, with Vicky in hot pursuit.

'I'll see you two at the pub,' called Blythe. She turned back to Sam, who was grinning broadly. It made something pleasant squirm in her gut but also made her wary. It had been a while since he'd smiled like that in her presence. Not since his moving-in day.

He beckoned her with his hand. 'Out with it then?'

'What?'

'I'm sure you've got something to say?' He pointed at his three pumpkins before leaning back.

Was he actually puffing his chest out? Blythe stopped herself from laughing. 'Nice job on the carving. Retro is always acceptable.'

'Not always appreciated though,' said Sam. 'Some little kid pointed at Pac-Man and said, "Is that meant to be an eye?"'

'Kids are rude and unappreciative of great art like yours,' said Blythe.

'Actually, they've been really well-mannered tonight. I have to admit I've enjoyed it more than I thought I would. But given I thought it would be on par with a prostate examination I have to say it's exceeded my expectations.' Sam went to put the bowl down.

'Hang on. I'm trick-or-treating too.'

He looked her up and down. 'I don't see any red basque and hot pants so I don't think you qualify.'

'Hey!' she protested. 'I'll stamp on your pumpkins.'

'Harsh.' He gave a look of mock horror. 'You'd best have some chocolate. But for that outfit just the stuff on the top,' he added, as he offered her the bowl.

She took a chocolate bar and popped it in her pocket. 'That'll do for pudding. That's assuming I've got any room after the buffet.'

'Ah, yeah.' He scratched his head. 'I think I'll give it a miss.'

'Why?'

'I've got stuff I should be doing.' He waved the Halloween sweets up the hall.

'We've all got stuff we should be doing. Come on. It's great and I wasn't wrong about pumpkin day now, was I?'

'I guess. It's just after the Christmas jumper woman accosted me—'

'Christmas Carol,' chipped in Blythe.

'Yeah, her. I really don't want to get interrogated again.'

'I'll be your wingman. I'll fend off the locals with a pitchfork,' she said, and for some unknown reason accompanied her words with a stabbing motion.

He chuckled. 'Isn't it meant to be the locals who have the pitchforks?'

'Yep, standard issue. You'll be getting yours soon.' She glanced at her watch. 'If we want one of Jassi's legendary samosas we'll have to hurry.' She could see he was wavering. 'And you still have a point to prove.'

He pulled his eyebrows together. 'How so?'

'You said you were fun.'

Sam opened his mouth wide. 'Are you saying my pumpkins aren't enough for you?'

Blythe snorted. 'They speak volumes of a misspent youth but very little about being fun.'

'Right. Give me two minutes. I'll show you fun.' A little ripple of excitement shuddered through her at the prospect but she felt that was jumping the gun. He was coming to the buffet not taking her to bed.

Where on earth had that idea come from? she thought, as Sam grabbed his coat.

Whilst it wasn't a particularly cold night Blythe was still grateful for the welcome warmth of the Highway Inn.

The pub was busy but Vicky had saved them seats. She waved them over. 'Grab a plate quick. Sarvan has just put out a new batch of samosas,' said Vicky, stopping Sam from pulling out a chair and shooing him towards the buffet.

'But I need to pay someone,' said Sam, pulling out his wallet.

'You can do that later. The samosas won't last.' Vicky pointed forcefully at the buffet table.

'She scares me,' he whispered to Blythe.

'Vicky's lovely. Almost as nice as me,' she said with a wink.

'You scare me too,' he said picking up a plate and a serviette festooned with ghosts.

Blythe leaned into his ear. 'Good!' she snapped, making him jolt.

'You're mean,' he said.

'I prefer unpredictable,' said Blythe, warming to the mild flirtation.

'Wind is unpredictable. You're just mean.' And he stepped in front of her to grab a samosa. They chatted as they made their way around the buffet table and Blythe was pleased at how much more relaxed Sam seemed. This was the breakthrough she'd been hoping for. Above everything she wanted Sam to be happy in Holly Cross and it looked like maybe this could be the start.

They took their plates back to the table and Vicky moved Eden's sweet pile to one side to make room. 'They've set up a tent in the garden for the kids. Arthur is out there telling them ghost stories.'

'Won't they freeze?' asked Sam.

'They're fine. They've got piles of blankets and they're high on sugar.'

'I was thinking more about Arthur.'

'He's a tough cookie,' said Vicky. 'Great with the kids. I think he sees them like substitute grandchildren.'

Sarvan appeared and Sam looked relieved to be able to pay for his meal. 'You're Turpin's new owner then?' asked Sarvan.

'Err... not really... he kind of...'

'Turpin was in here earlier. Made straight for the chimney. It's the first time I've had to put him out since Murray took him on. You two getting on okay?'

'We're a bit like housemates on different shifts. We don't see much of each other.'

'He's a funny little chap,' said Sarvan.

'I'm sure he is. We're just not in each other's faces. Although he has clawed my back,' said Sam.

'I'd like to—' started Vicky but Blythe willed her to stop with her eyes. Vicky shrugged and went back to demolishing a naan bread.

'Everything okay with the food?' asked Sarvan, scanning the plates.

'Fabulous as always,' said Blythe.

'Top banana,' said Vicky.

Sarvan waited for a response from Sam, who looked up from his plate. 'It's some of the best I've tasted.' A beaming smile spread across Sarvan's face and it stayed there as he went off to the next table.

'Is this better than your London Town fancy pants restaurants?' asked Vicky.

'I'm not really into those. But there are some excellent

places for Asian food and the street food in Borough Market is particularly good.' Vicky was frowning at him and Blythe could see the fear in Sam's eyes as he quickly added, 'But not as good as here.' Vicky's frown disappeared.

'I'm just going to check on Eden,' said Vicky, and she left the table.

'See, she's scary,' said Sam, pointing after her with his fork.

'She's not – you're just a big wuss,' said Blythe.

Phyllis slipped into Vicky's vacated seat and Blythe felt Sam's light mood instantly evaporate and saw his shoulders tense. 'Hello, Mr Ashton,' said Phyllis.

'You can call me, Sam. And you're Phyllis, right?'

Phyllis's cheeks coloured. 'You remembered my name.'

'Are you okay, Phyll?' asked Blythe, trying to draw her attention away from Sam.

'I'm fine. I wanted to ask Sam here a couple of questions.'

Blythe was already shaking her head. 'Can they wait? Because we're just having a quiet meal.' As soon as she'd said it she was aware of the loud noise level in the pub, and a burst of laughter from a crowd in the corner only emphasised it.

'Oh, I'm sorry. I didn't know you were on a date,' said Phyllis.

Sam choked on his bhaji and Blythe had to slap him on the back and offer him a glass of water.

'Not a date,' said Blythe, and Sam nodded vigorously. A little more forcefully than her ego would have liked.

Phyllis looked confused. 'Okay. Anyway, Blythe tells me you work with film stars.' Blythe could almost see Phyllis's eyes sparkle at the thought of it. 'Have you met Sean Connery?'

'I'm afraid not but I was once behind Daniel Craig in a coffee queue on the set of *No Time To Die*.'

Phyllis screwed up her features. 'He's not Bond. Well, not in my eyes. Too violent and he's not funny like Sean Connery or Roger Moore. Have you met Roger Moore?' Sam shook his head. Phyllis looked disappointed. 'How about Hugh Grant? I quite like him.'

'Sorry, no. I've met Simon Pegg a few times. He's nice.' Blythe could tell he was trying desperately to please Phyllis.

'Who?' Phyllis scowled at him.

'David Jason!' said Sam, as if the name had suddenly struck him.

Phyllis clapped her hands together. 'Oh, I love Del Boy! Is he nice?'

They chatted for a while and Sam regaled them with titbits from the sets he'd worked on and Phyllis was enthralled. When she went to top up her sherry he turned to Blythe. 'See, I told you I was fun.' She had to concede that tonight he definitely was.

Before Blythe could respond, Phyllis was back. She pulled her chair up close to the table and leaned in. 'What I wanted to know was did you find anything in Murray's cottage? Any clues?' Phyllis propped her elbows on the table and rested her chin on her hands, as if settling down for a long story.

'Clues to what?' asked Sam, drinking some more water.

'His family of course,' said Phyllis.

Sam looked at Blythe to fill in the gaps. 'Murray lived here for quite a while—'

'Definitely over ten years,' said Phyllis, with a firm nod.

'And he was a big part of the community,' explained

Blythe. 'We all thought we knew him well. But it turns out he must have had family up north because he was buried in Manchester. He's turned out to be a bit of a mystery and we're trying to piece things together.'

'That's not anyone else's business.' Sam had a stern look about him.

Phyllis waved a finger. 'But it is, you see, because the village is like a big family. We all look out for each other. Murray was one of us.'

'Doesn't give you the right to gossip about him,' said Sam, and Phyllis pulled her chin in fast.

Blythe didn't like his tone with Phyllis and stepped in. 'It's not that people are gossiping. They're just concerned.'

Sam turned his frown on Blythe. 'But Murray's dead. Any discussions about him now aren't because you care about his wellbeing.'

She felt put on the spot. 'I can see where you're coming from but it's not meant maliciously. It's friendly concern really.'

'I disagree.' He wiped his mouth roughly with a serviette. 'The only thing I despise more than Christmas and lying is gossip.' Phyllis was watching the exchange. 'I should probably go,' he said.

'You're suddenly not much fun at all,' said Blythe.

Sam shook his head, picked up his coat and left.

Phyllis sighed heavily as she patted Blythe's arm. 'Don't worry, dear. These actors are all rather highly strung.'

17

1st November

It was the first of November and Blythe had decided
to feed Turpin en route to an evening property viewing
and consequently was later than usual. She pulled up
outside Sam's just as he was coming out of the front door
in running kit. He was braving the breezy November day
in a muscle top and running shorts. Blythe couldn't help
but notice the muscle definition that had been previously
hidden under his clothes. Sam baulked at seeing her and
it irked her. She was done with apologising but Leonora
was becoming increasingly intimidating with every HCCC
meeting that Sam failed to attend and she needed to get her
off her back.

Blythe pasted on her best smile and got out of the car.
'Hi, Sam, you going for a run?' she asked, sticking to a
neutral subject.

Sam scanned his attire. Gave a look of mock surprise.
'It would appear so.' He pulled on a head torch and Blythe
had to stifle a chuckle.

'Great Dalek impression.' He glared at her so she returned
the chat to his jog. 'Going far?'

He checked his watch. 'Probably.' Which she took to

mean he was now going to be out long enough to ensure he avoided her.

'Well, have a good run,' she said and she gave him a pretend punch on the arm. She had no idea why she did that. They certainly weren't that pally. Sam stared at his arm where she'd touched him like he wanted to rip it off and throw it away. She walked past him and down the side of the cottage, only braving a quick look over her shoulder when she was almost out of view. Sam shook his head, put in his earbuds and set off at an impressive pace. She turned around and almost tripped over Turpin who was sitting at her feet scowling at her. If he had a watch she was sure he'd be tapping it in disgust at the late timing of his dinner.

'Sorry,' she said automatically and followed him round to the back of the cottage. She let herself in the utility and noted that the door from the utility into the rest of the house was now permanently locked. Sam clearly didn't trust her not to snoop around his home. Little did he know she had a key for that door too, not that she'd use it. Grey clouds were making it seem later than it was but at the thought of rain she fed Turpin inside and she hopped up to sit on the worktop while he ate. The cat always bolted down his food like he feared it was going to be taken away so she didn't have to wait long for him to finish. He sat next to the bowl and yowled for more. 'Sorry, that's your lot,' she said.

While she washed up the bowl she watched the droplets of rain smatter the windowpane. Poor Turpin. She didn't like the idea of him being out in bad weather. The utility doors each had a cat flap in them – one to the outside and one into the kitchen; both of them were fixed closed. Now it was starting to get colder would Sam really object to

Turpin sheltering in the utility room? She looked around. She couldn't see that there was much he could damage. There also wasn't anything cosy for him to sleep on, but it was still better than being in the garden sheltering from the elements.

Blythe eventually managed to dislodge the switch on the old cat flap in the outer door so that it would open in both directions and allow Turpin to come and go as he pleased. 'This is a cat flap. Basically, it's your own personal door. It works like this.' She pushed her hand through it and Turpin bobbed down to look out of it. 'You need to push it with... what am I doing? Come here,' she said, picking him up and unceremoniously popping him through it head first. She opened it and peered outside. Turpin wasn't looking impressed. 'You just need to do the same to come back in,' she told him. 'But you'll have to work that out for yourself because I have to go.' She grabbed her keys, opened the back door to leave and Turpin shot back inside. Blythe shrugged, locked up and headed off for her viewing.

Blythe rarely did evening viewings, and Ludo had drummed into them about personal safety, but she was meeting a young couple she had taken on viewings before so despite it being dark and the house a little remote she was sure that she wasn't putting herself in any danger. She let herself into the house, hung up her coat and started switching on the lights. Evening wasn't the best time to show off a house, especially an unoccupied one, but lots of light would definitely help. There was minimal heating left on to avoid any frozen pipes should the weather take a turn for the worse but it was still chilly. Blythe turned the dial on the thermostat and put the radiator in the kitchen onto max to give it a chance to warm up before her clients arrived.

The property was a probate sale and thankfully they hadn't cleared the stuff out as yet, which made it easier for clients to picture themselves living there even if the furniture wasn't to their taste. Blythe took off her coat and pulled a tin from her bag and placed it on the kitchen worktop. She carried a couple of scented candles with her precisely for days like this. She popped off the lid and lit the coffee candle and within moments the aroma was spreading gently. She dropped toilet blocks into the toilets, had a quick spray of air freshener in the other rooms and waited in the kitchen.

The clients were suitably impressed with the property and instead of being put off by the things that needed work, they were excited at the prospect of putting their own stamp on things. Blythe ended the tour in the kitchen as it was the most up to date and now also the warmest room in the house. 'Feel free to have a look around on your own. There's no rush.' Although her stomach was rumbling as it was way past her dinner time.

'Can we have a look in the back garden?' asked the male client.

'Sure,' said Blythe, although this wasn't the property's best feature, not least because it had been reclaimed by nature. She unlocked the back door and waved an arm to activate the security light, which lit it for all of five seconds before going off again.

'It's quite small,' he said, tensing a muscle in his cheek. These sorts of gestures had Blythe on red alert and she automatically jumped to counter any negative vibes.

'Actually, it's a very good size. It's a little unloved right now but it has huge potential. Let me show you.' She lead the way outside, waving her arms wildly to get the security light to come on. It obliged for the requisite five seconds before going off again. How annoying. It had started drizzling so she needed to give them a quick tour and get them back in the warm as fast as possible, especially as she'd not got her coat on. Blythe switched on the torch on her phone and headed off down the garden with the clients following her. They reached the corner which, if there had been some lighting, would have given the best perspective of the garden.

'Wait here and I'll set the light off again so you can see for yourself what a great size it is.' She began walking backwards with her hand in the air, hoping she wouldn't have to go too far before the light came back on. 'It won't take much to make – whoa!' Blythe had stepped backwards expecting there to be more solid ground but instead there was nothing until her foot hit water. It was too late to save herself. She toppled backwards in the dark, landing with a splash. At which point the security light came on as if to highlight her error. The clients came rushing over to find Blythe sitting in a shallow pond.

Thankfully they were lovely and were concerned for Blythe and her now very cold and soggy state, which she brushed away as nothing, like the professional she was. But the good thing was they were quite pleased that the garden had a pond. They'd gone off with lots to think about whilst Blythe had stripped off in the kitchen, bundled her wet clothes into a carrier bag, snuffed out the candle and returned the heating controls to how she'd found them.

She put her coat on and checked the coast was clear.

It was now chucking it down with rain, which was good because it meant there was nobody about. She locked up and dashed to her car wearing only underwear, her coat and a pair of very squelchy shoes.

The windscreen wipers had to work overtime to come anywhere close to clearing enough rain so she could actually see through her windscreen. The country lanes now resembled streams as the rain bounced high off the road. She was about five miles away from Holly Cross when she saw the figure of a jogger in the road dodging puddles. The outfit was familiar. Checking the road was clear Blythe slowed down alongside him and buzzed down the window.

A soaked and bedraggled Sam glared at the car but his expression changed when he recognised the driver.

'You want a lift?' she asked.

'Thanks,' he said, sounding quite exhausted. Maybe he wasn't as fit as he looked. He got inside and she gave him a cursory look while he did up his seat belt. Rivulets of water were cascading from his hair, down his face onto his already soaked top.

'Have you been out in this the whole time?' she asked, setting off again. He made a noise as he sucked his teeth, and a quick glance told her he was mulling something over. 'Is that a difficult question?'

'I was trying out a new running app and my phone battery died. I improvised on the route.' She could tell he was choosing his words carefully.

'You got lost in the rain,' she concluded.

'Not exactly. I was obviously on the right road back to the village.'

'But you must have been out for ages.' She couldn't help

the snort that followed. At least she wasn't the only one having a bad night.

Blythe changed gear and her coat pulled away to reveal her naked thigh. She instantly knew Sam was looking. She grabbed the edge and shoved it between her legs, making it quite hard to drive while she was squeezing her knees together.

It was Sam's turn to splutter a laugh. 'Are you naked under that coat?'

'I am most certainly not!' She was indignant.

'French maid's outfit or bunny girl? No, it's okay – I don't really want to know. Your boyfriend is a lucky man.'

She braked hard and her shoes made a wet fart sound. Not quite the statement she wanted to make. Blythe needed to explain and she couldn't do it whilst concentrating on driving. She pulled over and put on her hazard lights.

'I am not wearing some sex outfit under my coat.' She realised what she was wearing was possibly worse. 'I am wearing my underwear.' Sam's eyebrows jumped but she continued regardless. 'Because my clothes got wet. They're in a bag in the boot.'

'Apologies,' said Sam, although his grin implied he wasn't taking his apology that seriously. 'I didn't realise you'd got caught in the rain too.' He narrowed his eyes as he studied her fairly dry hair and dry coat.

'It wasn't the rain,' she said, reluctant to give him anything further to laugh at. But he was waiting for more information. 'I was showing a client around the garden of a property and I found the pond the hard way.' He started to laugh, a deep throaty laugh, and much to her annoyance she found herself joining in.

18

1st November

Blythe found the pond story was far funnier after she'd had a hot bath and slung everything in the washing machine. Unfortunately she'd had to bin her shoes because they reeked of stagnant pond. Her parents were out with friends for the evening so she was enjoying a rare opportunity to curl up on the sofa with a cup of tea and watch whatever she fancied on Netflix without her stepdad insisting that there was something far better she'd enjoy on Dave.

Her mobile sprang into life and she glanced at it – if it was work it could go to answerphone and she'd deal with it during office hours. It was Sam. An image of him in his wet running top clinging to his chest popped into her mind.

'Hi, Sam, you okay?'

'Are you downstairs?' he asked, in a hushed tone.

She glanced around her parents' front room. 'Yep. I'm watching Netflix. Why?'

'Not at yours. I meant are you downstairs at my place. Which obviously you're not. Never mind. It's okay.'

She had no idea what he was going on about. 'What's wrong?'

'I can hear someone snooping about downstairs,' he whispered. 'I thought it might be you.'

She was about to get the hump that he'd implied she was a snooper when a more pressing issue jumped to the front of her mind. 'If you think you're being burgled you need to call the police not an estate agent.'

'Helpful,' hissed Sam. 'If I put all the lights on perhaps they'll just leave.'

'Or they'll be able to see better when they bang you over the head. Don't be a hero. End this call and phone the police.' He went quiet. 'Why aren't you ending the call?'

'Because what if it's just the house creaking? I'll look like an idiot.'

'But at least you'll be a live idiot instead of one who has taken a golf club to the temple because he didn't want to call the police. The local constabulary are very nice around here. When the farmer's son went for a joy ride in his dad's tractor after one too many vodka shots they were very understanding.'

'Right. Again, most helpful. I think I'll go and have a quick check.'

'Shall I call the police for you?' she offered.

'Or you could stay on the line.'

'And listen to you being bludgeoned to death? Delightful. I guess it beats *Storage Hunters*.'

'What?' he asked, keeping his voice low.

'Nothing. Try to tell me there's something wrong without being obvious. Then I'll know to call the police and you can hide.'

'Great idea. I'm sure what a six-foot-four career burglar

wants to do on a November evening is play hide-and-seek with me.'

'Just say something that's not obvious like... do you want a cup of tea?'

'For heaven's sake I'm not inviting them for tea and biscuits,' whispered Sam.

'No, but if you say that they'll think there's more than one person in the house.'

'Huh. That's not a bad idea. Okay. I'm walking downstairs.'

She could hear the stairs creak a little and her heart started to pick up speed. She was feeling quite tense on Sam's behalf. What if there was someone robbing his home?

'Did you keep the door stop?' she whispered.

'What?'

'The door stop that used to keep the living room door open. Shaped like a chicken. Did you keep it?'

'Yes. Why?' His exasperation was evident but as he was possibly about to meet a hardened criminal, she let him off.

'Because it would make a good weapon. If you can get that far without getting whacked.'

'Oh, thanks.'

'Sorry.'

'Shhh now. I'm nearing the bottom.' She did as she was told. Blythe gripped the phone tighter. She could hear Sam breathing heavily. The long wait was agonising.

All of a sudden, there was a screech and a clatter and then silence. 'Sam. Sam! Are you all right?'

The phone had gone dead.

*

Blythe was racing across the village with her phone to her ear. She'd dialled 101 and ran outside. This was serious and she feared for Sam's safety. She wasn't much of a jogger but when she put her mind to it she wasn't a bad sprinter. Despite having to give her details to a police call operator whilst running she was still at the green in no time. A quick scan as she raced towards the cottage showed everything looked in order although she knew it wasn't. There were no lights on. She darted down the side of the property.

'How can we help?' asked the operator.

'I think there's a burglary in progress,' she said, in between puffs. She may have been quick but she wasn't that fit. She gave Sam's address and despite the operator asking her more questions she shoved the phone in her back pocket. Her focus was to get inside and help Sam. An image of him lying on the floor with a gash in his head shot unhelpfully into her mind. She took a breath and turned the key in the back door. It was dark in the utility but she knew her way around it so was at the internal door in two strides. Her hands were shaking as she carefully turned the key and tried the handle. The door opened a crack and she listened. All she could hear was her heart thumping.

When she'd been speaking to Sam he was at the bottom of the stairs heading for the living room. She carefully made her way through the kitchen, her senses on red alert. Was the burglar still here? Were they ransacking upstairs? She couldn't hear any footsteps above her and she recalled when she'd visited Murray that the floorboards above creaked in places. She returned her attention to the hallway. If the burglar wasn't upstairs, they had either left or they were waiting to surprise her. She very much liked the idea of the former. She gently felt along the worktop for anything she could use to defend herself. Her fingers touched something. It was kitchen roll on a wooden holder. It would have to do.

Blythe gripped the kitchen roll holder and stepped quietly into the hall. A shard of light from the tiny diamond window in the front door cast a distorted pattern across the space. The living room door was open and she was pleased to see no sign of Sam's prostrate body lying there. She crept towards the doorway. She held her breath as she inched forwards.

'Gotcha!' yelled Sam, grabbing Blythe by the shoulder.

'Arghhhhhh!' yelled Blythe, wielding the kitchen roll.

'Whoa! Blythe?' Sam shone the light from his phone in her face and they both jumped apart.

Blythe dodged out of the torch beam, scanning Sam's head for any sign of injury. 'You okay?' she lowered her voice.

'No, you almost gave me a heart attack,' he whispered. 'Nice dressing gown,' he added.

'Thanks. The phone went dead. I thought you'd been whacked.'

Sam tilted his head as if starting to understand her perspective. 'I called you back but it was engaged.'

'Because I was calling the police. Oh crap, the police.' Blythe pulled her phone from her pocket and explained quietly to a very patient operator that it was a false alarm. She ended the call and turned to Sam. 'I take it it's *definitely* a false alarm?'

They paused for a moment to listen. There was a small thud, which they both heard. Their eyes widened at the same time. 'Oh great,' she whispered. 'I've just stood the police down. You can call them back.'

'Shhh,' he said, and he pointed into the living room. He leaned in so close to her neck she could feel his breath against her skin as he spoke. 'I'll go in. You hit them with the…' He took in the streams of kitchen roll unfurled across his hallway. 'Kitchen roll?'

'The holder's wooden.' She held it up.

'Whatever. Hit them with it if they run out. Okay?'

She pulled her head back. She was about to explain the many things wrong with his plan but Sam had already disappeared into the living room. She stayed by the door, held the kitchen roll holder aloft, tore off the sheets of kitchen roll obscuring her view and stood poised ready to whack the burglar. This was a very bad idea indeed.

There was the sound of furniture being moved followed by Sam screaming. Blythe rushed into the living room ready to accost the burglar. She hit the light switch and the scene in front of her seemed to freeze for a moment. Sam was bent over as if lifting one end of the sofa and Turpin was on his back looking mightily pissed off and slightly alarmed as his tail was all puffed up.

'What the hell?' As realisation dawned, the adrenaline subsided and the giggles took over. 'Turpin, you gave us a fright,' she said, going over to stroke the cat.

'Uh. Excuse me. He has every one of his claws impaled in my back. Get him off!'

'Did nasty Sam scare poor Turpin?' asked Blythe, unfurling each of his paws and lifting him down.

'No. Nasty Turpin, scared poor Sam.' Sam straightened up and gave a little shudder. 'Well, not scared exactly.' Blythe was failing to hide her grin. 'It could have been a burglar. It sounded like one. I thought cats were meant to be agile.' Sam pointed at the ornament and candle lying on the floor in front of the fireplace, where they had presumably been knocked off the mantelpiece.

'I don't think he's been in here before. It's all unfamiliar to him.' Turpin immediately snaked around Blythe's legs, purring loudly, like he always did when he was expecting some food. She bent down to him. 'Turpin says he's sorry.' She looked up at Sam who was trying very awkwardly to rub his back.

'What I can't work out is how the hell he got in here in the first place.' Sam was frowning and Blythe took that as her cue to leave.

19

2nd November

Eden was at a birthday party so Vicky had roped Blythe into walking the dachshund clan with her, and five dogs between two people was working a lot better. It was a chance to have a catch-up too. Vicky loved Blythe's stories; they always made her laugh. 'It would have been funny if you'd attacked him with kitchen roll,' she said, setting herself off with another fit of the giggles as that image came into her mind.

'No, it wouldn't. What a nightmare. He's still puzzling over how Turpin got inside. He's hunting everywhere for an opening or a gap. I can't tell him that I unlocked the cat flap into the utility and that he must have got in from there when Sam opened the door.'

'He's a smart man. He'll work it out,' said Vicky.

'Thanks. I look forward to that moment. Anyway, there was something I needed to tell you.'

'Sounds formal.'

Blythe looked uncomfortable. 'Something I wanted to mention really.'

'Spit it out,' said Vicky.

'You know Owen friended me on Facebook?'

Suddenly nothing was funny anymore. 'You unfriended him.'

'I did. But he sent me this lovely message and…'

Thoughts raced around Vicky's head and a sense of foreboding stomped up her spine. 'What have you done?' she asked.

'Nothing really. Like I said, he sent a lovely message asking how I was, what I was up to, and why I'd unfriended him.' Blythe winced at the end of the sentence.

'And what did you tell him?'

'Nothing. I told him a bit about my job. He asked if I was married. I said I was single…'

'Ohmyword you're going on a date with him. This is the worst thing ever. This is worse than accepting his friend request. How could you?'

'If you'd let me finish.' Blythe looked a little irritated. 'It's definitely not a date. He just wanted to catch up, that's all. But I've said no because I knew you wouldn't be happy about it.'

Vicky sighed so hard it blew Blythe's hair about. 'Thank you. You gave me a fright there.'

'Sorry. I didn't mean to. I thought you should know what's happened. Not that anything has but I know you're a bit weird about Owen so…'

'I'm not weird about him. It's just…' There were so many ways she could finish that sentence. One of them being with the truth. Now wasn't the time. 'I don't like him.'

'I got that message loud and clear,' said Blythe, linking arms with her friend and almost tripping over a dachshund.

★

That evening Blythe was in Sam's utility feeding Turpin. Things had progressed slowly and now Blythe was able to stroke the cat while he ate. When the internal door opened and Sam popped his head in, Blythe hopped up to sit on the worktop while Turpin wolfed down his food. 'Ahh it's my favourite burglar duo.'

'Does that make Turpin a cat burglar?' asked Blythe.

'Very droll.' At the sight of the open door Turpin left his food and made a bolt for the gap. Sam wasn't quick enough. 'The little sod. Oh well.' He opened the door fully and stepped into the utility. 'It's a bit chilly in here,' he said, with a shudder.

Blythe put on a cockney urchin voice. 'You sees, the lord of the manor rations the coal, sir, so us paupers have to huddle together for warmth.'

'You should do stand-up,' he said. He took in Blythe sitting there in her coat with her arms wrapped around herself. 'Is the radiator on?' he asked, as he bobbed down to check it.

'It's stuck on minimum and only the bottom is warm,' said Blythe, who had tried a number of times to turn the thing up. 'But it's still warmer than outside,' she added, thinking that it was a little better for Turpin than sleeping in the garden. She stopped herself from saying anything else in case she let something slip. As far as she knew Sam hadn't worked out that the cat flap was back in use.

'Not much warmer.' Sam was wrestling with the radiator control.

'I'd best round up Turpin,' she said, hopping down from the worktop.

'Look, I'm not being a grouch about the cat. He's probably not house-trained.'

'You don't have to explain,' she said, as she went in search of her feline charge.

Turpin's escape gave her the ideal chance to have a good nose around the cottage. She hadn't planned to snoop but Turpin wasn't in any of the downstairs rooms so she headed upstairs. Sam hadn't made many changes. Some fresh paint and less clutter had brightened it up and yet it still had that warm cottagey feel to it. The stair carpet was still Murray's swirly one and she followed it across the landing into the only room with an open door. A giant sleigh bed dominated the room and in the middle of the plain white duvet was a lump. Blythe lifted up the duvet and peeked in the bed.

Two huge green eyes stared back at her. She was sure she detected a hint of disappointment that she'd found his hiding place so easily. 'Come on, Turpin. Back to prison you go.' She reached for the cat and he took a swipe at her. 'Hey! I'm the one who feeds you.' She knelt down and put her head under the duvet. 'I know it's cosy in here but Sam does not want to share his bed with a grumpy ginger pussy.' She heard a snort of a laugh from behind her. 'Did you know, Turpin, that some people, the worst kind of people, have really dirty minds,' she added for Sam's benefit although she was grinning under the duvet. She reached in, more slowly this time, and scratched Turpin's head. He let out a low menacing hiss. He wasn't going to be bought so easily. Blythe pulled her head out from under the covers.

Sam was leaning against the door frame with a broad grin on his face. 'Problem?' he asked.

'Kind of. I'll see if I can coax him out with some food.'

'Or,' suggested Sam, stepping forward and hoicking the duvet off the bed to reveal the crouched and now surprised cat. Turpin glared at Sam before jumping off the bed and skulking out of the room.

'I'll finish up downstairs and leave you in peace,' Blythe said, getting to her feet. 'I like what you've done to the cottage by the way. Murray would approve.'

'Thanks. I mean if I'm honest I'm hoping he's not stuck around to check it out but...'

'Scared of ghosts as well as cat burglars are you?'

'Again, that word *scared*. It's not what usually springs to mind when I think of my disposition. It's a good job you're not in PR. Although you do a top job of selling the benefits of living in this village.'

'Actually, I know you're not big on the community thing—'

'Hey, I did pumpkin day and Halloween. I should definitely be off the hook for community stuff for the rest of the year. And I should probably get some sort of prize or a badge at the very least.'

Christmas swam into Blythe's mind but she ignored it. Whatever Leonora said, or more accurately growled, it wasn't doing any good to keep badgering Sam about Christmas. Blythe had a more subtle plan, which was to gradually introduce him to village life – a bit like Turpin and the indoors.

'Sure. But it's bonfire weekend and I know the fireworks might not be your thing but we could really use your skills when it comes to building the bonfire. I'm guessing you're good with your hands because of the thatching,' she said. 'It was like a toppling Jenga tower last year.'

She hoped appealing to his expertise might be a good approach. She waited. He was mulling it over. 'It'd be a few hours on Saturday and you get a free jacket potato and entry to the event for your trouble. What do you think?'

He ran his lip through his teeth. 'I think you're very persuasive.'

'I think that describes my disposition perfectly.' She'd make Sam Ashton a part of this village if it killed her.

Saturday was the day the village were having their bonfire and Blythe's plan to avoid Leonora lasted for all of five minutes. Blythe and some others had cordoned off the end of the school field and were marking out the base of the bonfire when someone shouted her name and everyone turned to see Leonora marching over wearing her first aider tabard. 'Blythe, I urgently need an update on the Sam Ashton situation. He's on my critical path.'

Blythe didn't like the image that conjured up but tried to ignore it. 'Leonora, I know the situation with Sam isn't ideal but I know for sure that if we push him on this he definitely won't cooperate. If we are too forceful he's just going to dig his heels in.'

'But the Christmas display must be a priority. We have to—'

Blythe held up her hands to try to avoid a Leonora rant. 'I completely agree that we don't want any issues this year so I have a plan for how to get Sam on board. He is slowly getting involved in village life and he's even planning on coming to help us with the bonfire today. I think we need to build on that bit by bit. Ease him in gently.'

Leonora fixed her with a steely stare. 'We don't have time for easing anyone in. Tomorrow we go full steam ahead on Christmas. We have to.' Her voice went up a couple of octaves at the end of the sentence.

'Then Sam will retreat and we'll have a big gap in our Christmas display.' Blythe folded her arms. She'd put a lot of effort into encouraging Sam to join in with the community and she wasn't prepared to let Leonora steamroller all over it.

Leonora pursed her lips. 'I won't be blackmailed.'

'Nor will Sam.' The two women stared each other down.

'Fine. But I'm making a diary note for two weeks' time because that is an absolute backstop to get decorations up on his cottage.'

'And you promise not to mention Christmas to Sam today?'

Leonora's eyebrows danced. 'Well, I don't think—'

'Promise,' said Blythe, with a tilt of her head.

'Ridiculous. But if you insist.'

'Thank you,' said Blythe. Leonora muttered something and went off to badger someone else.

'Blythe!' called Eden, as she barrelled into her.

'Hey, you, have you come to help?' she asked, as she hugged the little girl. 'All helpers get a free hot dog or jacket potato at the fireworks tonight.' Eden screwed up her features. 'I thought you liked hot dogs?'

'They're okay.'

Blythe could give a very long list of reasons why Bonfire Night hot dogs were a lot better than okay. She wasn't a big junk food fan but there was something about a hot dog around the bonfire that whisked her back to her childhood. Or at least to a view through one of the windows onto happy times. Her, her mum and Greg all eating their hot dogs in between oohing and ahhing at the fireworks.

'Can I help make the bonfire?' asked Eden.

'I'm afraid not, but there are lots of things you can do to help instead.' Blythe could see it was a nice idea but they didn't let children help with the bonfire because a lot of the build involved rough pallets that were full of splinters. 'I hear that the plan is to build the biggest bonfire ever…'

'Wow!' said Eden, clearly impressed.

'But that means it needs more than one Guy Fawkes because one little itty bitty guy would look silly.' Eden giggled. 'That means you need to join the other children at the village hall where they're making them.'

'What?' asked a harassed-looking Vicky, as she finally caught up with her daughter. She had a rather tubby Labrador in tow who flopped down on the grass at the earliest opportunity.

'We're needed at the village hall. Come on, Mum,' said Eden, taking her mother's hand and tugging her back the way she'd come.

'What?' Vicky looked so confused. 'Fernando might have a heart attack if he has to walk that far. Let's give him a minute.'

Eden reluctantly let go of her mother and skipped off to greet some other locals. 'Is she all right? She said she doesn't want a hot dog.'

'She's had a bit of a tummy ache. If I'm honest I think she's been eating too many Halloween sweets.'

Blythe nodded her understanding. 'You okay?' she asked.

'This is my third dog walk today and I've four more to fit in somehow.'

'That's a lot for a weekend,' said Blythe.

'I'm doing a discount for weekends because I can't fit them all in Monday to Friday around work. I have lots of plates spinning,' she said, with a half-hearted grin. 'Spinning might be pushing it a little. More of a wobble. I was late in yesterday so I got another warning.' Vicky kissed her teeth.

'That's not good. Can't you walk some of them together?'

'It's a nightmare trying to work out who will walk with who. Virginia Woof the irritable pug has to wear a muzzle if she's with other dogs and that makes her look like Hannibal Lecter so she's better on one-to-one walkies.' Fernando looked up but it wasn't a joyful look on his face. Vicky gave him a pat. 'Unfortunately, most of the dogs I've got on my books are ones that are best walked alone. Like Fernando here who has his own pace, which is slightly faster than a lazy sloth.'

'That's tricky.' Blythe looked around. They still had a lot of work to do. 'I'm sure I'll be able to help you later today. Have you asked Norman or Phyllis?'

'I wasn't fishing for help. I'll be fine. Eden's got a playdate later so I'll be able to walk two then. Well at least one of them.' Vicky's expression didn't look certain.

Eden came running back. 'We need to go, Mum. I've got lots to do.'

'See you later,' said Blythe, waving them off and feeling pleased as she spotted the figure of Sam walking towards them.

'Hi,' said Sam to Vicky as she stomped past him. He turned to Blythe. 'Everything okay?'

She gave him a quick scan. Hair damp from the shower. A shadow of stubble on a chiselled jaw. Dark winter coat with the collar turned up. 'Yep, everything looks good to me,' she said.

'Where do you want me?' he asked. Now there was a question she had multiple answers for. This Sam was really very alluring. They were definitely building a rapport and he was becoming more and more attractive the longer she spent in his company. And as long as they avoided the subject of Christmas— 'You okay?' he asked.

Blythe snapped herself out of the little fantasy she had wafted away on. Flirting was just creepy if it was only one way and from the frown Sam was giving her she was definitely going solo. 'Yes. Let me show you what we're thinking.' She really needed to keep focused on the bonfire or they'd have another Tower of Pisa situation on their hands.

The morning flew by in a jolly bustle of stacking and building. Leonora hovered around them and Blythe saw the furtive looks she was giving Sam – obviously desperate to raise the question of Christmas with him. But true to her word, so far she hadn't mentioned the C-word. Sam was quickly welcomed into the small throng of dad helpers, and the bottom half of the bonfire quickly started to take shape. However, the great breadth of the base and the quickly diminishing pallet pile had Blythe starting to feel that perhaps they had been a little overambitious. There was a toot of a horn as a low loader with a stack of pallets on board pulled up, which gave Leonora something to occupy herself with. Norman and Arthur appeared. Norman waved as Arthur pushed his wheelbarrow across the school field.

'Refreshments!' called Norman, and everyone stopped what they were doing and came to investigate, much to Leonora's annoyance.

Inside the wheelbarrow were two catering flasks, a variety of green cups from the village hall and some cake boxes. Norman and Arthur set themselves up as an unconventional mobile snack emporium as everyone waited patiently. Blythe rubbed her hands together. 'Ow,' she yelped.

'You okay?' asked Sam.

Blythe studied her left hand. 'Splinter.' The dirty great thing was lodged in her middle finger.

'I'll get Leonora – she's designated first aider,' said Norman.

'No thanks. It's not that bad,' said Blythe, wincing as she prodded it.

'Let's see,' said Sam.

Blythe helpfully held up her middle finger and he smirked. 'Charming,' he said, taking her hand for a closer look. The sensation of his warm hand against her cold one made her start. At least that's what she assumed was making her tingle.

He stepped close to her and stared intently at her finger. 'I'll have that out in no time,' he said with a smile.

She was about to thank him when he pulled a large penknife from his pocket. 'Actually, it's fine,' she said, whipping back her hand.

'Don't be a baby.' He opened up the knife to reveal a rather large blade, which picked up the only shard of sunlight and glinted menacingly.

'I don't think amputation is the answer,' she said, sticking her finger in her mouth and trying to locate the end of the splinter with her teeth. She could feel it under the skin but there was nothing to bite onto so she couldn't pull it out. She took her finger out of her mouth and glared at it.

Sam took a cup of steaming water from Arthur and dipped the blade in it.

'It won't hurt,' he said softly.

'Liar.'

Sam grimaced. 'Okay. It might hurt for a second.'

'I don't think this—'

'Trust me,' said Sam, taking hold of her hand again. There was something oddly intimate about the moment. Despite her fearing for her fingertip.

Norman appeared at Blythe's side. 'I'll get you a coffee, Blythe. But the cakes are going quick so I thought you'd better choose one,' he said, holding the open cake box under her nose. The waft of sweet pastry had her full attention. 'Now I know you like an éclair but there's also one blackberry and apple turnover left—'

'Ow!' yelped Blythe, as a stabbing pain shot through her finger. She couldn't snatch her hand back because Sam was still holding it tightly.

'It's out,' said Sam, brandishing the tip of the pen knife like a trophy.

'I've got antiseptic wipes and plasters,' said Arthur, popping up between Sam and the cake box.

A few minutes later Blythe was sitting on a sheet of plastic with a coffee, a turnover and a plaster-covered finger. Sam sat down next to her. 'Have you forgiven me yet?' he asked.

'Definitely not. I'll probably need therapy to get over the trauma.' She took the last bite of her turnover, closed her eyes and savoured the perfectly autumnal flavours – there was even a hint of custard. She opened one eye to see that Sam was grinning at her. 'What?'

'Does that taste good?'

'Absolute perfection.' She nodded at his vanilla slice. 'Is this your first taste of Norman's cakes?'

'Yeah. But cake is cake right?'

Blythe became animated. 'Ohmyword. You could not be more wrong. Taste it. Go on.'

'Okay.' Sam shrugged a shoulder, took a bite and started to chew.

Blythe could spot the exact moment the flavours kicked in – Sam slowed down his chewing and his eyes conveyed how incredible it tasted. 'Told you,' she said, feeling smug. She sipped her coffee and waited for him to finish eating.

'That's astonishingly good,' he said, licking his fingers.

'That's Norman's bakery. One of the very many benefits of living in Holly Cross.'

20

6th November

Holly Cross always did their Bonfire Night on the nearest weekend to the 5th of November. And it was just the right amount of wintry when Blythe left home. She had a number of layers on, including the first outing for her Arran woolly hat with the double pom-poms and matching scarf.

She let herself into Sam's utility. There was no sign of Turpin who had taken to sleeping in the sink. She wondered if she could sneak in a cat bed or if Sam would object. She put down the cat food and took the empty tin outside. She tapped a few times with the fork. 'Turpin! Dinner time!' She waited but there was no sign of the cat. She put the tin in the recycling and returned to the utility. As she came in one door Sam came in the other.

'Oh, hi,' she said. 'Have you seen Turpin?'

Sam looked a little sheepish. 'Yeah, this way,' he said, showing her into the kitchen. She followed him through to the living room. She was scanning the sofas for any sign of the cat. Sam cleared his throat and pointed at the window. She didn't spot Turpin at first. But when she looked further up there he was sound asleep on the curtain rail.

'What are you doing up there, you cheeky boy?' Turpin opened one eye. 'Did he break in again?' she asked.

'It looks like he broke in the cat flap before so I shut it again but since then he's been using it like a door knocker. I wondered what the heck the noise was at three this morning so I came down to investigate to find him sat outside banging his paw on it. I opened the door to have a few choice words with him and he shot inside.'

'So, it worked.'

'Precisely. I also discovered at five o'clock that it works in reverse. He was knocking to go out.'

Blythe spluttered a laugh. 'He's a smart boy.'

'At least, on the plus side, I think it means he's house-trained if he wants to be let out. That or he has some perverse authority complex where he likes controlling people.'

'Could be a combination of the two,' she said.

'Anyway he's won and now both the flaps are open.' Sam looked resigned.

'Thank you, that's really kind. I was beginning to worry about him being out in all weathers. I've put his food down. Do you want me to put him in the utility?'

'Nah, he looks settled. He knows where his food is. If you give me a minute we can walk to the school field together.'

'Yeah. Okay.'

'Great.' Sam's smile was infectious. He left the room and Blythe tried to reach up to stroke Turpin but he eyed her superciliously as he clearly knew he was just out of reach.

Sam returned, dressed in coat and scarf, and held up his keys. 'Shall we get going?'

Blythe followed him out the front door, which felt slightly odd. She'd got used to using the back door. 'How's the finger?' he asked, as they strolled along. Blythe lifted her middle finger. 'I guess I asked for that.'

'It's fine. I put a new plaster on so I didn't get any dirt in it. Thanks for all your help today and I don't just mean with my finger. You worked hard on the bonfire.'

'I enjoyed it. And I have to admit, people here are nice.'

'Is this where I get to say I told you so?'

'You only get to say that once, so you need to choose your timing carefully.'

'Then I'll wait.'

They walked up the hill together, perfectly in time with each other. 'I'm quite looking forward to seeing the stack we built go up in the flames,' he said. 'I've never seen a bonfire quite that big before. And I can't remember the last time I went to a firework display.'

'When you were a kid probably.'

'No, we didn't do that sort of thing. I think it was when a group from work went to Battersea Park. That was a seriously impressive display.'

'Ahh then, I might need to manage your expectations a little. Holly Cross fireworks are special in their own way.'

Sam looked like he was going to question her further but they'd reached the school gate where people were waiting to take their tickets. It was a good turn-out and the queue for the hot dogs was already snaking out of the hospitality tent. Sam joined the queue and Blythe went in search of Vicky.

She found her friend near the boundary they'd made to keep people a safe distance from the fireworks. Vicky was eating one jacket potato and had another one lined up. 'You hungry or is that one for me?' asked Blythe.

'It's Eden's but she's changed her mind so you're welcome to have it.'

'You're okay. I've got my heart set on a hot dog.'

'Is that the only thing you've got your heart set on?' asked Vicky. Blythe was confused so Vicky elaborated. 'I saw you arrive with Sam. You two look like you have a connection. You were literally hanging on his every word.'

Blythe squeaked out an embarrassed laugh. She didn't like the thought that there was likely some truth in Vicky's observations. 'Nah, we were just chatting. I have to tilt my neck because he's so tall. Bit annoying really.'

Vicky gave her a look. 'All right. If you say so.'

Vicky's words were conjuring up interesting thoughts. Did she and Sam have a connection? She liked him when he wasn't being all weird about Christmas.

'Hello!' said a cheery woman in a bobble hat and puffer jacket, interrupting Blythe's thoughts. 'Are you local?' she asked.

'Err yes. You?' asked Blythe automatically, even though she knew the answer.

'No just here for the fireworks. It's busy. These people can't all be from this little village. Can they?'

'All of Holly Cross turns out for the fireworks and the food. Plus it brings in people from the surrounding area, like you. You should try the hot dogs.'

'Oh, okay. Thanks, bye.' And she disappeared into the crowd.

'You okay?' Vicky waved a potato in front of Blythe's face.

'Yeah. Where's Eden?' she asked.

'She's sitting on the hay bales with the other kids listening to our old history teacher spout on about the gunpowder plot and the very tenuous link to Holly Cross.'

Sam came to join them. He handed Blythe a hot dog and a large white wine and popped the ring on a can of Coke he'd got for himself.

'Thanks,' she said, taking them both and immediately biting into the hot dog.

It was as good as ever.

'First Holly Cross bonfire is it, Sam?' asked Vicky.

'Yep. Looking forward to it,' he replied, although he seemed cautious around Vicky. They ate their hot dogs in silence.

'Fireworks should be starting soon,' said Blythe to break the silence. The other two nodded.

When she thought things were feeling a bit awkward, someone else joined them and the awkwardness levels shot into the sky like an errant firework.

'Hiya, long time no see,' said Owen, opening his arms to hug Blythe.

'Oh, Owen.' Blythe froze and glanced at Vicky who looked crosser than a bulldog chewing a wasp. Belatedly Blythe hugged Owen. 'What a surprise,' she said. What she actually meant was: 'What the hell are you doing turning up out of the blue like this because in about ten seconds Vicky is going to kill me?'

'I thought I'd come over and see if I could catch up with you guys and enjoy the fireworks too. Hi, Vicky,' he said.

'Owen,' said Vicky, putting down her second jacket potato.

Owen glanced at Sam. 'All right?'

'Sorry,' said Blythe. 'This is Sam Ashton. He's new to the

village. Sam, this is Owen Hockley. We all went to the local comprehensive together.'

'Nice to meet you,' said Sam, and they shook hands. 'You escaped from Holly Cross then.'

'No, I never lived in the village. I did spend quite a bit of time here back in the day because…' His eyes alighted on Vicky's scowl and he ran out of words. Owen turned back to Sam. 'I bet you're dead excited about all the Christmas malarky that they do here.'

'I'm hoping to avoid all the celebrations,' said Sam.

Blythe wasn't sure what was worse – Owen turning up out of the blue or Sam being forced into a conversation about Christmas. Neither was fun.

'Good luck with that. I lived ten miles away and I still got roped in, thanks to this pair. You don't stand a chance.' Owen chuckled then seemed to note Sam's expression of dread. 'But, I mean, why would you want to avoid Christmas?' He waited for Sam to reply.

'I need to… um…' Vicky started to walk away.

'Vic, hang on, can we please talk?' Owen asked, walking in step with her and making her stop dead.

'Mummy!' called Eden. 'I don't feel very well. My tummy hurts.'

'Who's this then?' asked Owen.

Vicky swallowed hard. 'My daughter, Eden. Sorry, I need to take her home.'

'I'm not that bad,' said Eden, slapping on a huge grin. 'It'll be fireworks soon and I reeeeeeeally want to see the guys get all burned up. Please can we stay?'

Vicky looked from Eden to Owen. 'Fine, stay with Blythe while I speak to this man.'

*

There was a whistle from the PA system followed by a crackly announcement that the fireworks were about to start. The children were fizzing with excitement. More people came over to where Blythe and Sam were standing, making Sam move closer to Blythe. She looked up and he smiled down at her. Something in her stomach flipped. A hush descended and people moved even closer. Sam ended up standing behind Blythe. For a moment she imagined what it would be like if he wrapped his arms around her.

The first fireworks erupted into the night sky and showered down silver sparkles as the crowd oohed and ahhed. A series of rockets whooshed into the air and split into red stars.

Blythe felt Sam's breath on her neck before she heard him. 'Why aren't there any bangs?' he asked.

'Child- and pet-friendly,' explained Blythe.

He looked impressed. 'Turpin will be very pleased.' They grinned at each other and another series of whooshes drew their attention back to the display.

'Blythe, can I sit down?' asked Eden.

'You won't be able to see the fireworks too well from the grass and you'll get a damp bum.'

Eden stuck her bottom lip out. 'I can lift you onto my shoulders if you'd like,' offered Sam.

'Please.' Eden looked taken with Sam.

'That okay?' asked Sam.

'Sure. It's really kind of you.'

Sam took hold of Eden's waist and lifted her up. Immediately she screamed. And it most definitely wasn't a scream of excitement.

Sam returned Eden to the ground and she crumpled into a ball clutching her stomach. He eased her into the recovery position and checked her pulse.

Vicky was there in a flash. 'What the hell? What did you do?' snapped Vicky.

'Nothing,' said Sam. 'I was just lifting her and...'

'What hurts, sweetie?' asked Vicky, her mum voice back in place.

Eden let out a low groan. 'Tummy.' Her cheeks were very pale.

Leonora appeared wearing her first aider's luminous tabard. As a retired nurse she was more than qualified for the job. She crouched down next to Eden and after what appeared to be a quick scan she turned to the anxious watching faces. 'We need to get her to hospital.'

'I'll call an ambulance,' said Blythe.

'It would be quicker if someone drove her straight there,' said Leonora.

'I've been drinking,' said Blythe, feeling awful that she couldn't help.

'I'll run and get my car,' said Sam. 'We can sat nav the hospital.'

'My car is just over there and I know the shortest route,' said Owen. 'I'll take her.' His words were framed more as a question to Vicky.

Everyone paused for a second to await her response.

'Go!' instructed Leonora forcefully.

'I'm parked over here,' said Owen, leading the way.

Sam carefully lifted a balled-up Eden into his arms, making her whimper.

Vicky hovered at his elbow. 'Eden,' she said in a reassuring voice that masked her obvious distress. 'It's going to be okay.' The glance she gave Blythe told her she had little confidence in her statement.

They all rushed through the crowds towards the exit. The lights on the road outside the school gates guided them as they strode purposefully in silence. Out of the gates Owen stopped near a small white Kia, opened the door and pushed the passenger seat forward. 'If you put her on the back seat I think that would be best,' he said, shoving a large box already in the back to one side. He dashed around to the driver's side. Sam did as instructed and fitted the seat belt as best he could. Vicky tried to put the passenger seat back in place. Initially it didn't budge. She grabbed it and shook it with frustration. 'Bloody thing!' Sam leaned past her and flicked a switch, making the seat spring back into place. Vicky got inside, her features pale.

'Call me when you can,' said Blythe feeling helpless.

Vicky looked shocked. 'Aren't you coming?' Owen started the car.

Blythe glanced at Eden curled up in the back next to a large box. 'There's no room.' The distress on her friend's face pained her.

'We'll meet you there,' said Sam pulling his car keys from his pocket. In that moment Blythe was so grateful. Vicky nodded, shut the door and the car pulled away.

*

Vicky's heart hammered in her chest. She'd never been so scared. Something happening to Eden was her worst nightmare. And now she was living it. And to make that situation even worse she was sharing the ordeal with Owen. The man she had loved and the relationship she had monumentally stuffed up. She was twisted in her seat so that she kept her focus on Eden. The car was small enough for her to be able to reach her daughter's knee, the contact just as much reassurance for her as it was for Eden.

Despite what was going on it was hard to stop the memories from across the years invading her mind. Pictures of her first kiss with Owen aged seventeen outside the cinema after seeing a *Captain America* movie. Her twenty-first party at her mum and dad's where all their mates slept in the living room and Owen made bacon sandwiches for breakfast. Their last Christmas together when he'd bought her the hair straighteners she wanted. Closely followed by the sight of him kissing a Barbie-figured blonde in the town's only night club. And finally the sight of him storming off after catching her with Dim Wick – the latter blurred by hot tears.

'You okay?' asked Owen, flicking a look in her direction.

She realised tears were dripping off her chin and she roughly wiped them away, feeling slightly guilty that they weren't caused entirely by Eden's current condition.

'Fine.' Her tone was abrupt. She knew she needed to fight down the complicated emotions she felt for Owen. She'd been shocked to see him breeze into the Bonfire Night celebrations but the sight of him had made her heart skip. Exactly how it always had. The hurt and the years hadn't changed that involuntary reaction. And now here he was being a hero.

She turned back to Eden. The sight of her baby scrunched up in pain, sobbing gently, crumbled her heart. Eden had had some of the usual childhood illnesses – croup, chicken pox and a variety of cold and sickness bugs – but this was completely different. This was frightening. Vicky knew there was something very wrong and the thought made her feel sick.

'When I spotted the fireworks on Blythe's Facebook feed I didn't think tonight would end up like this,' said Owen jovially. A quick look in his direction revealed a broad grin, which made her blood boil. Did he not realise how serious this was?

'What did you expect, Owen? A big school reunion? Jolly waltz down memory lane?' He might be helping her now but he was also the cause of the fear, worry and uncertainty dashing around her system, which was an added burden she didn't need.

'Maybe. I thought it would be good to reconnect.'

'Reconnect? Our connection was broken a long time ago.'

'I didn't mean specifically with you, Vicky.' Owen's easy tone had gone.

Vicky decided not to ask what or who else he had hopes of connecting with because she really didn't want to know the answer. Her mind was whirring. She reassured herself that if even *she* didn't know if Eden was his daughter then there was no way he could. He probably meant Blythe.

'Can't you go any faster?' She wanted to get Eden to hospital as quickly as possible but was also driven by the desire to exit the car and get far away from Owen Hockley.

'I'm maxing out the speed limit as well as trying not to throw the kid around.'

Vicky huffily conceded that she would have to sit it out. She focused her attention on Eden who had gone very quiet. 'Eden, Mummy's here. Not much further. Eden?' There was no response.

21

6th November

Blythe and Sam were left standing on the pavement wondering what to do. 'Poor Eden and poor Vicky. I hope it's nothing serious,' said Blythe.

'She's going to get the best help at hospital. Try not to worry.' Sam reached out and squeezed Blythe's shoulder. The gesture was comforting. 'Are you okay?' he asked.

'I feel like I should be doing something.' A whistle behind her reminded her of the fireworks. They both turned to see a shower of silver light up the night sky. 'I'll get a taxi to the hospital.' Blythe pulled her phone from her pocket.

'Let me drive you. It'll be quicker to walk back to mine than it will be to call a cab.'

'If you're sure,' she said, but they were already walking. Sam had quite a stride and Blythe had to power-walk to keep up. She snagged a look at him in profile. He glanced in her direction and quickly changed focus to the street ahead. She felt immediately awkward. 'I felt so useless. When Eden collapsed like that, I just didn't know what to do.' She thought back to how Sam checked her pulse and eased her into the recovery position before Leonora took over.

'We can't all be good at everything,' he said. 'Vicky will

appreciate you waiting with her at the hospital. Having a friend there will definitely help her get through this.'

'Thanks.' He had a reassuring way about him.

The village was ghostly quiet. Everyone was at the fireworks. Sam's car was parked on his drive and as they approached they both came to an abrupt halt at the same time as they saw a beam of torchlight lighting up the side of the cottage.

'Burglar,' whispered Sam. 'Call the police.'

Blythe was in two minds. She'd already cried wolf once. She pulled out her phone but decided she'd wait and see. She didn't want to call the police out on a wild goose chase. Sam crept down the side of the cottage and very carefully opened the gate. Blythe followed him at a distance. Her pulse picked up. They inched closer. They heard the obvious sound of someone trying the back door. Blythe tapped Sam on the shoulder and he jumped. He mimed annoyance and surprise at her. 'Sorry,' she mouthed, with a grimace. 'I think it really is a burglar this time. I'll call the police.'

'I thought you were already doing that,' he whispered.

A clatter drew their attention. Sam inched his way towards the back garden. Blythe was experiencing a strange split loyalty. She knew she needed to alert the police but at the same time she wanted to see the burglar. An image of a giant rough-looking brute wielding a crowbar loomed into her mind and she dialled the police with trembling fingers. 'Be careful,' she hissed at Sam's back. Sam said nothing, but as he turned his expression of exasperation was clear.

He waved at her in an agitated fashion, which she took as a warning sign. The torchlight grew bigger and Blythe's heart thumped harder. They both peered around the corner of the cottage. The figure in the shadows crouched down and appeared to be looking underneath plant pots – how strange.

There was no sound as Blythe caught sight of Turpin creeping along the wall. She was relieved to see he was okay. There was a sudden movement and Turpin leapt from the wall, landing squarely on the back of the crouched figure. 'Argh!' came a woman's scream. She tried to stand up so Turpin climbed onto her shoulders and hung on as her arms flailed about.

'Help!' she yelled, her voice full of panic.

'Are you armed?' asked Sam.

The woman looked even more startled as Blythe and Sam approached. 'No, of course not.' She seemed surprised by the question.

'Stand still,' he instructed. Sam stepped forward and cautiously took hold of Turpin and lifted him up. But the cat had his claws firmly embedded in the woman's coat.

'Help,' said Sam, turning in Blythe's direction. She joined Sam and managed to free Turpin's claws with only a few warning hisses from the irritated feline.

'That gave me a start. But don't worry no harm done,' said the woman.

Blythe leaned past Sam to get a look at the intruder but the torchlight was blinding. 'Put the torch down,' called Blythe.

'Whoops, sorry,' said the woman, pointing the torch at her feet.

'What the hell do you think you're doing?' asked Sam.

'Oh, do you live here?' she asked, waving the torch in their eyes but realising and pointing it back at the ground.

'Yes, and right now you're trespassing.'

'It's lovely. Have you lived here long?' she asked, flattening herself against the wall and scooting past them both. 'Oh, hello again. Have the fireworks finished already?' she asked Blythe, and Blythe realised it was the woman in the hat who had spoken to her at the display, engaging with her like an old friend as she inched back down the path before turning and running into the night. 'Hey!' shouted Blythe but the woman had gone.

'Who was she?' asked Sam.

'I've no idea. I only met her about half an hour ago. She was asking if I was local. Maybe she was trying to get information about which houses were empty so she could rob them.'

Sam tried the back door and walked along the back of the cottage checking as he went. 'There's no sign of damage so I don't think she's a very good burglar.' At least that was a relief. But if she wasn't a burglar then who the heck was she?

Owen indicated and turned into the hospital car park. Vicky was expecting to feel a sense of relief but instead she felt a jolt of panic. This was really happening. The sight of the hospital brought the situation into sharp focus. Owen and their complicated past didn't matter. All that mattered was Eden. Owen stopped outside, jumped out and pulled the seat forward to get Eden out. 'Leave her. I'll take it from here,' said Vicky, reaching in to release Eden's seat belt and lift her out – which was a tricky manoeuvre as she was still scrunched up. As Vicky lifted her she vomited. The back of the driver's seat took the brunt of it. 'Sorry,' said Vicky, reversing out with Eden in her arms. 'And thanks for the lift.'

She rushed inside as fast as she dared and was relieved to see there was no queue at the desk, although a quick glance around told her they were in for a long wait. There were so many people waiting that every seat was taken and people were standing up.

'My daughter's sick and in pain. Please help me,' said Vicky, embarrassed at the sound of her voice cracking.

'It's okay, we'll get someone to triage her as soon as you give me some information. Name?' asked the receptionist.

Vicky gave Eden's details and the woman asked her to take a seat. Vicky stepped away from the desk and was frantically searching for somewhere to put Eden down when a door opened and they called Eden's name. For a moment Vicky felt relieved that they wouldn't have to wait but that was short-lived as she feared they would only call her in so quickly if this was urgent.

The triage nurse was lovely and he had a calming influence on Vicky as he took them straight through the back of the small room and asked Vicky to lay Eden on a bed that dwarfed her. He asked questions while checking Eden over. He even managed to make Eden smile despite her clutching a cardboard sick bowl. He pulled a large green curtain around the bed and popped out but soon returned with a woman about Vicky's age.

'Hi. I'm Doctor Karavadra. I'm going to take a look at Eden.'

'What's wrong?' asked Vicky as the doctor checked Eden over and noted when she winced.

'It could be a number of things. Let's get her up on the ward and run some tests.' She squeezed Eden's hand. 'We're all going for a ride in the big lift. I only get to go in that one with special patients.'

The nurse put a label on Eden's wrist and checked back her details again. It reminded Vicky of the label they'd put on her as a newborn. She remembered thinking how big the wristband had been and how tiny and delicate her daughter was. She still had that label, safely tucked in an envelope alongside a number of treasured items in a keepsake box. It had seemed special at the time; the first time Vicky had seen her daughter's name written down had been on that label. This label didn't seem special. It was a sign that they were expecting her to be in hospital a while. It was a worry.

The curtain swished opened and in walked Owen. 'Here you are. I've cleaned up the sick as best I could with a chamois leather and I've parked in zone B.'

She was so taken aback to see him that it took a moment to respond. 'Why are—'

'Right,' said the nurse appearing through the curtain. 'I've brought my mate Alan to move you up to the ward. He's the best driver of beds I know.' A large man appeared, pushed a pedal under the bed and it was suddenly on the move, making Vicky jump to her feet.

'I used to be a racing driver,' said Alan to Eden. 'We'll have you on the ward in no time.'

Vicky walked alongside the bed clutching Eden's hand as they strolled down a long white corridor with grey linoleum flooring and a mix of people darting around them. She was scared. She couldn't remember the last time she'd been this out of her depth. Eden groaned and threw up in the cardboard bowl. The nurse whipped it away and replaced it with another one. Eden looked so pale and small in the bed. They reached the lift and Vicky let go of Eden's hand for a moment to adjust her handbag, which was when she realised how much her hands were shaking.

Alan pressed the button to summon the lift. 'Only the most important patients go in the big one,' said Alan. As the lift pinged its arrival Doctor Karavadra joined them. The doors opened to reveal a steel interior; once the hospital bed was inside everyone else had to squish around the sides. Vicky turned around and was surprised to see Owen.

'What are you doing?' she asked, very aware that there were a lot of people in the small space, all listening.

'I thought you'd like some support.'

'That's kind, Owen, but I don't think we can have lots of people...'

'It's okay,' said the nurse. 'It's two per patient but that's really only at the bedside. There's a waiting area with a drinks machine and one that dispenses sandwiches but I had a cheese one out of it last week and swear there wasn't enough cheese in it to keep a mouse going to the end of my shift.' He grinned. Vicky frowned at Owen.

'Great. Thanks, mate,' said Owen. 'I'll keep you company, Vic.' He smiled. Vicky clenched her teeth. As if this wasn't bad enough, she now had to suffer Owen and be nice to him because he was being kind – it was a nightmare.

The lift doors finally opened and Alan pushed the bed out and everyone else followed. They were buzzed onto a ward and ushered into a small bay of three beds and three empty spaces. The doctor stopped at the nurses' station. Alan manoeuvred the bed into place and kicked the lever under the bed again – presumably the brake. 'This is where I leave you. No charge – just make sure you recommend me to your friends,' he said to Eden. As he passed Vicky he leaned into her shoulder: 'Best team in the hospital. She'll be fine, Mum.' Unexpected emotion swept over Vicky and she had to swallow hard.

The doctor returned with another nurse and they said goodbye to the one they'd met in A and E. The new nurse explained what she was doing as she swabbed the back of Eden's hand and put a canula in as she said they were going to give her something for the pain. She took some blood from Eden's other arm and Vicky thought she was going to pass out. Eden was becoming less and less responsive and Vicky's fear was rapidly increasing. Owen stayed on the periphery, which she was grateful for because she couldn't deal with him, along with everything else.

After a brief detour for a scan of Eden's middle they were back on the ward with Doctor Karavadra who pulled the curtain around Eden's bed and beckoned Vicky and Owen to one side. She clearly thought they were together but Vicky didn't want to delay any news on her daughter's condition by explaining her convoluted relationship with Owen.

'We're fairly certain it's her appendix,' said the doctor.

Vicky stifled a gasp. 'Does that mean surgery?'

'It does. We want to get her into theatre as quickly as possible. I'm just waiting on a colleague who is in theatre with an emergency at the moment and then we'll prep Eden.'

'Fairly certain?' said Owen, leaning forward. 'Should you not be dead certain if you're about to slice open a child?'

Vicky's hand flew up in the air. 'For heaven's sake, Owen! Not helping.'

He pulled his head in. 'I just thought that—'

Doctor Karavadra stepped in. 'All the signs are that it's appendicitis, but you can't be absolutely certain until you operate unless you do a lot more tests and given the stage I believe she's at, delaying for further tests is not what I would recommend. If the appendix ruptures that's life-threatening, so it's something we want to avoid. We're hoping to do keyhole surgery and go in through her belly button so she'll only have two small scars, but again we won't know until we operate if we can complete it safely by keyhole or if we need a bigger incision to remove the appendix without it bursting.'

Vicky felt her knees buckle. 'Can I come in with her?'

'Not for the surgery, I'm afraid. But you can come down to theatre and be with her while she's anaesthetised.' Doctor Karavadra smiled. Vicky wondered if they had any spare paper bowls because she had a feeling she was about to vomit.

22

Blythe and Sam's drive to the hospital was filled with chatter about who the trespasser might be and what she was doing snooping around Sam's cottage. Once they had exhausted a few theories Blythe's thoughts returned to poor Eden. She'd had no updates from Vicky, which was both understandable and worrying. Blythe tried to think positively. She needed to be upbeat for Vicky – anything less wasn't going to be very helpful. She took a deep breath. Sam's car had a new-car smell to it. Mixed with a hint of Sam's aftershave, it was quite appealing. She glanced over at him at the same time as he smiled in her direction. Blythe returned her attention to directing Sam to the hospital.

He pulled into a parking bay. 'Should I wait here? I don't want to intrude.' That was really thoughtful of him.

'You don't have to wait; it was kind of you to give me a lift.'

'I'm not going to dump you here and clear off. I'll hang around.'

Blythe felt bad but secretly pleased – Sam was turning out to be one of the good guys. 'How about you come in?

I'll buy you a cup of sludge masquerading as coffee and we can find out if I'm likely to be here all night or if Vicky and Eden are going to need a lift home.'

'Sounds like a plan,' he said, getting out of the car. 'This Owen, what's the deal there?'

'Ahh, now that is a long story,' began Blythe, and she gave him the potted history of Owen and Vicky's romance and its subsequent implosion; Blythe couldn't remember exactly what it had been about but there were accusations from each of them that the other had been cheating. They were still chatting as they entered the hospital. The accident and emergency department was heaving and a scent of disinfectant and boredom pervaded the air.

They were sent round the houses from accident and emergency to children's emergency and finally onto the children's surgical ward where they found Owen reading a women's magazine and sipping a coffee while Vicky stared through the glass of some nearby double doors. Blythe rushed in and Sam stood back.

'How is she?' asked Blythe, automatically wrapping Vicky in a hug.

'She's being operated on,' said Vicky, her eyes red and puffy and her features etched with worry.

Blythe's surprise must have shown on her face. She'd hoped they'd give Eden some medicine and send her home. Didn't kids get tummy ache all the time? 'Is she all right?' asked Blythe. Vicky gave her a look. 'Sorry. Obviously she's not all right but she's absolutely in the best place.'

'They think it's appendicitis.' Vicky bit her lip as tears welled in her eyes. 'I went down to theatre with her and they gave her this anaesthetic. One minute she was awake and the next she was out but her eyes were still open. It was horrible.' Vicky's lip wobbled.

Blythe gripped her friend's hand. 'You poor thing. It's good that they know what it is and it's easily fixed.' Blythe was scratching around for positive things to say.

'They didn't seem that certain to me,' piped up Owen, putting down his well-thumbed magazine.

'But the doctor explained about that,' said Vicky, and Blythe could hear the strain in her voice.

'My grandad came in here to have a bunion removed. He left with deep vein thrombosis and no dentures,' said Owen, nodding earnestly.

'I swear I'll brain him in a minute,' whispered Vicky.

'Hey, Owen,' said Sam. 'How about we see if there's a café open and I'll get you a decent coffee.'

'I should probably stay to support Vicky.'

'No, you're good. I've got Blythe now. In fact you could go home. Like all the way home to Oxford.' Vicky was virtually shooing him out of the chair.

'How'd you know that's where I'm living now? Have you been secretly stalking me on social media?' He gave a cheeky grin. 'Because it's cool if you—'

'Come on,' said Sam, seeming to sense the irritation practically radiating from Vicky. 'Before the café closes.'

'Oh, okay mate. If Vicky's sure.' He waited for her response.

'One hundred per cent,' she said.

'Cool.' Owen got to his feet and headed for the exit.

'What would you both like to drink?' asked Sam.

'Two teas, please,' said Blythe. 'Thank you,' she added, and surreptitiously pointed at Owen's retreating back.

'You're welcome,' mouthed Sam.

When the doors closed behind the men, Vicky's shoulders dropped. 'Bloody hell. He's a nightmare. He keeps coming out with all this really unhelpful stuff that's making my brain fizz. I'm so worried about Eden and all he can do is spout rubbish.' Vicky put her hands on her head as if expecting it to explode.

'He did give you a lift here. That was good of him,' said Blythe.

'It was but he won't leave and I've got enough to think about. They said she could be in there hours if it's tricky or if it bursts.' Vicky seemed on the verge of tears. 'What if she dies, Blythe?' Her face searched Blythe's for some hope.

Blythe was scared on Vicky's behalf but tried her best not to show it. 'That's not going to happen. She's getting the best care and she's got the best mum in the world.'

Vicky snorted. 'I'm a mess. I'm no help to Eden.'

Blythe took Vicky's hand. 'You're a brilliant mum. These are difficult circumstances but you got her here as quickly as possible and she's being treated already. That's got to be good. You need to hang on to the positives and try to stay calm.'

Vicky pulled in a deep breath. 'You're right. I know that but it's easier said than done. I need something to stop me thinking about someone cutting her open.'

'Here's something to think about. You remember the woman in the dark puffer jacket and a black bobble hat at the fireworks?'

Vicky looked beyond puzzled. 'Err I don't know... hang on. Yeah, she spoke to you and then she was talking to

Leonora. Actually, she looked like she was trying to escape from Leonora. Why? Who is she?'

'That's the million-dollar question.'

Blythe managed to keep Vicky's mind off things for a while by retelling the drama that had unfolded at Sam's cottage, although she could tell her friend was only half listening as her eyes kept checking the doors. Blythe thought the world of Eden and she was worried sick. She couldn't imagine what Vicky was going through as her mum. When the doors *did* open Vicky jumped to her feet only to be greeted by Owen and Sam returning with drinks.

'Teas,' said Sam, handing them over. 'Any news?' he asked.

'Thanks,' said Blythe. 'No update as yet.'

'That's good though,' said Owen, nodding encouragingly at Vicky, and Blythe was pleased that he was being positive. 'Because if anything bad had happened they'd have been out to tell you,' he added, unhelpfully.

'Bloody hell, Owen,' snapped Vicky. 'As if I'm not stressed enough, you rock up and you're about as useful as a tambourine to a fish. I don't need it,' she said, as she started to pace.

'Calm down,' said Owen. 'I said it was good news that nobody had been to update you. That's positive.' He looked to Blythe and Sam to back him up.

'It's not really helping,' said Blythe, and Sam shook his head. 'I know you mean well, Owen, but maybe we should all keep our thoughts to ourselves,' suggested Blythe.

They all sat in silence for a while, sipping their drinks, the sounds of hospital life taking over – the buzzes and beeps of machines, the swish of curtains and the muffled thud of swing doors.

Owen was scrolling through his phone. He made a sucking sound with his teeth. The others glanced in his direction. When he started tutting, Vicky snapped, 'What? What is it now?'

'It says here that the death rate for append—'

'You should go,' said Vicky, standing up quickly. 'All of you are free to leave. I'll be here all night anyway. You've been great. Thank you.' She splayed out her hands and for a moment Blythe thought she was going to take a bow.

'Oh, right,' said Owen, putting his phone away.

'I don't like to leave you,' said Blythe. Nobody wanted to face something like this on their own. She knew it was really only Owen that Vicky wanted to be rid of. 'I'll stay,' said Blythe, and she remained seated.

'But you've got a big day tomorrow,' said Vicky.

Blythe saw the interest from both Owen and Sam. 'It's nothing exciting.'

Vicky's eyes widened. 'Don't let Leonora hear you talking like that. It's T-Day tomorrow. The big kick-off. It's the start of Christmas in Holly Cross.' She seemed to be directing her information towards Sam whose frown deepened with every word. Blythe tried to alert her with a variety of twitches but Vicky was on a roll. 'There's a committee meeting bright and early when all planned decorations are confirmed and then everyone goes off to start putting them up. Leonora marches around the village shouting encouragement and co-ordinates whatever display is going on the green. Before you know it the whole of Holly Cross starts to look like a winter wonderland. The lot in the new houses have a bit of a race to see who can get... What?' Vicky seemed to have finally clocked Blythe's signalling.

'Maybe Sam and Owen should go. I'll stay,' said Blythe.

Blythe watched as Sam swallowed hard. He didn't say anything but he looked decidedly paler than he had before.

Vicky was chasing Owen with a giant chicken leg when her head felt like it was falling off and she jolted herself awake. She immediately panicked that she'd missed something. Her eyes darted around the small waiting room. Blythe was scrolling through Instagram pictures of what looked like Christmas lights. Sam and Owen had gone. Thank goodness Owen had left. Her feelings for him were very confused. She'd always assumed if she saw him again she'd want to lamp him – that all the anger she'd felt when they'd split up would still be there but it wasn't. He did aggravate her – that was definitely true – but that connection they'd had was still there and it had pulled at her like they'd been attached by bungee cords. He'd been just the same Owen she remembered before all the animosity and upset. The geeky, chatty boy she'd fallen for. Unfortunately he was also still the inept, tactless person who irritated the life out of her.

'It's okay,' said Blythe, who was sitting next to her on another of the hard plastic chairs. 'You had about ten minutes' nap that's all. Nobody has been around. I've been looking up sexy Santa outfits and now my pop-up ads are grim.' She showed Vicky a picture of a male model wearing elephant-trunk underwear. They both flinched.

'I can't ever unsee that.'

'Sorry,' said Blythe scrolling on.

Vicky sighed deeply. This was the most stressful thing she'd ever experienced. Even worse than the time she tried to get One Direction tickets in the three-second window that they were available. She checked her watch. Waiting was torture. However much she tried to stay positive her brain only seemed to want to remind her of all the terrible things that could go wrong. She'd had to sign a disclaimer for Eden to have a general anaesthetic and that was worrying her too. But what choice had she had? Don't sign and she can't have the operation and then she'd likely die. Do sign and they cut her open and she could still die.

'You okay?' asked Blythe, gently. 'Do you want something to eat or drink?'

'No. I'm fine.'

'You don't look fine. You don't have to be brave all the time, you know. This must be really tough for you. Is there anything I can do?' Vicky shook her head. 'Sit down. Read a magazine from ten years ago. They're quite nostalgic.' Blythe gestured to the chair next to hers.

'Thanks for staying, Blythe. You know you didn't need to.'

'Yeah, I did. It's what we do. We're here for each other. Whatever life throws at us, we have each other's backs. Unless Harry Styles turns up then all bets are off,' she said with a smile.

'Actually, there is one thing you can do for me?'

'Name it.'

Vicky scrunched up her shoulders. 'I've got lots of dogs booked in for tomorrow and...'

'No problem. Message me the details and I'll sort it all out.'

Vicky squeezed Blythe's arm. 'Thanks. And not just for dog walking but everything.'

Blythe smiled.

Vicky was about to choose a curly-cornered copy of *Hello!* when the double doors swished open and the ward nurse appeared with a beaming smile. That had to be good news, right? Or was she trying to prepare her for bad news? Vicky was on the cusp of shouting at the nurse to update her when she spoke. 'Eden's fine. The operation went to plan and she's in recovery. You'll be able to see her in about twenty minutes.'

Vicky burst into tears. She didn't know where they came from. She wasn't a crier but she couldn't hold the emotion in. She felt as if she'd won the lottery. Blythe hugged her and she could see she had tears in her eyes too.

'Thank you,' said Vicky to the nurse, who was already turning to leave.

'You're welcome. Help yourself to tissues.' She pointed at a box on the table. In that moment everything slotted into place. If Eden was well then everything in Vicky's life was fine. There was nothing she couldn't cope with or whip into shape as long as Eden was fit and healthy. She also realised how lucky she was to have a friend like Blythe – someone who was there for her no matter what. She felt like the luckiest person alive. Perspective was a very strange thing.

23

7th November

When Blythe's alarm went off on Sunday morning she'd had about five hours sleep, making it hard to open her eyes. She'd finally got a taxi once Eden was back on the ward and settled. It had been an emotional night but thankfully Eden was all fixed. With blurry eyes she fired off a text to Vicky and went to see if a shower would perk her up.

The eight o'clock meeting was usually an exciting affair as long as the weather was behaving itself, and today the forecast was overcast but dry. This was the point where the focus of the whole village turned to Christmas. Blythe and Greg walked through the village breathing in the crisp November air. The sky was a clear blue and the grass sparkled with frost. Greg was debating the pros and cons of battery lights versus mains but Blythe was only half listening. She'd not been happy about moving back in with Greg and her mum. She'd always felt like a gooseberry as a child – the third wheel, a spare part – but somehow it wasn't quite so bad now she was an adult. And she did love being back in Holly Cross. She reminded herself that it was only temporary. Soon she would need to get back on the property ladder. But this time she would be doing it on her own.

When Blythe and Greg entered the village hall it was already a hive of activity. Leonora was flicking back and forth through a variety of colourfully detailed flip charts, Norman was handing out cream horns decorated to look like Santa hats, and Phyllis appeared to be trying to tie a large ball of Christmas lights into a bow.

'You okay there, Phyllis?' asked Blythe, taking her coat off and unfurling her scarf.

'Yes, dear. I'm sorting these out for Leonora,' she said happily.

Blythe feared Leonora had given Phyllis the task to keep her busy and out of her hair.

'Ah, Blythe. Just the person.' Leonora marched over. 'Sam Ashton – what's the plan?'

Blythe took a deep breath. She'd mulled over all the options and come up with what she hoped was a good solution. 'I'm going to offer to decorate his cottage for him. I'm going with the snowman theme Murray had two years ago. I'm keeping it simple and front garden only.' That way she'd mused it wouldn't look too over the top – well that was how she was going to sell it to Sam. She was also going to take him some wine as a sweetener. 'And I'm adding the Christmas parcels Murray had on the roof last year to dot between the snowmen.' She waited for Leonora's reaction.

'I'd have liked something a little more impressive but at this late stage I suppose we are where we are. I'll add it to my flip chart.' She gave Blythe a curt nod, which she took as a good thing.

There followed a high-speed run-through of themed zones around the village and Leonora's plans for some signage. A number of dads had been tasked with erecting an elf house on the green and, once Phyllis had untied the lights, a winding path lit by a multitude of fairy lights would lead to it, with a variety of animated scenes for children to look at on the way. It sounded impressive and Blythe had to give credit where it was due: Leonora had got the whole village engaged. Her Christmas committee was a well-oiled machine of happy helpers.

'Other fast-approaching key events are the Christmas tree auction.' Leonora pointed at Christmas Carol who jumped like she'd been tasered.

'All on track,' said Carol. 'Trees ordered and paid for and are being felled as we speak. Will be delivered on the day. Greg has confirmed he'll be the auctioneer.' He gave her a double thumbs up. 'And as long as the PA system works tonight we're good to go.'

'Excellent,' said Leonora. Carol looked relieved. 'Christmas fayre is a sub-committee that I'm happy to report is all on track. Due to demand there will be more stalls than ever. Next…' She checked her flip chart. 'Sexy Santa dinner.' Leonora pointed at Blythe and she experienced the same fright as Carol – it wasn't fun being in Leonora's firing line.

'All on track. I've signed up the rugby club guys who were only too happy to be our sexy Santa waiters for the night in exchange for a barrel of beer for their Christmas party, which I'm getting at a reduction from Sarvan. Caterers are confirmed and menus have been approved by you.'

'Is it coq au vin?' quipped Carol, and everyone laughed, apart from Leonora and Blythe.

'Turkey dinner or vegan lentil bake.' Blythe ignored the continued tittering and returned to her list. 'Temporary event licence has been granted so there will be alcohol. We're using this hall, and Vicky and I will dress the tables. Tickets all sold out within a week.'

'I can't wait,' said Phyllis, clapping her hands together.

'I think most of the WI are coming,' said Blythe. There had been a stampede for tickets, with the WI leading the way and the rest of the local women close behind.

'Good work.' Leonora clicked her fingers. 'Let's stay focused on today. Now get going; there's a lot to be done. Chop, chop,' she said with a clap of her hands, and everyone scrambled to their feet and hastily put their coats back on.

Blythe was thinking over what she was going to say to Sam but as she approached the cottage it appeared she needn't have worried. There was Sam already up a ladder screwing something above the front door. Blythe could have hugged him if only he'd been at ground level.

'Good morning,' she called up, brightly.

'Hiya. How's Eden?'

'She's fine. Appendix removed by keyhole surgery. Vicky said she was sat up having toast and marmalade this morning for breakfast. She might even be home later today.'

'That's brilliant news.' Sam looked genuinely relieved.

'What's going to be hung up there?' she asked.

'It's a security camera,' said Sam, coming back down the ladder.

'Oh, right.' Her hope had been misplaced.

'State of the art. I bought it just before I moved because I knew this place didn't have one and then what with moving in and everything and the village lulling me into a false sense of security I didn't bother to put it up. Last night has taught me a lesson.' He admired the tiny camera proudly. 'Any movement and it automatically pings a message to my phone and streams the footage, as well as recording it so it can be used as evidence. How cool is that?'

'Yep. That's cool all right. As we're talking about putting things up I wanted to have a little chat to you about Christmas and decorations. Nothing scary so don't freak out. And I would do all the work and you could take the glory as the man who saved Holly Cross's Christmas. I'm thinking just a little sprinkle of festive. I mean, what could be more fun?'

'Root canal?'

'Ha, ha.' His expression had immediately changed so she hurried on. 'Please hear me out. There's no expense because Murray's lights are in the shed. I'll do all the work of decorating. I'll keep it as low-key as I can. Front garden only apart from lights along the guttering and around the windows. You don't need to do a thing. What do you say?'

'Absolutely not.'

Blythe blinked a few times. Maybe he didn't understand exactly how much work that was. 'But I'll be doing all the work. You don't need to lift a finger.'

'No way. I told you. I don't do Christmas. And that means my house doesn't do Christmas either. I don't want to be reminded of it every time I leave my home.'

'To be fair almost every house in the village and definitely all the houses around the green…' she indicated with a sweep of her arm '…will be screaming Christmas so I don't think a couple of snowmen on your own lawn is going to be an issue.'

Sam's nostrils flared. 'It's an issue for me. I appreciate the offer but no thank you.'

'But the whole village is coming together to make this year extra special. You don't want to be the one person who spoils it. I'll make sure—'

'No,' he said, firmly making Blythe blink again. This guy was the epitome of stubborn.

'Have you heard of aversion therapy?'

'Don't even go there,' said Sam, raising his palm. 'I mean it, Blythe. I don't want to fall out with you over this.'

'Okay.' It wasn't okay but she could see that pushing him on it wasn't the answer. She didn't have a clue what the answer was, which was a worry. She was firmly between a rock and a hard place and they were closing in like a scene from an Indiana Jones movie. It was either scary Leonora or unwavering Sam – she was going to disappoint someone.

'I did want to speak to you about Turpin though,' said Sam, changing the subject. 'I'm off to London in a couple of hours and I'm not back until Tuesday night. I don't want to banish him to the utility again so when you come to feed him, can you just check that he's not trashed the place?'

'Of course. I'd be happy to. You make him sound like a rock star.'

'He does give off those sort of vibes.' Sam ran his lip through his teeth. 'Look, I am sorry about the whole anti-Christmas thing. I know you don't get it and I know you think I'm being a pain about it. Can you just accept it?'

'Or how about you think about it and, who knows, living here as Christmas unfurls around you, it might make you change your mind.' He'd given her an idea.

He laughed. 'I love your optimism.'

'Ah, see, that wasn't a no,' she said, with a wag of her finger.

'Come in for a second and I'll show you how the alarm works.'

She followed him inside. 'But won't Turpin set it off?'

'Nope, it has a pet-friendly mode so only big things will trigger it – like you.'

'Rude,' said Blythe.

'Sorry, I wasn't meaning anything about your weight…' She raised her eyebrows. 'You're not overweight at all or a big thing…'

'Stop digging the hole and throw away the spade,' said Blythe. 'I'm joking with you.'

'Phew. You had me worried there. Right, this is the control panel.' Sam took her through the basics and let her have a go at setting and cancelling it herself.

'Do you think that woman has plans to come back then? I thought she was just a snooper.'

'I'm not taking any risks. Although I do wonder if she had heard that Murray had died and thought the property might be empty.'

'Ooh, now there's a theory. Murray, if you're listening we're taking good care of your place,' she said, with a giggle.

Sam looked alarmed. 'You don't think he's…' He looked up to the ceiling in an exaggerated eye movement.

'What? Haunting the cottage?'

'Do you?' Sam gave a little shudder and it made Blythe smile.

'I know someone with a Ouija board if you want to find out, or we could just see if we can contact him now.' Sam's eyes widened but Blythe was on a roll. 'Murray, if you're there send us a sign...'

They both listened carefully. At first there was silence. Then a strange whirring noise made them both jump.

'What was that?' whispered Sam.

'Why are you whispering?' asked Blythe, amused by his reaction and trying to hide that she was a little freaked out by the strange sound.

'I don't know,' whispered Sam.

The whirring went again. It had a sort of rhythmic rumble to it and this time it carried on. 'Murray?' Blythe's pulse was speeding up.

'It's coming from the back of the house,' said Sam.

They inched their way through the kitchen and Sam opened the utility door. He was right; the noise was definitely coming from the utility because there was Turpin using the old tumble dryer like a hamster wheel. 'What on earth are you up to, Turpin?' asked Blythe, relieved to find the answer.

Turpin glanced at her and carried on like a health-conscious jogger on a treadmill at the gym. 'I knew there would be a logical explanation,' said Sam, moving his neck as if trying to release tension.

'Did you? You sure about that? You didn't think it was Murray's ghost come back to haunt you because you won't decorate his cottage?'

Sam gave a tinny laugh. 'Nooo.' He opened a cupboard

and got out some treats, which immediately had Turpin mewing and snaking around his legs. 'We need to make sure this is properly closed; otherwise you could have been trapped in there,' said Sam, giving Turpin's head a rub before shutting the dryer door. It seemed that they were getting closer. Maybe Sam was slowly coming around to things.

24

7th November

Blythe spent the morning helping her mum and stepdad decorate their house. It was a joint effort with the attached semi so that the lights ran all the way along both properties. They had coloured lights in the conifer to make it look like a Christmas tree and white lights in the bushes on a low-speed flash setting. Nothing too gaudy as their house was more of a drive-by property, but when added to all the other homes on the street it gave a magical effect.

Blythe was hurriedly shifting boxes of decorations out of the way when one particular object caught her eye and pulled her up short. It was wrapped in tissue paper with just a tiny part showing, but even from just that she knew exactly what it was. She put the box down, picked up the tissue-covered ornament and gently released it from the paper. It was a robin. Pretty, delicate and perfect. She remembered every Christmas her father had insisted that it be placed up near the star so the robin looked like he'd just landed on their tree and was looking down on the celebrations. She smiled at the memory. But then, like so many things with her father, she remembered the harsh criticism in his words when she didn't get it right. However hard she tried she always seemed to disappoint him.

But not anymore. She straightened her spine. She would prove to Ludo that she was a worthy successor capable of managing his business when he was ready to step down. That would show her father exactly what she was made of. She had a point to prove and nothing would deter her from that course.

They wouldn't be putting up their indoor Christmas tree just yet, so she set the box aside and carefully replaced the little robin ornament. Things weren't exactly going to plan at work and she knew her dad would be in touch soon for their annual present exchange – it was also her one opportunity a year to see him face to face.

'You okay?' asked Greg, waving a hand playfully in front of her eyes.

'I zoned out.'

'Now don't be worrying about how you're going to afford to buy me an Aston Martin for Christmas because I'm sure you can pay by instalments,' he said with a wink.

'Yeah, a hundred pounds a month until I'm a hundred and fifty.'

'There you go. Don't worry about wrapping it either,' he said, giving her a one-armed hug. 'Come on, what's really up?'

What a question. Ludo and his disappointed expression flashed into her mind, closely followed by a stubborn-looking Sam Ashton. Leonora slapping a palm on her flip chart was right behind him and her dad pulling his 'I never expected you to amount to much' face. 'Just stuff.'

'Work stuff or boy stuff?'

His turn of phrase made her smile. 'A few different things. Work and some added Christmas stuff thrown in.'

'That's not good. Do you want to talk about it?' She shook her head. 'Want me to threaten to thump someone?' She smiled. Greg was so placid there was no way he'd ever hit anyone. 'Unless it's Leonora because that wouldn't be a fair fight. She'd deck me with her little finger.'

'No, you're okay. They're things I need to sort out myself.'

'How about a mince pie, not homemade so they're safe, and one of my special hot chocolates?' He looked keen and she wasn't sure if that was because she'd provide the ideal excuse for him to join her or he was just being especially kind.

'Go on then. Why not add diabetes to my list of problems.'

'There, that's the Christmas spirit.' And he gave her shoulder a comforting squeeze.

After finishing off the decorations with Greg, while her mum fed them her version of a roast dinner in a wrap – so it was transportable – she set off across the village to Sam's. The houses down to the crossroads were already getting their Christmas makeover – neighbours wrapped in scarves and hats, teetering on ladders, waved to her as she passed. Number seventy-two was pumping up his inflatable Father Christmas that would have at least four punctures before they got to Christmas Eve. The two elderly sisters at Rock Cottage had been knitting all year and they were yarn bombing their own hedge with festive creations. This really was a very special place to live and it made something tingle in Blythe's gut.

Putting up strings and strings of lights had been quite therapeutic and had given her time to think. If she didn't put some decorations up on Sam's cottage then it would completely spoil the look the village was working so hard to achieve but if she did put some up then Sam would be seriously unhappy. When she weighed the two things up it was an easy decision. She was far more scared of Leonora than she was of Sam. Also, the village winning the competition and making lots of money for charity was more important than Sam and his, quite frankly, ridiculous Christmas phobia. And if he genuinely hated it then she'd just have to take it all down.

Blythe went round the back and let herself in the utility room. 'Hi, Sam, are you home?' The house alarm began beeping. 'Bugger it.' She strode through the cottage and punched in the code. At least with Sam gone she had a chance to put some lights up. Perhaps if he just saw how pretty it was, how it fitted in with the rest of the village, and if someone was doing all the hard work for him as a surprise, who could be cross about that?

Blythe took the shed keys off the hook in the utility and went down the garden to check Murray's decorations. She opened up the door and stared at the contents. The last time she'd looked in through the window it had been crammed to the roof with snowmen, reindeer and some questionable penguins, which were an eBay purchase Murray had heartily regretted. Now all that was there were the extension cables and a rusty Christmas tree stand.

'You absolute swine, Sam Ashton.' Blythe was fuming. Not only because she had been outwitted but also because those decorations were part of the village display. If he didn't want them then fair enough, but getting rid of them on the quiet was unacceptable. She rang his number.

'Hallo,' said Sam, in a cheery voice.

'Where the bloody hell are Murray's decorations?'

'Hi, Blythe, I'm fine thanks – on a train to London. How about you?'

'Bloody furious because someone has stolen Murray's decorations. No, the village's decorations.'

'Hmm,' said Sam. 'Now why would you be looking in my shed, I wonder?'

He was making her blood reach jam-making temperature. 'Because the village needs those lights for the display. You had no right—'

'Now I can check with my estate agent but I think you'll find when I bought the cottage I paid for cottage and contents. Therefore, everything including all the tat in the shed was mine.'

'Tat!' She was appalled on Murray's behalf. 'I'll have you know that those were all professional display items… with the exception of the penguins.'

'Oh, is that what they were. I thought they were midget nuns. Really creepy-looking things. Their eyes were—'

'Don't dodge the issue. You knew the decorations were part of the village display.'

'And I also knew that you would probably use them to make my home look like Santa's brothel, so they went to my warehouse and will probably be in a Hallmark movie next Christmas.'

'You are unbelievable, Sam Ashton. What are you going to do to put this right?'

'Nothing.'

'Oh my word. You are the bloody Grinch. You can't—'

'Look out – tunnel.' And the line went dead.

'Arghhhhh!' shouted Blythe in frustration, and she slammed the shed door shut.

The next day Eden was discharged and sent home with some painkillers and although she was shuffling around like an old lady she was in good spirits. Vicky was so pleased to have her baby safely back in her own home. Whilst Eden seemed to be over the worst of it, Vicky was still feeling shell-shocked by the whole episode. It really made her feel for little Kal and his family who were regulars at the hospital because of his kidney condition. Other than the usual childhood illnesses Eden had been fit and healthy, so this had rocked Vicky more than she liked to admit.

It had been just her and Eden for so long she'd not considered how it felt when there was nobody on hand to share things like this with. She'd never worried about going to nativity plays alone or any of the good stuff, but realising that there was no one to share the tough times with was a bit of a jolt. Of course Blythe had been brilliant and that had meant a lot, but whilst she knew Blythe cared for Eden she couldn't fully understand exactly how Vicky felt.

For the first time in a while she wondered if she should do more to establish Eden's parentage. Should she get her DNA tested? But what would that tell her? Without DNA from a potential father she was none the wiser. A picture of Owen lolloped into her mind. She'd not had time to stress over why he'd turned up out of the blue to the fireworks display but on some level she was grateful that he'd been there. Aside from the unhelpful comments there had been a feeling. She couldn't quite put her finger on what that feeling was. What if he was Eden's father – did that make a difference?

She watched Eden snuggled under a blanket on the sofa, giggling at a cartoon on the telly. She was happy. Did she need anyone else in her life? Vicky had shied away from relationships because of Eden. Partly because when she had been brave enough to venture out and check out the dating scene, as soon as she mentioned she was a single mum the blokes disappeared quicker than a genie back into a lamp. And she'd also realised that dating was no longer just about her; anyone new she brought into her life she also introduced into Eden's, and that was when it really became complicated. No, she was better to leave things as they were.

The doorbell chimed and she went to answer it. 'Hello,' whispered Norman. 'We heard you were home. How's the patient?'

'She's fine. Doing really well thanks. Come in.'

'We don't want to disturb her,' said Phyllis, popping up from behind Norman. 'We just wanted to let you know we're thinking of you. And we've walked all the dogs on the list you gave Blythe.'

'And to give you these,' said Norman, handing over a cake box.

'Ooh, thanks,' said Vicky, touched by the gesture.

'Has Leonora been in touch?' asked Phyllis.

'No, why?' asked Vicky, having a sneak peek inside the cake box – doughnuts, yum.

'She's trying to track Blythe down. She and Sam have gone AWOL,' said Norman.

'Together,' added Phyllis with a *Carry-On*-worthy head tilt.

'We don't know that, Phyllis,' said Norman. 'But it does seem a bit of a coincidence. Especially as his cottage doesn't have any lights up.'

'Not one light,' added Phyllis.

'I've had a few text messages from Blythe but nothing else. If she'd eloped, I think she'd have mentioned it,' said Vicky.

'Shame,' said Phyllis, looking genuinely disappointed.

'Anyway. If there's anything we can do, you only have to say the word,' said Norman.

'Is that word doughnut?' asked Vicky with a grin.

Vicky had barely waved Norman and Phyllis off when her doorbell rang again. She left her cup of tea and her untouched doughnut and went to answer it. Leonora was standing on her doorstep wearing so many layers she looked like the sale table in Primark. 'Ahh, Vicky, you *are* in. How's the little one?'

'She's doing really well. Thanks for what you did at the fireworks. It all happened so fast.' Vicky replayed the events, and the panic she'd felt at the time came back.

Leonora waved her words away. 'That's what I'm trained to do. I still get quite a kick from making a correct diagnosis. I had a bet with myself that it was appendicitis. Anyway, the reason I'm here is it's T plus one and you don't have any decorations up.'

Bloody hell, thought Vicky, the friendly neighbour routine didn't last long. 'Given my daughter was in hospital until six hours ago I figured—'

Leonora held up a palm to stop Vicky's explanation.

'Completely understand, which is why I am offering to put your lights up for you. Well, not me but some volunteers who I will supervise.' Leonora fixed Vicky with a look.

'Wow. Yes, please – that would be terrific.' You could say what you liked about Leonora but underneath her power-crazed exterior was a kind woman full of the spirit of Christmas. Vicky felt a warm festive glow envelop her.

'Then I need all your decorations available by nineteen hundred hours today.'

'No problem.' Vicky knew exactly where all her decs were.

'Now, the more pressing matter is where is Blythe and what on earth is happening with Murray's cottage?' Leonora fixed her with a look that made Vicky feel instantly less Christmassy.

25

8th November

Blythe was screening her calls and so far she had managed to avoid Leonora but she knew she was on borrowed time because the woman seemed to keep popping up on her parents' doorstep like whack-a-mole. Blythe had a new plan but she couldn't sort anything out until after work. Usually things were quieter with house sales on the run-up to the end of the year, as people focused on Christmas, so it was a good time to get things up straight ahead of the new year when everything often went a bit crazy. Sadly, the festive season was frequently the trigger that blew relationships apart and with the new year came a new start, which meant an abundance of people wanting to move.

Amir was in and out of Ludo's office and kept telling anyone who would listen that they were working on next year's strategy. Blythe wasn't being drawn into it. Playing Amir's games had got her into trouble and she'd learned her lesson. She had a long-term goal to become the person who Ludo wanted to hand over the reins of the company to and, whilst she knew it was likely a few years off, that was what she wanted more than anything. She turned her attention to Mr Smith. She'd found him a lovely ground-floor flat with a small garden for Honey the dog and it was a short stroll to the park and the pub. She felt that until he was focused on leaving, it was going to be very hard to sell his current home.

Blythe was going over and above by taking Mr Smith to the flat viewing, but as he didn't have his own transport and inclination to move, it was likely he wouldn't turn up if she didn't intervene. She knocked at the door and retreated to wait in the car. The door opened and Honey dashed to Blythe's car, jumped up at the driver's window with her giant paws and started barking. It took a few moments for Blythe to realise she was on an extendable lead, not that Mr Smith seemed to have any control over it.

Mr Smith approached the car and Blythe buzzed the window down a fraction, which surprised the dog and made her bark all the more. 'I'm not sure there's time to walk Honey, Mr Smith. I said we'd view the flat at eleven.'

The man frowned. 'Honey's coming with us. It's her new home too,' he said, jutting out his unshaven chin.

It took Blythe a moment to realise the implications of this statement, by which time Mr Smith had already opened her back door and let the dog in. Blythe scrabbled in her coat pocket for the dog treats she now kept there thanks to having to pick up the dog walks that Vicky couldn't manage. She felt a warm breath on her neck and assuming it wasn't Mr Smith she thrust a treat over her shoulder in the hope the dog would eat that and not her ear. Her hand was momentarily engulfed by a tongue and the treat was gone. Thankfully her fingers weren't. Blythe let out a sigh as Mr Smith got in the passenger seat.

'Don't go fast,' he said, doing up his seat belt.

'I won't. You're safe as houses with me,' she quipped.

Mr Smith gave her a look. 'Honey gets carsick.'

After the day she'd had, Blythe was very pleased to see that what she'd ordered had been delivered. It was step one in her new plan, one that she hoped would appease both Leonora and Sam.

'When are you moving this?' asked her frazzled-looking mum as she peered around the phone-box-shaped container occupying the hallway.

Blythe squeezed past it and hung up her coat. 'Now – if Greg can give me a hand with it.'

'He's been summoned by Leonora to help put up lights. She has called here twice today. You are Holly Cross's most wanted – she'll be putting up posters on the church board next.' She waggled a wooden spoon at Blythe.

'Are you baking?' Blythe asked, failing to hide the trepidation in her words.

'I'm trying out a new recipe. I thought it might be good for Christmas leftovers. Sprout and cranberry parcels. Did you want to try one when they're ready?'

Blythe reached for her coat. 'Actually, I can probably manage this box myself. I'll get something to eat later. Bye, Mum, love you.' She grabbed the box, tipped it towards herself and dragged it out of the house. It was incredibly awkward but thankfully reasonably light and because it was downhill to the crossing and then flat across the green, with a bit of cajoling she could haul it along unaided.

When she had finally lugged it puffing and panting onto the green, she abandoned the box and went over to

Sam's. His cottage was standing out already, for all the wrong reasons. It was just before six o'clock in the evening and already dark. All around the village a myriad of fairy lights twinkled in hedges, on trees and around houses. The dads had done a good job of erecting a small house-like structure in the middle of the green, which was waiting to be decorated, but the path to it was already mapped out.

Sam's cottage looked sad and unloved, sat there in complete darkness. She didn't like to think what Murray would have said but she knew he'd have been sad to see it. If she could make her plan work perhaps things wouldn't be so bleak on this side of the street. Blythe went around the back of the cottage, let herself in and deactivated the alarm. She scanned the house for Turpin and called his name. She wasn't sure if he knew what his name was and given his attitude even if he did know it he was unlikely to respond. Downstairs all looked in order – no wild feline parties as yet, but then Sam had only been gone a couple of days. She went upstairs. Sam had left a drawer open under the bed so she had a quick look inside but it was empty, so she pushed it shut with her toe. No sign of Turpin but then he was probably out.

Blythe put down the cat food, reset the alarm, locked up and went to get what she needed from Sam's shed. She was walking back down the path when she heard Sam's voice. 'Hey, what's going on?' he asked.

She spun around expecting to see him at the front door but there was nobody there. 'Sam?' Unless he was hiding under a plant pot there was something odd going on.

'Oh, Blythe, it's you. I can see you on the security camera. Hi. I thought someone was stealing stuff from me.' There was a pause. 'Actually, what's that you've got in your arms?'

She scowled at the security camera. 'I'm *borrowing* Murray's cables. Is that okay with you?'

'Sure. I'm on my way home. Do you think...' Blythe turned her back and walked down the path. She wasn't having a conversation with Sam via the small black device, civil or otherwise. 'Blythe. Hey. Are you still there?'

She marched across the road to where Greg was now waiting by the giant box. 'Your mum said you needed a hand.'

'But I didn't want to drag you away from Leonora,' Blythe said, plonking down the cables.

'That was a quick job with so many of us helping. And talking of she who must be obeyed, Leonora is baying for your blood. I said you were busy at work and would be late home.'

'Thanks, Greg, you're a star.'

'That's as may be. What exactly are you up to?' He eyed the giant box suspiciously.

'I've had an idea.'

'If that's a fairy for the Christmas tree it's a tad on the big size.'

'You'll see.'

They worked non-stop for the next hour and were sorting the final pieces when everything seemed to happen at once. First there was the sound of her name reverberating around the green. Blythe looked up. Leonora was approaching and had spotted her from up the lane that led to the church.

'Blythe! I need to speak to you. Blythe! It's urgent!' This coincided with a taxi pulling up and Sam getting out with a small wheelie case. Sam scanned the front of his property before turning around to look across the green. The taxi pulled away and he crossed the road.

'What's going on?' he asked, taking in the large structure between Blythe and Greg.

Leonora joined them rather red in the face either from her speed walk down the hill or anger – Blythe wasn't sure which. Blythe held up a hand. 'I have solved both problems. Sam, your cottage is untouched by Christmas. Leonora, when we've added the final touches, we will have a striking Christmas display that includes every house on the green.'

'How can you include and not include that cottage?' Leonora stabbed a finger across the road at Sam's place, which was still sitting in darkness.

'Easy,' said Blythe. 'Flick the switch, Greg,' she instructed.

'Right you are,' said Greg and with that, fairy lights lit up all around them including the life-size figure of the Grinch next to Blythe – resplendent in countless green lights. The path snaking around the village green to the little hut was clearly defined and in the other direction it now led to the road directly opposite Sam's. Everyone followed the trail to a flashing sign and a giant arrow that pointed at his cottage and read: *The Grinch Lives Here!*

'What the hell?' said Sam.

'This is absolutely marvellous,' said Leonora, clapping her hands together. 'Well done, Blythe. You had me worried there but I must say this is a total triumph.'

'No, it's not,' said Sam, flapping his arms in the direction of the sign. 'You can't do that.'

'Why not?' Blythe put her hands on her hips.

Sam pointed at the sad-looking cottage and then back at the smirking Grinch. 'That's defamation of character or something.' He shook his head.

'There is nothing on your land, so I think you'd have a hard time finding a lawyer willing to take that on,' said Blythe, trying very hard to hide her smirk. 'But of course if you change your mind and decide to decorate your cottage and join in with the community Christmas spirit, then I'll be very happy to take this down.'

'Now let's not be hasty,' said Leonora, concern flashing across her features. 'This is probably the best display we've had for quite some time.'

'Your call,' said Blythe, fixing her eyes on Sam. They all waited for his response.

'This whole Christmas obsession the village has is ridiculous and I don't want anything to do with it,' said Sam.

'Then the Grinch stays.' Blythe smiled and was conscious that at that precise moment she probably looked a lot like the Grinch. Sam did a double take, huffed and marched off across the road, his wheelie case skittering behind him.

26

9th November

Blythe wasn't looking forward to going round to feed Turpin the next day. Perhaps now would be a good time to suggest that Sam took over the daily task. Although she knew Sam was frequently away, so she'd have to pick it back up then. Truth was she was very attached to Turpin. She couldn't have a pet at her parents' house because of her mum's allergies and she wasn't in a position to buy her own place just yet, which meant Turpin was the ideal adopted pet. At least she could put the food down in the utility and do a runner. She walked across the green and the sight of the Grinch made her smile. All the lights were now turned off in readiness for the big switch-on the following week. There were just a few sparkling on some of the hedges and a rogue elf on someone's lawn as people tested that everything was in working order.

Blythe let herself in the back door. The utility door was open. She opened the cupboard as quietly as she could, took out Turpin's food and bowl and promptly dropped the latter. It made a disproportionate racket as it clattered into the sink.

'Blythe?'

Oh great, she thought.

'Yep.'

Sam appeared in the doorway. He did not look happy. Clearly twenty-four hours had not improved his mood. 'Why did you shut Turpin in a drawer?'

Blythe was bamboozled by the accusation. 'I did nothing of the sort.'

'Then why was I woken at one o'clock this morning by what sounded like rats tunnelling under my bed?'

Blythe snorted a laugh. 'Oh, *that* drawer. But I checked and it was definitely empty when I shut it.'

'Apparently he likes to go in that drawer, crawl out the back and sleep in the one the other side of the bed, which has my spare covers in. They're covered in ginger fur.'

'Did he give you a fright?'

Sam scrunched up his shoulders. 'I dreamt I was in a coffin surrounded by rats gnawing at me.' Sam scratched his eyebrow and looked like he was reliving the nightmare.

Blythe giggled. 'Sorry. Is Turpin okay?'

'He's fine. It's me who was traumatised. He then decided that it was dinner time so I had to get up and feed him. And when I woke up this morning he'd managed to open the drawer again but I didn't notice and walked straight into it, bashed my shin and almost face-planted onto the wardrobe.'

Blythe bit her lip for a moment so she didn't laugh. 'Where is he now?' she asked, concentrating on forking some food into a bowl.

'Sulking under the bed because I've taken the covers out of the drawer to wash them.'

They regarded each other for a fraction longer than was necessary. Blythe looked away first. Her stomach was doing something strange, which was probably down to her mother's turkey and pineapple hollandaise.

'Right, I'll wash these up and be off.'

'Can we talk about the...' He pointed in the direction of the green.

'Weather?' She was being deliberately obtuse.

'No, the...'

'Big lights switch-on?'

'The Grinch,' he said, his voice taut.

'Of course. What would you like to know? I can probably get you a discount on some matching characters from the story if you wanted some for your front garden.'

He pursed his lips. 'I was hoping we could have a sensible conversation but if you're going to be like this.'

Blythe put on her most professional face. 'I'm sorry. What would you like to know about the Grinch?'

'When you're planning on taking it and the sign down.'

'Sorry, no can do. You saw how excited Leonora was about it. Best display yet. It's exactly what we need to win the competition and secure the prize money for charity. There's a lot riding on this year's display.'

'Come on, Blythe, it's a prank that's got out of hand. You're not seriously expecting to have that monstrosity flashing outside my window until Christmas. Are you?'

'Lights stay on until twelfth night, which is the fifth of January.' She did her Grinch smile and then stopped herself. Nobody liked a smart-arse.

'I don't want to go to war with you but I will if I have to.' His jaw tensed.

'It won't just be me though will it? You'll be taking on the whole village. Ooh, actually I had something to ask you.

The HCCC were wondering if you know any celebs who could switch on the lights next week. Might help get some press interest and steal a march on the competitors.'

He shook his head. 'You're unbelievable. Totally freaking unbelievable,' he muttered, as he walked away.

'Is that a maybe?' she called.

'No!' he snapped. Perhaps that wasn't the best time to ask for a favour.

Eden's recovery was coming on in leaps and bounds. Everyone kept telling Vicky how amazing the keyhole surgery had been and that years ago Eden would have been in hospital for a couple of weeks, but despite her speedy recovery her being at home was still causing Vicky issues. Until Eden was back at school she had to stay at home with her, which she loved, but it meant no work and no dog walking. The factory had been very accommodating and even had carer days for exactly this scenario, but her dog-walking clients were less understanding. But then they weren't getting the service they were paying for. Despite the best efforts of Norman, Phyllis, Blythe and a few others some dogs were not going out on all the walks they were due. Princess and Barnaby were a particular issue because nobody could handle them. As she was handing out refunds and apologies left, right and centre she'd decided she needed another income stream to bridge the gap. And she'd come up with just the thing.

Blythe stood and stared at the pile of wool on the kitchen table. 'Explain it to me again,' she said.

'It's pom-poms,' said Vicky, trying not to get exasperated.

'I get that bit. What I don't understand is why people are going to pay money for something they could make themselves.'

'Because everyone loves something handmade. Have you not seen how popular things like this are on Etsy? Come and look at the finished articles,' said Vicky, leading the way into the lounge where Eden was sitting on the sofa surrounded by yet more wool.

'Hello, sweetheart,' said Blythe, giving Eden a gentle hug. 'Blimey it's a proper little sweat shop in here.'

'What's a sweat shop?' asked Eden, not looking up from the brown pom-pom she was making.

'It's when children…' began Blythe, but Vicky was shaking her head so Blythe changed tack. 'It's nothing for you to worry about. Tell me about this brown pom-pom you're making.'

'It's going to be a robin.' Eden held up the brown lump of wool proudly.

'How?' asked Blythe.

Vicky picked up one from the sofa. 'Here's one I made earlier from a YouTube video.'

'How very *Blue Peter*.'

'I know right? See he's got a red wool tummy, googly eyes and a bit of orange felt for a beak.' She held up the pom-pom, now dangling from a long piece of wool on her finger. Vicky was very proud of her fat little robin tree decoration.

'That's actually really cute,' said Blythe, having a closer look.

'And there's Christmas puddings with white tops to look like sauce and when we add felt holly they look fab,' said Vicky picking up another.

Eden started to giggle. 'And sprouts in hats,' she said, holding up a green one with more googly eyes and a red felt cone on top.'

'These are surprisingly good,' said Blythe.

Vicky gave her a playful swipe. 'I figured if I sold them for three pounds each or two for a fiver I only have to sell forty to make a hundred quid! Or a hundred to make two hundred and fifty smackers!' Vicky was fired up at the prospect. That was easy money given that Phyllis had given her most of the wool and Eden already had a pom-pom-making kit. It was also money she desperately needed if they were going to have a decent Christmas.

'Smackers? Has anyone said that since Del Boy Trotter left our screens?' asked Blythe.

'You know what I mean.' Vicky stuck her tongue out.

'It's a good idea and everything but… how are you going to make a hundred of these in time for the fayre?'

'Because we're all going to make them.' Vicky picked up some wool and handed it to Blythe. 'Here you go. You can do sprouts because they're just one colour so they're easier.'

They all became engrossed in their task although Eden was a little distracted by Mr Tumble on the telly.

Blythe nodded at the screen whilst she dug the scissors into an almost finished pom-pom. 'He creeps me out.'

'I went through a phase of dreaming about him,' said Vicky.

Blythe looked mildly horrified. 'That's weird.'

'Oh no, not *those* sort of dreams. We were playing pass

the parcel and using sign language to communicate with each other about chips, that kind of thing.'

'You're right that's not weird at all.' Blythe held up her green pom-pom. 'How's that?'

'One sprout down, about thirty to go,' said Vicky.

'Slave driver,' muttered Blythe, picking the green wool back up and starting another one.

'What's a slave driver?' asked Eden.

'Someone mean,' said Vicky, cutting in before Blythe gave a more graphic response.

Blythe's phone pinged. 'It's Owen asking how Eden is.' She narrowed her eyes at Vicky. 'Did you not give him your phone number like I suggested?'

'Why would I want him to have my number?'

'So he stops texting me for a start. And because he's been nothing but kind since the fireworks.'

Vicky couldn't really disagree. Blythe had told her Owen had been messaging every other day to check up on the patient. But she needed to keep him at a distance. The closer he got the more complicated everything became. Owen was someone from her past and she wished he'd stayed there.

'What should I tell him?' asked Blythe.

'That she's fully recovered.' Vicky and Blythe both glanced across at Eden, who did look the picture of health.

Blythe shrugged. 'Okay. Shall I give him your number?'

'Definitely not.'

27

20th November

The Saturday of the big lights switch-on came around and, as usual, Leonora was banging her flip chart and having a rant about timings. Not many were listening because Norman was passing around the first batch of mince pies of the season. They were always a treat but Blythe felt there was something extra special about that very first one. And there was something particularly special about every one of Norman's mince pies. She didn't know what his secret was but wherever she'd been she'd never tasted another one like it. The pastry crumbled and melted into a buttery delight in your mouth and the filling was sweet but with a citrus kick. They really were completely and utterly delicious.

Vicky was juggling an overstuffed carrier bag in one hand and her mince pie in the other whilst trying to pull out a chair. 'What have you got there?' asked Blythe before popping in the last of her mince pie and savouring the flavours of Christmas.

'Wool,' said Vicky, tapping the side of her nose with her mince pie and leaving an icing sugar smudge. 'A dozen people sat doing very little for an hour – how many pom-poms can they make?'

'Is this like one of those how many reindeer does it take to change a lightbulb jokes?' asked Blythe.

'You're hilarious.' Vicky settled herself in her seat.

'You're not really going to ask the committee to make them, are you?'

'Watch me,' said Vicky, with a twinkle in her eye and icing sugar on her nose. 'How many reindeer does it take by the way?' she asked, through a mouthful of mince pie.

'Eight. One to screw in the lightbulb and seven to hold Rudolph down.'

Leonora raised her voice above the chatter. 'When you've finished stuffing your faces there's a competition we need to win, so if I could have your undivided attention,' she bellowed and everyone almost stood to attention. Phyllis had her teeth in a mince pie but she still froze on the spot. 'Shall we start the meeting?' Leonora waved a hand at the table and those still standing scuttled over to take a seat.

Vicky got up and began walking around the table placing wool in front of each person along with two circles of card. 'I've got a challenge for everyone. You all remember how to make pom-poms right?' There were lots of nods, a couple of confused glances and a look of alarm from Sarvan.

'A pom-pom's a gun right?' he asked.

Vicky laughed. 'No, it's one of these.' She pulled a sprout decoration from the bag.

'That's adorable,' said Phyllis. 'Is this what you're making with my old wool? Well I never.'

'Is this really appropriate?' asked Leonora, her hands on her hips.

'I think it's enterprising,' said Arthur. 'And I'm a bit rusty on making pom-poms but if my memory serves me correctly you just wind wool around these doughnut-shaped pieces of card. I can do that and listen at the same time.' There were nods of agreement.

'Fine,' said Leonora, with a dismissive wave of her hand. Vicky finished her lap of the table, handing out the remaining wool. 'Right off you go. See if you can all make at least one pom-pom by the end of the meeting.'

As people settled down Leonora turned over her flip chart with a flourish. 'Agenda item number one. Blythe.'

Blythe was whispering to Arthur as he'd asked for an update on Eden and the sound of Leonora barking her name made her jump. 'Yes,' she said, trying to speed read what was written on the board.

'Yes, you have secured a celebrity for the opening tonight?' questioned Leonora.

Before Blythe could reply, Phyllis was already clapping her hands together and scattering the remnants of her mince pie. 'Oh, how wonderful! Is it Sean Connery? Please say it's Sean.' She clapped her hands again and left them together as if in prayer.

'No, I'm sorry,' said Blythe.

'Not Sean.' Phyllis stuck her bottom lip out so far she looked like Eden when she'd been told she couldn't have any more sweets.

'Who is it?' asked Leonora, looking keen.

Blythe scanned the eyes all homed in on her. Anticipation filled the air. 'Nobody. I'm sorry but Sam is a bit grumpy about the whole decorations thing...'

'Grinch-gate!' said someone further down the table.

'Precisely. I'm not his favourite person and to be honest I'm not sure he has those sort of contacts anyway.'

She looked at the miserable faces and then at Phyllis, who looked the most dejected. 'Sorry.'

'Never mind,' said Greg. 'Well done for trying.'

'I'll have to sweet-talk the vicar again then.' Leonora tapped the flip chart. 'Item number two...' She went on to talk about timings and Blythe slunk down in her seat and tried to make herself invisible.

Arthur leaned towards her. 'You did a marvellous job with the Grinch. Ignore them; they'll get over it.' He patted her hand, which was comforting.

'Thanks,' she whispered.

The Holly Cross lights switch-on was obviously a big deal but Blythe felt it didn't warrant the amount of stress Leonora created. Everyone with lights, which was most of the village, were primed to switch them on at six o'clock precisely. Those on the green were operated by the committee and that was where the big countdown was performed, with most of the residents with properties around the green standing on their doorsteps and relaying the count to someone inside poised to flick the switch at the allotted moment – simple. Or it was until everyone tried to help.

Blythe was doing final checks and stationing her fellow hi-vis-vest-wearing marshals at key points to direct the cars through the village and up to the farm where they could park on the farmer's field for a suggested fifty pence donation to this year's charity.

Blythe saw the cottage door open out of the corner of her eye and Sam came across the road. She felt her hackles rise. Now was not a good time for an altercation.

'Blythe, can I have a word?' he asked.

She waved a hand at the hive of activity surrounding her as people scurried about like excited elves on Christmas Eve. 'Bit busy right now, Sam.'

'Sure. Won't take a minute.'

'Right, fine,' she said, and she marched him away from where Arthur and Norman were arguing about the speaking clock's accuracy versus Siri.

'That's definitely your colour,' said Sam, pointing at her bright orange vest.

'Well, it worked for the Oompa Lumpas. How can I help you exactly?'

Sam beamed at her and she was immediately suspicious. They'd hardly spoken a word to each other in almost two weeks and she was sure he was making a point of leaving the cottage when she was there feeding Turpin. 'Any chance of you not lighting up the Grinch arrow sign tonight? I get that you need the character.' His eyes travelled up the six-foot figure. 'But the huge flashing arrow pointing at my place isn't really necessary. Is it?'

'Sorry, Sam. Leonora would likely strangle me with fairy lights if we changed things at this stage.'

'You're not scared of her surely?'

'Totally terrified and so should you be.'

'Oh, come on, Blythe. Don't be so stubborn. I'm being reasonable here. I thought we could compromise.'

'You had your chance to join in. You chose not to. The Grinch *and* the sign are both key to the display. I'm really sorry but it has to be a no. If that's all, I need to go and prime the vicar.'

Sam sniggered. 'Why what's happening to him tonight?'

'He does the countdown. Have you met him?' Sam shook his head. 'You should – you've got a lot in common. He hates Christmas too. Gets triggered by "Away in a Manger".'

They were both pondering this when the local TV van pulled up and Blythe thought Leonora might spontaneously combust with excitement. Sam clocked it too and he scowled at Blythe.

She was considering whether or not to apologise again when Vicky appeared at her side. 'There's a problem with an elf,' she said, before clocking who Blythe was talking to. 'Oh hi, Sam. You joining in the fun tonight?'

'Nope. How's Eden?'

'She's sulking because she says she's well enough to come out but I've made her stay in with Phyllis and switch our lights on.'

'That's probably wise. I'll be staying inside too.' He shot Blythe a look but she wasn't interested.

'I'll be there in a minute,' Blythe told Vicky, and she disappeared. She turned back to Sam. 'I hope you're not going to sulk for the whole of the festive season because the only one who will miss out is you.'

'You think I'm just being awkward, don't you?'

'You *are* being awkward.'

He puffed out an exasperated sigh and shook his head. 'You don't think that maybe I've got a good reason to not want to be involved?'

'No,' she said, honestly.

He looked like he was considering something but in the pause they were interrupted. Vicky tapped Blythe on the shoulder but addressed Sam. 'Is that the woman who was creeping around your place?' She pointed through the crowd but with so many people milling about it was difficult to see who she meant.

'Right,' said Sam, and he stormed off in the direction Vicky was pointing.

'Oh great, a confrontation on the news is just what we need,' said Blythe, charging off after Sam. At least he was tall and easy to keep in her sights despite the crowds.

'Sorry!' yelled Vicky, belatedly.

Sam weaved in and out between people, narrowly missing a tray of mince pies; however, he didn't see the small fluffy dog on an extended lead that dashed across his path, sending him flying. He landed with an oof. A woman talking to Arthur nearby spun around to see what the fuss was about. And Blythe recognised her. It *was* the same woman. She clocked Sam and Blythe but before Blythe could say anything she disappeared into the mêlée of people and was gone.

'Hey!' said the dog owner trying to tug the lead from underneath a prone Sam. The little dog seemed overjoyed to have a face at his level and he showered Sam with doggy kisses.

'Eurgh,' said Sam sitting up, which released the lead and the little pup was almost bungeed across the green to be reunited with his owner. The owner picked up his dog and shook his head at Sam.

'You okay?' asked Blythe, offering him a hand to pull him to his feet.

'Been better.' He looked rather cross.

Their hands met and something shot through Blythe's system at the touch. She concentrated on hauling him upright. 'Come on, let me buy you a drink. Everything seems better after mulled wine.' As if on cue Jassi was serving someone and a whiff of the spicy-sweet drink wafted in their direction.

'No, you're all right. And I can see this is your priority so I'll feed Turpin tonight.' He walked off without giving her a chance to respond. Blythe let him go.

'Hey, Arthur, who was that lady you were talking to?' asked Blythe.

'In the bobble hat?'

'Yep, that's the one.'

'No idea. She seemed very interested in the village. Why?'

'Because we caught her snooping around the back of Sam's place on firework night.'

'I thought I recognised her from somewhere. She was at the fireworks too.' He scanned the crowd to see if he could spot her. 'I wonder what she was doing around Murray's cottage.'

'Thieving, we thought, but then would you keep popping up in the same place and chatting to the locals if you were planning on robbing them? What was she asking you?'

Arthur seemed to be thinking. 'She wanted to know if there was parking in the village and any local nature reserves.'

Blythe couldn't work out if that was suspicious or not. 'If you see her again, can you think of an excuse to bring her over to me so I can quiz her?'

Arthur pulled his shoulders back and he almost matched Blythe's height. 'I can question her.'

'Okay, Arthur, but be careful. We don't know what she's up to.'

The vicar took to the podium and the PA system squealed

like an excited child. The vicar gave the same welcome he did every year from the same curly piece of paper and the countdown commenced. Blythe had one of those sensations that someone was watching her; she scanned the crowd but everyone was focused on the vicar. She glanced over her shoulder where Sam was standing by his front door with his eyes fixed on her.

'… two… one…' The lights on the green burst into a fit-inducing frenzy of sparkliness, closely followed by the surrounding properties. A cheer went up from the assembled crowd followed by a round of applause. Leonora was being congratulated by those around her and Blythe couldn't help but feel a little glow of pride. The Grinch looked magnificent and the sign pointing to Sam's cottage flashed happily, in direct contrast to Sam who shook his head, went inside and slammed the door.

28

1st December

Blythe had an afternoon viewing at a property where the couple were out at work all day. She'd dropped them an email to let them know she was showing someone around and the wife had replied that everything was neat and tidy and she was happy for Blythe to go ahead and work her magic. They were keen to sell as they had found their dream property to start a family in and it was hanging in the balance.

Blythe was chatting to the prospective buyers outside; a young couple keen to buy their first home together. The outside was modern and well maintained, with parking for two cars and in an excellent school catchment area. All of which was making them nod – a lovely sign to any estate agent. Blythe opened the door and let them in first. It was warm and welcoming, which was just the ticket. Blythe closed the door and for a moment she thought the owners had left a radio on because she could hear some rhythmic sounds coming from nearby. Blythe pushed open the living room door and was alarmed to be greeted by a naked bottom bobbing along to the soundtrack of a woman hitting a particularly high note.

'Oh, goodness, I am so sorry,' said Blythe to the naked bottom, which stopped mid bob. A head popped up above the back of the sofa. 'Ah Mr Gardener...'

'What the hell are you doing?' barked Mr Gardener disappearing for a moment before reappearing at the side of the sofa hopping on one leg as he speedily tried to get his trousers on.

'I messaged your wife earlier. Hello, Mrs Gardener,' said Blythe, going on her tiptoes to peep over the sofa only to see the face of a woman who was not Mrs Gardener.

'Wife?!' snapped the woman, now doing up her shirt. 'You bastard! You said she'd left you.'

'I think she might now,' muttered Blythe, as she retreated into the hall. She gave the viewers her best apologetic smile. 'Perhaps we should start upstairs,' she said, leading the way.

Blythe was relaying the story in the office as there were no clients about and everyone was laughing hard. 'Have you told the wife?' asked Heather.

'You're not going to rat him out to his missus, are you?' asked Amir. He was watching her closely. 'You've already grassed him up, haven't you?'

'All I have done is message his wife with feedback from the prospective buyers as they said it wasn't quite what they were after and they did seem particularly alarmed by the Pampas Grass out the front of the property. And I may have mentioned that her husband was at home and I was sorry if I had startled him and his friend.'

'Good call,' said Heather. 'Cheaters need outing.'

'Unprofessional,' muttered Amir.

'Who's unprofessional?' asked Ludo, coming out of his office and immediately looking at Blythe. That look hurt her more than she cared to admit.

'Blythe here has just exposed a man's extramarital affair,' said Amir, rather too quickly.

'He exposed himself,' said Blythe. 'In more ways than one.' She feared it would take a while to rid her mind of the picture of his bare bum.

'Not really for us to get involved,' said Ludo.

'I was there with prospective buyers and I'm certain the only reason they didn't place an offer was because of his antics. How was I supposed to explain that to his wife? And anyway, what woman wants to buy a new home, take on a bigger mortgage and think about starting a family with a cheating arse like him?' There was the image of his bum again flashing into her mind. Blythe blinked quickly to rid herself of the mental picture.

'Again, not for us to decide,' said Ludo.

Amir moved to stand at Ludo's side and he nodded sagely. 'We shouldn't be getting involved in the private lives of our clients,' said Amir.

Ludo did a double take as if Amir had crept up on him. 'No, but I have to say that morally what this man has done is deplorable.' Ludo watched Amir for a response.

'Oh, yeah. Totally. He deserves all he gets.'

Blythe shook her head at Amir. He was such a weasel.

The Christmas tree auction was the next big event in the Holly Cross Christmas calendar and Blythe's family were heavily involved as Greg played the part of auctioneer. *Played the part* was the key phrase because Greg's only experience of auctions was the few episodes he'd watched of *Cash in the Attic*. Otherwise he hadn't got a clue what he was doing but when had that ever stopped him? Greg was one of life's carefree folk who actually enjoyed making a fool of himself so when he got on the podium his main aim was to make people laugh as well as sell some trees. Blythe could see Leonora already tensing up as Greg tapped the microphone and grabbed the attention of the amassed crowd.

'Evening, everyone, and welcome to the hundred and seventy-second Holly Cross Christmas tree auction,' he said with a theatrical wink. 'Tonight you have the opportunity to purchase a one-off...' He waved his hands in an upward motion and paused. 'This is where you whoop with enthusiasm.' The crowd tittered. Greg cleared his throat and tried again. 'These trees are one-offs...'

'Ooh!' replied the crowd.

'Better,' said Greg, with a smile. 'They are top quality...'

'Ooh.'

'And they are guaranteed to drop needles all over your carpet.' There was laughter and confusion from the crowd. Greg pretended to check his notes. 'Oh, sorry. Guaranteed *not* to drop needles. Anyway they are beautiful firs, the like of which are already gracing Buckingham Palace and every posh pad from here to Balmoral...'

'Doesn't the king spend Christmas at Sandringham?' asked Leonora, scratching her neck and looking particularly stressed.

'Relax, Leonora, they know he's joking. Nobody's going to sue us because they've not got the same tree as the royal family,' said Blythe.

'Right,' said Greg. 'We are starting with the big trees. The seven-footers. Here's an example modelled by my lovely assistant.' Sarvan held one of the biggest trees steady so everyone could get a good look at it. The rest of the trees were wrapped in mesh, waiting on the back of a truck with some village lads poised to pass them down to the winning buyers. 'How this works is we auction them off for the highest bid. The highest bidder in each size category also receives a handmade door wreath. Everyone else is encouraged to pay the same amount for their tree or within ten per cent of the winning bid. Remember it's all for charity, folks.

'I need to see clear hand gestures for bids. Not that sort of hand gesture, Phyllis. Really?' Greg playfully shook his head while Phyllis giggled. 'Are you ready?' There was a mumble from the crowd. 'I said, are you ready?!' This time they roared and the auction began.

The thing with Greg was that whilst he had no idea about being an auctioneer, he did an excellent comedy impression of one. Most of what he was saying was inaudible but had the rhythm of an actual auctioneer. He interspersed this with the occasional marker so folk knew what was going on. 'Forty pounds I'm bid by the man in the Christmas pudding bobble hat – excellent headgear, sir.' And then he was off on his incomprehensible babble. When he was confident they had topped out the bids he slammed down his gavel. Greg yelped as he pretended to smash it on his thumb and took a round of applause from the crowd as happy punters went to pay and collect their trees. While that was happening, Blythe went to grab a mulled wine from Jassi who was manning a pop-up pub stall for the night. She was in the queue when someone tapped her on the shoulder – it was Sam.

'Ah, the Grinch himself. Good evening and how are you?'

'I'm bearing up given the level of festivities. Have you been at the mulled wine already?' he asked.

'It's a lack of mulled wine that's causing the problem. What's made you venture out this evening? You're never buying a Christmas tree, are you?'

'No way. Dead shrub in the corner of the room, festooned with the tat of Christmases past. It's not for me.'

'And yet you paint such a charming picture,' said Blythe. 'So what brings you here?'

'Someone asked me.'

She was surprised by his answer and intrigued as to who had sufficient allure to entice Sam out to a festive event. 'I asked you out, but you turned me down.'

His eyebrows rose. 'When did you ask me out?'

Blythe was glad it was dark because she could feel her cheeks heating up. 'Not *out* out. But I did ask you… to come out for Christmas.' Sam was smirking at her growing awkwardness. 'Anyway, who was so much better than me that you came when *they* asked?'

Sam gave an annoyingly long pause. 'Owen.'

Blythe looked around both sides of Sam like a boxer dodging blows but there was no sign of Owen. 'What, Vicky's Owen?'

'Is he Vicky's Owen? I got the distinct impression things were frosty between those two.' A timely gust of wind across the green made them both shiver and smile at their own synchronised shuddering.

'You're right. Those two were over years ago so she will not be happy that he keeps popping up.'

'He seems like a nice guy,' said Sam.

'Apart from forcing someone with a festive phobia out of the house to face more Christmas than an elf could shake a candy cane at.' She gestured to the flashing lights of the decorations and the large truck of Christmas trees.

'Apart from that, yes.' He shoved his hands deep into his pockets, making his scarf ruffle up around his ears. 'It's not exactly a phobia. More of an aversion.'

'Nope. Still don't understand it.'

They'd reached the front of the queue so their conversation was interrupted. 'Hiya, Blythe,' said Jassi. 'And Sam, good to see you here tonight. Two mulled wines?'

'Two each please,' said Blythe, and Jassi raised an eyebrow. 'They're not all for us.'

'I believe you,' she said, swapping the warm mugs for the cash they both handed over. 'Don't forget to bring the mugs back,' Jassi reminded them.

They made their way through the crowd to where Owen was bidding furiously on the six-foot trees. Sam tried to pass him his mulled wine but he was too engrossed. 'Does he realise that he'll still get one if he stops pushing the price up?' Sam asked Blythe.

'Possibly not.' She tried to see who he was bidding against as they sipped their drinks and enjoyed the drama. Greg was looking over by the elf hut and the bidder was the other side. 'Owen, let it go. There's plenty of trees.'

'But I want that one,' he said to Blythe. 'One more pound!' he shouted at Greg.

Vicky appeared, looking fraught. 'What are you doing?'

'Getting a Christmas tree. This is ace.'

'No, it's not. The idea is it's a bit of fun. You're pushing the price too high.'

'But I thought that was the whole idea?' Owen looked confused.

'Sold!' shouted Greg. He gave a firm nod towards the elf hut but none of his usual insightful banter regarding the winning bidder.

'Awww,' said Owen. 'I lost my tree.'

'Come on, let's get you an equally good one,' said Blythe, towing Owen off to the truck.

After rejecting four others he settled on a fabulous-looking tree that was barely being held in place by the mesh. 'That's a bushy one for sure,' said Blythe.

Owen happily handed over the money and tried to lift the tree. 'Blimey, that weighs a bit,' he said, lifting it onto his shoulder and almost knocking off Norman's bobble hat. Sam and Vicky strode over carrying their drinks.

'What are you going to do with it now?' Vicky asked.

Owen looked puzzled. 'Take it home and decorate it. I've not had a real tree before.' He grinned at her.

'How exactly are you getting it home?'

'In my car.'

'Lord, give me strength,' said Vicky, throwing up her arms and almost showering them in mulled wine.

'Have you still got that little Kia?' asked Sam with a grimace.

'Oh. Right.' Owen started to laugh. 'I'm a doofus.'

'Grade-A doofus,' muttered Vicky.

'Thanks, I've never been an A at anything,' said Owen, holding her gaze. 'Here. You'd better have the tree.' He tried to pass it to Vicky but thankfully Sam intercepted it.

'I can't accept that.'

'Sure you can. Eden will love it,' he said.

Blythe was standing next to Sam, sipping her mulled wine like she was watching a soap opera.

'Could someone make a decision because it's surprisingly heavy,' said Sam, setting the tree down.

'Seeing as you can't get it home, I guess I could take it off your hands,' said Vicky, with a shrug.

'Great. Can I help decorate it?' asked Owen.

'That would be a nice gesture given you've got a free tree,' suggested Blythe, and Vicky glared back at her.

'Here comes your rival bidder,' said Sam, nodding behind Blythe.

She glanced over her shoulder and was surprised at who she saw walking towards them.

29

1st December

Blythe was taken aback to see her father emerge from the crowd. No wonder Greg hadn't made a quip about his appearance. Hugh looked a little greyer than last year but still cut an imposing figure as he strode towards them in a long black overcoat. 'Good evening, Blythe,' he said, kissing her on the cheek. He eyed the small group around her.

'Hi, Dad,' she said, and noted the interest on Sam's face. 'What are you doing here?'

'That's not exactly a warm welcome now, is it?'

'Sorry, it's just a surprise.' Shock would have been a better word. He never came to see her without booking in advance. Or more accurately without getting his secretary to book it.

She was aware of the eyes on her. She looked at Owen. 'Weren't you going to help Sam take the tree to Vicky's?' She fixed them all with stern looks, which got them moving.

'Yes, we were. Nice to see you again, Mr Littlewood,' said Vicky, giving Blythe's arm an encouraging squeeze. She leaned in. 'Call me later.' They all gave Blythe their empty mugs.

'Bye,' said Owen, oblivious to the frosty atmosphere.

There was a slight delay before Sam lifted the tree up onto his shoulder and followed the others. Whilst Blythe had wanted them to leave, it felt even more uncomfortable to be left with her dad. 'Is this visit as well as your annual Christmas trip or instead of?' she asked.

'It's an extra because your present hasn't been purchased as yet.' It didn't sound like he was buying it, but then given she usually received a selection of bath accessories when she only had a shower at home, she had suspected this for some time. He seemed to have a flash of inspiration. 'Although I could get it sent directly to you and save an additional trip.' Blythe was sure he didn't realise how he came across sometimes.

'If you like, but I've not wrapped your present yet so I can't give you that today.' She always spent a lot of time seeking out a fitting gift for him. She felt it was important to find just the right present for people; it was part of the fun of Christmas for her. Not that she got much feedback on the things she bought her father, although he did always say thank you. And knowing her dad, if the gift wasn't suitable, he'd likely tell her.

'You could always post it?' he suggested.

'Oh, okay,' she said, feeling deflated as Hugh nodded cheerfully.

Another large tree came through the crowd and they moved out of the way. Greg announced the next auction and people surged forwards as there was always a lot of interest in the five-foot trees. 'Maybe we should take a stroll,' suggested Blythe. 'How long are you here for?'

'I've been here all day. I thought I would kill two birds with one stone.'

'And buy a Christmas tree?'

'Oh, I'm not taking it. It was more of a gesture. I've told them to resell it.' Poor Owen could have had that one after all, she thought.

'If not a Christmas tree what are the two birds then?'

'Well, you.' She'd worked that out for herself. 'And a business meeting.' Blythe tried not to be niggled that he'd lumped her onto the end of a business trip.

'Around here?' Her interest was piqued. Her father usually stayed within the boundaries of the North Circular, never venturing far from his beloved London.

'It's important to diversify and grow, Blythe. Business is constantly evolving. You have to stay on top of it. Which leads me to you. How is your career progressing?'

Did all children have conversations like this with their parents? she wondered. It was like having an annual appraisal but without the positive praise, nice lunch and occasional bonus payment. 'I'm still senior negotiator...' As she said it, she thought of Amir. 'Ludo took on another senior negotiator at the end of last year but I'm the senior, senior negotiator if you get what I mean.'

'Not really. Why would Ludo bring in another member of staff at the same level?'

It was something she'd pondered at the time. 'There was a lot of work and Ludo is keen not to work long hours now he's getting older.'

'Is that the only reason I wonder?' said Hugh, although she wasn't sure it was a question.

Fearing he was going to suggest she wasn't doing her job properly she tried to think of positives to share. She remembered the competition. 'Back in May I beat the office sales record. A whole year of top monthly sales – something you said wasn't achievable. I emailed you about it at the time.' She found she was nodding furiously in an attempt to make her father understand the magnitude of the feat.

'Every so often I delete everything in my inbox. If it's urgent people will message again. This thing with Ludo and the new negotiator...' He appeared to be pondering something. 'Perhaps Ludo was trying to mix things up a little by bringing in an outsider to test you. Or maybe preparing a replacement.' He tilted his head. 'What do you think?'

She'd taken Ludo's explanation at face value. 'Ludo said he was expanding the team because we were doing well and extending our area.'

'Hmm, surely you'd bring in junior staff and train them up. Much cheaper and less likely to upset the balance.' His eyes had a glint. 'Unless upset the balance was exactly what he was trying to achieve. You know about the Tuckman model?'

'Form, Storm, Norm, Perform. Yeah, I'm familiar with it.'

'Sounds to me like Ludo brought someone in to thrust you all into the storming stage. Yes, I bet that was the reason. Smart old fox, that Ludo.'

Blythe had had enough of work talk. Her relationship with her father was an unconventional one. He and her mum had split up when she was six. She didn't remember too much about the actual split, although she remembered her mother sitting on the stairs and crying as her dad walked out. At the time she'd cried too, thinking that her daddy had gone on holiday without them. As the visits dwindled to the annual event they had been for many years, Blythe had felt obliged to squeeze all their conversations into that one meeting. There were the regular scheduled phone calls, but her father was always distracted and she could sense he was itching to get off the phone.

She didn't like that she'd not been able to prepare for his visit. Not that she did a PowerPoint presentation or anything, although her father would likely respond better to that, but she felt she had so much to cover off. She liked to jot down all the things she'd achieved. She longed for the day he might say he was proud of her, but unless she could somehow match his success she feared that day would never come. That didn't stop her trying. While she ordered her thoughts on that front Blythe decided to tackle what she saw as the other key reason they met up – to cultivate and improve their rapport. Perhaps one day they would have the easy relationship she saw others enjoy with their fathers – *or perhaps not*, she thought as Hugh checked his watch.

'How are you, Dad?'

'Business profits have increased by three-point-four per cent on last year, which is ahead of my own stretching growth projections and I'm forming some ambitious plans for next year.'

Blythe sighed deeply. 'But how are you? Not the business. You.' She realised she was waving the empty mugs around so she stopped.

He seemed momentarily perplexed by the question before recovering. 'My annual health check was all clear.'

'That's good.' Not exactly the chatty response she was after but at least he'd answered the question. Her father was hard work. 'How's your love life?' she asked, with a smile.

He frowned at her. 'I don't have time for that.' *Just like you don't have time for me*, she thought bitterly. And not having time didn't mean he didn't have some poor woman trying to cultivate a relationship with him. 'Are you dating anyone?' he asked.

'No, not at the moment. Like you, I don't really have time.' That wasn't strictly true but common ground with her father was hard to come by so she'd grab what she could. 'But a life of all work isn't healthy. I'd like to meet someone special.' An image of Sam marched into her head, shocking her.

'I suppose you need to factor in children, if you're planning on having any,' said Hugh. 'They frequently decimate a woman's career.'

That was a depressing thought. 'Thanks, I'll think about that and add it to my plans.'

He nodded and they stood there in silence. Blythe was grateful for the cheer that went up. 'I think the auctions are over.' She watched Greg shaking hands with people as he left the podium, heading straight for them.

'Hello there, Hugh,' said Greg, grasping his hand and pumping his arm like a long-lost friend. 'Great to see you here. Has Blythe been telling you what a fabulous job she did with the display this year?' Greg instinctively put his arm around her shoulders and gave her a squeeze.

'What display?' asked Hugh.

'This.' Greg waved with his free arm. 'The Holly Cross Christmas extravaganza. The Grinch was all her idea.'

Hugh glanced around as if he hadn't noticed he was standing in the middle of a myriad of flashing Christmas lights. 'Oh, right. They pay you for this do they?'

'No, she volunteers all her time,' said Greg, proudly.

Hugh winced and shook his head. 'You missed an opportunity there, Blythe.'

Vicky wasn't sure how she found herself making multiple mugs of hot chocolate while Eden, Phyllis, Sam and, of all people Owen Hockley, were in her front room putting up a Christmas tree. She threw the marshmallows on the top of the cream and took the tray through. The tree was a beauty, but it seemed to have grown between the village green and her house. It looked twice the height it had done and, now out of its protective mesh, considerably bushier too. They had to move her frog ornaments off the mantelpiece and windowsill and there was no way she'd be able to draw the curtains properly again until after twelfth night. Sam was holding the tree near the top. Owen was lying underneath it, fiddling with the base. Phyllis was sitting on the sofa giving them contradicting instructions, whilst Eden danced about excitedly.

'Left a bit. No, more to the right. No, your right. Sorry, no, it was my left,' said Phyllis, tipping her head to the side as if checking it was the tree tilting and not her.

'Ooh, hot chocolate,' said Eden, dashing over and almost bumping her nose on the tray in her keenness to be first to be served.

'Sit down and be careful,' said Vicky, waiting for Eden to wriggle into position on the sofa next to Phyllis before handing her a mug. Owen scrambled out from under the tree and plonked himself in the armchair. Clearly he'd assumed the instructions were aimed at him.

Phyllis took the proffered mug. 'This looks scrumptious. Thank you.'

'Thanks,' said Owen, taking his.

'Can I let go now?' asked Sam.

'Is it secure?' asked Vicky, having images of the thing keeling over and taking her telly with it.

'I've screwed it in tight,' said Owen, coming up from his hot chocolate with a cream moustache, which made Vicky smile despite his very presence putting her on edge.

Sam let go and gingerly crept away. The tree leaned to the right but didn't topple. Vicky relaxed and let out a breath she'd been holding in. She and Sam both mirrored the tree and leaned to one side.

'It's not straight,' said Vicky.

'Don't worry, we'll fix it,' said Owen.

'Hmm.' She wasn't convinced the skill set for that was in the room. Vicky handed Sam a hot chocolate.

'Thanks. I can't remember the last time I had a hot chocolate,' said Sam.

'Does your mummy not know how to make it?' asked Eden.

Sam had a melancholy look about him. 'No, she never made me hot chocolate.'

Eden stroked his arm. 'That's sad.'

He took a sip and his dejected demeanour disappeared. 'It's really good. Maybe I'll get a hot chocolate the next time I'm at the coffee shop in town.'

'Is the Bean Machine still there?' asked Owen.

'Yep, it's changed hands umpteen times since you left,' said Vicky, 'but they still do the best milkshakes.'

'Aww, Crunchie milkshake,' said Owen. 'My mouth's watering at the thought of it.'

'Is that any good?' asked Sam.

'Ye-ah,' said Owen. And the others all nodded their agreement.

Vicky thought back to their school days and could picture the two of them sitting in the little coffee shop after school on a Friday having saved some of their dinner money to be able to afford the weekly treat. They used to sit opposite each other to drink their milkshakes. Slurping, chatting and laughing. They'd laughed all the time back then. Owen looked her way and grinned. That same cheeky grin she knew so well. They had been happy once and he didn't seem to have any agenda for showing up other than genuinely wanting to reconnect with old friends. She realised she'd fabricated most of the concerns she had. Yes, their relationship had ended badly but that was a long while ago. Perhaps she'd been too hasty in pushing him away.

Owen finished his hot chocolate with a slurp. 'That was awesome.' He stood up quickly. 'Right, let's get this tree fixed so we can decorate it,' he said.

'Do you like fixing stuff, Owen?' she asked.

'Yeah, that's pretty much what my business is – me fixing stuff. Why?'

'Because I might have a few jobs for you.'

'Ace,' said Owen, and he crawled back under the tree.

30

11th December

It was the Saturday afternoon of the Sexy Santa dinner; Eden was on a pantomime visit with the Rainbows and Brownies, and Blythe and Vicky were in the village hall sorting through bags of decorations.

'It's like the crap of Christmas past in here,' said Vicky, her head still in a giant bag.

'I've bought some new stuff too, so I think it'll be fine. Maybe if we tip it all out and put what we're going to use on one of the tables that'll help,' suggested Blythe.

Vicky pulled her face out of the sack. 'Let's see.'

Blythe unloaded the masses of goodies she'd built up over the past few weeks. 'Holly tablecloths, a big candle for the middle of each table and a plastic holly wreath to go around each of them. Holly serviettes and some table confetti with—'

Vicky held up her palm. 'Let me guess.' She closed her eyes for a moment. 'Is it holly by any chance?'

Blythe took a playful swipe at her. 'You'll never know because I'm not showing you now. But it is the Holly Cross Sexy Santa dinner, so I figured it made sense as a theme.'

'Or you could have gone with sexy as a theme. Did you

know you can get tablecloths with naked men on them wearing strategically placed Santa hats? And pasta shaped like—'

'That's enough to put you off your dinner,' said Blythe. 'I thought we'd try and keep it tasteful.'

Vicky looked disappointed. 'I thought the men were going to be topless.'

'They are.'

'Oh, that's good then. Not *too* tasteful.' Vicky grinned.

They sorted through all the old decorations, pulling out some tinsel with holly additions, strings of fairy lights and a lot of plastic ivy, and they began decorating the hall. Blythe moved the stepladder and Vicky handed her a length of ivy and the staple gun. 'How's things with you and Owen?' asked Blythe, trying to sound casual as she pinned ivy to the window frame.

'There is no me and Owen.' Vicky's voice was stern.

'I know that. I only meant how are things between you. He seems to have been at yours a few times since the Christmas tree auction.'

'That's because he's been doing some odd jobs for me.'

Blythe couldn't help feel a little disappointed. She knew there was history but Vicky and Owen had always been good together and she felt they could be again if only Vicky would let down her barriers, which seemed to be built particularly high when it came to Owen. 'What jobs?' she asked.

'The sliding wardrobe door in Eden's room came off the track so many times I just left it off, so he's fixed that and it works a treat now. He put up a coat hook in the hall and stopped the leaky tap in the kitchen.'

'What did all that cost you?' Blythe plunged another staple into the ivy. There was no immediate answer so she turned to look at Vicky who was studying the next piece of ivy. 'You didn't pay him did you?'

'He offered!' Vicky threw up her hands and the ivy went with them. Blythe caught it mid-air. The stepladder wobbled and she clung on tight.

'You can't do that,' said Blythe.

'You said *you'd* be better up the ladder.'

'Not this. What you're doing to Owen. You know he likes you. You can't use his goodwill to get jobs done around your house.'

Vicky's head flopped from side to side in a very teenagery way. 'I know. But he offered and I don't have much spare cash and I really *really* wanted them fixed.'

'Oh, if you really, really wanted them fixed then it's okay.'

'Is it?'

'No! Obviously not.' Blythe shook her head and went back to vigorously stapling ivy.

'I know, you're right,' said Vicky in a small voice. 'It's also kind of nice having him around.'

Blythe spun around so fast she almost toppled off the stepladder. 'Hah! I knew it. You still like him. You do. Don't you?'

'Wind back the arrows, Cupid. I'm not getting back with Owen. No way. All I meant was it's not easy being a single parent. Everything ends up on your to-do list. It felt nice to have someone else doing some jobs around the house. That's all.'

'Is it though? Is that all it is?' Blythe waited.

'Yeah. That's all.' But Vicky broke eye contact and that made Blythe doubt her words.

After a couple of hours the hall was transformed. Ivy and fairy lights were placed at key points around the room and the tables were decorated. Vicky was bundling up the unused decorations, having sorted out the very tatty and broken ones, when Blythe's phone pinged and she checked the message. 'Caterers are all on track,' she said to Vicky. Everything was going to plan. She had plenty of time to go home, shower and change ready for the event. Technically she was working because she was compere and therefore hosting the event, which was a grand title for someone who was there to make sure it all went to plan, but she was also getting a meal and looking forward to the evening as a whole. She was about to put her phone away when it rang. She didn't recognise the number, which meant it was probably a work call because she gave her number out to prospective clients all the time.

'Good afternoon, Blythe Littlewood. How can I help?'

'Blythe, it's Steve from the rugby club. I take it you've heard?'

She was immediately concerned. 'Heard what?'

'It was the rugby club Christmas party last night.'

'I knew it was yesterday because I paid Sarvan for the beer. Did it go well?'

'Yeah. Only we all went out for a kebab afterwards and they've been dropping like flies all day. Food poisoning has gone through all of them. When I say gone through I mean—'

'I can imagine,' said Blythe, cutting him off before it got too graphic. 'But not all twelve of them surely?'

'Hang on, let me count up who I've heard from.' There was a long frustrating silence while Steve muttered names as he counted and Blythe sent up a silent prayer to Father Christmas that at least some of them had avoided the dodgy kebabs.

'Ten definites. As in definitely got the runs.' Blythe started to feel very uncomfortable. 'Only Slim and Turtle not accounted for,' he added.

Why did blokes use such stupid nicknames? 'And which are those two again?'

'Oh, right.' Steve laughed. 'Seb and Fraser.'

Blythe was trying hard not to panic. 'Hopefully that's three then. Let me see who else I can rustle up.'

'Where'd you get three from?'

'Seb, Fraser and you makes three.'

'Oh no, I'm on the loo right now and let me tell you it's like the Somme down there.'

Time to hang up. 'Okay, Steve. Hope you're feeling better soon. Thanks for letting me know.' She hastily ended the call and oddly felt the need to sanitise her phone.

'What's up?' asked Vicky.

Blythe quickly relayed the issue. And glanced around the hall, which was set up for ninety-six people who would be arriving in less than three hours. 'Twelve tables and two sexy Santas.'

'Two *unconfirmed* sexy Santas,' pointed out Vicky.

'You're right.' Blythe rubbed at her forehead where a headache was brewing.

'You call Seb and Fraser, and I'll rope in Sarvan and ring round the playground dads. Only the fit ones, mind.'

'You're a star, thank you,' said Blythe.

After five minutes of frantic phone calls they came back together. 'How'd you get on?' asked Vicky.

'Seb and Fraser are both fine. One vegetarian and one vegan. Seb has a brother he's persuaded to help us out who I am very much hoping is as toned as he is. How about you?'

'Sarvan's up for it but it leaves Jassi a bit short at the pub. Only two dads can do it, I'm afraid, because most of them are staying in because their wives are out at the sexy Santa dinner.'

'Bugger it,' said Blythe with feeling. All the usual babysitters, like Phyllis, were also on the guest list. 'That's only six Santas for twelves tables. Call Owen,' she said in a rush.

Vicky looked like she'd been hit in the face with a sleigh. 'I don't think so.'

'It's okay for him to be fixing your odd jobs but it's not okay for him to help me out?'

'This is different. This is asking him to be a sexy Santa.' Vicky looked uncomfortable.

'Come on. He's good-looking. I bet he's pretty toned with the sort of work he does and he's a good laugh. I'm sure he'd do it. Especially if you asked him.' Vicky was scowling at her. 'Please. Or I'll have to cancel, in which case Leonora will chop me into little pieces.'

'Fine. But you owe me big time.' Vicky wagged a finger at Blythe.

'And ask if he's got any mates he can bring.'

'Will do. But if I'm asking Owen, you need to ask Sam.'

★

Blythe texted Steve because she couldn't face another phone call via his toilet and because he had been in charge of the costumes, what there was of them, and she needed to get hold of them quickly. He'd replied that he'd get his dad to drop them at the hall. There was a moment where Blythe considered asking if his dad was up to the job but she decided against it. She was not looking forward to asking Sam and could predict his response but Vicky was right – she had to at least try. She was going over how best to pitch it as she let herself in the back door of his cottage.

'Blythe, is that you?'

'No, it's the crazy burglar lady. Why?'

'Because I've got a bit of a problem. Can you come here, please?'

He was being very polite and he needed a favour – this was a good start. 'Of course, Sam. Holly Cross residents always help each other out,' she said, moving through the downstairs rooms trying to find him. 'Where are you?'

'Stairs,' said Sam.

Blythe walked through the hall and turned to face up the stairs. Sam was standing towards the top, holding onto the banister – he looked perfectly fine. Turpin was sitting a couple of steps down. 'What's wrong?' she asked.

'It's Turpin.'

'He looks okay to me.'

Sam looked a bit embarrassed. 'He won't let me come downstairs.'

Blythe smiled. Sam was well over six feet tall and what Phyllis would refer to as a strapping lad. 'You're not scared of a little cat. Are you? Just walk past him.'

Sam pursed his lips, gripped the banister and gingerly

came down one step and then the next, which was level with Turpin's head. The cat whipped around and dived on Sam's bare foot.

'Ow!' he yelped and retreated back up the stairs to inspect the damage.

Blythe fell about laughing.

'It's not funny. He really hurts. He's scratched my feet.' Sam waved one as evidence.

'I heard about this on the radio,' said Blythe.

'It would not surprise me if Turpin had called in to complain about me but given he's been sitting here the whole time, I don't think it was him.'

'Very funny. I meant they had a feature on the radio about it. It's called podophobia.'

'What?'

'It's an irrational fear of feet. Maybe Turpin has podophobia,' she suggested.

'What's it called when you like inflicting pain on feet? Because I think it's more likely he has that.'

'Sadism?'

'Sounds about right. Now whilst the chat is lovely, do you think you could perhaps do me a favour and persuade Turpin to move out of the way so I can come downstairs?'

Blythe rolled her lips together. 'I could, but I might need a teensy-weeny little favour in return.'

'Name it,' said Sam, giving one of his injured feet a rub. 'As long as it has nothing to do with Christmas,' he added hastily.

31

11th December

Blythe gave Sam a whistle-stop update on the sexy Santa issue and from shortly after her first mention of Santa he began shaking his head.

'Sorry, I'm going to have to say no,' he said.

'Because you don't like supporting charity, or you have some hideous skin condition that would put people off their dinner, or because of your Christmas phobia?'

'It's more—'

But she didn't give him a chance to finish. 'Then you leave me with no choice. I'm going to have to leave you stranded up there with Turpin here on guard.' She went up a couple of stairs and rubbed Turpin's head. 'There's a good boy. If he so much as twitches you bite him. Got it?' Turpin stood up and attempted to walk along the stair but he only made a couple of steps before he limped as soon as he walked on his back foot. Blythe glared at Sam. 'He's limping. What's wrong with his paw?'

'I dunno. I've not seen him walk today. He's either been asleep in the sink or he's been sitting here taking a swipe at me.'

'No wonder. Poor boy is in pain. He's scared you're going to step on him and make it worse.'

'I'm not sure he's capable of that level of deduction.' Blythe gave him her sternest look. 'But it's not good that he's hurt himself.'

Blythe tried to get a better look at Turpin's foot but he wasn't letting anyone too close – not even her. 'There's a big lump on one of his back legs.'

'Offside,' said Sam.

Blythe shook her head. 'This has nothing to do with football. Right now we need to get him to the vet's. I'll let you off the sexy Santa dinner. You have a more important job to do. Please can you message me from the vet's so I know what's happening.' She turned to leave.

'Oh no, hang on,' said Sam, running the gauntlet down the stairs and getting scratched again by Turpin, his tail swishing menacingly. 'Ow! I can't take him.'

'Why not?'

'For a start I don't have a cat carrier basket thingy.'

'Phyllis will loan you the one she had for her cat. Number ten, Penny Hill.' She pointed to the back of the cottage and carried on through to the utility with both Sam and Turpin hopping after her.

'You'll have to help me get him in the thing or he'll savage me. Look what he's done to my foot.' Sam pulled up a trouser leg and lifted a red and bloodied foot towards Blythe. 'I dread to think what he'd do to my face and hands.'

'Use gardening gloves.' Blythe put some food down for Turpin, which he ignored, and she made to leave.

Sam held up his palms. 'Okay, you win.'

'Win at what?' Blythe was confused.

'I'll do the dinner thing if you take devil cat to the vet's.' Sam looked defeated.

'Nice idea but I've not got time.' Blythe checked her watch. It would be extremely tight even if the vet could fit Turpin in now.

'Please,' said Sam. 'I can't believe I'm virtually begging to dress up as sexy Satan—'

'Santa.'

'It's just an anagram of Satan.' Sometimes he did make her smile. 'Come on, I'm sacrificing a lot here and Turpin needs you.'

'Okay. I'll take him but you need to sort a few things out at the hall for me too.' He nodded. 'And you have some black trousers right?'

'Yep. Casual and dinner suit.'

'Dinner suit would be perfect.' It seemed sometimes things did just work out how you needed them to.

Turpin was easily lured into the cat carrier with some of his favourite treats. The local vet was able to squeeze him in as an emergency because he was clearly in pain. He was surprisingly well-behaved at the vet's – almost like he knew they were going to make him feel better. The vet explained that the lump on his foot was an abscess, most likely from a fight with another cat. Turpin yowled and spat when the vet lanced it but didn't make a sound when he gave him an injection of painkillers, although he was quick to slink back inside the carrier and curl up. He was silent on the way back to Sam's, where Blythe left him along with the antibiotics he needed to have daily.

Blythe dashed home, showered, changed and did her hair at record speed and got Greg to drop her at the village hall, which saved her the walk in the rain. When she walked in it was a hive of activity. The caterers had arrived, Vicky was in the middle of the room waving her arms about like she was directing traffic and there was no sign of any sexy Santas.

'Where are the men?' asked Blythe, taking off her coat and trying not to get flustered. They had forty minutes before a stream of overexcited females descended.

'Five are in the kitchen changing into their outfits, Fraser is on the drag because his tractor broke down – long story – and one of the playground dads is in the loo.' Vicky lowered her voice. 'Nervous tummy.'

Owen came speed-walking out of the kitchen wearing a T-shirt and black leggings. 'Hi, Blythe,' he said cheerily.

'What are you wearing?' she asked, trying hard not to focus on a particularly bulgy bit of his outfit.

'They're my leggings,' said Vicky. 'He didn't have any black trousers so I improvised.' Owen lifted up his T-shirt to reveal just how high the leggings went – nipple height.

'They're quite warm really,' he said, with a wriggle. 'Bit restrictive in certain areas though.'

Blythe was hastily trying to count up the men in her head. 'Is Sam here?'

'He was but he's gone—'

'Bloody typical. I keep my end of the bargain but he wriggles out of his. I swear I'll swing for him next time I see him.'

'Swing for who?' asked Sam, walking in behind her.

Blythe turned around to be faced with Sam bundled up in a coat, holding up a pair of trousers.

'Ho, ho, ho,' he said, passing the trousers to Owen who scurried off to the kitchen with them. 'How's Turpin?' he asked.

'He's got an abscess, so he's going to be sore for a few days but he's fine.' She decided to save the news about the antibiotics until later; there were more pressing issues to address. 'Why aren't you dressed? You're backing out, aren't you? After I've kept my side of the bargain. It's not fair. I blooming well knew you'd let me down.' Anger was bubbling in her gut. She'd trusted him and he'd reneged on their agreement. Why was she not surprised? Because men frequently let her down. A picture of her father swam into her mind. 'I'm just disappointed, that's all.'

Sam pouted. 'But I am dressed.'

Exactly what she didn't need was Sam trying to be a smartarse. 'I meant dressed for the sexy Santa dinner.'

'Ahh, that's easily sorted.' In a couple of swift movements Sam removed his coat and whipped off his jumper to reveal a bare torso accompanied only by a bow tie and white cuffs. He pulled a Santa hat from the back pocket of his dress trousers and put it on. Blythe was momentarily stunned. He had a very nice body. Lightly sculpted with some definition around his abs and quite impressive biceps. He was the very essence of sexy Santa. 'How about now?' He grinned at her.

For a moment she struggled to find any words. 'Oh, well that's different. It's good. Thank you. I'll be getting on with...' She pointed to the kitchen, hoping to quickly escape before the rush of embarrassment she knew was coming reached her cheeks. She turned swiftly and, in her haste, immediately bumped into a chair. 'Whoops, sorry,' she said. As she reset that chair, she bumped into another and apologised to that too.

She tried to enter the kitchen, but the door only half opened. 'What's going on?' she asked the back of Vicky's head.

'Too many people,' said Vicky.

Blythe peered inside to see a number of men in various states of undress and some worried-looking caterers putting things in the oven. 'Let's get the men out of there. They can finish getting dressed in the office, then we need to brief them. How many of them know the routine?'

'Just two but they can learn it before people arrive.'

'Problem?' asked Sam behind her.

She spun around and came very close to his chest. He had a lemony, just-showered smell to him and she had to drag her eyes up to his face. 'There was meant to be a sort of dance routine in between courses, nothing fancy. Just a bit of fun but only two people know it.'

'Oh, come on. I've dressed up. You didn't say anything about prancing about.'

She feared he was going to bolt. 'It's fine. You don't have to dance. But let me show you the two dances on TikTok and then if you want to sit out you can.'

'Sit out? Like a maiden aunt?'

'Your words not mine,' she said, getting out her phone.

'Send me the links,' he said, opening the TikTok app on his phone.

'You're on TikTok?' Blythe was surprised and it probably showed on her face.

'I am. I don't post much. Film clips showing sets we've been involved with mainly. People love that sort of thing.'

The kitchen door opened and five topless men paraded out, followed by Vicky who had a bigger grin than the Grinch.

'We've not got enough Santas to have one per table,' said Blythe, grabbing Vicky by the arm and stopping her following the men into the office.

'Can't they double up?'

'With eight per table? It'd mean people waiting for their food.' Blythe closed her eyes so she could think.

'If you and I waited a table each and roped in two more people that would work. Although I'd definitely rather have one of them serving my meal than you. No offence,' said Vicky.

'But we could switch tables so each table has at least one course served by a Santa.'

'There you go,' said Vicky. 'We just need two more servers.'

With twenty minutes to go, Blythe managed to persuade Greg and Arthur to make up the numbers.

She popped her head around the office door to see ten Santas of varying degrees of sexiness gyrating to 'Here Comes Santa Claus'. Sam glared at her but Owen beamed in her direction. 'I think we've nailed it,' he said, wiggling his pelvis. She nodded her agreement and exited swiftly.

As ladies started to arrive, Christmas Carol took their coats and they were directed to the seating plan by Vicky. A particularly rowdy bunch came through the doors and in the middle of the excitable women were Phyllis and Arthur, who was sporting a wide grin and an apron emblazoned with a naked man apart from a strategically placed Santa hat.

'I know I'm not what they ordered but I thought this was fun,' he said.

'It's perfect, Arthur.' And Blythe ushered him through to the office. 'Thanks for coming. It's all hands on deck,' said Blythe.

'Ooh, which one's Dec?' asked Phyllis, eyeing the Santas and rubbing her hands together with glee.

32

11th December

Vicky had been looking forward to a fun evening of being waited on by sexy Santas but found she actually quite enjoyed the slightly manic dashing about as the catering staff directed them all out with the starters and instructions for who had special dietary requirements. She couldn't get over Owen. It had been a long time since she'd seen so much of him but the sight of him topless had brought all sorts of memories rushing back – most of them X-rated. He looked gorgeous in that innocent cheeky way he had. Every time she looked over at him he was watching her and he beamed that smile of his that made her insides melt. On one occasion she'd almost tipped a plate into someone's lap because she was watching Owen rather than what she was doing. With the starters delivered she'd only been a couple of minutes late sitting down to her meal, and the chatter on her table was hilarious.

A lot of the ladies hadn't experienced anything like it and some clearly hadn't been out for quite some time. The wine was flowing and the food was so delicious Vicky felt a little sad as she ate her last mouthful. From the back of the hall the music started, a whoop went up from the tables and people hurriedly finished their starters. The Santas, led by Seb and Fraser, strutted down either side of the hall to 'Walking in a Winter Wonderland' and the women began to clap. When it got to 'Here Comes Santa Claus' the crowd went wild. Arthur followed the others down and gave the crowd a flash of what was underneath his apron – which was his cardigan and brown corduroy trousers – but it still elicited a scream from the hyper audience.

The Santas lined up with Seb and Fraser at the front and they ran through the TikTok routine but there was only one person Vicky was watching – Owen. He was loving every minute of it and it reminded her of how much fun they used to have. She wondered when that had changed.

'It's the Grinch,' shouted someone, and for a moment Sam looked wrong-footed.

'Wow, he's gorgeous,' said a lady on Vicky's table. 'He can rummage in my Christmas box any time!' There was a hoot of laughter from those around her.

'Come on, let's clear away while they're doing this,' said Blythe, as the Santas began repeating their little routine. Vicky reluctantly stopped watching Owen wiggling his peachy little bum at the crowd and hastily collected up the plates from her table and ferried them into the kitchen, where the caterers were ready with main meals. A cheer went up from inside the hall, followed by a round of applause and whistles before a bevy of Santas descended on the kitchen with more plates.

'Did you like my moves?' asked Owen, his eyebrows dancing.

Vicky had planned to play it cool. Stick to all her reasons why resurrecting something with Owen was a really bad idea, but the sight of him in that bow tie and cuffs was too much. She grabbed him by the shoulders and pulled him towards her. He didn't resist and a whoop went up from the packed kitchen as they kissed.

'Oh my,' said Phyllis. 'Do we all get one of those?'

Blythe tapped Vicky on the shoulder and thrust some plates of turkey into her hands. Owen gave her a little wave as she was bustled back out into the hall. It had been a brief kiss but it had been exactly what she needed. Whatever her head was telling her, it was wrong. She still loved Owen and she really wanted to show him just how much but another five plates of turkey needed to be delivered to the next table along.

As everyone settled down to their main courses Blythe took to the floor. 'Just a quick announcement from me. Your entry ticket was also a raffle ticket and the raffle will be drawn by two of our sexiest Santas…' she paused for the inevitable whoops, which came on cue, '…between your main course and dessert. And please remember no touching,' she said, giving Vicky and Phyllis hard stares. Phyllis tried to look innocent.

Given how many meals the caterers had had to produce, the main meal was exceptionally good. But then, Vicky reasoned, you couldn't go far wrong with a turkey dinner, pigs in blankets and a shitload of wine. Everyone on her table was clearly having a great evening and a quick look around the hall showed her that was replicated twelve times over. Blythe gave her an anxious look. Vicky responded with a double thumbs up, which made her smile.

More music announced round two of the Santas and the same routine although they seemed to be growing in confidence and were definitely more polished and, if she wasn't mistaken, even more suggestive this time. When Owen thrust his hips in Vicky's direction she almost lost her sausage. More hooting, clapping and general merriment ensued until the music ended, the Santas took a bow and left Fraser and Greg to draw the raffle, while the others cleared away the plates.

The kitchen was a hive of activity and Vicky was working out where best to stand so she was out of the way while she waited for the Christmas pudding slices to be put into bowls when someone grabbed her hand and bustled her out the back of the kitchen and into the car park.

Blythe thought she could finally relax when everyone was tucking into pudding but someone on Arthur's table started a chant of 'One more time!' She glanced around but the Santas were already getting to their feet to the delight of the audience. Seb's brother took his bowl of Christmas pudding with him to the back of the hall while Christmas Carol scuttled through the tables to restart the music. 'Walking in a Winter Wonderland' blared out much louder this time and the Santas trooped down to the front. It may have been the wine but they were definitely embracing their roles now. She couldn't look at Greg – there were some things you could never unsee and your stepdad twerking to Christmas songs was one of them. Blythe did a quick Santa count. There was one missing. As she scanned them again she caught Sam's eye. 'Sorry, last time I promise,' she mouthed at him.

'It'd better be,' he mouthed back. The happy faces, empty plates and ear-splitting shrieks told her the evening had been a success. They rowed up at the front in time to the music and she realised Owen was the missing Santa. Oh well, he'd been there for most of it. Missing the impromptu encore was allowed. For the other performances she had been fretting that everything was going to plan, worrying about the two dads at the back bumping into each other and whether the plates were hot enough. But now the meal had been devoured and the evening was drawing to a close she could sit back, sip some wine and enjoy the entertainment.

The Santas all appeared to be enjoying themselves this time around. Even Sam seemed to be finding his groove. His thrusting was subtle but compulsive viewing. She would have liked to have put the sensations she was experiencing down to the wine but given she'd barely touched hers she knew it wasn't the alcohol causing her giddiness. The routine ended and the Santas took a bow. The women were on their feet. Across the room Sam locked her in a stare. A twitch of a smile on his lips, he gave her the briefest of nods. He'd done her proud – they all had.

Seb waved his arms to try to get the crowd to lower their volume. 'The guys have all agreed to photos if you'd like to take some selfies with us. Arthur will be taking donations for charity.' Arthur appeared with his trusty collecting bucket and there was a great deal of rummaging in purses.

'I want a picture with the Grinch!' shouted one lady, and a queue quickly formed next to Sam.

Blythe finally waved off the caterers and surveyed the mess. The evening had been a huge success and the sexy Santas a definite hit but now the clean-up operation started. Arthur,

Phyllis and a few others had volunteered to help and were diligently putting rubbish into black sacks. There was no sign of Vicky but then she would have to get back for Eden. The Santas had got changed while she had been restacking the dishwashers; only Seb and Fraser had put their heads around the door to say they were leaving and to sign up for next year as they'd had a ball. Blythe was disappointed not to see Sam but he had kept his side of the bargain and she was grateful to him for that. It was likely the sight of him in his sexy Santa outfit would stay with her for a lot longer than it should – Greg's too, for completely different reasons. Arthur poured each of the helpers a glass of wine from a bottle he'd kept back and that spurred them on to finish.

'My, my, that was a night. Wasn't it?' said Phyllis, putting on her coat.

'We raised a lot,' said Arthur, rattling his bucket.

'Leonora will be over the moon,' said Phyllis.

'Bum, I was meant to text her,' said Blythe. 'You guys go and I'll lock up here.'

'If you're sure,' said Arthur, ushering Phyllis to the door.

Phyllis diverted to whisper in Blythe's ear. 'If you've got any of those bow ties and cuffs spare…'

'I'll drop a set through your door,' said Blythe.

Phyllis's face lit up. 'Happy Christmas.' Blythe had a feeling it would be for Phyllis but she feared for poor Norman.

Blythe locked the back door and sat on a chair in the kitchen while she whizzed off a text to Leonora. She grabbed a bow tie and cuffs for Phyllis, along with her coat, and began switching off lights as she made her way to the main doors. She opened them to leave and almost bumped straight into Sam.

'Thank goodness you're still here. Turpin's gone AWOL.'

'He can go out, Sam. The vet said it was okay.' She shooed him out into the cold and locked the door.

'But he's not eaten anything and I've checked his usual places and there's no sign of him. I called him but he's not exactly one of my fans.'

'You made plenty of those tonight,' said Blythe, pulling on her woolly hat as they turned to walk towards the green.

It was hard to tell in the light but he seemed to go a bit pink around the edges. 'Were you one of them?'

The question caught her off guard. 'I'm very grateful to you for keeping your end of the bargain. I bet it wasn't as bad as you were expecting. Was it?'

'Far worse,' he said with a laugh. 'Those women were wild. And Phyllis…' He shook his head in mock disapproval.

'It's always the quiet ones.'

'I'm not saying it was my favourite thing but I did have more fun than I expected to. A couple of the lads have invited me out for a beer in the new year and I'll probably catch up with Fraser for a game of squash.'

'Now look at you – making friends,' she said, and he playfully bumped into her as they walked. 'I told you the locals were friendly.'

'I'd like to get to know some of them better.'

She wasn't sure what he meant by that, but they were nearing his cottage so it was easier to not think about it and focus on the cat. 'Shall we check around here first for Turpin and then inside?'

'Makes sense. If he hears you he might follow us.'

Blythe began calling Turpin as they walked along the edge of the green and up to Sam's cottage but there was no sign of him. They walked on past and doubled back – nothing.

'I'll check the garden if you want to see if he's inside,' said Sam.

'Sure.' Blythe let herself into the utility. Turpin hadn't touched his food. She was walking through the kitchen to check the rest of the house when something caught her eye and she reversed back.

Sam joined her in the kitchen. 'I can't see him,' he said.

'I can.' Blythe pointed to the top of one of the kitchen cupboards where Sam kept his wok and there, just visible, was the end of a ginger tail. Turpin had curled up and gone to sleep in it.

Sam followed where Blythe was looking. 'Seriously? How the hell did he get up there?'

'I guess he feels safer hidden away. Poor thing. Hey, Turpin, you okay?' she called up. An ear popped up above the edge of the wok.

'How do we get him down?' asked Sam.

'I'd leave him. Maybe you could put a chair on the worktop so it's not so far for him to jump down.'

'Good idea. Look, I'm sorry I dragged you over here but then again I'd never have spotted him up there. It's like extreme "Where's Wally?"' He picked up one of the bar stools and put it on the counter to aid Turpin's descent from the wok.

'No worries.' They held each other's gaze a moment too long and Blythe felt a rush of something that scared her – desire. A picture of Sam in his sexy Santa garb danced into her head and made her flustered. 'I should go. And thanks

again for tonight. For being a sexy Santa. And dressing up...'
Why did it sound sexual? She needed to leave. 'Leonora will
be delighted.' She scanned her phone to see if she'd had
a reply. When she looked up Sam was standing very close
to her.

'You don't have to go. You could stay for coffee.' He
raised an eyebrow.

Could she? Did he mean just coffee? But the look in his
eyes told her he didn't mean just coffee. They *never* meant
just coffee. Blythe felt herself heat up but that was because
she was wearing too many layers indoors. 'Maybe I'll take
some things off.' Sam's other eyebrow jumped up to join
the first. Blythe pulled off her gloves and shoved them in
her coat pocket in an attempt to cool down. 'I mean I'm
a bit warm but yes, coffee would be nice. As long as it's
decaffeinated. I only drink decaf.' What was she rambling
on about? It had been a while since she'd been in this
situation and it had taken her by surprise.

'You sure?' he asked, stepping closer. 'Because I have tea.'
He carefully took off her woolly hat and she feared her
hair was sticking up in all directions as it usually did, but
Sam wasn't looking at her hair. 'Coffee will be fine.' Her
voice had gone all breathy. What was she doing? This was
Sam. Sam was a flight risk. But then everything didn't have
to be about long-term relationships. *A hook-up could be
fun*, she thought. There was the sexy Santa outfit again.
But who was she kidding? How awkward would that be
living in the same village with someone she'd had casual sex
with? Or worse, would he see her as a friend with benefits?
Nothing more than a shag buddy. 'No!' She said it a bit
louder than she intended and they both jumped. 'I should

go,' she said, diving a hand into her coat pocket for her gloves and pulling out the bow tie and cuffs she'd taken for Phyllis.

Sam blinked. 'Wow, you did come prepared.'

'Actually, no. Whilst you did look amazing in them... these are for Phyllis.' Sam tilted his head. 'Try not to think about it. I'm not sure I'll be able to face Norman and his iced buns after this.'

Sam chuckled. 'You're funny. I don't know if this will sway your decision about the decaf coffee but I really like you, Blythe. You're smart, funny and you're on my mind a lot. In summary, I think you're great. Aside from all the Christmas and Grinch shenanigans that is.'

'Sam, that's lovely of you to say. And I like you too apart from the strange Christmas phobia. I don't know what I'm looking for but I know it's not a one-night stand so... Thanks but no thanks.' She shrugged.

Sam was giving her an odd look – one she'd seen him sport a few times before. 'The Christmas thing. It stems from my childhood.' He looked tense as he scratched his ear and looked away. 'This is in confidence, right?'

'Of course.'

'My father left when I was a baby and my mum struggled with drink and drugs.' Blythe knew her shock at his statement showed on her face. Sam held up a palm. 'Not the hard stuff, mainly weed and ecstasy but that's where all her money went. I was the kid on free school meals, with a uniform that didn't fit and plimsolls instead of school shoes whatever the weather.' Blythe's heart broke for the little boy Sam had been but didn't feel she could interrupt his story.

'We muddled along but at Christmas it was the worst. I wrote letters to Santa like all the other kids did. I never understood why he never wrote back.' Sam let out a derisory snort. 'At Christmas I'd still put up a pillowcase for him to fill but he never did. My mum told me it was because I was on the naughty list. One year I was desperate for a Tamagotchi – all my mates had one. I didn't put a foot wrong for weeks because of the threat of not getting one for Christmas and still there was nothing on Christmas morning. For years I believed I was too bad to get a present. I was so ashamed. I'd pretend I was sick so I missed the first day back at school after the holidays. I couldn't face my mates when they were telling me about all the stuff they'd been given because they were the kids on the "nice" list. I couldn't tell them I was one of the others. I bet I was the only kid who cried happy tears the day I found out Santa wasn't real.'

Blythe hadn't realised she was crying until a sob escaped. 'That's awful,' she said, pulling a tissue from her pocket. 'I'm so sorry.'

'I didn't mean to upset you.' He swallowed hard. 'It's why I hate Christmas. I guess it's kind of triggering and when I hear people lying to their kids about this wonderful guy who's going to bring them presents because they've been good all year I want to scream at them. I just can't cope with people who lie; it does so much damage.'

Blythe blew her nose. A little voice in her head unhelpfully reminded her that she'd lied to Sam all those months ago when she'd sold him a cottage that wasn't for sale. But that wasn't a big lie. Not a brutal one like the one his mum had told him as a child. 'You shouldn't lie to kids. Not like that.'

Sam shrugged. 'It was better at secondary school.'

'Because you knew it was a fairy tale?'

He gave a wan smile. 'Because my mum got done for possession and I was taken into care. I was in and out of a children's home. But it was okay. I was the kid who hated Christmas. The weirdo. Looks like I still am.'

Blythe felt terrible. 'I'm so sorry I said those things. I had no idea.'

'It's okay, really. It's my issue. I know that. A lot of expensive shrinks have told me that over the years. I can deal with it now. It's why I try to keep away from Christmas but I've realised over these past few months that I can't keep away from you.'

Blythe dried her eyes. 'But I'm always going to remind you of Christmas.'

'Maybe you're the aversion therapy I need.' He stepped closer and took her in his arms. For a moment she hesitated. Men always left her. How long before Sam did the same? But then sometimes didn't you have to take a chance? Their lips touched and Blythe melted into his kiss. It was suddenly cut short when Turpin jumped out of the wok sending it flying in their direction. Thankfully Sam had lightning-fast reflexes and grabbed it a moment before it whacked one of them on the head. Unfortunately, it brought their kissing to an abrupt end.

'I should probably go,' said Blythe, touching her lips. 'But I'd like to see where this leads. If you can stand dating someone who loves Christmas.'

Sam hugged the wok to his chest. 'I think I'm prepared to take that risk.'

33

The Christmas fayre was a big deal for Holly Cross. They closed off the roads around the green and filled them with stalls selling every conceivable thing you could want for Christmas along with an array of homemade crafts and gift ideas. As well as being a great money spinner for their chosen charity it was also a fun evening. People came from far and wide as it was also a good opportunity to see the village lights.

Various volunteers spent the morning getting the stalls in place so the vendors could set up from midday, but it was really after dark that it all got going. Blythe managed to slip out of work early so she could lend a hand. The fayre was entirely Leonora's domain but as this year Vicky had a stall, Blythe was going to give her a hand. Vicky had been making pom-poms at every available opportunity for weeks and Blythe was hoping it would all be worth the effort.

It was a crisp December evening, and Blythe's breath plumed out in front of her as she walked. As long as it wasn't raining she liked it cold. Somehow it felt more Christmassy that way. She had no idea how she'd cope in a warmer climate at this time of year. She doubted it would feel the same to be on the beach in a bikini opening your pressies. She drew closer to the green, where Christmas music was mingling with chatter and laughter. The smells of gingerbread, chestnuts and mulled wine filled the air as she strolled past the first stalls. The two elderly sisters from Rock Cottage had excelled again with their knitting skills – their stall was filled with blankets, scarves and an array of interesting woolly hats. Lots of stalls vied for her attention – there was everything from handmade jewellery to penguin slippers, and the crowds were already pouring in.

Blythe found Vicky's stall over near Sam's cottage between a stall selling chocolate stirrers and another adorned with festive birdhouses. Blythe glanced across the road. The night of the kiss was etched in her mind. They had exchanged frequent texts but Sam had been away on business again, although he was due back soon. She was trying not to think too much about it and certainly not to read too much into it. It was just a kiss. Although it had been a fantastic one, she had no idea where things would lead. She knew she liked Sam but she also knew she didn't want to get hurt.

'Hiya, how's it going?' she asked, standing back to get a proper look at Vicky's stall. There were big bold signs clipped to the table and the overhead canopy detailing prices and some interesting slogans including: *One day only! Exclusive to Holly Cross Christmas Fayre* and *You're the only person who hasn't bought one!*

Vicky pointed to the pile of pom-pom decorations on the table and then to the boxes underneath. 'Slow. I'll not rival Elon Musk yet. But thanks for coming.'

'No worries. I figured we could take it in turns to man

the stall and then go for a look around the others. I might get Greg some penguin slippers.'

'Ooh, good idea,' said Vicky.

'Where's Eden?'

'The Rainbows, Brownies and Guides are doing Christmas songs on the green in an hour so Snowy Owl is filling them full of hot chocolate and going over the words of "Give Me Joy in My Heart" one more time. I can't convince Eden that it's not "sing lasagne to the king of kings".'

Blythe came around to Vicky's side of the stall and realised there were two piles of green pom-poms. She picked one up. It had a Santa hat on, wild eyebrows and a creepy smile. 'This isn't a sprout. Is it?'

'It's the Grinch.' Vicky grinned at her. 'After Sam was such a hit at the sexy Santa night, I had a flash of inspiration. People who come to see the lights will want a souvenir. What better than a lovingly handmade Grinch tree decoration?' Vicky was nodding furiously. 'I whipped them up at record speed.' Vicky held up another sign that read: *Get your Grinch souvenirs here!*

Blythe had to admire her initiative. 'Anyone bought one yet?'

'No, but it's early. I figured if I had a stand near Sam's cottage I could lure a few people in when they were admiring the lights.'

'Good idea.' The mention of Sam had Blythe overheating. Thoughts of their kiss made her roll her lips together.

'Any chance of him making an appearance? Preferably in his sexy Santa outfit?' asked Vicky.

'When it's two degrees outside, and just to sell your pom-poms?'

'Fair point. But I figured now he's got over his Christmas strop we'd see more of him.'

This was uncomfortable. What Sam had told her about his childhood was weighing heavy on her and how she'd reacted to his dislike of all things festive. She also felt bad about what she'd done. The Grinch sign flashed at her as a reminder. Previously she'd been vocal about Sam's loathing of Christmas and how silly she'd thought it was. Now she knew the reason, she felt awful about what she'd said. But how could she put that right without betraying a confidence?

'I'd not call it a strop exactly. More an aversion. Maybe I was too quick to judge. And I'm not sure him helping out one time means he'll be embracing the festive season.'

'Miserable git,' said Vicky, rearranging her Grinches.

'No, he's really not...'

Vicky pulled her chin in and gave Blythe a sideways look. 'You've changed your tune. Why's that I wonder?'

'No reason.' Blythe felt her cheeks flush.

'OMG you've hooked up with Sam. And you've not told me about it!' Vicky's voice was rising.

'Shhh!' Blythe waved at Vicky to keep her voice down. 'There's nothing to tell.' Vicky flicked her hair over her shoulder dismissively and stared at Blythe. 'Well, not much to tell. We kissed that's all.'

'That's all? That's huge. He's the first guy you've kissed in, what, a year?'

'Bloody hell, Vicky. Keep your voice down.' The man from the chocolate stirrer stall was inching closer as he rearranged the same stirrers for the umpteenth time.

'I'm pleased for you. I really am. I like Sam. I especially liked...' Vicky did an impression of the sexy Santa thrusting.

'Stop it. I don't know if it's going anywhere.'

'Surely that's up to you. If it was me, I'd be heading straight to the bedroom dragging Sam by his sexy Santa bow tie.'

'But if it turns out to be just sex, how awkward would that be living in the same village?'

'Probably worth it though,' said Vicky, repeating the thrusting. 'And what if he sweeps you off your feet, you get married at St Bart's and this time next year there's three stockings hung up for Santa?'

Blythe blinked rapidly. 'Bloody hell, Vicky, slow down. Married and pregnant by next Christmas are two things that are definitely not in my plans.'

'Plans change,' said Vicky with a shrug as Owen approached the stall, leaned over and gave Vicky a passionate kiss. It all got a bit fervent and Blythe feared Owen was going to mount the table.

When pom-poms started to roll, Blythe had to intervene. 'Hey there, Romeo and Juliet,' she said, grabbing some of the rolling pom-poms.

'Oh, hi,' said Owen, finally pulling away from Vicky.

'I think of us as more Jay-Z and Beyoncé,' said Vicky, rearranging her bobble hat. Owen gazed at her adoringly.

'And when were you going to tell me about this little development?' But it made Blythe feel a whole lot better about not telling Vicky about her kiss with Sam sooner.

'I kind of did tell you. Well, I hinted.' Vicky looked coy – not a look Blythe associated with her friend.

'You didn't.'

'You know I said I couldn't see you this week because a thing came up?' Owen sniggered and Vicky batted him on the upper arm. 'Owen was the thing. I would have said before only I wasn't sure where it was going. Sorry.'

Blythe was feeling exactly the same, which was why she hadn't mentioned her kiss with Sam. 'That's okay. But we need to have a proper catch-up before Christmas.'

'Definitely. Thanks for understanding,' said Vicky.

'Why don't you two have a look around the fayre before it gets too busy and I'll keep watch on your stall,' offered Blythe. She was so pleased that Vicky was letting Owen back into her life. Some people were just meant to be together.

'Great, thanks,' said Owen, taking Vicky's hand and pulling her away.

'Don't watch. Sell!' instructed Vicky as she was towed away.

Thirty minutes later Blythe was getting flustered by the big crowd of people around the stall. Where was Vicky? She'd been ages browsing the fayre. Blythe tipped some more pom-pom decorations out of the box and tried to attend to the customers in an orderly way. One lady had two in her hand and her head down studying more.

'Can I help you with those?' asked Blythe.

The woman looked up. There was a moment where they both smiled before placing the other. 'You!' said Blythe, recognising her customer as the woman who had been creeping around Sam's cottage. The woman dropped the pom-poms and turned to disappear into the crowd. 'Oh no you don't!' Blythe was determined not to lose her again. 'Hold the fort!' she yelled to the stallholder next to her as she dashed from behind the stand and grabbed the hood of the woman's coat.

'Ow!' she shrieked, and the crowd all turned to look.

'Didn't pay,' said Blythe by way of explanation.

'I'm back!' called Vicky, holding up an armful of brown paper bags. It appeared she'd spent her profits before she'd earned them.

'Great. Can you take over while I have a chat with this lady?'

'Sure.' Vicky dumped her packages, clapped her hands together and turned her attention to her many customers.

Blythe linked arms with the mystery woman. 'I think it's time you and I had a talk.'

'I can't stop – I need to be somewhere,' she said, although she was walking in step with Blythe as they moved away from the crowded stalls.

'It won't take long. All I want to know is who you are, what you were doing snooping around that cottage over there and why you keep popping up in Holly Cross.'

The woman sighed heavily. 'It's going to sound crazy.'

'Try me.' They had reached Sam's cottage so Blythe sat down on the wall and gestured for the woman to join her. 'I'm Blythe, by the way.'

The woman hesitated then sighed resignedly. 'Dawn,' she said, dusting the wall before gingerly perching on it. She glanced over her shoulder at the cottage. 'I'm not sure what I was hoping to find here. It's all a bit of a mystery really.'

'I love a mystery,' said Blythe, now completely hooked.

Dawn pressed her lips into a flat line. 'You see, I came here because I was given this car and the only address in the sat nav was this cottage.'

Blythe felt this wasn't much of a mystery at all. 'The previous owner probably came to see the lights once.'

'From Manchester?' asked Dawn, with a tilt of her head.

Blythe had to concede that was a fair way to come. 'It's very popular.'

'He travelled all over the country visiting nature reserves. So why would this be the only address?'

'I don't know,' said Blythe, wondering why this woman was so interested in what her car's previous owner had got up to. Vicky was now waving at her to come back as the queue to the stall was snaking across the pavement and into the road. 'Maybe they knew their way to those other places.'

'He always said he liked exploring *new* places. Tracking down rare bird species. But I've only found one spotters' book with anything detailed in it and the last entry was August 2010. I'm not sure he was going birdwatching. I thought perhaps he was coming here. But I don't know why. I feel like I didn't know him at all.'

'Know who?' Blythe was losing track of what Dawn was talking about. Vicky's waving was getting more frantic. Blythe was going to have to apologise and go and help.

'My dad. He left me the car in his will.' Dawn looked dejected.

'Oh, I'm sorry to hear that. Perhaps he was thinking of moving here. Retiring to the countryside. A lot of people do. I'm an estate agent. In fact, I sold this house just a few months ago.'

Dawn perked up. 'I don't suppose you'd be able to tell me who lived here. Confidentiality and all that.'

Murray was gone, what harm could it do. 'Well, don't go broadcasting that I've told you but the previous owner was a friend of mine so I'm sure he wouldn't have minded. It was Murray Henderson.'

Dawn turned so fast she almost toppled off the wall. Blythe steadied her. 'You've got that wrong. It can't have been.'

Blythe hated it when people challenged facts. 'I knew Murray really well. He lived in this village for years. I can assure you he did live here.'

'But how is that even possible?'

'You've lost me,' said Blythe, ignoring Vicky jumping up and down across the road in a desperate attempt to get her attention.

'Murray Henderson lived in Manchester. I know that for a fact because I'm his daughter.'

34

18th December

Blythe almost toppled off the cottage wall herself. She'd not been expecting that. 'Maybe there's been some sort of mix-up.' Although Blythe was struggling to think what it could be. How could one person live in two places? They couldn't.

'My dad, Murray Henderson, died in May. This is him,' said Dawn, opening her purse and showing Blythe a dog-eared graduation photograph of much younger versions of Dawn and an unmistakable Murray.

'But that makes no sense.' As she said it a few queries pinged into Blythe's head to challenge what she thought she knew. 'I mean he used to go away quite regularly because he was a big birdwatcher.'

'That's what he told us...'

'Us?' questioned Blythe.

'Me and Mum. Well, before she died five years ago. He was always off to different places all over the country. And after he died, I wanted to feel a bit closer to him and I thought perhaps visiting those same places might help. But when I started looking there was no information anywhere. I'd inherited his car but not used it so I checked the sat nav expecting to find a long list of addresses and postcodes. The only address was this one.' She pointed over her shoulder at the cottage.

'That's why we caught you checking the place over,' said Blythe.

'I'm sorry. I don't know what I was expecting to find. Some answers to my questions I suppose.' She turned to face Blythe and took a deep breath. 'Who lived here with him?' she asked.

'No one. Murray has always lived alone.'

'That's good. I think. I can't really get my head around him having a home here as well as... well, at home. Was there someone local he was close to?'

'Only Turpin the cat,' said Blythe.

Dawn sighed heavily. 'Really?' She looked doubtful. 'He'd never let us have a cat when I was a child because he worried it would hunt the garden birds.'

'He didn't buy this cat. Turpin got evicted from the pub...' Dawn was giving her an odd look. 'Long story.'

Dawn studied the cottage. 'It's a beautiful place. Maybe renting this cottage was his way of escaping from life at home.'

'It wasn't r—' Blythe stopped talking. Walking through the crowd carrying a holdall was Sam. The last thing she wanted was to have to explain to Dawn in front of Sam that she'd sold Murray's cottage without it actually being for sale.

'Blythe! Help needed now!' hollered Vicky, who was no longer visible thanks to the swarm of people around her stall.

'I'm sorry, I need to help my friend,' said Blythe, getting to her feet. She was relieved when Dawn did the same.

'That's okay. I've taken up too much of your time as it is. Although I still have so many questions.'

So did Blythe. Not least of all why Murray's next of kin didn't seem to have inherited his property. Otherwise, why would she think it was rented? Blythe handed Dawn her business card. 'Next time you're visiting…' Was visiting the right word? Blythe wasn't sure. 'Or passing this way, call me and we can have a coffee. I'll tell you what I can. It might help you solve the puzzle.'

'Thank you. That's really kind of you.'

'Blythe! Drowning here!' yelled Vicky.

'Sorry,' said Blythe. 'Bye.' And she hurried across the road and into the Christmas fayre crowds.

'Thank goodness you're back,' said a flustered-looking Vicky. 'I'm rushed off my trotters here.'

'Where's Owen?'

'He got waylaid by Norman's monster sausage.'

Sam was making his way around the throng of people. 'Actually, hang on. I'll be back in a mo,' said Blythe.

'What?' But before Vicky could protest Blythe slunk into the crowd and headed for Sam.

She darted around the back of the stalls, and popped out by the toffee apples. 'Hey, you,' she said, walking in step with Sam.

His beaming smile told her he was pleased to see her and that made her heart give a happy skip. 'Hello. I was just thinking about you.'

'All good I hope,' said Blythe. She gave a cursory glance at Vicky's stall as they passed at a safe distance and was pleased to see Owen had now turned up.

'I was thinking maybe we could grab a bite to eat this evening?'

'Ah.' Blythe pointed at the Christmas fayre. 'I'm going to be a bit busy until late as I promised Vicky I'd help her out. I could ask Norman to save us a couple of his monster sausages. The fayre closes at ten o'clock if you can wait until then.'

He checked his watch. 'No problem.'

The Holly Cross brass band started up, which drew everyone's attention. The children were all rowed up and looked rosy-cheeked as they broke into song. Blythe couldn't help her grin – it was such a cute thing. Sam leaned into her ear. 'Too festive for me. I'll see you later.' And he strode off.

Blythe was taking down the signs from Vicky's stall and Vicky was selling off the last of her pom-poms at a discounted price when Sam strolled over. He was freshly showered and she got a whiff of aftershave as he leaned in to kiss her cheek. 'Are you all done here?' he asked. 'Because I'm starving and all I can think about is Norman's monster sausage.'

'Oh man,' said Owen, appearing with a cardboard box. 'Norman's sausage is the best.' He put the box down. 'It's like this big, man,' he said, holding his hands about eight inches apart. 'The thing is huge.'

'Okay,' butted in Vicky. 'Enough about Norman's monster sausage.' She linked her arm through Owen's. 'We will finish up here,' she said. 'Go on. You two love birds can clear off now.' She gave Blythe her bag of things she'd bought from the fayre as well as a big hug. 'Thanks for your help tonight.' She whispered in Blythe's ear, 'I bet Sam's sausage is even bigger than Norman's.'

Blythe snorted a laugh. Vicky was incorrigible.

There was a buzz of tired happiness as they weaved their way between people dismantling stalls and packing up their Christmassy contents. Sarvan was handing out free mugs of hot chocolate to the remaining helpers and waved Blythe and Sam over.

'Here you go,' he said, handing them two steaming mugs. 'How did Vicky get on tonight?'

'She pretty much sold out. Only a few pom-pom sprouts left.'

'Did you bag some bargains?' he asked nodding at her bag.

'Penguin slippers for Greg but shhh they're a surprise.'

They waved their goodbyes and walked on cupping their drinks. 'Guess who turned up this evening?' asked Blythe.

'Santa. The real Grinch. Elvis?' suggested Sam.

'Even more unlikely than them. It was the woman who was snooping around your cottage and you'll never guess who she is.'

'A Jehovah's Witness on overtime?'

'Nope. She's Murray's daughter!' Blythe was expecting a suitably shocked response from Sam but he just nodded. 'This is huge,' she said, lifting her arm and almost spilling her hot chocolate. She brought Sam up to speed on what she had learned from Dawn. 'You see,' she concluded. 'He was living a lie this whole time.'

'I thought you said Murray was a good person.'

'I did and he is... well... he was.'

'But there never is a justification for lying to people. Not people who you claim to care about.'

Blythe was going to protest some more but her own failings flooded her mind and instead she kept quiet. They sipped their drinks as they made their way over to where Norman and Phyllis were packing up.

Norman splayed out his arms. 'I've been looking forward to seeing you all day.'

'Really?' Blythe was intrigued.

'Yes, because you're my last customer and I can't wait to get home to bed. I think I might be getting a bit old for this.'

'Nonsense!' cut in Phyllis. She unsubtly looked Blythe and Sam up and down before pulling in her chin. 'Now what do we have here, I wonder.'

'Leave them be,' said Norman, handing over two hot dog buns with sausages hanging out of either end. Sam got out his wallet. 'Blythe has already paid. Looks like you owe her dinner,' said Norman with a wink.

'I guess I do,' said Sam. 'Thank you.'

They made their way over to one of the benches and sat themselves down to eat. Blythe munched away happily whilst watching Vicky and Owen larking around with Eden. It was lovely to see the two of them behaving like teenagers again, with the addition of Eden who was giggling wildly. Sam made a noise and it drew Blythe's attention.

'Sorry,' he said. 'Owen is right; Norman's monster sausage really is the best thing ever.'

'Shall I add it to the growing list of things you like about Holly Cross?'

Sam gave her a look that made her insides flip. 'You know you're top of that list, right?'

'I do now,' said Blythe, concentrating on her sausage and trying to be nonchalant.

'You see the thing is…' began Sam.

'Oh no. I don't like it when there's a thing. This never ends well for me. Does there have to be a thing?' asked Blythe popping in the last of her hot dog.

'I just want to be completely honest with you, Blythe.'

Blythe braced herself. 'Okay, out with it.'

Sam's eyebrows twitched but he quickly regained focus. 'The meeting I've just come back from was with a company that sets up shared warehouse space. It's nearer to London and they're offering competitive rates. Most of the film work is in London so it would save on transportation, but it would mean moving my business lock, stock and authentic traditional beer barrel back to the city.'

'But you're settled here. Aren't you?' asked Blythe.

'A year ago, I would have jumped at it.'

'And now?' Blythe swallowed hard.

Sam turned to look at her. 'I don't know. Something has changed. I've changed. It's not the easy decision I thought it would be. When I bought this place I was looking for somewhere that worked with the business. I wasn't looking to put down roots.'

'So, you're still thinking about selling up then?' asked Blythe.

Sam reached across and took her hand. 'I've got a lot to think about.'

35

23rd December

The money Vicky had made at the Christmas fayre together with her dog walking had enabled her to buy all the things Eden needed, as well as a couple of presents on her list. She enjoyed the dog walking and she'd lost a couple of pounds thanks to the exercise, but it was hard to juggle her job, being a mum and walking the dogs. If she was honest if it wasn't for Blythe and a number of other locals she'd have lost most of her clients weeks ago.

It was the end of a busy day that had seen Owen call round to join them for tea and they'd ended up playing snakes and ladders until it was Eden's bedtime. She loved being back in a relationship with Owen. There was something familiar and yet exciting at the same time. So it was all good as long as she ignored the little voice in her head that was obsessed with who Eden's father might or might not be. Vicky came downstairs from putting Eden to bed. 'She's zonked but I doubt I'll get a lie-in tomorrow.'

'You would if I stayed over,' said Owen, taking her in his arms.

Vicky very much liked the thought of both Owen staying the night and of having a lie-in. Add to that a full cooked breakfast and that was pretty much Vicky's idea of heaven.

'I don't know,' said Vicky. 'It's Christmas Eve tomorrow. I'm sure there's lots you should be doing.'

'You for one thing,' said Owen, with a cheeky grin.

Grabbing a few hours alone was proving tricky, but Vicky was enjoying the time the three of them were spending together.

'It's a big week in Holly Cross, with the lights at their busiest and the judging of the Christmas village competition. Leonora will be stressing everyone out, there'll be last-minute niggles and the forecast is rain – you'd be best to avoid that pantomime if you can.'

Owen gave her a quizzical look. 'I love all that. And Leonora is a pussycat really.'

'She's a sabre-toothed tiger but with a bigger roar.'

'Maybe I like my women feisty.'

'Your women?' Vicky laughed. 'She'd tear you into a paper chain in a blink.'

'But *you* wouldn't.' He pulled her close. 'How about I stay over and I don't just mean tonight.'

Vicky knew exactly what he was suggesting and she'd been expecting it. It was the step she wasn't sure she was ready to make. 'I would love that.' Owen's face lit up and she hastily continued. 'But I have to think of Eden.' And that was truly how she felt. It was fine if Vicky's heart got broken but she couldn't let that happen to her daughter, who was becoming increasingly close to Owen.

'Why would Eden be a problem?'

'She's not. I just don't want us to play at happy families and then when our relationship ends for her to be disappointed.'

'Why would it end?' asked Owen. 'Are you planning on dumping me?' He did a comedy pout.

'No, but things happen. Children get attached and they think something is forever and it's not fair to let her think you're going to be part of her life if you're not.'

Owen smiled. 'I'll always be a part of her life.'

Vicky wobbled her head. 'You might like to think that, but things change.'

'I know maths was never my strong subject at school. Actually, I didn't have any strong subjects at school. But anyway, I've done the sums. I know Eden is my daughter.'

In the office Blythe was busy helping Heather put together some new property details. They were looking through the photographs Amir had taken, and Blythe was pointing out good and bad points about each of them. The next one she clicked on was of a dark and dingy living room absent of furniture but with an abundance of shadows and a carpet stain that looked like someone had just dragged out a body. 'This one we could caption – "Rare opportunity to purchase set from low-budget horror movie",' said Blythe, and Heather giggled.

Ludo called Blythe into his office. As she got to her feet the door opened and Sam walked in. She was thrilled to see him. 'What can I do for you?'

'I wondered if you fancied lunch,' said Sam. Blythe knew that was the moment everyone else in the office tuned in.

'Give me ten minutes and I'll meet you at that little Italian on the corner of—'

'It's okay, I'll wait,' said Sam, picking up a local property flyer and taking a seat.

'Blythe?' came Ludo's voice.

She had no choice. 'I'll be as quick as I can,' she said to Sam. She dashed into Ludo's office and really hoped it was just a quick word he wanted.

'Have a seat,' he said, shutting the door behind her. Blythe tried to position herself so that she could keep one eye on Sam through the glass. 'I wanted to talk to you about some changes.' Now Ludo had her full attention. 'I've received an offer for the business. Don't worry, I'd insist the new owner keep on my staff. It's a fair offer and I do want to cut down my hours. But there is another way I could do that and that would be to have someone step up to associate partner.'

'Who?' she asked, holding her breath. If it was Amir she may batter him with a stapler.

'You, of course,' said Ludo, with a chuckle. 'I've been thinking about winding back my hours for some time now and I think you're ready, Blythe. And this way I could still tinker around the edges.'

When Blythe glanced out of Ludo's office she could see Amir perched on her desk talking to Sam. She did not like the stern expression on Sam's face. She realised Ludo was still talking. 'Ludo, this is all brilliant and I am truly grateful. Don't you think it would be best if we sat down this afternoon and went through the details then?'

'I don't want to push you for an answer. You've got the Christmas break to think about it, but for now we could talk over how it might work in practice.' He looked keen.

This was her dream; Sam would have to wait. 'Okay, just let me put off my lunch date.' Blythe nodded into the shop.

Ludo looked in the same direction and the sight of Sam pulled him up. 'Well now, you didn't say there was a young man involved. You should go. This can wait,' he said, with a smile.

'Are you sure?' she asked, but Ludo was nodding enthusiastically. 'Thank you,' said Blythe, getting up and giving him a brief hug. He self-consciously shooed her out of his office.

'What's going on here?' asked Blythe, walking straight up to Amir.

'Amir was just telling me how you sold me a cottage that wasn't even for sale just to hit a sales target. Something you never bothered to mention to me. In fact, I'm certain you said it was new to the market.'

'Whoops. I'm sorry if I've said anything out of turn,' said Amir, looking like the snide tattletale he was.

'Shut up, Amir,' said Blythe. Amir slid off her desk and moved around to sit in his own chair where he had a front-row seat for whatever was about to play out.

Blythe turned back to Sam. 'Technically the cottage was for sale; I just didn't know that it was when I sold it to you.' Sam's eyebrows rose. 'But then I very quickly tracked down the solicitor dealing with the sale and the rest of the story you already know. It all ended well, didn't it?' Blythe smiled at Sam in the hope he would see her side of things.

'But it was basically lying, Blythe.'

She wobbled her head. 'I wouldn't call any of it lying. Maybe I didn't tell you everything but...'

'You didn't mention that Holly Cross was the Christmas capital of the world either, which makes me wonder what else you failed to tell me,' he said, getting to his feet.

'I didn't, but to be fair – look at you now. You've debuted as a sexy Santa and been to the Christmas fayre, which means Vicky owes me some crackers.' She said the last part more to herself than Sam.

'Why would Vicky owe you crackers?'

'Because she bet that I couldn't persuade you to like Christmas and I have.' Blythe was grinning but she didn't like the look on Sam's face.

'So, everything. You and me. It was all about winning some stupid bet?'

'Not at all. Look, let's go for lunch and I'll explain,' said Blythe, grabbing her coat.

Sam checked his watch. 'Actually, I'm not sure I'm free after all. I need to go.'

A weight hit the bottom of Blythe's stomach like one of her mum's mince pies. Her defences kicked in. 'That's fine because you were always going to choose something else over me,' she said, jutting out her chin. 'Men always do.' Sam paused as if thinking how to respond. 'It's fine, Sam. Go. It's not like it was a big thing anyway.'

Amir sniggered behind her until she held her stapler aloft and he stopped.

'Everything all right?' asked Ludo, emerging from his office.

'This client was just leaving,' said Blythe, opening the door for Sam.

Sam shook his head but walked out anyway, closing the door behind him.

The chill of December made her shiver. 'Are you all right?' asked Ludo, looking concerned.

'I'm not sure,' she said. The high and low she'd just experienced had given her emotional whiplash.

*

Blythe walked home with a heavy heart, two bottles of wine from Ludo and a box of chocolates from Mr Smith and Honey, who were looking forward to moving into their new flat in the new year. Noddy Holder was blaring out from the kitchen radio as her mum and Greg danced into the hallway and at the sight of Blythe fell about laughing. 'Hey, you've finished for Christmas. Get a snowball down you,' said Greg, dashing off to the kitchen while her mother readjusted her blouse.

'You're okay,' said Blythe. 'I'm not really in the mood for a snowball.'

'What's wrong, love?' asked her mum.

Where should she start? 'Ludo has offered me associate partner.'

'That's marvellous. I'm so proud of you,' said her mother, wrapping her in a tight hug. 'Greg, open the prosecco I bought for Christmas.'

'And Sam's dumped me,' mumbled Blythe into her mother's shoulder.

'On second thoughts, Greg, we need tea. Put the kettle on.' Her mum directed Blythe into the living room. 'Sit down and tell me all about it.'

Blythe flopped onto the sofa and gave her mother the short account of what had happened with Sam and how it had ended. What she didn't tell her was how stupid she felt to have messed up something that had the potential to be so special. 'It's my own fault,' said Blythe.

'If it wasn't meant to be it's nobody's fault,' said her mum.

'He's probably going to sell up and move back to London

anyway. If I look at it like that I've actually had a lucky escape.' Blythe tried to find a smile.

'Where is that tea, Greg?' called her mum.

'Stop your shouting,' said Greg, coming in with steaming mugs. 'I've put the prosecco in the fridge. We might be up to celebrating later. Would you like a mince pie with that?' he asked, handing one of the mugs to Blythe.

'I'm not feeling very Christmassy.' Blythe wrapped her hands around the hot mug.

'This Amir sounds like a right little stirrer. He got you into trouble over the sales targets and he should have kept his nose out of your relationship. If you ask me, it's all his fault.'

'Thanks, Mum.'

Blythe looked over at Greg who was perched on the arm of the chair. His eyebrows twitched and he stared at the carpet. His expression told her he didn't agree with his wife. Blythe felt a pang of guilt. 'It's not Amir's fault. It's mine for getting caught up in his stupid competition and agreeing to the silly bet with Vicky. And I should have come clean with Sam months ago about the situation with the cottage, especially once I knew how important honesty was to him.'

'I think honesty should be important to all of us,' said Greg.

'I know,' said Blythe, beating herself up a little bit more. She couldn't bear the look of disappointment on Greg's face. 'I've learned my lesson.' She puffed out a sigh.

'And this Sam, the boy who hates Christmas, was it serious with him?' asked her mum.

Blythe pouted. She thought back over the many arguments they'd had, as well as all the special little moments. Despite everything she'd felt and the hopes she'd had for her and Sam, sadly it didn't amount to much when she analysed it. 'Not really.'

'Hmm.' Greg was watching her. 'I think you two had something. Are you sure you can't retrieve it?' he asked.

Blythe shrugged. She thought back to Sam's face as he left the office. 'I don't think there's much point.' Perhaps there was never much there on Sam's side after all; maybe she'd imagined more than there was because it seemed to be very easy for Sam to walk away. Then again was she the common denominator here? Apparently everyone found her easy to walk away from.

'I think he's over-reacting,' said her mum. 'Any man would be lucky to have you. Don't you sell yourself short. I need to prepare the sprouts.'

'I don't think they need to go on yet,' said Blythe, but her mum just planted a kiss on her daughter's head and left the room.

Blythe and Greg exchanged glances and then both studied their mugs.

'What do you think I should do?' asked Blythe.

'Not really for me to say,' said Greg. He'd always been circumspect when it came to advising Blythe; as her stepfather he had explained long ago that it wasn't his place.

'I could do with a little help here and I really value what you think.'

Greg smiled. 'Then if I were you, I'd invite Sam here for Christmas.'

36

Christmas Eve

Blythe was in two minds about meeting Dawn. Part of her wanted to share her memories of Murray but at the same time she didn't want to inadvertently betray him. He'd been living a double life, that was for sure, but however hard she tried Blythe couldn't figure out why.

Dawn was already seated at a table in the pub when Blythe went in. 'Hi, Dawn. Nice to see you again. What can I get you to drink?'

'I'm fine, thanks.' She pointed at her coffee cup. 'I've only just got this.'

Blythe went to the bar and ordered a coffee. Arthur was in his usual seat. 'Who's the stranger in town?' he asked.

'You'd not believe me if I told you,' said Blythe, feeling that whilst she was fond of Arthur she didn't want rumours circulating about Murray. It didn't seem fair when he was no longer around to defend himself.

Arthur raised one eyebrow. 'Now I'm intrigued,' he said.

'I'll bring your coffee over,' said Sarvan, and Blythe was happy to escape Arthur's gaze.

'How was your journey?' asked Blythe, taking the seat opposite Dawn.

'The roads were busy and it struck me how many times Dad must have done that same trip. I really didn't know him very well at all.' Her voice cracked with emotion and she blew her nose. 'Thanks for coming.'

'It's no trouble. How are you?' asked Blythe, unsure what else to say.

'I'm good, thanks. I've been thinking about Dad and his two homes a lot since we spoke.'

'Have you come to any conclusions?' asked Blythe.

'An affair really is the only explanation. That was what it must have been. He found some other woman but couldn't bring himself to divorce Mum. Was there someone special in his life here?'

'No. Not romantically at least. He had lots of friends but not a partner.' Dawn's assumption didn't sit neatly with the kindly older gentleman Blythe had grown fond of. But why else would he be living two separate lives? It made no sense to her.

'I know this puts you in a really awkward position and I've been thinking a lot about it. If Dad did have a lady friend here in Holly Cross I'm okay with it. I want to know all about his life here and I know you're going to try to protect whoever it is, but you don't need to. I'm not angry. Whoever she is she must have been very special to Dad and he was never anything but a loving husband to my mum. And it was really tough for him when he couldn't cope with her at home anymore and she had to go into residential care.'

'I'm sorry to hear that,' said Blythe. 'How long ago did that happen?'

Dawn pouted with thought. 'Eight or maybe nine years before she died. So about fourteen years ago.'

'Murray moved into the village thirteen years ago,' said Blythe. At least that was the last time the cottage had been sold – Blythe had been doing some investigating herself. Sarvan quietly put down Blythe's coffee and she mouthed a thank you.

'That fits,' said Dawn. 'Dad had always been a keen twitcher but he became more immersed in it after Mum was diagnosed with multiple sclerosis. He was brilliant with her. Always patient and kind. And when he was home, he visited her every day. He always went straight to the nursing home when he came back from his birdwatching trips. He did all he could for her and he was there at the end.'

'That sounds like the Murray I knew,' said Blythe. 'He was kindness to a fault.'

Dawn sniffed. 'Look at me getting all teary. Tell me about him. What he was like when he lived this part of his life.'

She fixed Blythe with interested eyes. Blythe's mind whizzed through her memories of Murray. 'We often chatted. I'd pop over and we'd sit in his garden with a cuppa and have a bit of a gossip about village life and things in general. Although now I realise I did most of the chatting whilst he listened.'

'That sounds like Dad,' said Dawn with a wan smile. 'Please go on.'

'He took in Turpin the cat and was very patient with him. At first, Turpin lived at the bottom of the garden in the log store and freaked out if you went to touch him. It was Murray who slowly coaxed him until he'd let you stroke him. Murray was always on hand to help with whatever was happening in the village. He threw himself into the events – we've really missed him this Christmas.' Blythe swallowed down a lump. Murray had been such a presence at all the activities but especially at Christmas. 'He was on the HCCC.' Dawn gave her a confused look. 'Holly Cross Christmas Committee.'

'Crumbs, he had immersed himself into life in the village. But you've not told me who he was close to.'

Blythe twisted her lips. 'I'm honestly not keeping anything from you, Dawn. I don't think he was in a relationship with anyone here. Murray was close to pretty much everyone but nobody specifically. If that makes sense.'

'If that was the case then why didn't he ever tell me? Why keep his life here a secret?'

'I'm sorry, I have no idea,' said Blythe. She stared into her coffee. 'But there is something you should know. The cottage where he lived. It wasn't rented.' She saw confusion on Dawn's face. 'I sold it. The sale went through in September.'

'Are you saying Dad owned it?'

'That's where things become a bit unclear. The sale was all dealt with via a solicitor. I just assumed they were acting for Murray's whole estate. But as you knew nothing about it that clearly wasn't the case.'

'There was just his flat in Hale. He sold the house I grew up in a few years back. Said it was too big for him with Mum not there but I knew it was really because he needed the money to pay for Mum's nursing home. What happened to the things in the cottage like furniture and knick-knacks. I assume he had some?'

'Most of it was sold with the cottage. Although I did give the solicitor a box of personal items. I say personal but to be honest there wasn't much like that in the cottage. No photographs. Only a few books, a seagull ornament, some keys that didn't fit anything at the cottage and which I'm now thinking were probably for his place in Manchester. And a couple of awards he'd won in various local competitions. He was the star in the pub quiz team.'

'Does the solicitor still have them?' asked Dawn.

'That's the thing. I rang and they told me that the box had been picked up. But for confidentiality reasons they can't tell me who collected it.'

Blythe put up her umbrella as she left the pub. It was tipping it down so hard the rain was bouncing back up off the pavement. This wasn't the light dusting of snow Leonora had ordered and she'd not be pleased with the substitution.

She rushed along with her brolly at an angle to try to keep the worst of the weather off her. She dashed across the road and immediately bumped into someone. 'Oh my word, I am so sorry. I didn't see—' As she moved her umbrella, there stood Sam rubbing his chin, which from the red bump coming up was likely where she had stabbed him with her umbrella.

'It's okay,' he said, his voice tight. He went to walk past her.

'Sam, let's not leave things like this. Can we talk?'

Sam shook water from his hair and swept a hand over his outfit. He was clearly out running. 'I need to get on,' he said, jogging past her.

Blythe drew in a breath. She'd tried and she certainly wasn't going to beg. Not even Sam Ashton was worth that. And what sort of fool went for a jog in a downpour anyway? When the sound of the rain on her umbrella made her realise she'd just been standing there on her own, she pulled herself together and carried on to the village hall at speed.

Blythe was pleased she wasn't the only person who looked like a wet dog. Eden was one of a number of small soggy children playing with Lego in the corner and Leonora was marching up and down only occasionally pausing to look at her flip chart. Blythe left her brolly with the other dripping items and went to join everyone at the table.

Blythe sat down next to Vicky. 'Everything okay?' she asked, with a nod towards Leonora.

Vicky leaned in and spoke in hushed tones. 'Not really. It turns out Owen is a lot smarter than I gave him credit for. I mean, I know I was never unkind enough to say he was a reindeer short of a sleigh team but he was never on the list for Mensa either. Turns out he's worked out that he could be Eden's father. Actually, he's convinced that he is. Now he wants to play happy families whilst I'm wondering whose sperm swam the quickest.'

'Tart?' asked Norman. Vicky and Blythe both spun in his direction. Vicky glared at him. 'Cranberry and orange tart?' Norman tentatively offered Vicky the cake box.

'Ooh yes, ta,' said Vicky reaching inside.

'No thanks,' said Blythe. Vicky stared wide-eyed at her, as did Norman, as if she had uttered cake blasphemy. 'Maybe later,' she added, and they both relaxed.

When Norman and the cakes had moved on Blythe whispered to Vicky. 'Are you really not sure who her father is? I thought you said it was that bloke from the factory.'

'That's the thing – I don't know. It's not like it could be a whole rugby team. There's only two possibles. What should I do about Owen?' she asked, before sinking her teeth into the tart.

'Be honest,' said Blythe. 'He deserves that. If he has all the information then it's up to him what happens next. If you deceive him, it's likely he'll never trust you again. And if you're not straight with him now you could lose something very special.' Blythe thought of Sam and sighed deeply.

'Blimey, that's a bit profound. But you're right. If I tell him and he cops a strop then that tells me all I need to know. Thanks.'

Blythe wished she could go back in time and heed her own advice. The look on Sam's face when she'd bumped into him flitted into her mind. The harsh look in his eyes would stay with her for a long time. She hated that she'd hurt him and let him down. He'd had enough of that in his life. But then she couldn't help thinking that he'd been very quick to walk out on her. Wasn't she worth fighting for?

'You okay?' asked Vicky.

'I saw Sam on the way here. He can barely look at me.'

'Can I offer you some advice?'

Blythe needed all the help she could get. 'Please do.'

Vicky placed her forearms on top of each other in front of her, making Blythe wonder what was going to happen next. 'You are too closed,' said Vicky, nodding at her arms held rigidly across her chest. 'You need to open up your doors and let him in.' She turned out one arm and then the other.

'I think we're past that point.'

'It's never too late. Look at me and Owen. I opened up my doors and—'

'I'm not sure I'm ready to let anyone in. Every time I do they—'

'Piss on your doormat?' offered Vicky.

Blythe shook her head. 'I was going to say, they let me down.'

'But if you don't let people in you could miss out on the one person who won't let you down.' Vicky repeated the arm gesture.

'I love your optimism but I fear that person doesn't exist. Perhaps it's the way men are programmed or at least the ones in my life anyway. Or maybe it's me.'

'Yeah, that could be it,' said Vicky with a grin, making Blythe give her a friendly swipe.

'What's with the arms?' asked Blythe.

'I'm not exactly sure but you get the gist,' said Vicky, still opening and closing her metaphorical doors.

A few late arrivals dripped into the hall and Leonora called the meeting to order. Her face was grave as she tapped her flip chart. 'This is it, team. This is D-Day.' She looked around the room. 'Thanks to all your efforts we are in a fine position to win the title of UK's Most Perfect Christmas Village.' Leonora pulled her shoulders back as she spoke. 'But we must not rest on our laurels. We have...' she said, checking her watch, '...precisely three hours and eighteen minutes until the judges arrive.'

'Heaven help the judges if they're a minute late,' whispered Vicky in Blythe's ear. Leonora glared at them and Blythe felt like she was back in school and about to get a detention.

'We must remain focused at all times. I have a list of

checks we need to undertake to ensure everything goes smoothly, as well as a late addition that I think will make a difference – we are piping music out across the village.' She placed her palms on the tables and scanned the expectant faces. 'This is our joker. Our trump card. The icing on our Christmas cake. And we must pull it off. Agreed?'

There was an uncertain ripple of agreement but Leonora was hyped. 'Are we agreed, team?' she asked in a rousing pitch.

'Hell, yeah!' said Vicky. Others joined in with positive responses and Arthur started a round of applause.

Leonora looked suitably happy. She turned over the page on her flip chart to reveal a long list of tasks with names assigned. Blythe was busy scanning for her name when the hall doors banged open and in true dramatic movie style the wind and rain came in in a flurry along with Sarvan, who looked like he'd swum there. 'There's been an accident. You need to come quick.'

37

24th December

Vicky had taken Eden's hand, grabbed her things, along with the last of the cranberry and orange tarts, and followed the others as they rushed from the village hall. Sarvan had delivered the news and immediately left, leaving everyone none the wiser as to what had happened or more importantly who had been hurt.

Outside, the rain was relentless but Vicky's curiosity had got the better of her and she was swept along with the rest of the group as they made their way to the green. In her head she ticked off the people she knew were safe. Owen immediately popped into her mind. Her heart thumped harder just at the thought of him being hurt, making her realise how much she cared about him.

Vicky heard Leonora's cry just before she came upon the scene. As she had Eden with her, she held back just in case it was a bloodbath. She blinked through the teeming rain to see a white builder's van on its side. Two men were standing near the vehicle checking it over and Vicky felt instantly relieved that nobody appeared injured and that Owen wasn't involved. For a moment it seemed there wasn't too much to worry about and that Sarvan's dramatic entrance appeared unjustified.

However, as the group crossed the road the whole horror became apparent. The van was wrapped in fairy lights and as Vicky traced them back she was able to see the trail of destruction. The white van appeared to have left the road on the other side of the green and crashed through the fencing, dragging a multitude of lights along with it as it skidded and churned up the wet ground, taking out first the Christmas tree, then the elf house, before hitting the Grinch and finally toppling onto its side.

While Blythe was trying to calm down a distraught Leonora, Vicky went to look at the van. She approached one of the two men standing nearby. 'Is anyone hurt?' she asked.

'Only him,' said the older of the two as he pointed at the tangled frame of the Grinch.

Vicky winced at the sight of the figure's head hanging to one side. 'What on earth happened?'

'He was driving.' He pointed at the younger man, who Vicky could now see had a complexion the same shade of white as the van. 'Just passed his test,' he added, with an eye-roll. 'Tyre blew as we were coming down the hill and he swerved to miss a jogger and before we knew it, we ended up like this.'

'We need Superman – he'd sort this out super quick,' said Eden. 'Does anyone have his phone number?' she asked, and the men shook their heads.

Leonora marched up to them, her face the colour of holly berries. 'Look what you've done. You've ruined everything.' Her eyes alighted on the logo on the man's shirt. 'Were you delivering something locally?' she asked.

'Yeah, some sound equipment to a Leonora Clarke.'

'I'm Leonora. Is it...'

The man walked around to the back of the van and opened the door. Vicky and Leonora peered in at the mass of smashed equipment. 'I am not signing for that,' said Leonora. 'And you need to move this now!' she added, waving her arms about wildly.

'I've called for recovery and I'm waiting to hear how long they'll be,' said the white van man. 'But we're going to need a crane and a low loader, I think.'

'A crane?' Leonora scanned all the faces. 'We can't have a crane in the middle of our Christmas display!' Her voice was escalating.

'Sorry, love. But if you want the van moved there is not a lot else for it. That's assuming we can find one and an operator on Christmas Eve.'

Blythe gave up trying to keep her umbrella over Leonora as she paced up and down and went to stand next to Vicky. 'Did I hear right?' asked Blythe. 'Did he say he swerved to miss a jogger?' She was scanning the green.

'Yep. You don't think...'

'I do,' said Blythe, and they both turned to look at Sam's cottage. A blind moved in the front window. 'You try and keep Leonora calm while I sort out Sam Ashton.'

'Keep her calm? How? Look at her. She's crosser than a frog in a Christmas stocking,' said Vicky, but Blythe was already striding across the road.

Blythe knocked at the cottage. Sam opened the door looking like he'd taken a shower fully clothed. 'I understand you were involved in the accident. Are you okay?' she asked, as she scanned him over. He rubbed his hair with a towel, giving it a sexy tousled quality. His wet top clung to his frame, which appeared far more muscly than she remembered from the sexy Santa night. His sturdy thighs glistened...

'I'm fine. Nobody was hurt thankfully. The guy was hurtling down the hill and I was running in the road trying to avoid the puddles when there was an almighty bang. But thank goodness it was loud or I might not have heard it as I had my earbuds in. He swerved and I dived out of the way. Couple of scratches.' He pointed to his upper thigh. 'Otherwise a lucky escape.'

The pause made her drag her eyes back up to his face. 'Try not to feel too bad about it.'

Sam looked confused. 'Bad about what?'

'The state of the green. That van has pretty much wrecked our chances of winning the competition. And it was partly your fault.'

'How do you work that out?' He stopped his hair drying.

'Because the driver swerved to avoid *you* and did that!' She pointed forcefully across the street where Leonora was still waving her arms surrounded by a group of sullen-looking villagers.

'Look, I'm sorry, but I'm not going to get upset about a few Christmas decs being trashed. Why does everyone around here get worked up about something so silly?'

His derision of the effort the village went to as *silly* made her blood boil. 'Haven't you worked it out yet? Holly Cross isn't about Christmas.' Sam glanced past her at the green. 'Well, it is partly,' she conceded crossly. 'But what it's *really* about is community. It's the people. Christmas is just an excuse. It gives them a purpose to get together, to support each other and create something special that benefits others. It's the people who make Holly Cross, *not* Christmas. Without the festivities this village would be very different. What Norman makes in December subsidises his business for the coming year. How else would a little village bakery survive? The sisters from Rock Cottage spend all year knitting and embroidering things, either as decorations or to sell at the Christmas fayre, which keeps them busy and gives them a purpose. And Leonora threw herself into all this after her husband died suddenly. It's helped her deal with the shock and the grief.

So yes, I know you think it's *silly* and you don't care and that's fine, but other people do. I care about Holly Cross because *I* care about the people and if that makes me silly then I'm fine with that.' She was done with Sam Ashton. She turned around and went to see what she could do to help.

Blythe realised she'd well and truly killed any possible chance of a reconciliation with Sam, but she felt some things were more important and she'd had to speak her mind. After twenty minutes of milling around the green in the rain, with Leonora picking up broken lights and muttering to herself, and no sign of a recovery vehicle, Blythe decided someone needed to take charge.

She and Vicky rounded up the bedraggled bunch of helpers and Blythe hopped up onto a bench and waved her brolly to get everyone's attention. 'I don't think we're making any real progress and we're all cold and wet so I suggest—'

'We can't give up,' came Leonora's considerably deflated voice. There was disgruntled muttering from the crowd.

'I'm not suggesting we do,' said Blythe. 'I think we should all go home, get warm and changed into dry clothes and meet at the hall to work out what we can salvage and how best to present what we have to the judges.'

'Good idea!' shouted Vicky. 'And we need to think about all the punters who will be planning on coming tonight.'

'They're more important than the judges. We can't let them down,' said someone and there were mumbles of agreement.

'Shall we meet back at the hall in one hour?' Blythe scanned the faces and her eyes rested on Leonora who eventually nodded. 'Okay. Two o'clock in the hall – bring ideas, solutions and enthusiasm.'

The disheartened crowd murmured their agreement and dispersed. *Oh well*, thought Blythe, it wasn't quite the rousing response she'd hoped for but the people of Holly Cross had put in too much effort to let this ruin things. And whilst their hopes of winning were now thinner than her mum's gravy, they had an obligation to visitors to make their trip worthwhile and spread some Christmas cheer, and that was what Holly Cross was all about.

Greg was coming out of the shower, having finished work early, when Blythe arrived home, so she sent him off to buy as many strings of outdoor lights as he could lay his hands on. He also pledged to round up as many additional volunteers as he could on his way back. She felt instantly revived after a hot shower and a change of clothes and she hoped the other committee members felt the same.

It was still raining when she walked back through the village. The deep tyre tracks gouged across the green were filling up with water. If they weren't careful they'd have people stuck in a quagmire. She called by the village stores en route to buy pop and biscuits to give everyone a much-needed sugar boost and she walked into the village hall ready to lead them into battle.

Members of the HCCC were first to arrive, closely followed by a steady stream of villagers all keen to lend a hand. There was no sign of Leonora so Blythe grabbed the flip chart and made some notes. When the hall was half full Blythe stood next to the flip chart and gave it a tap. She surveyed the many faces and found Greg's. 'Thank you,' she mouthed.

'You're welcome,' he replied.

'Has anyone heard from Leonora?' she asked, and everyone shook their heads. 'Okay, then let's do the best job we can.' She turned over the flip chart and went through the revised plan. Blythe explained that now it was so wet they had to keep visitors off the grass area so they needed to move all they had to the edges so it could be viewed from the pavement or road. She allocated teams to fixing the Grinch, rebuilding the elf house and righting the Christmas tree and replacing lights; and, ambitiously, she decided she would try to get some music sorted. She pinned up the respective charts around the hall. 'Now this is where you guys come in. I want you to spend the next fifteen minutes jotting on your flip chart what you need to make your thing happen and how you are going to do it. Okay?'

There were tentative nods. 'So we get to write on the flip chart?' asked Phyllis.

'Exactly. I can't do all this by myself. We all need to own it.'

'Brilliant,' said Phyllis, taking a marker pen and pulling off the top with a flourish.

They dismissed Vicky's idea to plug in the festive lights currently wrapped around the stranded white van and make a feature of it, as if the Grinch had crashed while stealing all the presents. Blythe had taken on the role of contact point for the van recovery but there was still no news on that. The noise in the hall was an excited and slightly manic jumble as ideas and suggestions were shouted out and jotted down. When Blythe called them all back to the table, everyone looked eager to get going. A quick walk-through of each of their flip charts showed that they had come up with workable solutions for every problem.

'Right, in conclusion,' began Blythe, as someone near the door cleared their throat. Everyone turned to see Leonora. Blythe didn't know how long she'd been standing there but she beckoned her over. 'I'll take you through the recovery plans in a mo, Leonora, but we're confident we'll have something to show the judges as well as the visitors tonight. It might not be exactly what you'd planned but it'll be something worthy of Holly Cross. Did you want to say anything?'

Leonora joined her at the front of the hall. 'I know I take this very seriously and perhaps a bit too seriously sometimes.' There were half-hearted contradictions. 'No, it's true. I get caught up in things. I just see so much potential in what we can and have achieved as a team of volunteers.

I might be the one with the flip chart but it's each one of you that makes Christmas in Holly Cross special for so many people. Maybe I don't say it enough but you're all doing a brilliant job. From the bottom of my heart – thank you.'

'It's thanks to you that we're all here,' said Arthur, starting a round of applause.

'Let's make this another special Holly Cross Christmas,' said Leonora. This seemed to rouse the troops and in a buzz of excitement people started making phone calls and grabbing up their things.

Leonora scanned Blythe's flip charts now Blu-Tacked around the hall. 'I know it's not how you would have approached it but—'

Leonora held up a hand. 'Thank you for doing this. For seeing past the disaster. I was ready to give up and I'm ashamed of myself for that.'

Blythe waved her words away. 'No time for that. We've got a Christmas display to save. Are you okay to schmooze the judges when they arrive?' Blythe pointed to a flip chart with Leonora's name on it.

Leonora pulled back her shoulders. 'Absolutely.'

'Then it's time to show them what Holly Cross is made of.'

38

24th December

Blythe was feeling empowered and invincible as she grabbed her soggy brolly ready to face the weather again. She looked up to see Sam Ashton standing in the village hall doorway. This was all she needed. Her treacherous heart gave a happy skip at the sight of him. She wondered how long it would be before she could break that habit.

'Have you got five minutes?' he asked.

She held her head high. 'Sam, I think we've both said everything there is to say. Ours is the relationship that never was and I think it's best not to dwell on it. If you don't mind I need to join the rest of the village in trying to save the display.' She went to walk past him but he didn't budge.

'It was the display I wanted to talk to you about.'

Crap. Embarrassment crept over her. 'Right. Yes. Of course. The display. What about it?'

'I'd like to help.'

Blythe was about to give him the 'It's a bit bloody late for that' lecture when behind her Vicky cleared her throat. Blythe glanced in her direction.

'Let him in,' mouthed Vicky, whilst doing her elaborate door-opening gesture, which looked a lot like she was opening an imaginary coat and flashing at them. Blythe shook her head at Vicky good-naturedly.

Sam was giving them both an odd look. 'Is she okay?' he asked, nodding in Vicky's direction.

'She's learning a new TikTok routine,' said Blythe, trying to explain away Vicky's odd behaviour. 'Anyway, we're wasting time. Let's get going and we can talk on the way.'

They left Vicky and Eden manning the village hall like a WW2 war room (but with better biscuits) and started walking towards the green. The weather was a little kinder than it had been earlier, but it was still drizzling, so Blythe put her brolly up. She noted that Sam kept a safe distance away.

Up ahead Blythe could see the green was a muddy mess with so many people traipsing across it. 'Look at the state of that,' she said more to herself than to Sam. Whatever they did they weren't going to be able to hide that from the judges but at least it would be less obvious once it got dark.

'If anyone can turn this around it's you,' said Sam.

The unexpected compliment caught her off guard. 'Thanks for coming to help. What did you have in mind?' asked Blythe.

'I was kind of expecting you to tell me what you need,' said Sam.

'All tasks have been allocated. It's really a recovery job at this stage. Talking of recovery, is that a tow truck?' Blythe quickened her pace towards the van.

'Sam, over here!' called Greg, who was up a ladder holding on to the Grinch's head while someone tried to shore it up.

'Shall I?' asked Sam, pointing to Greg.

'Sure, just help wherever you can.'

Sam jogged off across the road. Blythe pulled her eyes away from him to focus on the van. Unfortunately, the white van was still on its side. Blythe went over to the two men who were standing in the bus shelter eating sausage rolls. And from the looks they were exchanging they were from Norman's bakery. 'What's happening?' she asked.

'No cranes available but this vehicle has a winch so they're hoping to right it and then cart it off to a garage,' said the older one. 'Once it's loaded we'll be off.'

It was terrific news but Blythe was in organiser mode and here were two idle people she could utilise. 'Not so fast. I know it was an accident, but you very nearly wrecked our biggest night of the year. I'm thinking you'd like to be useful while you're waiting…' She paused long enough until eventually they both nodded. 'Great. If you see the man in the red jacket you can help him to repair the fencing around the green.'

'Fine,' said the older one, popping in the last of his sausage roll and reluctantly leaving the cover of the bus shelter with his colleague in tow.

The sisters from Rock Cottage approached. 'Blythe, what can we do to help?' asked one.

'We've got some embroidered bunting left over from the fayre,' suggested the other.

'Brilliant,' said Blythe and the ladies looked delighted. 'As soon as the elf house is reconstructed it needs decorating to cover up the broken bits so can I leave you to do that?'

'It would be our pleasure,' they said in unison.

The village was a hive of activity and Blythe felt like Queen Bee. She could see how easily Leonora had been carried away by it. As things were completed, Blythe called them through to Vicky and Eden, who ticked them off. By half past three the van had been removed, the elf house had been reconstructed, although this time it was a more rustic affair involving pallets, and the Grinch's head was back in place, although sadly there was still an issue with his lighting.

'I can't get his sack to flash,' said Greg. Phyllis chuckled naughtily as she rushed by. 'But I'm working on it,' he added.

'Is Sam still helping you?' asked Blythe, trying not to make it obvious as she scanned the green for a glimpse of him.

'Went off about half an hour ago. Said he needed to make some calls.'

'Typical,' said Blythe.

'Is it?' asked Greg. 'Because he's done loads today and only had good things to say about you.'

Blythe couldn't hide her surprise but before she could ask Greg more, Leonora was hurtling towards her. 'Judges ETA twelve minutes.'

There began a frenzy of activity as things were hastily finished off and tidied away. Members of the Holly Cross brass band were assembling around the now upright Christmas tree, so they would have some music even if it wasn't piped around the village as Leonora had planned. With about ten minutes to go, a white van came around the green at speed, making the ladies from Rock Cottage gasp.

'Not another one,' said Blythe, watching it pull up nearby. She wasn't expecting to see Sam get out of the cab. She marched over. 'Sam, the judges are arriving any minute—'

'Ten minutes to judges!' yelled Leonora.

Blythe pointed over her shoulder. 'Obviously you can park here but it would be better if you didn't. I think we've all seen enough white vans for one day. Any chance you could move it please?'

'Trust me we'll be five minutes and then it'll be gone.'

She really didn't have time to ask, she just wanted the van out of the way. 'Okay.'

While villagers scurried in various directions and Leonora headed up to the village hall to greet the judges, Blythe spotted Sam and some other men carrying something across the green. She couldn't worry about it now but she was curious.

The white van moved off as Vicky and Eden appeared. 'Blimey, this looks good,' she said, squinting across the green in the half light. 'Do the lights work?'

'We've only tested in batches. We'll only know when Greg flicks the switch,' said Blythe. 'We're waiting for Leonora to walk the judges down. Did you meet them?'

'Not really; we got shooed out as they arrived. There's four of them.'

'Will they have big buzzers to press if they don't like it?' asked Eden.

'Oh, they'll like it,' said Vicky, giving her a squeeze.

'After all this I really hope so,' said Blythe, nibbling at a hangnail. Greg raised a hand from the middle of the green to let Blythe know he was ready. At least the rain had stopped, which was a bonus. She could see Sam standing there with him. She wondered what they were talking about.

'It's getting dark,' said Eden. 'Why don't the houses have their lights on?'

'Because we're going to do it all at once like we do for

the switch-on to impress the judges,' explained Blythe. *Assuming everyone is ready when I hit send on this message*, she thought, her thumb hovering over her phone. A few moments later Blythe spotted Leonora with four others coming down the hill. She waited for Leonora's signal. Her heart was racing. She felt like a starter at the Olympics. As if the world was scrutinising her. Of course they weren't but the people who mattered in *her* world were watching and for everyone involved she wanted to get it right. She held her breath.

Leonora raised her arm and then dropped it dramatically. Blythe waved at the band sergeant, hit send on the message and gave a thumbs up to Greg. There was a moment's delay and then it happened. The display on the green burst into life as decorations around the village went on in almost a domino effect. The band broke into 'It's Beginning to Look a Lot Like Christmas'. Blythe was about to breathe a sigh of relief when she became aware of an unfamiliar noise. A motor? She looked around to see where it was coming from, which was when she noticed something unexpected.

'It's snowing!' shouted Eden.

Blythe glanced upwards – nothing. Then she looked across the road and sure enough snow was billowing across the green covering the muddy mess as a snow machine sent flakes flying into the night sky. Snowflakes caught in the lights and sparkled. The effect was magical. She was trying to work out where the snow machine had come from when she saw Greg pointing frantically at the snow and then at Sam who was grinning broadly. She gave him a thumbs up, which he shyly returned.

It seemed Sam had really thrown himself into helping

them finish the display. Thanks to everyone getting stuck in they'd done it. Holly Cross had a Christmas display to be proud of.

The judges spent a good half an hour walking the village but now it was dark the visitors were arriving in droves, so Blythe and Vicky were directing cars and people. Arthur and his collecting team were busy, as were many other HCCC members.

'Blythe!' called Leonora, the usually sharp edge gone from her voice.

'Have the judges gone?' asked Blythe.

'Yes.'

'And?' Blythe was on tenterhooks.

'We won't know until Boxing Day who's won,' said Leonora. 'They've seen seventeen villages and they had one more to see after us.'

'Did they give any hints?' asked Blythe, feeling a bit deflated.

'They made the right noises but what they really thought and how it compares to the others, who knows?'

'Oh well. We did our best,' said Blythe, looking around. Happy smiling faces everywhere were oohing and ahhing at the lights as artificial snow dusted the festive scene and a slightly lopsided Grinch sneered over the prettiest Christmas village scene.

'We did. Thank you,' said Leonora, opening out her arms and looking awkward.

Blythe realised a moment too late she was offering her

a hug. 'Oh...' She stepped forward and they tentatively embraced.

Leonora cleared her throat. 'Anyway, if you want to get off early, there's plenty of us.'

'Does that include me?' asked Vicky, her face appearing at Blythe's shoulder, making Leonora start.

'Of course. Merry Christmas.'

'And to you,' said Blythe.

Blythe lost count of how many people wished her a merry Christmas as she walked through the village. It was the happiest she'd felt in a while. The village was drenched in Christmas spirit and it was lovely to see. It almost didn't matter what the judges decided because the village looked a picture, people were happy and it was Christmas Eve.

Up ahead she saw someone struggling with two heavy collection buckets and she rushed to help them.

Arthur was breathing heavily. 'Let me take those,' said Blythe, grabbing the buckets. It was a shock just how heavy they were. 'Goodness, these weigh a ton.'

'Thank you. We've made a lot tonight,' he said in between breaths. 'Would you mind popping them inside?' he asked, opening his gate.

'Of course not.' Blythe went with him up the path, waited while he unlocked and followed Arthur inside.

'Put them down anywhere. I'm looking forward to counting up how much we've raised. I think it might be another record breaker,' he said. 'Now you must get home. I don't want to delay you.'

'Merry Christmas, Arthur.' Blythe was smiling as she

turned to leave. But something caught her eye and made her twist back around.

On Arthur's hall table Blythe had spotted something very familiar. A wooden seagull. 'You okay?' asked Arthur.

'It's just that I've seen one a bit like that somewhere before,' said Blythe, walking over and picking up the knick-knack. 'Murray had a seagull a bit like this one.'

'Kittiwake,' said Arthur.

'That's right. Murray corrected me for calling it a seagull more than once.' She smiled at the memory as she turned the ornament over in her hand. As she went to put it down she noticed something. The beak had been glued back on. She stared at it before glancing at Arthur. Arthur looked like he'd been frozen in time. 'Oh my G— This *is* Murray's seagull.' She held it up as if presenting evidence to Arthur.

'Kittiwake,' said Arthur.

Blythe shook her head. 'Okay, kittiwake, but that's irrelevant. It's Murray's. And I packed this in the box with the rest of Murray's personal effects from the cottage and it went to the solicitor.' She waved the wooden bird about and then fearing that she might drop it she put it back on the table. Things started to slot into place although she still wasn't entirely sure what it all meant.

She fixed Arthur with a hard stare. 'What's going on, Arthur?' she asked.

Arthur grimaced. 'I think perhaps I have some explaining to do.'

39

24th December

Arthur walked away leaving Blythe standing in the hallway stunned. Her mind was trying to fill in the blanks. She could hear the sound of a cupboard opening and glasses clinking and she followed it through to a small living room where Arthur was pouring himself a drink.

'Port?' he asked. 'It's a rather nice one that I brought back from Portugal.'

'Yeah, go on then, I certainly need something. I've had a bit of a shock.'

'I am truly sorry about that, Blythe.' He passed her a glass and they sat down. 'I'm not sure what else to say other than I'm sorry.'

'I could do with you filling in a few blanks for me please, Arthur.' Blythe sipped her drink. 'That's really lovely, thank you.'

Arthur sighed deeply. His sad eyes fixed on Blythe. 'Please don't judge me. Or Murray.'

'As if I would,' said Blythe. 'I'm sure you know I think the world of both of you.'

Arthur smiled. 'That's lovely to hear.' He stared into his

glass and swirled the dark red liquid. 'I'm sorry. I really don't know what to tell you.'

Blythe decided if she wanted to know anything she was going to have to ask. 'Were you and Murray lovers?'

Arthur's head shot up. 'No, that makes it sound sordid but we were in a relationship of sorts. I don't know how to describe it. It's complicated.'

'In my experience relationships always are,' said Blythe. 'Try starting at the beginning.'

Arthur sucked in a heavy breath. 'We met many years ago whilst birdwatching. We spent a day together in virtual silence in a hide, and it's the most at ease I've ever been with another human being. Neither of us said anything at the time but we both knew that we had a connection. We kept in touch and saw each other whenever we could. We simply wanted to be in each other's company. Does that sound odd?'

'No, it sounds like love.'

'I really did love him.' Arthur smiled. 'Murray couldn't stay with me here. It would have raised too many eyebrows in a small village and he had a family he desperately wanted to protect. He split his time between them and me, and that worked rather well. It was easier after I bought the cottage on the green.'

'It was you Sam bought the place off. Was it you who kept the garden tidy too?'

Arthur nodded sheepishly. 'I'm sorry for all the cloak-and-dagger shenanigans but I wasn't ready to face the rest of the village.' He looked a little alarmed. 'I'm still not ready to face them.'

'That's okay. I won't say anything. But you know, people would be more understanding than you'd think.' Arthur looked doubtful. 'And there's one person I know who would be relieved to hear about you and Murray, and that's his daughter – Dawn.' Blythe pulled a pen and pad from her bag and jotted down Dawn's number from her phone. She passed it to Arthur. 'When you're ready.'

He nodded. 'I miss him terribly,' he said, his lip wobbling slightly.

'We all do,' said Blythe, touching his arm 'If you ever want to chat about him just call me.'

Arthur managed a weak smile. 'I'd like that.'

'Me too,' said Blythe.

Thanks to the port, Blythe was feeling quite festive when she walked into her house. That feeling disappeared when she saw who was waiting for her. The sight of her father standing in the kitchen doorway was a surprise. Belatedly, she greeted him. 'Dad. Hi, merry Christmas.' She tried to hug him; he kissed her cheek. 'I already received your card and present,' she said, trying to work out the reason for the Christmas Eve visit.

'My PA thought a label maker might be useful and the book on setting goals was my idea.'

'Oh, I've not opened them yet.' Blythe couldn't hide her disappointment.

'Anyway, to business,' he said, pulling out his phone. 'Everything is digital these days. I'll send you the link to the document and—'

Blythe waved a hand to interrupt him. 'Sorry, I don't know what you're talking about.'

'I thought Ludo told you I was buying the business?'

Blythe narrowed her eyes in thought and she rewound the conversation in his office just before Sam broke up with her. 'Ludo said there was an offer on the table.'

'I wonder why he omitted to tell you the offer was from me?' He dismissed it with a shake of his head. 'Anyway, I need you to sign an employment contract and—'

'Stop, stop, stop,' said Blythe, waving her hand in front of her father's face to distract him from his phone.

The front door opened and Greg reversed in. 'Ho, ho, oh,' he said, turning around and seeing Hugh. Greg clumsily hid a carrier bag behind his back. 'Hello, Hugh. Everything okay?' he asked, looking directly at Blythe. It was like Lego bricks clicking satisfyingly into place. Here was Greg who, without question, had given up most of his day at the drop of a Santa hat to help Blythe. Next to him was her father who had swanned in to get her to sign a contract of employment she hadn't read for a job he hadn't actually offered her but merely assumed she would take.

'I was just about to explain to Dad that I'm accepting Ludo's offer.'

'Darling, that's brilliant,' said her mum, appearing in a cloud of steam from the kitchen and throwing her arms around her.

'Good decision,' said Greg, giving her a hug. Her mum and stepfather stood either side of her as she faced Hugh.

'What offer's this?' Hugh scowled at them.

'Ludo was debating whether to sell up or to put me in as associate partner while he took on an advisory role and enjoyed semi-retirement. Seeing as I have no idea what you're offering me I'm going to go with Ludo.'

'It sounds like you're telling me that you're blocking my

expansion by doing this. Quite frankly I'm hurt, Blythe. We're family,' said Hugh.

Blythe looked at the two people flanking her. 'You're my dad, and I love you, but that's a biological connection and family is something quite different.' She reached out her hands and they were both grasped automatically.

'I'm not sure what you're getting at.' Hugh shook his head. 'But as your father I expect your support.'

'No,' said Greg. 'She should expect yours.'

Hugh looked at Greg as if he'd just materialised out of thin air. 'Are you suggesting I don't support my daughter? Because here I am offering her a job. I don't think you're in a position to do that now, are you, Greg?'

Blythe let go of her mum's hand and held her own hand up to stop things turning into an argument. 'Thank you for your kind offer, Dad, but I'm going to politely decline.'

'Fine,' said Hugh, putting his phone in his inside coat pocket and turning away.

'Happy Christmas, Dad,' said Blythe.

Hugh turned back and with a tight jaw said, 'And to you all.' And like the ghost of Christmas past he left a chill in the hallway as he walked out.

'Right,' said Greg, letting go of Blythe and clapping his hands together. 'It's Christmas and we've got lots to celebrate. Let's get that fizz open.'

Blythe took him by the arm. 'Thanks for everything, Greg. You've been more of a dad to me than Hugh ever has been.'

'I'm sure there's a place for both of us. Now let's celebrate!'

'I'll join you in a bit. There's just something I need to do.'

★

Vicky was knackered by the time she got in, but Eden was hyper because she was running on hot chocolate and marshmallows, with a heavy sprinkling of the Holly Cross Christmas magic. Vicky wondered if she'd ever manage to get her to bed. Eden got out a plate and put a mince pie and a carrot on it for Santa and Rudolph while Vicky poured a large glass of white wine, having persuaded Eden that Santa would have had more than enough dairy by the time he got to their house and would probably enjoy a cheeky little Chardonnay instead of a glass of milk. Eden wasn't convinced but she dutifully put the treats on the fireplace. That was one thing Vicky could cross off her long list. Thoughts of the presents she needed to wrap tumbled into her mind along with emails she still had to write for her dog-walking clients and the Christmas dinner she needed to prepare. She was just beginning to feel overwhelmed when the doorbell went.

'Is it Santa?' chimed Eden.

'If it is he can crack on with the sprouts,' said Vicky, heading for the door.

At first she couldn't see who was there due to the pile of presents they were carrying, then Owen's grinning face peeped over the top. 'Can I come in before I drop this lot?' he asked.

She had not been expecting him and for a moment it threw her.

'Owen, Owen, Owen!' squealed Eden with delight. 'Are they for me?' she asked, her eyes wide with wonder.

'I'm not sure,' said Owen. 'But this big fat guy in a red

suit asked me to put them under your tree and said we mustn't touch them until tomorrow.'

Eden sucked in a breath at his words and whispered, 'Santa.'

'Let's put these under the tree then I have a top-secret job for you, Eden.' Owen gave her a wink. 'Can you put the kettle on please, Vicky?' he asked, disappearing into her living room with Eden skipping behind him. What the hell was going on? She decided she definitely needed something to drink. She wasn't sure it was tea but she put the kettle on anyway. After a few minutes Owen joined her in the kitchen.

'You're not allowed in the front room for five minutes, which is just enough time for a festive snog,' he said, stepping closer.

'Whilst this is lovely it's not what we agreed. We said we would see each other on the 27th. You were spending Christmas with your mum.'

'I know and I've been thinking about that a lot. Families should be together at Christmas. And that's what we are, the three of us. Aren't we?' And there it was, not so much the elephant in the room as the elephant that had been following her around for years.

Vicky shut the kitchen door, leaned back against it and took a deep breath. 'Owen, about that. I know you think you're Eden's father but the truth is I don't know. It could be you, but it could also be the other guy I slept with. There is no way of knowing for sure without doing a DNA test.' She braced herself for the backlash.

'I don't need a test to know she's mine,' he said, stepping towards her. 'Now we're down to about three and a half minutes for that kiss.'

Vicky couldn't believe how blasé he was being. 'Owen, this is serious. You can't just brush it under the carpet. It matters.'

'Why does it?'

'Because what if she's not yours? What then? At some point you're going to resent caring for another man's child. What if we have another child together?'

'Now, I like that idea,' said Owen, trying to put his arms around Vicky but she ducked out of the way.

'But where would that leave Eden? You'd have one child that was definitely yours and Eden with a big question mark hanging over her. I can't let that happen.' Vicky didn't like the sound of the wobble in her voice.

Owen held his hands up. 'I can see this is an issue for you so how about we do the test?'

Vicky felt everything tense up. 'Okay.'

'But, I don't want to know the result.'

'What?' said Vicky.

'You do the test if you want to know but it makes no difference to me. What I want is to do the school run, read her stories and teach her to ride a skateboard. I want to be Eden's dad and I think she'd like that. And before you say anything I know this is a lifetime commitment and I'm here for it. And I don't need a scientist's permission for that.'

Vicky saw the love in Owen's eyes. 'Really?'

'Really. Now can I please have that kiss?'

Vicky smiled. 'I guess.' She stepped into Owen's arms.

'Mummy! Owen! I think I heard Santa's sleigh on the roof!'

They started to laugh.

25th December

Christmas Day

Sam was woken by Turpin trying to get inside his pillowcase. It was the cat's new favourite place to sleep and it was a minor inconvenience to him that Sam's head was on it. Sam had hoped he'd be a long way from Holly Cross today but all the drama on the green the day before had made him cancel his plans to escape to a cottage in the Cotswolds. So now here he was. He was going to treat it as he usually did – as just another day. The only difference was that he avoided the television, internet and his phone. All those things would do their best to remind him what day it was.

He yawned as he made his way downstairs. He was surprised to see a large white envelope on the mat. There would be no post today. He hesitated. If it was a Christmas card he didn't want it. He picked it up. His name was on the front in black marker pen. It didn't look very festive. Sam went through to the kitchen and put it on the table while he made himself some toast.

With no TV or phone it was quite boring sitting eating his breakfast. The envelope intrigued him. He opened one end and peered inside. It wasn't a card and he was hugely relieved. He tipped out the contents onto the table.

He blinked at the handwritten map. His eyes were drawn to the title: *Sam's Treasure Hunt*. It made him smile for a moment. He knew exactly who was behind this. He studied the map. All the key places and people in the village were featured on it and he had to admit he was intrigued. At the bottom it read – *Clue Number One: Hot on the tail of a highwayman.*

Sam had a shower and got dressed but all the while the map and its clue were on his mind. He made the bed carefully so as not to annoy Turpin, whose paw darted out of the pillowcase each time Sam came too close. A possible answer to the clue popped into Sam's head. Without thinking too much about it he picked up the map, grabbed his coat and rushed out of the cottage. It would only take a few minutes to find out if he was right and then he could squirrel himself away for the rest of the day.

The pub was busier than he had expected but at least that meant nobody was really focusing on him. He made his way between the people to the big fireplace. For a moment he was stumped. He'd assumed this was the answer to the clue but as there was a full log fire burning he wasn't sure where the next clue might be. People had come in behind him and were now wishing each other a merry Christmas. This was a bad idea. Sam turned to leave.

'Hiya, Sam,' said Sarvan. 'Over here a minute.' He beckoned Sam into the restaurant area.

'It's okay. I'm not stopping,' said Sam.

'I know, but I thought you might like to see where some of the Holly Cross charity money goes.' Sarvan pointed to a long table surrounded by elderly folk. 'If it wasn't for the money we raise they'd be on their own today. Have a chat to them.'

'Actually, I've—'

'Are you Sam?' called out a lady at the head of the table.

'Er, yeah.'

'We've been expecting you,' she said, and she waved an envelope.

Sam went to get it, but the woman wouldn't hand it over until they'd had a chat and she'd sung the praises of the village and shared how much the Christmas lunch meant to her. Sam eventually escaped with the envelope. Outside, his breath plumed in the cold as he ripped it open. The piece of paper inside read – *Clue Number Two: Knit one, purl one.*

He was sure it was something to do with the two old ladies but where did they live? Then he remembered the cottage on the way into the village where the wall and gate were festooned with crochet and he set off in that direction, checking the map as he went.

Sam knocked on the door whilst trying to think what to say when they opened it.

'Sam! You worked it out. Come in,' said the first sister, ushering him inside.

'Right, I'm just after the next clue really,' he said.

'We know,' said the other sister, appearing with a white envelope. 'We've been briefed not to say…' She lowered her voice. 'You know what.'

'But we are allowed to give you this.' She handed Sam something wrapped in tissue paper.

He tentatively unwrapped it. It was a beautifully knitted scarf. 'Thank you. I feel bad that I didn't get you anything.'

'But that's not why you give presents, Sam. We love to knit and the best thing is to see our knitting find a happy home. Really, that's a gift to us right there,' she said, watching Sam put the scarf on. 'Anyway, here you go.' She handed him the envelope. 'This one might be tricky so you may want to open it in here.'

'Thanks.' Sam took out the clue and read it out. '*Clue Number Three: Carry yo-**ur hart** in a bucket.*' The ladies looked at it with him.

'Odd spelling,' said one.

'And some letters are highlighted,' pointed out the other.

'Anagram of u, r, h, a, r, t perhaps,' suggested Sam, running a finger over the bold letters.

The three of them looked at each other. 'Ah!' said one of the sisters. 'Arthur always has the collecting bucket.'

'Arthur! That's it,' said Sam, delighted. 'Where does he live?'

'Further up the hill, opposite side, with a green front door. Off you go.' And they shooed him out.

Sam was soon being welcomed at Arthur's. 'My word. I wasn't sure I'd see you today. Then I wasn't sure I'd see anyone today,' he said with a melancholy smile.

'You not going to the pub?' asked Sam.

'Not this year. I'm not feeling very sociable.'

'I can relate to that,' said Sam.

'You'll be wanting this.' Arthur offered him a cracker.

'Actually, I'm after a clue. Probably in an envelope.'

'This is all I was given,' said Arthur, proffering the cracker. 'I guess I can't pull it on my own.'

'Of course you can't,' said Sam, taking the other end. On three they pulled and the cracker snapped open. Out fell the usual hat, joke and a plastic frog along with a slip of white paper. Sam quickly unfolded it and read it out: '*Clue Number Four: I'm a prize turkey.*'

'Whatever does that mean?' Arthur's puzzled face was peering at the clue.

Sam smiled. 'I think it means I've come to the end of the treasure hunt.'

'Then where's the treasure?' asked Arthur.

'I think it's at Blythe's house.'

'I'm just heading off there now. I'll walk with you if you like?'

The question was, did Sam want to go?

'This plan of yours,' began Greg. 'How confident are we?' he asked Blythe, as he popped another peeled potato in the pan.

'Not at all. But I've tried not to be pushy. There's a note on the front door.'

Greg pulled a face. 'And what does that say?'

'Congratulations, you've won a meal for one (available as a takeaway if you'd prefer). Buzz once for takeaway, twice to join us for dinner.' Blythe ran her lip through her teeth. 'Was the treasure hunt a bad idea?'

'No, it was a kind and thoughtful one. But that doesn't mean he'll want to stay for Christmas so don't be disappointed if—' The doorbell buzzed once and they both froze.

Blythe held her breath and Greg squeezed her hand. The doorbell buzzed again.

'Thank Santa for that,' said Greg. 'Go get your man.'

Blythe kissed Greg's cheek and dashed to open the door.

Arthur was standing on the doorstep alone. 'Merry Christmas, Blythe. Was I right to buzz twice?'

Blythe's stomach plummeted but she slapped a smile on her face for Arthur. 'Of course, Arthur. Merry Christmas.' She gave him a hug as he came inside. Her mum went into hostess mode, taking Arthur's coat and showing him through to the living room. Blythe leaned out of the front door and scanned the road in both directions – not a soul about. She shut the door and turned to see Greg watching her.

'It was always a long shot,' he said. 'Try not to let it spoil your Christmas.' He opened his arms and she stepped into them. Greg gave the best hugs. The sort of hug that told you however crap things seemed they would turn out okay.

'Thanks for being my dad,' she said.

'It's been an honour.' He kissed the top of her head. 'Let's see what I can make with the bottle of absinthe I won at the fayre. Although I warn you now, it may taste like antifreeze.'

Despite everything, Greg was able to make her smile.

But as they went into the living room the doorbell buzzed twice, making Blythe's heart leap.

She raced to open the door, not caring if she seemed a bit too keen. An unsure-looking Sam greeted her. 'Hey.'

'Hey,' she replied, not too certain what to say knowing that merry Christmas was the last thing he'd want to hear. 'You went for option two then.' He nodded. 'I need to warn you that option two includes Greg reading out all the cracker jokes and laughing at every one. Are you sure you're ready for this?'

Sam gave a weak smile. 'Not entirely but a prize is a prize.'

'You're letting all the heat escape,' called Greg from the living room doorway. 'Let the lad in!' Blythe stepped out of the way and Sam edged furtively inside.

'Come in,' said Blythe, taking Sam's coat and hanging it up.

'Hi Sam, don't mind me,' said Blythe's mum, giving him a quick peck on the cheek as she passed. 'I'm juggling dinner after three sherries—'

'Four!' shouted Greg. 'Don't worry, her cooking is better if there's alcohol involved.' She gave him a swipe.

Blythe went into the living room, where Arthur was admiring their Christmas tree. Sam hovered in the doorway. His vulnerability was endearing. Blythe was conscious he was a flight risk and was unsure how much festiveness he'd be able to handle. She was thinking through how best to ease him in when Greg intervened.

'Get that down you,' said Greg, handing Sam a glass.

'What is it?' asked Sam.

'Probably best you don't know,' said Greg. 'Right, you and Arthur are behind on the present opening. You'd best catch up.' Greg reached under the tree and handed Arthur two neatly wrapped gifts.

'Ooh, thank you,' said Arthur, sitting down to open them.

'Here you go,' said Greg, passing Sam one of the bright red stockings from the mantelpiece.

'For me?' Sam seemed surprised.

Greg showed him the tag hanging from it which read, *Sam – Nice*.

Blythe saw Sam swallow hard. He downed his drink in one, winced and took the stocking from Greg. Sam stared at the label before peeking inside. 'Are these all for me?' he asked.

'It's not much really,' said Blythe. 'Just a few things I saw that made me think of you, and the usual stuff you have to have in stockings.'

'I don't know what the usual stuff would be… but thank you.' Sam reached in and began pulling things out.

Arthur gasped. He'd just unwrapped a framed photograph of him and Murray. He shook his head, his eyes full of tears. 'But it was only last night that—'

'I did a last-minute dash around the supermarket for a few things. That frame was one of them,' explained Blythe. 'And the picture is from last Christmas when you and Murray were on car park duty together. I just printed it out.' It was a lovely picture of the two of them laughing.

Arthur held the frame to his chest. 'Thank you,' he mouthed, through happy tears.

'You're welcome,' said Blythe, feeling a little choked herself.

'Here,' said Arthur, passing her a present.

'Thanks,' she replied, ripping off the paper. She loved opening presents. Inside was Murray's little wooden bird. 'The kittiwake.' A lump of emotion caught in her throat. 'Are you sure?' she asked.

'I know he'd want you to have it,' said Arthur, patting her arm.

'Have you got to the bottom of that stocking yet?' Greg asked Sam as he hovered nearby with a refilled glass.

Sam was surrounded by gifts: a chocolate orange, chocolate coins, socks and a variety of toiletries. Sam held up a clementine and a walnut. 'Can someone explain these?' he asked.

'Yes,' said Greg, passing Sam his drink and putting his Penguin slippered feet up on the foot stool. 'Back when Noah was a lad we were poor and we only ever had fresh fruit and shelled nuts at Christmas. They were unusual things and getting them in your stocking was special. Food was cheap and came in a tin. I was eleven before I realised pineapples weren't ring-shaped.'

Blythe mimed playing a violin and Sam smirked.

'You can laugh,' said Greg good-naturedly, 'but if you didn't have much you had to make the best of it. I'm right, aren't I, Arthur?'

'You are,' said Arthur, trying on his other present: a pair of thermal gloves.

'Right,' said Sam, putting down the walnut and clementine but not looking much better informed.

'They're a family tradition I guess,' explained Blythe, scanning what Sam had unwrapped. 'There should be one more present in there,' she added, nodding at his stocking.

Sam put his hand inside and pulled out a small package. Blythe tried hard to hide her grin. She'd been dying to see him open this ever since she'd bought it a couple of weeks ago. That was back when she'd hoped they would still be together at Christmas. Sam kept glancing at her as he opened it. The look of realisation on his face was a picture. 'A Tamagotchi?' He shook his head. He spontaneously got to his feet and hugged her. 'Thank you. I love it.'

'Santa said he's sorry it's a couple of decades late.'

Sam snorted a laugh. 'Tell him it's okay. I forgive him.'

'I might not see him until next year. Will you still be living in Holly Cross then?' She held her breath.

'I've decided not to move my business if that's what you're asking.' Sam's lips twitched at the edges. 'I think you, Turpin and Holly Cross are stuck with me.'

'Right,' said Blythe's mum appearing in the doorway looking slightly flustered. 'I need to know who wants what. There's carrots, parsnips, cauli cheese, sprouts, red cabbage, pigs in blankets, roasties. Well, everything really.'

'Let's bung it all in dishes and everyone can help themselves. I'll give you a hand,' said Greg, jumping to his feet and beginning to clap. 'I'm giving her a hand. Get it?' he asked.

'Gregory, you're such a clown.' And she hooked a tea towel around his neck and towed him off to the kitchen.

'I'll see if I can be of any help too,' said Arthur, following them out.

'Sorry about them,' said Blythe, feeling a wave of embarrassment similar to the many her mum and Greg had triggered during her teenage years.

'Don't apologise,' said Sam. 'I think they're amazing. I'd have killed to have parents like them growing up.'

Blythe felt the mood dip a little. 'I hope this isn't all too much.'

Sam looked around the room at the decorations, the tree and his pile of presents. 'It's actually okay.'

'Really?' Blythe feared he was putting on a brave face.

'Yeah,' said Sam. 'This is nothing like Christmas.' Blythe twisted her lips in confusion. 'Well, it's nothing like any Christmas I've ever had. All the stuff on the run-up to today reminds me of my childhood and that triggers me. It makes me remember the hurt. The unfulfilled expectation. But this...' He splayed out his hands. 'This makes me feel kind of happy.' He seemed surprised by his own words.

'That'll be whatever Greg gave you to drink.' They both laughed.

'Actually,' said Sam, taking Blythe in his arms, 'I'm pretty certain it's you who makes me happy.' Before Blythe could question it he kissed her.

'Grab your indigestion tablets because dinner's ready!' called Greg, interrupting their kiss.

Blythe's mum always kept the dining room door shut until it was time to eat. Her Christmas table was different every year and something she took a lot of time over. When Blythe was little they used to tell her that the elves had been and decorated the table for Christmas dinner but even now she had that familiar sense of excitement at seeing it. Greg rapped out a drum roll on the dining room door before opening it. This year they had gone for a navy and silver theme with a navy tablecloth, sparkly silver table runner and a multitude of matching sparkly items. 'Mum, it's fantastic,' said Blythe.

When all the food had been brought out Greg tapped a glass to get everyone's attention. 'I just want to say this looks amazing.' Everyone murmured their agreement. 'I'm so happy that you're all here.'

'That'll be the absinthe again,' whispered Blythe to Sam.

'Here's to those we love who are not here today,' said Greg, raising his glass. 'Very merry Christmas to you all.'

'Merry Christmas,' they chorused, including Sam. And they all clinked glasses.

'One more thing,' said Greg. 'Crackers!'

'Here we go,' said Blythe, shaking her head, and Sam laughed.

They all tucked into the food, rolled their eyes at Greg as he belly-laughed at every cracker joke and watched the king's speech; and Blythe fell asleep in Sam's arms wearing a wonky cracker hat. It was exactly how Blythe believed Christmas should be.

Epilogue

26th December

Boxing Day

Boxing Day in the pub was always a bit manic, but meeting there was a Vicky and Blythe tradition, and this year they had an added incentive because Leonora was expecting an email from the Christmas competition judges.

Blythe heard her name above the chatter and turned to see Vicky waving from the door. Close behind her was Owen carrying a grinning Eden aloft. It was a sight to warm her heart. Blythe placed a drinks order as the others made their way through the crowd, which took a little while as every other person was greeting them. At last Vicky enveloped Blythe in a hug. 'Happy Boxing Day!' she said, holding Blythe tight.

'And to you.' Blythe tipped her head at Owen who was chatting to Norman. 'How was your Christmas?'

'A-maze-ing!' said Vicky. 'Thanks for the bath bombs, hoodie and the posh crackers.'

'You're welcome. Did Owen—'

'A number of times,' said Vicky.

'I was going to say – stay for Christmas?'

'Oh, right.' Vicky giggled. 'Yep. Turned up Christmas Eve with more presents than Santa. We talked about *who's the*

355

daddy and it turns out he really doesn't care. Anyway, here's the scoop. He's moving in!'

'I'm so happy for you,' said Blythe, as they hugged again.

'Thanks. And once Owen has built up his business locally I'm going to reduce my hours at the factory.'

'And the dog walking?'

'I'm going to make sure I don't take on too much because between me and you I've been relying on a couple of people in the village to help me out.'

'You don't say?' said Blythe with a smile. 'But I think some of your helpers have really enjoyed it so maybe offer to pay them a little something rather than lay them off,' suggested Blythe.

'Ooh, good idea.' On her third attempt Vicky managed to perch on the bar stool.

'Hiya, Blythe, we're off to play pool' said Owen, pointing up at Eden. Blythe handed him a pint and a glass of lemonade as he passed. 'Ta,' he said, taking them from her and catching a quick kiss from Vicky who visibly shivered at the contact.

'Get a room,' teased Blythe.

'Sorry. I take it you didn't get any festive action?'

'Well—'

As if on cue Sam appeared and kissed her lightly on the lips. 'Sorry I'm late. Turpin wouldn't let me out of the utility room. He says thank you for his Christmas dinner doggy bag by the way.'

'That was all Mum's doing, although I don't think her alternative suggestion of calling it a pussy bag will catch on,' said Blythe, cringing at the memory.

'I think you have some explaining to do,' said Vicky,

looking primly at the two of them. 'I do not like being last to know juicy gossip.'

'Ah, long story,' said Blythe, as Sam nuzzled into her neck giving her goosebumps.

'I have time.' Vicky leaned her elbows on the bar top.

Sarvan rang the bell to get everyone's attention. 'It's okay, it's not last orders but Leonora has an update for us.' Everyone looked around but there was no sign of her. 'Hang on,' said Sarvan, hastily grabbing a crate and helping Leonora to stand on it so she could be seen.

'Hi, everybody,' she said. 'I will keep this short and sweet. Holly Cross is more than just a village—'

'So much for keeping it short,' mumbled Vicky.

'Shh,' said Blythe.

'It is a group of friends – some close, others a little more distant – but I call them friends because when you need them, friends are there for you no matter what, and that's the spirit of Holly Cross. Each and every one of you should be proud of what we have achieved. I don't have final figures but Arthur assures me we have beaten last year's record-breaking total for fundraising.' There was a spontaneous round of applause and Sarvan lifted a clapping Kal onto the bar top.

'But did we win?!' called someone.

'I'm coming to that.' Leonora took a deep breath and pulled out a piece of paper. 'The judges said – *a wonderful display, imaginative and original. Holly Cross embodies everything Christmas should be about – generosity, fun and community. They are worthy winners of this ye—*' But nobody could hear anything else as Leonora was drowned out by the deafening spontaneous cheer.

Everyone congratulated each other; hugs, kisses and handshakes were shared.

'We only bloody did it,' said Vicky, grabbing Blythe and squeezing her tight.

Owen took Vicky in his arms and kissed her deeply while Eden giggled. It seemed they weren't the only ones sharing a kiss. Blythe spotted Norman and Phyllis sneaking a quick peck on the lips. Leonora was swamped by people but managed to wave an arm in the air. 'Sarvan says there's fizz for everyone!'

Another cheer went up.

When it had been announced, even Sam had punched the air. 'Feels good to be a part of this doesn't it?' said Blythe.

He studied her. 'You're not going to make me say it out loud, are you?'

'I won't ever make you do anything you don't want to.'

He took her in his arms. 'Really?'

'Really.'

'Not even sexy Santa?' He raised one eyebrow.

'Of course, but private showings only.'

Sam grinned. 'That sounds good to me.'

Acknowledgements

I must start with the biggest THANK YOU possible to my editor Rachel Faulkner-Willcocks, who championed this story from the very beginning and gave it a home at Aria, Head of Zeus. Thanks to Laura Palmer for seeing this one over the line. Thank you also to all the fabulous team at Aria. Special mention to Harry Woodgate for the original illustration, and Jessie Price at Head of Zeus for the cover design.

I am beyond grateful to my agent Kate Nash, who is there through thick and thin and secured a publisher for this story when I feared it would never be published. You are worth your weight in custard creams.

Huge thanks to my technical expert, Nick Owen, for allowing me to tap into a wealth of estate agency knowledge and for answering all my questions for the price of a coffee. Any errors are entirely my own.

I am incredibly lucky to have so many wonderful friends in the writing world who are there to celebrate all the little successes but also there to help me through the low moments – and that's when you really need them. Special shout out to Christie Barlow, Jules Wake, Sarah Bennett, Darcie Boleyn and Phillipa Ashley.

Big hugs to my family for their ongoing love and support.

I will be eternally grateful to book bloggers, booksellers and library staff for their support and to all my wonderful readers – every share, review and recommendation helps people to find my books. Thank you!

Thanks to everyone who as at some point suffered me getting excited about Christmas!

A little shout out to the wonderful village of Eathorpe, Warwickshire, which was the inspiration behind Holly Cross. If you ever get a chance to visit on the run up to Christmas you won't regret it!

About the Author

BELLA OSBORNE has been jotting down stories as far back as she can remember but decided that 2013 would be the year that she finished a full-length novel. In 2016, her debut novel, *It Started at Sunset Cottage*, was shortlisted for the Contemporary Romantic Novel of the Year and RNA Joan Hessayon New Writers Award.

Bella's stories are about friendship, love and coping with what life throws at you. She likes to find the humour in the darker moments of life and weaves these into her stories.

Bella believes that writing your own story really is the best fun ever, closely followed by talking, eating chocolate, drinking fizz and planning holidays.

She lives in The Midlands, UK with her lovely husband and wonderful daughter, who thankfully, both accept her as she is (with mad morning hair and a penchant for skipping).